## FORGE BOOKS BY WARD LARSEN

*The Perfect Assassin*
*Assassin's Game*
*Assassin's Silence*
*Assassin's Code* (forthcoming)

# ASSASSIN'S
# SILENCE

## WARD LARSEN

FORGE®

A TOM DOHERTY ASSOCIATES BOOK
NEW YORK

This is a work of fiction. All of the characters, organizations, and events portrayed in this novel are either products of the author's imagination or are used fictitiously.

ASSASSIN'S SILENCE

A Forge Book
Published by Tom Doherty Associates
175 Fifth Avenue
New York, NY 10010

www.tor-forge.com

Forge® is a registered trademark of Macmillan Publishing Group, LLC.

ISBN 978-0-7653-8578-9

Our books may be purchased in bulk for promotional, educational, or business use. Please contact your local bookseller or the Macmillan Corporate and Premium Sales Department at 1-800-221-7945, extension 5442, or by e-mail at MacmillanSpecialMarkets@macmillan.com.

First Edition: May 2016
First Mass Market Edition: February 2017

Printed in the United States of America

0  9  8  7  6  5  4  3  2  1

*For Dr. Jack*

# ACKNOWLEDGMENTS

This novel could not have been created without the assistance of others. My enduring thanks to my editor, Bob Gleason, who is never at a loss for either ideas or enthusiasm. To Elayne Becker and the staff at Tor/Forge, you are second to none. Also, much appreciation to NaNá Stoelzle for her faultless, and much-needed, copyediting skills. As always, thanks also to my agent, Susan Gleason, for her intrepid guidance and irrepressible good nature.

Of particular help in deciphering medical physics was my brother, Dr. Kent Larsen. For both detail and inspiration, thanks to my longtime friend and raconteur General Walter "Nap" Bryan, USAF (Ret.). I have taken a few minor liberties for the sake of convenience, in particular the precise location of Wujah Al Hajar Air Base and the standard crew complement for a USAF C-17. Any other technical inaccuracies are fully my responsibility.

Finally, thanks to my family, both for your inputs to the early manuscript and your perpetual understanding. Rose, Lance, Jack, and Kara—without you there would be no stories to tell.

# ASSASSIN'S SILENCE

# PROLOGUE

 Al Qutayfah, Syria

The final bolt was always a contest of will. Suleiman Malouf paused to wipe sweat from his brow, then set his feet wide, locked his arms straight, and leaned every ounce of his weight into the iron pry bar. The water pump from the old engine was stubborn—but he was more so. He pushed down on the bar with locked arms, his feet nearly coming off the ground, and finally the last hex bolt snapped. The corroded pump housing fell to the dirt with a hollow thump.

Malouf stood back, expelled a long breath, and mopped his face with a filthy shirtsleeve. The engine block, taken from an abandoned military truck of Russian manufacture, was now separated from all its accessories. A clean two-hundred-pound block of metal would bring five dollars at the scrapyard. Maybe more if the tight-fisted Marwan was in a generous mood.

He kicked the water pump across the workshop floor, perhaps with a bit of victory, and it came to rest in a pile of alternator housings, engine starters, and fuel pumps. He stood back and began cleaning his hands with a rag. Through the doorless entryway Malouf looked out across his domain, half an acre of dirt populated by automobile engines, corrugated roofing, and rusted oil drums. Like everything else, his collection had lost value since the war, the laws of supply and demand taking hold as ever. He was eyeing the shack he called home, and thinking about dinner, when he spotted his two nephews coming up the path. They were pushing the wheelbarrow and clearly struggling with its weight.

Malouf smiled.

When it came to picking up the pieces of Syria's civil war, children had proven to be the best scavengers. Their senses of sight and smell were sharp, and their small supple bodies ideally suited to delicate steps over unstable rubble and worming into crevices. In the harshest of truths, they were also the least likely to set off unexploded ordnance. Best of all—as the young had proven in wars through the ages—they were rarely distracted by matters of risk or mortality.

"And what do you have for me today?" he asked as they approached.

Neither boy answered, yet he could see they were excited. Ten-year-old Naseem was the leader, sixty pounds of bone and sinew that might, if he lived long enough and found the barest of nourishment, someday develop into a hard man. Massoud was two years younger and softer, a follower if there ever was one. Their father, Malouf's eldest brother, had been a lifelong day laborer before the uprising. Before he had traded his shovel for defiant slogans and a Kalashnikov as old as the Dead Sea. Glory has many contrivances, and the boys' father had found his at the wrong end of an Alawite artillery barrage.

An exhausted Naseem set the wheelbarrow down in the shade of the big acacia tree. Malouf's eyes narrowed as he studied what was inside.

"What do you think it is?" Naseem asked.

Malouf stuffed the rag in his back pocket. "Where did you get it?" he asked.

"From the old shed outside town," young Massoud replied.

Malouf frowned. "You went inside?"

"Yes," said Naseem proudly. "I used a long plank to cross over the collapsed back wall."

They all knew the place. It had been a stout building, older than most, which here was saying something. Thick-walled and thin-roofed, rumor had it that a tank commandeered by the rebels had been hidden inside at the height of the war. When the government got wind of it, they launched a spirited air attack. Two of Assad's MiGs had scored direct hits, sending the roof to the heavens and toppling the old stone walls from the inside out. There had indeed been vehicles inside, but no tank among them.

Ever since that day the building had been off-limits, the old mullah from the nearby mosque insisting that unspent ammunition lurked in the rubble. Inevitably, however, the recovery ran its course. In the mosaic of devastation, the center of town was the first to be reclaimed. Unrecognizable since the hostilities, the once-vibrant sandstone apartment buildings were forever lost, two- and three-story affairs reduced to piles of rubble no taller than the malnourished urchins who rifled through them. Malouf's nephews had already scoured those streets, as had a small army of other young businessmen. Tin pots and copper wire were becoming scarce, and the metal carcasses of crushed washing machines and microwaves had long disappeared.

As things became increasingly picked over in town, places like the old shed became more attractive.

Naseem, apparently, had decided it was time to test the rumors.

"Was it stable?" Malouf asked.

"Nothing has fallen recently—you can tell by the dust, the way it lays in patterns."

He contemplated telling the boy he should be careful, but doubted it would do any good. Malouf moved in for a closer inspection. He tried to lift the thing, but found it incredibly heavy. It was a steel cylinder, roughly the size of a one-gallon paint can, yet it weighed at least five times as much. The outer shell was dusty and scarred, yet clearly high-grade steel—probably high in nickel content, Malouf guessed, and perhaps some chromium. There seemed to be no lid, nor any handhold, which implied it was not designed to be regularly handled. The only irregularity to suggest its purpose was a small port on one side that gave access to . . . something.

"I have never seen anything like it," he admitted. "It is too dense to be a bomb—and too well-machined. The outer case is steel, certainly. There is more metal within, judging by the weight." He drew a wrench from his pocket and rapped on the side. They all heard a dull clang.

"It has to be worth a lot, whatever it is," Malouf reckoned.

The two boys beamed at their uncle.

"You have done well," he said. "The metal alone is worth four dollars—eight if there is lead inside. Are there more?"

"Yes," Naseem said, "twenty that I could see, but I think there might be more. We covered everything so no one else would find them, and then I half-buried a spent rocket casing nearby—it looks very dangerous."

Malouf smiled. "My brother's son has the instincts of a thief."

Naseem smiled back, knowing his uncle was pleased.

"You boys will make good traders someday. Now go, I have work to do. I will deal with this thing later and let you know what I find."

"And the rest?" Massoud asked.

Malouf thought about it at length before saying, "Leave them where they are for now."

It was later that evening, the high summer sun having mercifully retreated, when Malouf got around to the canister. With some trouble, he hoisted it to his heavy bench and went to work. He concentrated on the side aperture, attacking it with a broken screwdriver, a hacksaw, and finally a hammer and chisel. Having no luck whatsoever, he graduated to heavier implements. It was the combination of a sledgehammer and a metal punch that ultimately breached the opening.

Closing one eye, Malouf peered inside, and that was when he got his first surprise. In the poorly lit workroom he noticed a blue glow emanating from a cavity inside. Intrigued, he jammed a flat-bladed screwdriver into the opening and scraped out what looked like two glowing grains of rice. They were not warm to the touch, yet somehow shone, like the toy light sticks he handed out routinely to the children during Ramadan. He scraped out a few more grains and turned them in his hand. Perplexed, Malouf took them to the house.

His wife, who was preparing supper in the kitchen,

instantly stopped what she was doing when he showed her his find. Always a mystical sort, she was rendered speechless by the lustrous grains that seemed to hold their own light—this in itself a miracle—and she demanded that he hand them over. Old Malouf, more interested in the value of the metal canisters, surrendered his find with a shrug.

His wife rubbed the blue grains on her arm, and then on her aching bunion. Sensing perhaps some relief, she asked him for more to give to her friends. Malouf agreed, but only on the condition that she finish making his dinner. One flatbread and goat cheese sandwich later, his fifth this week, the bargain was consummated.

Over the next two days the magic crystals found their way to three other homes. One woman used them as a topical cure for her rheumatoid arthritis. Another compelled her husband to fashion a ring, setting the luminescent blue nugget into an old pewter band. A third ground the crystals into a powder which she then ingested to promote relief from a series of chronic digestive disorders.

It was this last woman who displayed the first signs of trouble. Within twenty-four hours of drinking her concoction she fell violently ill, subject to violent bouts of vomiting and diarrhea. Old Malouf was next to feel the effects. By the third evening after opening the canister, he had severe blisters on his hands, blood in his stool, and the next morning found clumps of hair on his pillow.

By Friday that week no fewer than eighteen men, women, and children had presented themselves to the clinic in Aadra. The attending physician—indeed the *only* physician—was a steady and well-meaning man named Dr. Kibrit.

He was roundly flummoxed.

Overwhelmed on the best of days, particularly during the heat of summer, he recognized that he was witnessing some kind of contagion. Yet Dr. Kibrit had never seen such a disparate array of symptoms. Some patients were vomiting blood and had severe diarrhea, suggesting a gastrointestinal malady. Others complained of dizziness, and ocular bleeding seemed prevalent. In a handful of patients he noted clear indications of kidney and lung involvement, yet this was not universal.

Over the weekend ten more patients arrived.

By Sunday night six were dead.

A frantic Dr. Kibrit made calls to the main hospital in Duma. Two physicians there asked the same questions he already had, but in the end were no help in identifying the epidemic that seemed to be sweeping Al Qutayfah. Dr. Kibrit, whose residency had been in infectious diseases, ran tests for cholera, malaria, and shigellosis. He wanted desperately to have autopsies performed on the deceased patients, but since there was no formal medical examiner within fifty kilometers, he played the hand he was dealt. For eighteen hours a day he went from one bedside clipboard to the next, ordered basic tests, and interviewed patients about their diets and sanitation and common contacts. By candlelight at night—the power grid was still unreliable—the doctor pored over books on infectious diseases. He tried to find relationships and build a map of what was happening, all while his selfless nursing staff did their best to comfort the ill—and console the families of those who fell from that side of the ledger.

Within a week of the first deaths, another dozen patients arrived with like symptoms. Dr. Kibrit knew from his interviews that there were others who'd been affected, men, women, and children who refused to come to the clinic. This he understood all too well. The Aadra clinic was run by the government, such as it was, and therefore subject to widespread suspicion. Indeed, in this corner of the world—a region that seemed to have cornered the market on mindless violence and ethnic cleansing—public suspicion ran rampant that outbreaks of illness were only some new method of terror, a weapon introduced by one tribe in order to thin the ranks of another. Dr. Kibrit considered that he might be seeing the results of a chemical or biological weapon, something the clinics had been told to watch for, yet none of the symptom profiles seemed to match.

The clinic's rudimentary lab produced no shortage of results: aplastic anemia, low platelet and red blood cell counts, all correlating to precipitous drops in blood pressure. Unfortunately, when summed with his clinical findings, the lab data only added to Dr. Kibrit's disheartening volume of ambiguity. He elected to not share this diagnostic vacuum with his hard-working staff, nurses and technicians whose efforts had been nothing short of heroic. Things continued to degrade, each day bringing more patients, more deaths, and increasingly conflicted test results.

It was the end of the second week when a young man arrived from Beirut on a mission to repair the clinic's only viable X-ray machine. A beleaguered Dr. Kibrit let loose his frustrations, and over endless cups of sweet tea he vented while his guest listened politely.

The younger man was a trained health physicist. He had an earned PhD, with a thesis in medical physics, and had been hired to calibrate and repair machines that either contained radionuclides or emitted radiation. There were few such devices in this part of the world, and none of the more advanced models: no radiation therapy with intensity modulation or image guiding techniques. But there was enough to keep one educated man busy—particularly when he was responsible for Syria and Lebanon in their entirety, and the bulk of Jordan.

After two hours, a disconsolate Dr. Kibrit went back to his work, leaving the young physicist both highly caffeinated and pensive. Regarding Dr. Kibrit's story, the man thought, but did not say, that the collection of symptoms presented was not altogether inconsistent with radiation poisoning. His interest piqued, the young man performed his own investigation into the outbreak, one that was simple and highly focused. It took no more than one bedside to get positive results.

By that time the physicist's caffeine was ebbing. His thoughtfulness, however, was not. At the nurses' station—with Dr. Kibrit's blessing—he requested and was given a list of addresses for every patient involved in the epidemic. In a quiet side room he used his tablet computer to plot the addresses on a map. The subsequent collage of red dots only hardened his convictions. He quickly repaired the clinic's X-ray machine—a vacuum tube on the fritz—and bid the staff of Aadra's besieged clinic good-bye and good luck.

In his rattletrap car he drove eight kilometers north to the village of Al Qutayfah. He navigated to the densest grouping of dots on his map, and at the southern edge of Route 7, where the gravel siding relented to dust, he found a collection of small farmhouses. Pulling the car off the road, he presented himself at the first residence, claiming to be a hospital representative on a mission to return personal effects to the families of the recently deceased. He spoke tactfully and with respect to a frightened old woman, who told him she was happy to at last see some kind of official interest in the neighborhood plague. Three front doors and two cups of tea later, by a combination of gossip and logic, the physicist suspected he was nearing ground zero.

He found it at the fourth house—if five hundred square feet of corrugated tin and scrap lumber could be referred to as such. The place was completely vacant, which he suspected was for the best. The physicist nudged the door open with his toe, and saw unwashed dishes in a tub and clothing on the floor—signs of a hasty departure. In his hand was a small case, inside which were not pairs of old shoes or wedding rings, but rather a small and very accurate dosimeter, the same one he had used at the clinic bedside. He began at the kitchen and found a high radiation exposure rate, enough to cause him to wish he had brought protective equipment.

Analysis of the rest of the home was less convincing, and so he moved outside. On the path behind the house the meter again went wild, particularly in a small ditch that had been graded to drain the property. He gazed over the place, and in the distance saw row after row of salvaged machines and cars in various states of disassembly, which only deepened his suspicions. The physicist followed his dosimeter probe into a workshop, and then out the back door. There, in late morning air that carried down from the Lebanon Mountains and across the Bekaa Valley, an old wheelbarrow leaned against a wall, and in the shade of a towering acacia tree he saw what he was after.

Or at the very least, what he expected. If there was a hesitation, it was brief.

The man, whose name was Moses, knew precisely what he had to do.

# ONE

 Twenty months later

Centered on the sun-soaked island of Malta, the ancient city of Mdina stands tall and brusque, a defiant island of brown whose vaulted bastions amplify the country's most prominent hill. Though incorporating no more than one square kilometer, the palaces and narrow streets of the medieval city have stood the tests of a thousand harsh summers, dozens of military campaigns, and in a more contemporary test of endurance, the annual invasion of a million tourists each year. For all these reasons, Mdina is a place in constant need of repair.

Most in demand are good stonemasons.

On the falling afternoon, with a classic portrait of burnt orange clinging to the western sky, a solitary mason put his finishing touches to the foot of an arch near the Nunnery of St. Benedict. The repair, a reissue of a simple decorative façade that bore no weight, was the kind of touch-up that had played out regularly over the last millennium. And while the cement was perhaps a more uniform mix than the mud used by craftsmen of past eras, the hammer and chisel the mason used to shape the flat faces and fitted angles were virtually unchanged, notwithstanding the likes of rubberized handles and carbide tips. Stoneworkers in other towns on the island had relented to more contemporary instruments—heavy masonry saws and compressed-air power tools—yet such advances were not favored in the Old City. The patron who today commissioned repairs here, a city formerly administered by the likes of knights and noblemen, was the Maltese Ministry for Tourism, Culture, and Environmental Affairs, a body with an unyielding eye for absolute authenticity. In a curious twist of fate, the fact that this craftsman was not a native Maltese was squarely in line with tradition. Having existed for so long at the geographic crossroads of Europe, the Middle East, and Africa, the time-tested stonework of Malta had been raised almost exclusively by journeyman masons.

The man stood back to regard his work, a chisel and damp cloth in his calloused hands. After a ten-hour day he was gray-suited in sweat and dust, the only exception being a pair of clear gray eyes, and tiny streams on his face and neck where rivulets of sweat had washed the skin clear. The heat and sun were a constant here, although in early February the Mediterranean winter was at the height of its relief. All the same, the city seemed to draw a long breath as its shadows leaned to darkness.

The mason compared the column he'd repaired to its sister four meters away. It was good, he decided. The cuts were accurate, and the color of the stone a reasonably close match. Those effects he could not simulate were the ones carved by time—the gentle erosion of mortar channels, edges nicked by handcarts, stains from spilled wine. These would come in due course.

He bent down with his hammer and chisel and made his mark next to another, an artisan's signature that had, he guessed knowledgeably, most likely been hewed sometime in the late sixteenth century. That done, he began packing his tools in a hand case. Tomorrow he would regard his work in better light, perhaps make a few alterations, and wash things down for the last time. And then? Then he would move on to his next job—two collapsed pillars in the Catacombs of St. Paul. For a mason, Mdina and the surrounding city of Rabat were not a series of day jobs—they were a career.

A spindly young boy scurried up the street with a broom in his hand and stopped next to the mason.

"All done, sir?" he asked in Maltese.

The mason kept to the language he'd picked up over the last months, if only in a colloquial sense. "Done for the day." He reached into his pocket, pulled out a two-euro coin, and flipped it through the air. The boy snatched it cleanly.

"When you're done cleaning up, take the tools with you. Meet me tomorrow at the Catacombs."

"The Catacombs? That is very far from here, sir."

The mason grinned and reached into his pocket. His second coin was a one-euro denomination, and his second toss less accurate. Not that it mattered— the kid caught it effortlessly. Indeed, in the three months of their association he had never once missed. He was ten or eleven years old, the mason guessed, although never having raised a child himself he couldn't say with any authority. They didn't know each other's names because neither had ever asked. Sir and Kid sufficed, both words conveniently shared between English and Maltese. "Kid" was a straight bean of a child with a mop of curly black hair, and he invariably appeared in worn tennis shoes and a shirt with a corporate sponsor's name on the front and a large number on the back. He loved soccer with a passion, and lived in the Old City with his mother. That was all the tradesman knew—indeed, all he wanted to know. The kid did what he was asked to do, smiled more often than not, and showed up on time.

He was the perfect employee.

"*El Clasico* is tonight," the boy said, referring to the semiannual clash of Spanish soccer giants Real Madrid and Barcelona. "You should watch. Their new forward is better than Messi."

"I'll try to catch it," said the mason as he raised his ladder against the crest of the arch for the day's final inspection.

"There is a man up the street watching you."

The mason stopped what he was doing. "A man?"

"He has been there since I brought you the water."

"The water? That was two hours ago."

"Yes."

A long pause ensued. "And you think he's watching me?"

"Oh, yes."

The mason stood very still, his eyes locked on the sturdy stone arch. It began as no more than a tremor, a cautionary jolt he'd felt twice since arriving on the island. Once it had been a gunshot out of a quiet night, probably a misguided celebration from some drunk who didn't realize that bullets sent into the sky still come down. The second occurrence had greater basis, a team of policemen with weapons maneuvering outside his rooming house—as it turned out, there to raid a nearby apartment where a drug dealer had bunkered up. In both instances he'd felt the surge of adrenaline, but waited with well-practiced patience until the threat was disproved.

Now he did it again. In the ensuing minutes of uncertainty, the mason went through the motions of his business. "Where is he exactly?" he asked the boy, his hand flicking away a bit of loose mortar.

"You can't see him from here—he's near the Cathedral Museum, sitting in the courtyard behind the gift shop. It was very shady there this afternoon, many customers. Now he is the only one remaining, and still watching you through the open door of the shop. I walked past twice to be sure."

"He's alone?"

"Yes. But I saw another tea cup on the table."

Right then, the mason decided the kid had a future. One that didn't involve kicking a ball.

The boy smiled eagerly. "You want me to go look again?"

"No," said the mason quickly.

He considered his position. The archway he was repairing was situated at a T-shaped intersection. He glanced ahead, along the length of Triq San Pawl, and saw the gift shop with the open front door. In the opposite direction the street reached its southern end near the Xara Palace, and the third leg of the intersection was made by Triq Mesquita, a narrow cobbled path that ran toward the Piazza Mesquita. The walls bordering all these streets ran the same, indeed like every other street in Mdina, thirty-foot tan stone faces with minimal ornamentation. There were no windows at street level, and the doors came at odd intervals, brilliant blue and red invitations that the mason recognized as no more than temptations to chance—doors here were famously sturdy, and some had been bolted shut for centuries. He admonished himself for not knowing in advance which were accessible. In years gone by he would never have made such a mistake.

He turned to face Triq Mesquita. The crowds had thinned considerably with the setting sun. A street vendor was pushing his handcart home for the day, and an old man walked an old dog, a pronounced resemblance in their uneven gaits.

He spotted the second man easily.

He was standing with a gelato, his back against a wall, a stone-sober image in a spill of stray light. On appearances he wasn't Maltese, and he showed no apparent purpose beyond scooping ice cream from a cup. He was dressed in khaki trousers and a loose-fitting shirt, dark wraparound glasses in the waning sunshine. He was tall and thickly built, with fair skin and hair, the trim a close burr-cut that would have passed any military inspection. What concerned the mason most, however, was how the man wore his shirt—free and untucked. It might have been a carry-over from an unseasonably warm afternoon, or perhaps he'd eaten too many gelatos and his trousers were tight.

*Yes,* the mason reasoned, *it could be any of that.*

He turned and looked to the third leg of the T, the far end of Triq San Pawl. He saw a mother and a small girl walking toward him in a flurry of skipping legs and bright fabric. Two men walking in the opposite direction wore matching yellow bibs of the Cleansing Directorate, the pair deep in an animated conversation whose words and cadence were clearly Maltese. The mason saw no one on this street that he could stamp as a threat, yet he noted a number of intersections and alcoves. The kinds of places he might once have sought himself.

Altogether, three avenues of escape—two covered and the third in question. The first possibility was that he was being overly suspicious, sensing another false alarm. If so, no reaction was necessary. The second option: he was being watched. This implied trouble, though not necessarily a threat. The third possibility was more problematic, and one that demanded immediate resolution.

"I need you to do something for me." The mason took the broom from the boy's hand. "I'll clean up. I'd like you to take the tools and walk toward the gardens. Keep a good watch until you make the turn onto Triq Inguanez."

Kid looked at him quizzically.

"You have good instincts—trust them. If you see any other men up the street, anyone who looks out of place, put the toolbox on the ground as if it's too heavy, then switch hands and keep going. Don't look back at me, and whatever you do, don't stare at anyone."

The boy nodded.

"If there is someone else," the mason continued, "don't go home tonight. Do you have a relative who lives nearby?"

"An uncle in South Rabat, near the old seminary."

"Good. If it comes to that, go straight to his house and stay inside. Tomorrow take my tools and sell them. You know what they're worth."

The boy nodded again, a teasing smile at the corners of his mouth. The prospect of a good payday? the mason wondered. Or was it the implications of what he was being asked to do? He would lay odds on the latter—the excitement of his first op plan.

"And if there is not anyone else?" the kid asked.

"Then meet me at the Catacombs tomorrow morning. And don't be late."

The kid grinned openly at that. He was never late.

He picked up the tools with a show of effort and waved, adding a loud, "*Arrivederci,* sir."

The mason turned toward the ladder. He climbed two rungs and began running his hand over a stone cornice. He glanced when the boy was thirty meters away, then again at fifty. He was just past the alcove of the Nunnery of St. Benedict, standing in a strong shaft of light, when he set down the tool case. The kid shook out his arm as if it was cramped, then picked up the case with his opposite hand. He walked no more than ten steps.

Then he did it all over again.

# TWO

For the second time in his life David Slaton had become careless. The first had occurred not long ago, at the end of a problematic year in Virginia. He had gotten too comfortable, and his wife and child had nearly paid the ultimate price. He vowed never to let that happen again, and carried through on his pledge by the most tried and true method—distance.

For fourteen months Slaton had taken up a quiet and solitary existence in Mdina. He never made international phone calls and avoided the Internet. He rarely left the city, and had not once ventured outside the country. His lone contact with the outside world was an obscure e-mail account he rarely accessed, and then only from random Internet cafés across the island. He rented a small flat and made a few casual friends—to be a complete recluse would only raise suspicion—and allowed the occasional dinner out, even then only during off-hours. As far as he could tell, he'd blended in perfectly. Or as perfectly as a six foot two, sandy-haired stonemason could manage on a Mediterranean island.

Someone had found him anyway.

He knew how it had happened—his mind-set. That healthy mistrust so essential to his former life had gone slack. He had become a stonemason. Slaton knew because he went to sleep each night with fading thoughts that did not involve safe houses or zeroed sight pictures. Now it was corner joints and rubble veneer, and in the morning vague dreams recalled of a family he would never know. At some point, he had stopped taking precautions, the result being that a ten-year-old boy had seen what he should have seen. Four men covering all the angles.

The questions of who they were and why they were here he discarded for the moment. Of far greater relevance were the where, when, and how of the situation. The answers came quickly.

A man emerged from the shadows of the café, tall and lean, with wireless glasses over high cheeks and a patch of black chin whiskers. He moved with the air of a hurried mortician. Slaton thought he looked familiar, although in that moment he couldn't put a name to the face. He next spotted the two in the alley, where the kid had alerted. This pair were swarthier, two-hundred-pound sacks of muscle with comparable squat builds. The most discriminating feature between them was the color of their shirts—one drab green, the other mud gray. The crew cut was still there on Triq Mesquita. Slaton watched him scrape the last gelato from his cup before taking to the cobble street.

Was there a chance they were here to talk? Could they want to hire him?

No, Slaton decided. He had never been a mercenary, and anyway, such negotiations would not require four men. He gave up pretenses and looked directly at each man, one by one. If their pace did not alter, there might still be a peaceful way out. All four began moving more quickly. They dodged passersby with quick, purposeful strides, and when one put a hand under his shirttail the charade was officially over. Slaton was watching a well-orchestrated takedown, and from the worst point of view.

They were doing a good job of it. The time of day was ideal, indeed when he would have chosen. Minimal street traffic led to fewer bruised elbows, fewer bystanders to accidentally screen a shot. The light was nearly gone, but adequate for a marksman and offering the target no cover of darkness. It was also the time of day, Slaton knew, that shift changes took place at police departments, leading to a period of sluggish response. The opposing pincer along Triq San Pawl was nicely staggered, the twins shouldered against the eastern wall, and the man with the glasses keeping to the west. Slaton recognized this for what it was—an attempt to deconflict firing lanes. They were smooth and well-coordinated. Certainly disciplined. In sum, they were very much like him.

They were assassins.

Slaton found himself under a stone arch and surrounded by high walls. He had no weapon with which to respond. With his closest pursuer a mere thirty yards away, he saw only one viable option. He scrambled up the ladder.

He was halfway up when the first shots rang out, followed by shouting all around. The wooden rung near his head shattered, and Slaton bypassed the step and vaulted upward, launching himself the last few feet onto the top of the arch. A kick sent the ladder tumbling sideways to the ground. It gave them a way up, of course, but hopefully bought precious seconds.

More shots echoed, and bullets chipped stone all around him. The arch was three feet wide, enough to cover him shoulder to shoulder if he hugged close and kept his face planted. But he had to move. They would soon find elevation, better angles that would leave him exposed. The rooftop behind him was blocked by a knee wall, but straight ahead the arch blended perfectly into a flat roof. Slaton fast-crawled on his elbows and knees, bullets pinging into the stone on either side. Then the first impact—a vicious bite in one thigh.

He kept moving.

Reaching the relative safety of the roof, he rolled until his attackers no longer had line of sight, then rose to a crouch and ran. His right thigh hurt like hell. He dashed right, paralleling Triq San Pawl, as the gunfire gave way to shouted commands—he didn't understand the words, but the accent was distinctly eastern European. Slaton kept to the center of the roof for cover and at the first side street encountered a ten-foot chasm. He jumped across in full stride and landed in a heap, gravel grinding into his hands and arms. He scrambled to his feet and a shot rang out, the round pinging into a water tank to his right. Slaton glanced back and saw the crew-cut soldier—he had climbed the ladder and was giving chase. The others were likely below, moving by his instructions. The high ground that had briefly protected Slaton would quickly become a snare, limiting his avenues of escape.

But he was not without advantages. Slaton knew a great deal about rooftops, as all men with his training did. He was also on familiar terrain, and no amount of reconnaissance on their part could match the local knowledge he'd acquired by living and working in these neighborhoods for nearly a year. He found the place he wanted, a raised stairwell shaft with a crumbling stone exterior—the very façade he had been hired to repair last October. Slaton knew the door would be open because he had personally removed the old rusted lock, and the owner, who enjoyed stargazing with his mistress, had insisted he not replace it.

Slaton burst inside and slammed the door shut behind him. The stairwell beckoned, but he paused and studied his surroundings. Over his head a pair of thick wooden beams supported the vaulted tile roof, and the doorjamb was sided by a vertical series of cavities where he'd removed the ancient hinges of the original door. Slaton put a foot into the first notch, testing. He gripped a higher one with his hand, and lifted himself up. Seconds later he was perched high in the rafters.

It took ten seconds.

Slaton heard a one-sided conversation, this time in hushed, heavily accented English. *"No contact. Do we pull back yet?"* A pause, followed by more words that were indecipherable. The man outside was talking over a tactical comm unit.

The door flew open under a heavy boot, and Slaton watched the crew-cut soldier edge inside. He cleared the space expertly from the threshold, the muzzle of his weapon methodically sweeping left and right. But not up.

Slaton dropped like an anvil, his knee aimed at the man's head.

His adversary reacted, but too late as Slaton's two-hundred-plus pounds crashed down mercilessly. Both men tumbled onto the stairs, a rolling mix of arms and legs that came to a hard end at the first stone landing. Slaton heard the metallic clatter of the man's gun skittering down the staircase. The soldier was dazed, but he was also big and strong, with the thick muscles of a weightlifter. Slaton had a more pragmatic strength, earned from ten-hour days hauling stone and mortar. He began with an elbow to the face, the crush of cartilage audible. A knee to the diaphragm hammered the air from his opponent's lungs. The man doubled over, and a kick to his temple with a steel-toed work boot finished the job. He nearly back-flipped down the next flight of stairs, ending facedown and completely still.

Slaton rushed down and rolled him over. The man was out cold, his breathing shallow and ragged. Slaton performed a quick pat down but found no ID, nor any weapon besides the one that had bounded down the stairwell. He also noted a lack of body armor. They'd known he would be unarmed. A comm device was clipped to the man's belt, a unit Slaton didn't recognize with controls labeled in English. It looked damaged and he left it where it was. Then he found something more useful—on the man's inner bicep, a familiar tattoo. A swooping, long-winged bird of prey with a lightning bolt in its talons. Polish Special Forces—GROM.

The breathing stopped, and in the next moment he heard a sound from below. Reinforcements had arrived. Slaton strained to see down the darkened stairwell. The man's gun was nowhere in sight. Ignoring the burn in his thigh, he ran back out to the roof. A siren blared in the distance, the police responding. He doubled back in the direction he'd come, retracing his steps, loose stones and broken bits of tile scattering as he ran. It was a counterintuitive move, and not without risk. Mdina was a classic fortress, hundred-foot walls and gated entrances, an ideal design for repelling marauding Byzantines. Yet as with any such defense, once the bastions are breached the fortress becomes a trap.

At the roof's end he looked straight down and saw what he wanted—twenty feet to his left, a second-floor balcony. They were common in the otherwise flat-faced tenements, added by noblemen over the centuries as platforms from which available daughters could be advertised for marriage. Slaton slipped over the roof's edge, hung briefly by his fingertips, and dropped ten feet to the balcony. The next fall was slightly more, and he landed on the cobbled street in a parachutist's landing, bent knees followed by a roll onto his left hip and side. He ran east, away from the building where he imagined his pursuers were cautiously climbing stairs and clearing rooms.

He was wrong.

Thirty meters ahead, at the next corner in the medieval maze, he saw one of the squat twins. The man spotted him immediately, and after a frozen moment Slaton turned. The man with the glasses was behind him, reaching into a shoulder holster.

Cut off in both directions, there was only one option—he sprinted up a staircase that led to an observation deck. The overlook was empty, no lingering tourists appreciating the glittering jewels of Malta at dusk. Slaton veered right, and where the deck ended he mounted a two-foot-wide ledge that topped the outer bastion. A sheer stone wall vaulted upward on his right, and to the left was simply a black precipice. Arms outstretched for balance, he traversed the granite ledge like a man on a high wire.

A bend in the wall approached, and Slaton knew what lay beyond—the patio of a popular restaurant, a sea of comfortable wooden chairs and square tables under candy-striped umbrellas. He had dined there some months ago, a lazy Sunday with pasta and bread, a steaming espresso his companion afterward. He remembered looking out over the island on that bright autumn day and seeing all the way to Sicily. Now he saw only distant lights and blackness, felt a chill wind swirling.

Rounding the bend, the restaurant was there. The place was alive: waiters scurrying beneath strings of naked bulbs, early diners waiting for meals and drinking down bottles of the harsh house red. He rushed past a waiter who was furling patio umbrellas, cranking them closed one by one as the sun had given way to stars. Slaton jumped down from the wall, ran inside, and skidded to a stop near the maître d' station. Diners and servers looked at him uneasily, and a hush fell about the place.

The realization struck too late—from his earlier visit he recalled crates of greens and wine being wheeled in through the front door. Which meant there *was* no back door. He looked through the entrance and saw a street bordered by old revetments—the restaurant had been wedged neatly into an otherwise dysfunctional corner of the district. He spotted two familiar silhouettes trotting up the street, alert and purposeful. The only other way out was the way he'd arrived, the narrow ledge that was certainly covered.

Slaton was trapped, and reckoned he had a ten-second window. He saw white bulbs and brightly colored canvas. Stone walls and a black night. He saw a hundred eyes fixed on him.

Ten seconds.

The rest of his life if he didn't do something.

# THREE

The man with the glasses was on the ledge, his gun level as he approached the bend where his target had disappeared. His name was Ben-Meir, and he cursed with each step along the precarious bastion wall. Finger on the trigger, he rounded the corner and was surprised to see a busy restaurant. His target was nowhere in sight.

Keeping to the shadows, he bent his chin toward his tactical microphone. *"Position."*

*"Near the restaurant entrance,"* said his second-in-command, a Bulgarian named Radko.

Radko's partner, who'd been in charge of mission planning and was thus the most familiar with the city's layout, added, *"I recognize the place—there's no back door. I repeat, no back door!"*

Ben-Meir cursed again, this time more loudly. *"Does anyone see him?"*

A long pause, then two negative replies.

They had their man surrounded, his back to a wall. Not good. Ben-Meir had wanted to finish things quickly and cleanly, but the mission had proved costly and taken far longer than it should have. He activated his transmit switch.

*"Pull back!"*

He had no sooner unkeyed the transmit switch when he heard a loud crash and a chorus of screams.

*"Pull back! Pull back!"* he repeated.

It happened in a flash. Near the outer wall a bolt of movement and color. In a defensive instinct, Ben-Meir shifted his weapon to the spot. His target was there, a blur in the transition between the restaurant's bright lights and the darkness beyond. He seemed to be clinging to something, and then, incredibly, the man in his sights flew over the rampart ledge and into the black void beyond.

Ben-Meir fired once, a certain miss as gravity accelerated the crazy, cartwheeling silhouette into the night sky. He ran into the restaurant while patrons bolted toward the exit. Ben-Meir knocked aside an empty table in his scramble toward the ledge, and to compound the confusion he waved his gun and yelled, "Police! Police! Everyone out!" It might buy thirty seconds.

At the ledge he leaned over and looked down, but saw only a void, the lights all around spoiling his night vision. He did, however, hear a series of crashes that rang like muted gunshots. Then a more imperative sound from behind—a fast-approaching siren. With one last look down, he ordered the egress.

It was fifteen minutes later, with their car withdrawing quietly through the Mdina gate, that Ben-Meir and his team realized how badly things had gone. Kieras was dead, and there had not been time to recover his body. He'd been the youngest and most fit of the lot. Not the most lethal, perhaps, but a good fighter all the same. Radko had found him in the stairwell, and while there was nothing to be done, it never sat well with soldiers to leave comrades behind. Ben-Meir would at least not have to notify Kieras' next of kin—a minor consolation of commanding an off-the-books army.

"How could this have happened?" said Radko.

"Shut up," said an irritated Ben-Meir. "It's our own fault. We knew he was good."

"Apparently not good enough. You saw how it ended—our mission failed in the worst way. What will we report?"

"I said shut up!" roared Ben-Meir. "We report nothing until we're sure."

The ensuing ride was short and silent, weaving through Howard Gardens before a loop around the city to the north. The driver pulled onto a gravel siding where the road reached its nearest point to the calamity. Ben-Meir and Radko got out, and from the lower elevation they jogged a kilometer uphill to the foot of the bastion walls. They had no trouble finding the spot—the restaurant above was lit like a carnival—but they were stunned by what they *didn't* find. The body of their target was nowhere to be seen.

"I don't understand," said Radko. "No one could survive a fall like that."

Ben-Meir cupped a hand over his chin, but said nothing. In the spill from the lights forty yards above, he saw something on the ground. He moved closer, recalling the flash of color as their quarry had gone spinning over the wall. One of the big red-and-white patio umbrellas from the restaurant lay on the ground. Partially open, most of the fabric had been ripped from its bent frame, and metal rods jutted out at odd angles.

His lieutenant looked on with disbelief. "He jumped from a cliff and survived by holding that? The man is suicidal, I tell you."

The commander scanned the ground with his flashlight and found branches that appeared freshly broken, one as thick as his arm. He shifted the beam upward, into a thick bay tree, and followed from top to bottom where the arboreal gauntlet had been run.

"No," he argued. "To stay above, from his point of view—*that* would have been suicidal." He reached down and picked up the bent aluminum frame. "This? This was a calculated risk. The umbrella alone would never stop his fall. Yet if he knew the trees were here, and if he could jump out far enough to find them. Ten meters, no more. The only question would be holding onto the thing during its run through the branches. That would require a certain . . . tenacity."

The two exchanged a look, and the lieutenant said, "We need to be careful with this one."

"We *were* careful—now Kieras is dead."

Ben-Meir bent down and examined the fabric strips that had been torn from the umbrella. He was studying a bloody smear when voices from above drew his attention. He looked up to see a policeman in the half-light leaning over the granite ledge, next to him a waiter pointing downward.

"Come," he said, snapping off his flashlight and turning back toward the road on a fast walk, "there is nothing more for us here."

The driver set a brisk, professional pace, and the city fell behind them. In the front seat, Ben-Meir studied a map of the area on a tablet computer. "This is useless—he could have gone anywhere." He addressed Radko's partner, Stanev, who'd been their primary shooter. "You are *certain* you hit him?"

"No doubt," the man said. "I saw him react. He was limping afterward."

Ben-Meir stared at the empty map display. He

removed his glasses, pinched the bridge of his nose, and took out his phone. He placed a call that was picked up immediately.

"Well?"

"We reached him," said Ben-Meir, "only things didn't go completely as planned. He got the better of our point man."

"Were you able to clean it up?"

"No. There was no time to retrieve the body."

A pause. "And your target—where is he?"

Ben-Meir looked at the topographical image of Malta on his laptop, thinking it looked bigger than ever. "We don't know."

"How can that be?"

"I don't know—there could be any number of reasons. We cornered him perfectly and scored a hit, but then he started taking chances. At the end he jumped off a goddamned cliff."

"A cliff?"

"He survived, but he's definitely injured."

"Badly?"

"I can't say."

Another pause, then, "This wasn't what we intended."

Ben-Meir thought silence the best option.

"All right," said the distant voice, "assuming his injuries are not severe, there is still a chance. We know where he has to go. Be ready—and next time make no mistakes."

# FOUR

Situated halfway between Manaus and Belém in
northern Brazil, the Santarém–Maestro Wilson Fonseca Airport was carved from the forest in the early
1970s. Designed and funded by the Brazilian Air
Force, it was intended as a replacement for the original airfield—ten acres of crumbling asphalt that was
eventually rehabilitated into a clumsily conceived commercial district, the wide runway becoming a street
that could have supported ten lanes of traffic, and
the tall control tower transformed into a neon-dressed
advertisement for a disreputable nightclub.

In the intervening decades, the new and improved
Santarém airfield had not risen to meet expectations.
Never more than the fortieth busiest airport in Brazil, it today offers a meager schedule of flights from
small airlines and air taxi operators, and manages an
anemic flow of air cargo. The facility does, however,
hold at least one unique claim—it is the only airport in
the world named after a Brazilian operatic composer.

From another perspective, the new Santarém airport can be likened to many others in the Amazon
basin—it is home to a rusting boneyard of forgotten
aircraft. Like a collection of flightless birds—twelve
if one were to count—they stand in varying degrees

of decomposition on crumbling back lots. The oldest is little more than a steel tube with a tail—a Boeing 727 by consensus opinion—that had thirty years before slid off the notoriously slippery runway during a fierce microburst, and ended with its nosewheel sunk in three feet of muck on the southern bank of the Amazon River. All the aircraft here have stories, most far less dramatic and involving the collapse of one ill-managed airline or another. In more economically developed countries such surplus aircraft exist as a managed commodity, mothballed by airlines and lessors in desert airfields, valuable components like engines and avionics sealed and preserved for their value on the global spare parts market. In Santarém, however, a place strung by a bureaucratic jungle no less dense than the surrounding rain forest, these orphaned aircraft are largely left to rot in the torrid heat and tropical rain, their sleek shells assailed by mildew, nesting birds, and that most deadly of all infestations—corrosion.

From a distance the two men walking across the weed-corrupted tarmac could not have been more alike. Both wore loose trousers and billowing shirts under the heavy afternoon sun. Both were slim and of average height, and on the lee side of fifty, this last point upheld by like crops of dark hair edged in gray. In every other aspect, the two men could not have been more different.

Umberto Donato was the airport caretaker. He was a lifelong resident of Santarém who had only once traveled outside the city, nine years ago taking a tour of the Santos headquarters of BAM Airlines, during a rare interval of corporate largesse and expansion, spending two afternoons at the airline's general offices learning about flight operations, and two evenings in a nearby bordello overlooking his marriage vows. Umberto was responsible for the airport grounds, to include whatever drove in from town, crawled out of the forest, and fell from the sky. For a facility that covered nine square miles, plus or minus, it was no small task. He saw to it that the grass was cut, the trash cans emptied, and the vagrants booted. He'd implemented a system to have illegally parked cars towed, and made sure that the remains of flattened caimans and pythons were promptly removed from the steam-shrouded runway. And when people abandoned airliners on the fringes of his domain, Umberto's job was to look after them—at least, as best he could given his laughable budget.

Umberto Donato was Brazilian, mostly honest, and a man who held few grievances with life. The man walking beside him was none of those things.

He had arrived this afternoon on the 1:15 flight from Brasília which, by an evident act of blessed providence, had been ten minutes early. In the air-conditioned passenger terminal the man had introduced himself as Gianni Petrecca, and produced an Italian passport to that effect. He spoke Portuguese with an accent Umberto supposed was Italian. His black hair and dark shadow of beard were decidedly Mediterranean. Gianni said he was from Naples, and that he was both a pilot and a broker of used aircraft, none of which the Brazilian had any reason to doubt. Indeed, after five minutes of conversation, Umberto was sure the man knew something about airplanes.

"Is it always like this?" the Italian asked, wiping sweat from his forehead with a shirtsleeve.

"Only in summer," said a smiling Umberto, before adding, "but of course, here there is no other season."

With Umberto in the lead, the two men skirted a little-used taxiway on the airport's east side and approached the aircraft in question. It was situated on the largest parking apron, a square pocket of asphalt the size of a soccer field that pushed insolently into the forest. The pad was surrounded on three sides by walls of vegetation, waxen green leaves the size of doormats and thick vines that seemed like arteries, binding everything into a single living organism.

The airplane looked better than most of Santarém's sky-tramps. It had all its engines, wheels, and entry doors, and the exterior access panels appeared to be in place, although a few hung open, waving limply in the moist air that was stirring on schedule. Two reflective panels in the cockpit windshield gave the impression that the jet was taking a nap behind blinders. All these details, however, were overshadowed by one overwhelming highlight—before them was the largest aircraft ever to land at Maestro Wilson Fonseca Airport by a factor of two.

"Yes," Gianni said, "it looks like the photograph in the listing. How long has it been on the market?"

"Only two weeks," said Umberto. "The airport has only recently taken legal possession."

"Nine hundred thousand U.S.—that is a lot to ask. I understand it will need a D-check soon. Heavy maintenance for such aircraft is very expensive. More than your asking price."

"But she *is* a low-cycle airframe," Umberto countered, parroting what he'd been told to say by the city fathers, even if he wasn't sure what it meant. "Another four to six years of use, depending on how hard she is flown." *She,* Umberto thought. *Yes, that's very good.*

Gianni seemed unconvinced.

"I am not authorized to discuss financial matters," said Umberto, "yet there is always room for compromise." He did, in fact, have some knowledge of the negotiations, which were being overseen by Santarém's *município,* or community council. A broker from Brasília, well-versed in resale markets, had been consulted, and he explained that each month the jet didn't sell lowered its value in the neighborhood of 3 percent.

"What is the history of the craft?" the Italian asked.

Umberto made a show of checking the paperwork he'd brought. It listed all the prior owners, the most recent being a Canadian leasing firm. They had bought the hull, in turn, from a highly specialized U.S. government contractor in California. Before that had been Air Ethiopia, who'd purchased it out of receivership after the collapse of Pan Am. "The original owner was Pan Am," Umberto said, keeping with the most respectable maintenance outfit on the list, and glossing over the detail that Pan Am had acquired the jet in its takeover of National Airlines. "After that there were a few other operators, all reputable."

The Italian nodded thoughtfully and walked closer.

Umberto let out a long-held breath, relieved that Gianni hadn't asked how the aircraft had ended up here. For the most part, aircraft histories were an open book in the age of online registries. CB68H, her tail-displayed registration number, was a McDonnell Douglas DC-10 wide-body built in 1976. The chain of ownership was there for all to see, as were the heavy maintenance checks, these documented in painstaking detail as per regulations. More oblique was that the aircraft sat where it was because last year, on its way to Buenos Aires, it had caught fire at thirty-seven thousand feet and diverted to the nearest suitable airfield—Santarém–Maestro Wilson Fonseca Airport. The captain on that flight, a native of Belarus with only sixty hours in command of the type, had gotten excited and misjudged his flare over the short, narrow runway, planting two hundred tons of airliner in a landing so hard it had pressed permanent dents into the grooved asphalt.

The fire, as it turned out, was a minor issue, a bit of residual oil in the auxiliary power unit that had flashed in an instant and sent a wave of malodorous, if quite harmless, vapors into the air-conditioning system. The aircraft might have flown out the next day had the shaken captain not documented his hard landing in the aircraft logbook, an admission that instigated a long series of missteps. Extensive inspections and modest repairs became necessary to place the aircraft back in service, and it was here that the owning company, DGR Aviation, ran into a host of regulatory roadblocks.

The Brazilian authorities, contemptuous as ever, took unkindly to aluminum overcast falling from the sky. In the ensuing wrangles, DGR's insurers balked at making damage payments. The bank holding a lien on the jet filed legal papers to protect their interests, and the Santarém Airport Authority instigated a lawsuit to cover unpaid landing and parking fees, adding by way of codicil an estimate to repair their newly dented runway. For six months claims were met with counterclaims and the system whirred like a blender, the only result in the end being an aircraft with a pureed airworthiness certificate. Already nearing the end of its useful service life, CB68H sat chocked in place like an impotent dinosaur, hope dimming with each day that a new operator might come to its rescue. So it was, in the ensuing months, the aircraft fell to be owned and maintained, for all intents and purposes, by a slight Brazilian named Umberto Donato.

Umberto padded behind the Italian as he circled underneath the aircraft, and it struck him that the man looked very much like a pilot conducting a preflight inspection.

"You can fly this?" Umberto asked.

"Yes, I have a type rating on the MD-10. About four hundred hours in command."

"MD-10? I thought this was a DC-10."

"When it came off the assembly line, yes. At some point the cockpit was modified to a new standard. The flight engineer's station was removed, and now it can be crewed by only two pilots."

Umberto nodded, then asked, "Will you be the one to fly it out?"

"Perhaps . . . yet first it must be decided if the craft holds any residual value."

Gianni paused underneath the central hull, directly between the main landing gear, and looked up at a pair of large doors on the bottom of the aircraft.

Umberto followed his gaze, and said, "I have spent my whole life around aircraft, yet never have I seen such access panels. Do you know their purpose?"

"I couldn't say," replied Gianni. "Some kind of cargo modification, it seems—something I will leave to the engineers. Our interest is whether the aircraft can be repaired and either operated or resold at a profit. What people have done with her in the past— that is no concern to my company."

The two men rounded the tail, looking up at the two-tone paint job that split the aircraft around its waist, the upper half faded blue and the bottom a dusky gray. The exterior tour ended near the front where Umberto had hours ago wheeled in place a set of boarding stairs. The pilot led the way up to the forward entry door. The air inside was sweltering, and the cabin smelled like all cargo jets Umberto had encountered—an acrid stench of spilled oil and hydraulic fluid. Looking aft there were no seats, as one would find in a passenger version, but simply a mammoth cylinder carrying forty yards toward the tail. The only interruption in the massive tube was a holding tank of some sort amidships. To Umberto it looked like a covered swimming pool in the middle of a train tunnel. He assumed it was a long-range fuel tank, given its position at the midpoint of the hold—even for an airplane this size, weight and balance could be critical. All the same, the tank seemed to waste a great deal of the jet's usable cargo volume.

Gianni turned toward the front, and Umberto followed him to the flight deck. He watched the Italian study the instruments with a pilot's eye. Minutes later they were back outside.

"Well?" Umberto asked.

"It is possible," Gianni allowed. "Only the price is far too high. I will have to forward my findings to our engineering staff. If they can allay certain concerns, a bid might be forthcoming. But then, that is something for me to discuss with your *municipio*. Thank you for allowing an inspection."

"*Prego*," Umberto replied, expending the full range of his Italian.

The two shook hands, and Umberto offered his guest a ride to his hotel. Gianni said he preferred to find a taxi, and walked away toward the terminal. Umberto watched him go, then turned back to the aircraft and began buttoning things up. In a way, he hoped the airplane didn't sell. The money would quickly be swallowed by one city project or another, and for him there would be no commission, not even a bump in his dismal operating budget. This DC-10—no, MD-10—was something special, a signature display for his little museum. Indeed, as he neared the end of his career, that was how Umberto increasingly viewed the airfield grounds—an accidental museum of which he was the curator.

He climbed the stairs and reached for the handle to close the entry door. There Umberto paused. He stepped once more into the cavernous belly of the beast and looked aft, regarding the big fuel tank between the wings. Perhaps it was only natural that the jet should sell. Fill that tank with Jet A fuel, he imagined, and she would carry pallets and boxes to cities across the world, one more cog in the world's economic machine.

He would never come to know how wrong he was.

# FIVE

Slaton hobbled over the first mile as his body adapted to new bruises and contusions, the most prominent being the wound on his right thigh. Things began moving more smoothly, and he managed a jog for the next three miles.

He rounded the national stadium in Ta' Qali before bogging down in the Meridiana Vineyard, the trellis-rowed ground soggy from recent rains. Outside the village of Mosta, Slaton approached a farmhouse, and from a clothesline near a courtyard wall he requisitioned a pair of dark pants and a shirt, both roughly his size. Crouching behind a low wall—these everywhere on an island with little precious soil and a tireless wind—he removed his torn and filthy work clothes, and donned the new ones. That done, he ripped a cotton strip from his old shirt and wrapped a hasty field dressing on his wounded leg.

Slaton set off into the heart of Mosta trying to mask a limp, his right leg having stiffened during the pause. He was determined to move quickly, but with twelve euros in his pocket his options for travel were limited. He had to either find a free ride, or quickly obtain more money. At this hour of the evening, nearing seven, the latter seemed more attainable.

The first prospect he encountered was a night-club, but Slaton bypassed it for two reasons: the crowds would be thin at this early hour, and the place would have crude but effective security. He next by-passed Speranza Chapel, as he did so remembering the old legend. Centuries ago, during a Turkish inva-sion, a young girl had injured herself running from a group of attackers. She took refuge in a cave under the old chapel, and there prayed to the Holy Mother for salvation. According to the tale, her prayer was answered when a spider cast a web across the cave's entrance. The invaders, reasoning that no one could have passed and left the web intact, ignored the cave and kept going. Slaton had always thought it a fine story—but to his thinking, one that spoke less of the Holy Blessing than of a poorly disciplined squad of Turks.

The invaders chasing him tonight would not be so easily sidestepped.

On the next street was a pair of restaurants, and these drew his interest. One was a formal establish-ment with a menu posted under glass at the main en-trance. The other appeared to be a small family-run business, humble meals offered at accordant prices— and of the two, the place far more inclined to do business on a cash basis.

He entered Salvino's, and what he saw was encour-aging. Fewer than half the tables were occupied. At a glance Slaton regarded a split layout, fifteen tables on one side of the room, a fully stocked bar on the other. The walls hadn't seen a paintbrush in years, and the only thing that might be called a decoration was a line of Christmas lights strung over the liquor rack— they looked like they'd been put up twenty years ago and never taken down. Behind the bar was the kitchen, and through a wide passageway Slaton saw a steel oven and a stove with pots on the boil.

He went to the bar and took a seat on a high stool. A heavyset man in an apron, whose last name was almost certainly Salvino, said in English, "What can I get you?"

Owing to his Nordic-leaning features, Slaton was typically addressed in English by native Maltese. "I'd like to see a menu."

The man slid one across the hardwood counter. "The chef's special tonight is scallop ravioli," he said, not missing a beat as he pulled a pair of beers from a long-handled tap and set them on a tray.

A call rose from the kitchen, urgent and in Maltese, "Did you call the plumber? This leak is getting worse. I am going to shut it off."

Salvino wiped his hands on his apron and went to the kitchen entrance where he stopped and looked up. Slaton followed his eyes before switching his attention to the bar in front of him, in particular a central spot along the mirrored back wall. He cross-checked the menu and saw exactly what he wanted.

Fish and chips.

Salvino came back. "You decide on something?"

"I'm still thinking."

Just then a large party came in the door. They were boisterous and familiar, clearly regulars. Slaton pegged Salvino for the kind of owner who would give a personal welcome—hugs and back slaps and an assortment of free appetizers. The proprietor did not disappoint, steering around the bar with outstretched arms.

Slaton pushed the menu away and headed to the front door.

He wasn't sure if Salvino noticed his departure, but

it mattered little. At a brisk pace he circled the block, rounding a pharmacy and a luggage shop, both closed for the night. In back he found a narrow lane, something between a street and an alley where a handful of cars were parked as if abandoned in a nuclear war, wheels on curbs and situated at odd angles, the occasional window left ajar. Trash cans and beaten crates were stacked against flaking mortar walls, most overflowing with garbage, and the smell was like all the world's backstreets, a pungent mélange of rotting organic matter.

The back door of Salvino's was obvious enough, framed by two brimming cans of kitchen refuse, and on an overturned crate an aproned teenager sat smoking a cigarette. The kid, perhaps eighteen years old, seemed lost in brooding self-reflection—a young man staring hard at life. He said not a word to the tall stranger who walked crisply past him into the kitchen.

Once inside Slaton paused, and he was instantly struck by fragrances far more pleasant than those outside: sautéed garlic, spices, fresh bread. He saw the expected accessories—steel sink, commercial oven, and a hook-lined wall where large spoons and dented pots hung in wait. He heard Salvino out in the dining room, still bantering with his new customers. With the kid outside clearly on break, there was only one man in the kitchen, a rotund cook who was busy dressing a pizza in shredded cheese and sliced sausage.

"I'm the plumber," Slaton said in Maltese.

The cook looked up and stared. "Where is Marco? He is our usual plumber."

"He couldn't come, so he asked me to fill in."

The cook shrugged, then pointed up at a fire sprinkler that was dripping water. "That one is bad. I shut the supply off but we need to have it fixed right away.

We are due an inspection by that idiot from the Fire Authority—the last time he ate here he claims his wife got food poisoning."

"You have a screwdriver?" Slaton asked.

The cook looked at him oddly.

"I had to park down the street," Slaton said. "I didn't want to drag all my tools here until I knew what I was dealing with. It will be easy."

With a pained look, the cook reached into a drawer and pulled out a long, flat-bladed screwdriver. Every commercial kitchen had one.

Slaton took a quick look around, and saw what he needed near the foot of the deep fryer. He took the screwdriver from the cook and began tinkering with the main supply valve.

The cook went back to his pizza.

Mario Salvino was kissing the cheek of a very attractive cousin when he heard a shout in Maltese.

*"Fire!"*

He looked up and saw smoke billowing from the kitchen. Salvino moved quickly, and was halfway there when he heard it again.

*"Fire!"*

It did not register to Salvino—not until later—that the warning came in an unfamiliar voice, nor did he question why the fire alarm had not sounded. He only saw flames billowing from the kitchen entrance, and heard the hiss of a fire extinguisher discharging. He paused long enough to shout to his customers, "Everyone outside! And call the fire department!"

Diners began scrambling for the door, at least three with mobile phones to their ears. At the very moment Salvino reached the kitchen entrance, he was struck in the face by a burst of noxious vapor. He tripped over something and went down hard, his eyes stinging from the chemical bath. There was a crash, followed by shouting, and he called out to the cook. "Vincente! Where are you? Help me up!"

Vincente didn't come.

Salvino rubbed his eyes, trying to regain his vision, and finally someone—he couldn't say who—helped him stand and find his bearings. He staggered back toward the dining room, ricocheting between chairs and tables, and finally groped his way to the front door. Outside he was guided to safety by a circle of concerned relatives. In the next minutes his sight began to return, a haze-stricken world behind a sea of tears, and the first thing he recognized was an arriving fire truck.

The firemen were inside for ten minutes, after which Salvino was able to see well enough to notice the captain beckoning him with a wave. "Come, Mario, I must show you something."

"Please—tell me it is not Vincente. Is he all right?"

The fire captain, a regular customer, grinned and said, "Vincente is Vincente—no worse than usual."

The air inside the dining room was clearing rapidly, smoke venting through open windows, a light cloud of vapor clinging to the ceiling. The kitchen was equally improved, the back door open to dismiss smoke that had seemed liquid only minutes ago. Vincente was there, leaning against the walk-in freezer and looking stunned but otherwise unharmed.

"We found him in the cooler," the captain said to Salvino. "The outer handle had been barred with a broom handle."

"What? But . . . but the fire."

"There wasn't really a fire. Somebody threw a can of

used fryer oil into the hot oven. It created a tremendous amount of smoke, but nothing was damaged. Whoever it was emptied both your fire extinguishers."

"But . . ." stuttered Salvino, "who?"

The captain took the bewildered restaurateur by the elbow and led him to the bar, stopping halfway down the mirrored wall. "Whoever did that," he said.

Salvino looked down and his blood rose. The cash register was empty, a flat-bladed screwdriver jammed into the drawer.

"*Bastardo!*" he bellowed at the top of his voice.

As Mario Salvino was calling the police, the man who'd cleansed his cash drawer was already four miles east in the Birkirkara district, stepping out of a cab near the municipal bus depot. In the back of the cab Slaton had discreetly counted his haul, the total falling in the middle of his estimate for what might be mined from a second-tier restaurant on an early Tuesday night: three hundred and two euros. He committed the number to memory, put it in the same mental file as the address from the takeaway menu.

He reached the station just in time to catch the last mainline departure to Valletta. Slaton purchased a ticket from a vending machine, and eight minutes later stepped onto an aquamarine bus. There were perhaps a dozen riders already there, scattered antisocially, and Slaton took an empty seat directly behind the driver, which gave a buffer of three rows to the nearest passenger. He molded into the cloth seat, and for the first time took stock of his injuries.

His thigh remained the biggest problem. It throbbed in pain, and a stain on his newly acquired workpants made him glad he'd stolen something dark in color.

The last passenger to board was an elderly woman, and when the gentlemanly driver stood to help her up the steps, Slaton seized an opportunity. Secured to the floor next to the driver's seat was a first-aid kit, and while the man was distracted, he unlatched the metal box and quickly requisitioned a handful of gauze and antiseptic, and an assortment of bandages. He had the half-empty kit back in place seconds before the driver returned, and when he reached for the swing handle to close the door, Slaton engaged the kit's anchoring latch with the toe of his left boot.

The bus came to life in a rumble of diesel and hissing brakes. Slaton eased back in his seat. By his best estimate, he would arrive in Valletta shortly after midnight.

# SIX

Characterized by Disraeli as, "A city of palaces built by gentlemen for gentlemen," Valletta, Malta, is perhaps more aptly described as a fortress built with style. In 1530, Charles V of Spain granted the long-drifting Knights of Saint John sovereign rule over the island, the annual fee being one Maltese falcon. Knowing a bargain when they saw one, the order of knights, who had a strong proclivity for mingling war with religion, rebranded themselves as the Knights of Malta. To make the place their own, the Knights set about fortifying the main harbor of Valletta. They built sentry stations and watchtowers, all looming high over the city's elegant cathedrals. With their defenses in order, the Knights set a more leisurely pace to fashion the first planned city of Europe. They stayed for two hundred and sixty-eight years.

In the intervening centuries, the city has endured battles great and small. Valletta was where Suleiman the Magnificent was proved to be something less, his forty thousand troops sent packing by an entrenched force one quarter of its size. Even at the height of World War Two, enduring an enthusiastic bombing campaign by Axis air forces, Valletta remained largely intact thanks to the Knights' robust design standards, not to mention brigades of sharp-eyed Allied antiaircraft gunners. By any measure, Valletta is a city built from the ground up with a defensive mind-set.

And defense was exactly what Slaton needed.

By cab he reached Senglea shortly after midnight, one of three harbor districts on the east side of the capital. In a country barely larger than Martha's Vineyard there were few places to hide, so he'd opted for the densest population center, even if it was a predictable move. The neighborhood was an eclectic mix, a place where expatriate accountants lunched with tenth-generation cobblers, and sailmakers shared jugs of red wine with computer hackers. Yet there was no denying Senglea's underlying soul—the massive Valletta shipyard was pervasive, infused into every brick, gutter, and shingle.

The temperature dropped markedly as morning took hold, and Slaton wished he'd stolen a jacket as well. His pants were bloodstained in spite of his efforts at a washbasin in the bus station restroom. His thigh throbbed in pain, and his hands still showed marks from a gravel rooftop in Mdina. A deep bruise on his elbow was a reminder of the Pole—the man he had killed in the stairwell. Slaton easily let that thought go. He hadn't set out to kill anyone today. The other man had.

He selected a shabby boarding house near an empty dry-dock berth. The Inn, as proclaimed by a hand-drawn sign, was three stories of stone, mildew, and mortar that looked every bit as inspiring as its name. The night clerk was a man near sixty, and weathered was the word that came to Slaton's mind—his channeled face and weary eyes spoke of a life less lived than endured. A lit cigarette was perched on a soda can, the ashes centered over the hole on top. The clerk barely registered Slaton's approach.

"Do you have any rooms?" Slaton asked in English.

The man picked up his cigarette, the ashes missing the can completely and scattering over a scarred wooden counter. Once it was hanging from his slack lower lip, he said, "I have lots of rooms. Do you have any money?"

Slaton wondered if he looked that bad. He pulled out his wallet. "Two nights," he said, knowing he would stay only one.

"Sixty euros . . . in advance." As Slaton handled his wallet, the night clerk noticed the abrasion on his hands. "Been in a tussle, have you?" he asked, his tobacco-stained breath carrying across the counter.

"Accident at work. I'm a stonemason—I fell off a ladder. It was my hands or my face."

The man curled fingers under his chin to think about it, a knurled thumb and forefinger that reminded Slaton of the branches of an old tree. He nodded as though it made perfect sense.

Slaton slid three twenties across the counter, and a key came in return, the old-school type with metal teeth and an engraved number 6.

Registration complete.

"Are you expecting company?" the desk man asked.

"Yes," Slaton lied. "If a dark-haired woman comes looking for Max, please send her to my room."

The Maltese nodded to say he would.

Slaton turned to go, but then he paused. He stepped back to the front desk and put his palm down on the moldering wood. When he pulled it away an additional twenty-euro bill appeared. "And if a man should come looking for me . . . or her . . . call my room and let the phone ring only twice."

The man eyed him, and then the cash. "I don't want trouble."

"That's my point."

The twenty disappeared under the proprietor's hand.

Another precaution was in place.


Slaton found room 6 on the second floor at the end of the corridor. The hallway by the door was nearly dark, the three-light fixture at that end of the hall having failed completely. He walked back to the staircase where a twin fixture was working perfectly, and in less than a minute he had switched out two of the three small bulbs. The hallway in front of room 6 was again bright. He did not reinsert the two dead bulbs into the staircase fixture. Instead, he studied the runner on the floor, a worn stretch of carpet ornamented with flowering vines and songbirds, all long ago trampled into submission. He raised the end of the runner nearest his door and placed the bulbs underneath, one at the end, the other a few feet farther on. When the carpet fell back in place the tiny rises were virtually indistinguishable.

Inside the room Slaton found what he expected, maybe a little more. The bed had been made and the floor seemed clean, although it was hard to say given the feeble light—every room at The Inn seemed a few bulbs short. There were dings and scrapes on the wall, but no damage that breached through to the next room. He rapped his knuckles on random sections and was rewarded with something old and solid, not the wood-framed drywall you got in newer buildings that was easily penetrated by small-caliber arms. The floor was old hardwood, worn and stained, and might have been recently swept. There was even a tiny bar of soap and a half-used bottle of shampoo in the bathroom.

Slaton swept the place for electronic devices, less because he expected to find anything than as an exercise to establish the right mind-set. Finding the phone unplugged, he reconnected the cable in case the night clerk had to make good on their arrangement. He checked the peephole at the door and saw an empty hallway, and through the room's lone window, partly covered by plastic drapes that hung like lead, he saw the gray-brick siding of the adjacent building.

Slaton laid on the bed and closed his eyes, hoping for sleep. What came instead was the question he'd been evading for hours. *Who would want me dead?*

Regrettably, it was a long list. Family members of those he'd dispatched. Their tribal brethren. Even entire countries. Slaton had served for years as a *kidon,* a Mossad assassin, doing Israel's dirtiest work. A thing like that followed a man, no matter how well he concealed himself. The accomplishments of his career, if they could be called that, were branded for eternity in minds and souls across the world. Including his own.

Yes, he decided, that had to be it. His past was responsible for what had happened tonight in Mdina. But what part?

One detail narrowed the field considerably. The man he'd dispatched in the stairwell, he was quite sure, was former GROM—Polish Special Forces. Yet the others were different. He knew because the Pole had used heavily accented English on their tactical frequency—likely the attackers' only common tongue.

Everything about the group screamed high-end mercenary. Which led to more troubling questions.

Who had hired them? What did it relate to?

Finally, the most vexing question of all. Given such a team—experienced and heavily armed, with a well-designed plan, and facing an unarmed and surprised target—how on earth was he still alive?

# SEVEN

Slaton slept as well as a hunted man could. Which was to say, not well at all.

To walk through life with a target on one's back instills a measurable degree of fear—indeed, a lack thereof would border on psychosis. It was something Slaton had long ago come to terms with. More intolerable was the unpredictability. During his years in the field with Mossad he had rarely lived by routine, habitually leaving open where he would eat, travel, and sleep the next day. One could set a general course, but in the end life became no more than a series of reactions. No flights scheduled in advance, no meetings on a calendar, no lunch dates with friends. Unpredictability was the key. It was what kept you alive.

Late-morning sun coursed through the dirty window of room 6—the tilt mechanism on the slatted blind was broken, stuck in the open position. He went to the window, and the blunt wall of the other building was still there, only with color now, a dreary oyster-gray that would have looked right at home on any battleship. The inside of the room appeared worse in the truth of day. Wallpaper peeled from every corner, and what had appeared to be crown molding at midnight was actually a band of mildew riding the ceiling's perimeter. The design he'd seen on the rug at the foot of the bed was in fact a terrible stain, the source of which Slaton had no desire to speculate upon.

He went straight to the bathroom and checked the mirror. A coarse man stared back, but a marked improvement over last night. The abrasions on his face had lessened, one scrape on his left cheek remaining. His thigh still hurt like hell, and Slaton stripped down and pulled the bandage back to inspect the wound. It appeared no worse, no obvious infection. After a lukewarm shower he tamed his hair with a quick finger-comb, then did his best with the antiseptic ointment and a fresh bandage. He dressed in the same dirty clothes he'd arrived in.

He compared his circumstances to yesterday's: a dreary studio outside Mdina, a half-full fridge, and a dresser drawer stocked with clean shirts and socks. He envisioned that room today being swarmed by detectives. There would be little to find. The furniture and books had come with the apartment. There would perhaps be a bit of DNA—these days one could only do so much—yet there would be no computer or smartphone, and correspondingly no Facebook or Twitter. Slaton had long existed to the inverse of those privacy-killers. His good jacket he would miss, so too the wedding band mortared behind a bathroom tile, likely never to be found. Not unless he returned, and he never would. Christine would understand, he told himself.

Or would she?

Slaton was contemplating this point, standing at the washbasin and scrubbing a stain from his shirt, a towel wrapped round his waist, when a distinct *pop* caused him to freeze. He shut off the tap and listened.

A second *pop*.

The muffled implosions of two broken vacuums—the lightbulbs under the rug outside his door. Gentle sounds that in the context of events arrived like cannon shots. With soft steps Slaton followed the wall to the door. He heard a hushed curse in Maltese, a female voice, and then the rush of a broom and the tinkle of broken glass. He took the towel from his waist and waved it twice across the viewing port. Nothing happened. He leaned in and ventured a look, and saw the best possible scenario—an irritated maid sweeping up glass shards.

Slaton expelled a long breath. This was how makeshift precautions often ended—teasing false alarms. The warning system he'd set last night was disabled. It hardly mattered. The Inn had served its purpose. He took a moment to study the evacuation diagram below the viewing port—every hotel door in the world had something like it.

Twenty minutes later Slaton stepped silently down the hall, past the busy housekeeper who was sheeting a bed in an adjacent room. He trotted down the stairs, took a turn before reaching the front desk, and pushed through an alley-side fire door into the bright midday sun.

The meeting was arranged for eleven that morning, and so shortly after ten, from his hotel near the airport, the man registered as Gianni Petrecca took a cab into the center of Santarém. With thirty minutes to kill—to be early would be a sign of enthusiasm—he veered to a roadside *rodízio,* and carried away a plate of rice and beans that was remarkably tasty. As a former airline pilot, he was something of a scholar of the world's cuisine, although a series of nuisance stomach ailments had instilled a preference for the bland over the exotic.

His true name—one he had not used in months—was Osman Tuncay. He had been born fifty-one years ago in the Turkish village of Sariyer, at the head of the Bosphorus Straits, a clear sign of providence for a child who would flow into the world and never return to his source. He kept a Turkish passport in his given name—perhaps in the Beirut flat?—along with a European-sourced JAA pilot certificate and medical document. He doubted he would ever use any of them again, as his years of lawful flying were clearly at a sunset. Tuncay had flown for Arabian Air for eighteen years, and two smaller airlines before that. His abrupt termination at Arabian had not been an issue of discipline, but rather the economics of revolution. The Arab Spring, notwithstanding all its hope and fervor, in the end had the far more material effect of putting millions of men and women out of work. The airline industry was more susceptible than most, and Tuncay had been notified of his dismissal by form letter, attached to which was a check for one month's severance pay. The contents of his locker were summarily shipped to the flat in Beirut. Fees due upon delivery.

For the next year he sent resumes across the world, a shotgun approach that was as sobering as it was hopeless. Watching his flight currency expire like sand from the top of an hourglass, his longtime hobby of carpentry rose to become his only source of income. Then, four months ago, just as he was debating whether to commit to a new set of hand tools, this new job had found him. There had been no job posting, only a quiet recommendation from the friend of a cousin in Haifa. The man who came to see him made an unthinkable offer, indeed a once-in-a-lifetime contract. For two months' work, and a measurable amount of risk, the villa in Mallorca that Tuncay had always dreamed of could be his.

He'd been doubtful at first, yet the six-figure advance, landing forcefully in his sinking bank account, had done the trick. Tuncay threw his allegiance behind an initiative that relied on seven men from across the hemisphere. They'd met as a group only once, gathering in a quiet villa on the Lebanese coast. Besides Tuncay, there was one scientist, a second pilot, and four others who were certainly soldiers. The scheme was audacious, yet with the right planning and backing he thought it might actually work. An Israeli named Ben-Meir, one of the soldiers, had governed that meeting, although Tuncay and the others had sensed a higher authority. An unseen underwriter of considerable means. A point further proven by what Tuncay today carried in his briefcase.

At a quarter past eleven, under a torrential downpour, he arrived at Santarém's municipal hall. The building was inundated, overwhelmed gutters feeding a temporary river that circled the foundation, and a crumbling roof that leaked like a colander. He was ushered to a small conference annex—as far as he could tell the only dry room in the place—where he shook hands with the mayor and two city councilmen. Rounding things out was the township's lead—and Tuncay imagined only—staff attorney.

The mayor opened things up. "We are happy you have come to do business in Santarém, sir."

Tuncay answered in his ambiguous Portuguese, "You have a lovely city. Unfortunately, I will not be able to stay long enough to enjoy her more subtle charms." Without sitting down, which would imply patience, he set his briefcase on the conference table and unlatched it theatrically. "The corporation I represent has performed its due diligence with regard to the airframe. Our engineers have evaluated all maintenance records, and our legal department has determined that there should be no barriers with regard to an export license."

Tuncay pushed a purchase agreement toward the lawyer, underneath which was a Brazilian application for the title transfer of an aircraft, pending purchase, along with the associated security license. It all looked devastatingly authentic—a particular specialty, it seemed, of the group he worked with. Were the lawyer to cross-check records in Brasília, he would find that a slightly altered application had indeed been filed, only the associated fee not paid, an oversight which anchored the process, for the foreseeable future, deep in the administrative eddies of the Ministry of Transportation.

"This aircraft is near the end of its service life," he continued, "and considerable maintenance will be required to restore the airworthiness certificate."

"Yes," said the mayor, "we are aware of all that. But we also know the market prices of such aircraft." He produced papers of his own and presented them to Tuncay. "This is a list of all transactions across the world involving MD-10s during the past two years. Sixteen sales have taken place, proving that significant demand remains among cargo operators."

Tuncay sighed. He was a pilot, not a negotiator—which was perhaps why he'd been given clear instructions. He pulled a certified check from his briefcase and slid it across the table, ending the brief volley of papers. "The amount, I suspect, is less than you would like, but it is the only offer I am authorized to make. If you have other buyers on the pitch you may wish to decline." Tuncay said, "I will give you ten minutes to confer amongst yourselves, then I must get back to the airport. The last flight to Brasília today leaves in two hours."

Leaving the check on the table in front of four grim faces, Tuncay excused himself and left the room. At the entrance portico he smoked two cigarettes in twelve minutes, and marveled at a lashing rain that showed no hint of relenting. The streets became rivers, seeming to fuse a sodden city with its surrounding jungle. He had seen such storms before, in places like Africa and Indonesia, and he wondered if this one might affect his flight schedule. When his second cigarette was done, Tuncay twisted the toe of his shoe over the butt and kicked the remains into the gathering mote.

He returned to find everyone in character—the lawyer was studying the purchase agreement language with a furrowed brow, and the two councilmen were in a hushed argument with the mayor.

"Well?" Tuncay asked. "Have you reached a decision?"

All went silent, and everyone looked at the mayor, who after a lengthy pause said, "Yes, let's do it."

Their guest smiled.

Papers were signed and the deposit banked, effecting the transfer of the airframe known as CB68H to a Seychelles-based concern that no one in the room, including Osman Tuncay, had ever heard of before—Perseus Air Cargo.

The ersatz Italian was at the airport thirty minutes later waiting for his flight to Brasília, a scheduled 1:20 departure. The storm had subsided, but others were on the horizon, hinting at certain delays. As he waited in the boarding area, Tuncay pulled out his cell phone and dialed a number that was not listed among his contacts.

"It is done," he said.

"When will it be ready?" the Israeli asked.

"For our acceptance flight? Two days, perhaps three. I will talk to our lawyer in Brasília this afternoon. The more errors he makes in the paperwork, the more time we will have. The maintenance contractors should arrive today, and I will get their opinion when I return. After that I'll have a better idea as to when we can fly."

"These mechanics can be trusted?"

"They are very capable, and have charged us accordingly. As long as the money flows, the aircraft will fly—it is only a matter of when."

"But are they discreet?"

"I hired Spanish speakers in a Portuguese-speaking country. No one will question what they're doing."

"Even . . . the day after?"

A pause before Tuncay understood. "*Especially* the day after. The mechanics work for a reputable aviation maintenance, repair, and overhaul facility. For such companies, reputation is paramount. They will make every effort to distance themselves from what's going to happen."

"All right. I am trusting your judgment."

"Where is my copilot?"

"Walid is on the way. Are you sure he's the right man for the job? Does he not need special training for this aircraft?"

Tuncay said, "He needs a pilot certificate and a pulse," and by the time he added, "just leave everything to me," he was already dreaming of the sun-drenched Mallorcan sea.

# EIGHT

Zan Ben-Meir.

The name came to Slaton as he crossed a narrow street with church bells ringing in the distance. Maddeningly, there was little else, but that was who he'd seen yesterday. He associated the name to Mossad's training grounds, and perhaps the café and halls of the service's headquarters building. But there it ended. While it was not a large intelligence organization, Mossad spanned thinly across the world, and so there were countless operatives Slaton had never met, let alone worked with. Zan Ben-Meir was in his mind as a name and a face, but nothing more. He pushed it away, and focused on his principal reason for coming to Valletta.

On first arriving in Malta, early last year, he had taken a succession of minor masonry jobs in the city with a specific purpose in mind. For Slaton it was an investment, the way other people might put money in a brokerage account. His first commission, a chimney in need of refacing, had proved unsuitable, as had the second, a terraced retaining wall near a gas station that had been marred by an auto accident.

The third job, however, had been ideal.

The wall, a standard two-meter affair no different

from a thousand others in the city, bordered the play-ground of a private school. For two days Slaton had made repairs, refurbishing the edges and joints, and adding new mortar where necessary. He arrived each day at sunrise, stayed until dusk, and took special care that the school's headmaster was happy with his work, going as far as to offer an unconditional guarantee of his work—in truth, less out of good business practice than to ensure that no other masons would be called upon if subsequent restoration became necessary. In the end, the two hundred euros he earned for his work was no more than an afterthought.

He approached the school now on a quiet mid-afternoon to find the recess yard mostly empty. There were puddles from recent rain, and a group of robust-looking children, raised on fish and goat cheese and the southern sirocco, sat circled under a tree with a teacher on the far side of the grounds. He rounded the outer perimeter on a little used sidewalk, and followed the wall to the end where it abutted an adjacent building. He paused long enough to isolate the correct section of wall, an acute alcove where the stone face was hidden from the street. Slaton scanned a half-dozen high windows on the far side of the street, and the only eyes he met were those of a listless cat on a ledge, presumably scanning the sidewalks below for mice it would never chase.

He quickly went to work, happy he'd had the forethought to conceal a short pry-bar behind the inset mounts of a rain gutter. It took twenty seconds to retrieve the bar, which was red with rust, and far less to remove the keystone. Slaton reached his hand into the fist-sized gap, curled his wrist, and found the small package. He pulled it clear and stuffed it under his shirt, the plastic covering he'd so meticulously wrapped still in place. He repositioned the stone and tapped it into place with the bar. There was a fleeting urge to seal things properly with mortar, which made him wonder—had his profession of the last year made such deep inroads? No, he decided, it was only the other profession clawing back into his life. If anyone saw a problem with the year-old repair, it might give reason to recall the light-haired stonemason who'd performed it.

Slaton dropped the bar in a shadowed corner and made his way back to the main street. There he turned left, and walked purposefully in the direction of the harbor.

There is no better place to find a private moment than in a church. And with over three hundred to choose from, there is no better place to find a church than on the island of Malta.

Slaton slipped silently into the Chapel of St. Phillip. He ignored the timeless stonework and mosaic portraits of saints, and solemnly took a seat in the pews three rows from the front. A pair of women were kneeling at the head of the nave, while a nun tended candles at the foot of the holy altar. The silence was overwhelming.

As a child Slaton had worshipped regularly, albeit in a very different house and, as with most children, under a degree of duress. Over the years, however, somewhere between a sun-hewn kibbutz in Wadi Ara and the deep-shadowed campuses of Mossad, he had lost his way. Perhaps it wasn't his belief in God that had faltered, but rather the concept of faith itself, gone skidding into oblivion under the weight of what he had seen. Under the weight of what he had done.

Slaton kneeled devoutly and bent his head, and with his hands hidden from sight he extracted the plastic-encased package from under the tail of his shirt and opened it deftly. Everything was still there. On first arriving in Malta, old habits still intact, he had set up the drop and filled it with the essentials of a quick escape. While murmured prayers bounded softly between the cavernous walls, Slaton counted eighteen thousand euros in mixed denominations. There were two passports, one of which was accompanied by a credit card. He'd considered adding a weapon to his get-well kit, but even assassins have morals, and the idea of concealing a loaded weapon in a playground wall violated his low-slung threshold of decency.

The first passport was a throwaway item bought locally from a known purveyor of gray identities, a man whose usual clientele were of two sources—either salt-encrusted Africans who'd survived the Mediterranean, or desperate Maltese fugitives about to tackle it. That document would never hold to close scrutiny, yet might stand in certain circumstances, allowing the other to be kept in reserve. The second document, as far as Slaton knew, remained pristine, and he'd kept the credit card in that name active.

He had purchased the identity in Marseille from Henri Faber. A hound-faced man—and a jewelry engraver if one went by the sign in his shop window—Faber was, in Slaton's opinion, the preeminent forger in western Europe. For fifty thousand euros the officious Frenchman, who attributed his illicit leanings to a vein of Corsican blood, had presented to Slaton a perfectly legitimate E.U. passport. It was written in the name Eric Risler, who was in fact a young Austrian tragically institutionalized in a clinic near Lienz following a motorcycle accident that had left his spine severed and his brain damaged. This was Faber's preferred strategy, situations he harvested by spending weekends in cafés poring over regional dailies and tabloids, reviewing the lesser misfortunes of greater Europe. Car crashes, equestrian tragedies, ski-slope falls, stroke victims. In a world of pixels and metadata, Faber was a well-grooved disciple of newspaper clippings and word of mouth. He kept an extensive file on every candidate, and most critically a photograph, as he insisted his clients bear a reasonable likeness to the original identity-bearer.

Once a match was made, the simplest method was to steal the original, oft-forgotten passport. Faber kept ties to a good thief, a man who could be relied upon not only to do a dishonest day's work, but to do it with discretion. Once a targeted passport was acquired, the most straightforward path was to renew the document if it was near the expiration date. Otherwise, Faber saw to it that enough physical damage was done to justify a replacement, paying particular attention to the watermarks and embedded electronic chips that authorities so heavily relied upon. Faber worked with the utmost caution, and all attendant paperwork was handled through a series of accommodation addresses. Properly done, the scheme left little chance that the families, let alone the victims, would ever catch on. All the same, Faber monitored each of his unfortunate principals for death, legal proceedings, or miraculous recoveries for the term of what he referred to as his "standard warranty"— five years.

The original Eric Risler, before his accident, had been very near Slaton's height and build, and within two years of his age. When a passport renewal laced through the system, bearing a marginal photograph of the man born as David Slaton, not an eyebrow was raised, this in one of Europe's most rigorous bureaucracies. It was time to put Faber's work to the test.

The nun went about her duties, her black habit flowing as she lit fresh candles on behalf of the ill and downtrodden. One of the kneeling women stood and made the sign of the cross before shuffling to the side exit, the clipped echo of coins clinking in a metal tray as she passed the door. Slaton pulled an assortment of coins from his own pocket and folded them neatly into a twenty-euro note. He divided the rest of his cash evenly and placed it in his two back pockets, then separated the passports and slid them into the two in front, Eric Risler on the left. The tough plastic bag he discarded in a seat-back holder next to a dog-eared book of hymns.

Slaton heard a shuffle of fabric from the nun's habit in the still, virtuous air, and outside the distant thrum of a passing bus. He remained still for a long moment with his head bowed reverently—in truth, filled with thoughts that were little removed from prayer. Unlike the others here, he did not petition for divine intervention, but rather something along the lines of inspiration. The question that had dogged him since last night continued to weigh heavily.

*Who is hunting me?*

The mere fact that he had been found was troubling enough. What concerned him more was his family. If someone had tracked him to this remote corner of the earth, might they also know about Virginia? Slaton's life in Malta was distilled to one theme—he had abandoned the two people he loved in order to protect them from his troubled past. Yet by erasing his existence, even to them, he had effectively rendered himself helpless, unable to protect his wife and child if things went wrong. It had always been a gamble—one that now appeared lost.

But what to do about it?

Going to America himself was not an option. He didn't know whom he was dealing with or if he'd eluded them, so a straight line back to his family was out of the question. There seemed only one course—he needed help. It had to be someone he trusted, someone capable, and most restrictive of all, someone who knew he was still alive. That cross-referenced list came to a single name.

Slaton rose quietly, made the sign of the cross at the aisle, and walked to the side portico. Not even the nun looked up when the muted sound of coins wrapped in a banknote touched the offering tray, nor moments later when the big door swung open to expose the brilliant light of day.


Slaton paid cash for a throwaway phone at a small grocer, and made his call from a bench overlooking Valletta's Grand Harbor. The western sun was touching the flagpole in front of him, the Maltese Cross snapping smartly in a crisp onshore breeze as he dialed the number from memory.

On the fourth ring, "Hello."

The voice was familiar, perhaps more subdued. "Hello, Yaniv. Is this number safe?"

There was a long pause as Yaniv Stein contemplated first the voice, then the question.

"As safe as any these days."

"How are you?" Slaton asked. The question was more than polite chatter. Sixteen months ago he had pulled a delirious Stein from the Iranian desert, a torrid patch of sand where he'd been stranded and left for dead after a botched Mossad mission. The man's leg had been mangled, and the next day when Slaton put him in the care of a doctor in Kazakhstan there had been talk of amputation. He'd not seen Stein since.

"I still have the leg," Stein said, "only it's not worth much. I walk with a cane and they gave me a medical retirement—as if they were doing me a favor. Nobody cared that I could still shoot straight."

"You never shot straight." Slaton was sure there was a smile behind the ensuing silence. "Where are you?" he asked.

"Tel Aviv. I have a small room in Holon—on a clear day I can almost make out the sea. I won't bother to ask where you are."

"Actually, that's why I'm calling. After I last saw you . . . I tried to find a quiet place where no one would bother me."

"Tried?"

"It worked for a while, but somebody tracked me down yesterday. It wasn't a happy reunion, and it's put me in a position where I need help."

"Me help *you*? On principle I'd be happy to repay you for pulling my dehydrated ass out of the Dasht-e Kavir. But realistically? I'm a gimp who's been dumped into retirement."

"I know exactly what you are. Same thing you always were. One bad leg? That's only an inconvenience."

A hesitation, then, "What do you need?"

"Two things. First of all, did you ever know a guy in the service named Zan Ben-Meir?"

"Not well, but yes, I remember him. He was Metsada, a former army officer. I remember he got in trouble for something a few years back."

"Any idea what?"

"I can't remember, so it must not have been any-thing spectacular. But I do think he was forced out. Did you run across him?"

"You could say that." Slaton explained what had happened in Malta.

"You were lucky to survive."

"Maybe so."

"Any idea *why* they came after you?"

"None at all. If Ben-Meir isn't Mossad anymore, he may have gone soldier-of-fortune . . . which means he could be working for anybody."

"I suppose . . ." Stein hedged. "Then again, you know the new Mossad director. I've heard he tries to bring back operators after they've fallen off the radar."

"Tell me about it," said Slaton, who was himself the victim of director Nurin's first clawback scheme.

"Sorry I can't tell you any more," Stein said. Then after a pause, "You said you needed two things."

Slaton explained his overriding reason for calling.

Stein took a long time to think it through. "I never knew you got married."

"Mistake on her part."

"Big mistake. But yeah, I can do that for you."

"I'm not sure how long it will take."

"Time is something I have a lot of these days," said Stein.

"And there is one complication."

"What's that?"

"My wife, Christine—she has no idea I'm still alive."

# NINE

Dr. Christine Palmer saved the stroller, but at the price of falling on her backside in an entirely graceless flop. Davy, her eleven-month-old, overwrapped bundle of boy, gave a gurgly chuckle.

"I'm glad to see you have a sense of humor," she said, sitting waylaid on the icy steps at the threshold of her front door. Christine reasserted her balance, one hand on the door handle and the other on the umbrella stroller, and pulled herself upright on the slippery stone landing. "I suppose I'd have laughed at you for the same thing—but you have a diaper to cushion your fall."

Her son looked at her hopefully, as if waiting for mom's next trick. She disappointed him by moving carefully, and they reached the sidewalk uneventfully. Two right turns later she was sinking the doorbell of the house next door.

Almost immediately the door swung open, and Davy chirped when he saw the sixtyish woman in a flowered housedress with a steaming cup of coffee in her hand.

"It's my Wavy-Davy," the woman exclaimed in her best singsong voice.

"Hi, Annette. Be careful on your steps—mine were

frozen solid." Christine pushed the stroller inside, and as soon as the door closed she began to unwrap Davy. When he was down to a sweater and pants she plopped him on the floor amid a circle of colored blocks.

"Yes, it was a hard freeze," Annette said. "Davy and I are definitely going to stay inside today. Can I get you a cuppa?"

"Sorry, maybe when I pick him up. I have to get to work right away. One of the other doctors has the flu and I have to help cover. But the good news is I should be home early, in time for dinner with any luck."

"It's nice that you have such flexibility. Are many doctors working part-time these days?"

"Only the poor ones," Christine answered dryly. "But it's getting more common. My practice has two other women in my . . . well, in similar situations. We look out for each other."

"I know it's not easy being a single mom, but I think you're going about it in the right way. Roy never understood anything but putting his nose to the grindstone," she said, referring to her late husband who'd been a family practice man for thirty years.

"Yes, so I've heard. I wish I could have known him."

"Three years since I lost him," Annette said, "but it seems such a blur. It was only last month that I started going through his things in the garage."

Christine thought, but didn't say, *Is that how long it takes?* She'd been staring at David's side of the closet for nearly a year, and had yet to take the first load of clothes to Goodwill.

"I don't suppose you need a wooden tennis racket, do you?" asked Annette.

"No, we already have a pair. Edmund was going to give me lessons right before . . . right before he died."

Annette didn't let the silence sit long. "I'm glad I got to know him. Just this morning I was admiring the stone planter he built for me out back. I'll fill it with annuals every spring. Edmund was good at what he did."

"You can't imagine."

Annette seemed ready to say something, but then held back.

"What?" Christine asked.

"Well . . . nothing much. But I'll always remember one day last summer. He was sitting on your back deck reading a book, and I came over for something or other. Edmund went inside to get me a glass of iced tea and . . . well you know me, book fiend that I am . . . I looked to see what he was reading. I recognized it as *History of the Persian Empire,* by Olmstead. A very comprehensive book, one might even say academic."

"Well, yes . . . for a stonemason I suppose he had some eclectic tastes."

"It wasn't so much that," said Annette. "You see, the version he was reading was a Swedish translation."

Christine's response was instantaneous and right on legend, "He went to school in Sweden as a young boy." Not, *Yes, he was perfectly fluent in four languages, and had a working knowledge of another three.*

"That explains it," said Annette. "Every once in a while I caught the trace of an accent I couldn't place."

They watched Davy play with the blocks, mesmerized like campers watching a fire. Christine realized she'd never seen a picture of David as a child. *Was this what he looked like?* "So tell me," she asked, wanting to change course, "have you asked Anson out to coffee yet?"

"Anson?"

"The new tenor in the choir—you were talking about him last week."

"Oh, Lord. He's one of two widowers in the entire church, and there must be thirty of us who've lost our husbands. The poor man is besieged."

Christine smiled. "I don't know. If you don't pursue these things—"

Annette's eyes widened a bit, as though she'd just made her own point. Christine began fishing through her purse. "Here's your February check."

Annette took it and set it aside.

Christine said, "I need to get going. I may need you one or two weekends next month. I'll let you know."

"Not a problem, as long as I can make a service on Sunday." She peered obviously out the bay window in front. "Have you seen our new neighbor yet?"

"What new neighbor?"

"A young man, although I've only seen him once. He moved into the Mooreheads' place."

Christine looked out the window, toward the house set on a diagonal from her own. "Oh, right. I forgot Ed had been trying to rent it out."

"It's kind of odd. I saw him pull his car in the garage a few days ago, but he hasn't left since."

"How could you know that?"

"No tracks in the driveway."

Christine laughed. "I'll say it again, Annette, you've been staying up too late with your mystery novels."

"I suppose you're right—wishful thinking. Nothing exciting ever happens around here."

"Don't knock it. There's a lot to be said for boring."

Davy squealed, and a red block went tumbling toward the unused fireplace. Christine handed over the daily diaper bag. "Cereal for lunch, and use the office number if you need to reach me. My cell has been giving me trouble lately."

Christine leaned down and kissed her son, who ignored her in favor of a picture book, and minutes later she was backing her car out of the driveway. She tried to avoid it, but found herself glancing at the Mooreheads' house. It looked just as it had for months, ever since Ed had taken a promotion in San Diego. The only thing new was a dim light burning behind the blind of the top-floor window. Maybe someone *had* rented the place. But there was nothing else. No smoke from the chimney, no snow-shoveled path to the front door. And Annette was right about the driveway—it was covered in snow and there wasn't a single track.

Christine shook her head, frowned, and accelerated down the hill. *No,* she thought, *that's a mentality I'll never allow again.*

# TEN

Slaton slipped easily into his old ways. Needing to replace the work clothes he'd stolen the night before, he found a secondhand store and paid cash for khaki pants and a tan cotton shirt, making sure both were a loose fit. At a sporting goods store he splurged on a beige weatherproof jacket and a pair of quality trail shoes to replace his beaten work boots. He also bought a cheap yellow raincoat that came in a tube and a pair of wraparound sunglasses. In the gallery of deceit Mossad had instilled in him, one basic tenet prevailed—multiple small changes were the most effective.

He stepped into the street and was washed by a warm evening breeze, burnt shocks of orange painting the low western sky. He stood still for a long moment and, registering no threats, set out downhill. There was little choice but to leave Malta. The problem was that departing any island offered but two options: by air or by sea. With only one international airport for his pursuers to monitor, Slaton's hand was forced.

He spent two hours that afternoon canvassing the Valletta waterfront. Across the harbor, moored like a floating city block, was a massive cruise ship sided by tourist shops and cab stands and vendors selling trinkets. South of this was the Virtu Ferry Terminal where scheduled boats departed to the Sicilian ports of Catania and Pozzallo. All were public, monitored by authorities, and funneled passengers to fixed destinations. Which meant all were problematic.

He meandered around the piers, memorizing the names of cargo ships and bulk carriers. At the Port Authority office he inquired politely about the mooring fee schedule for private vessels, and was steered toward an office near the back of the building. Slaton never entered that suite, but instead spent ten minutes rambling through the place, and in a dreary side office he encountered a dry erase board on which was listed the scheduled time and date of departure for every vessel in the harbor. Unfortunately, the subsequent destinations for these sailings were not included, but he reckoned at least half would take him in the direction he needed to go—north to Europe. There his passport would be at its strongest, allowing him to move with the least amount of scrutiny, and from any port on Europe's Mediterranean shore he could easily cover the remaining ground to the only destination that made sense—Zurich. A place where he could acquire the means to carry whatever battle had found him.

Satisfied with his reconnaissance, he turned away from the piers, and after no more than fifty steps Slaton found what one found within a block of all the world's wharfs—a squalid watering hole topped by a sputtering neon sign and footed by beer-fouled gutters. Most intelligence operatives liked bars—people were drunk, talked a lot, and made bad decisions they often couldn't remember the next day. Slaton disliked them for the same reasons. He ducked inside and let his eyes adjust to the dim light. It was barely six in the evening, but the place was busy. Ships docked and sailed, he knew, on schedules drawn by profits, no consideration given for human circadian rhythms. It explained why merchant seamen rarely wore watches, and never drank by them.

The building was likely a converted warehouse, stone-walled and ancient, not dissimilar from the Catacombs of St. Paul where he'd originally expected to work today. Leather-skinned sailors and bulky longshoremen were planted behind tables, and a round-bottomed waitress swerved between them taking leers and pats, and certainly large tips, with an all-knowing smile.

Most of the patrons were here to socialize, a few simply to drink, yet there was always an underlying element of those looking for work. They held at the fringes, mostly alone, a brackish blend of the down-trodden, fugitive, and otherwise unemployable; journeyman sailors hoping to haul lines and scrape rust all the way to the next port where they would squander their earnings in another bar as they waited for the next ride.

Slaton went to the bar, and when the aproned man behind it made eye contact, he said, "Coffee, black."

Slaton reckoned this was not a breach of etiquette. He had an abrasion on his cheek and hadn't slept well, the edges of his rough night there for all to see. The barkeeper didn't hesitate. He drew a tall steaming cup from a dented pot on a burner.

"I've been stranded," Slaton said in decent Maltese as the cup was slid in front of him. "Need to get back home. You know of any skippers taking passengers? Something to Italy or France?"

The bartender was a surly sort with lined jowls

and sad eyes that afforded him the aura of a basset hound. He looked Slaton up and down, and said, "People order whiskey, I give them whiskey. The travel agency is across the harbor."

Slaton pulled a twenty-euro note from his pocket and edged it across the table.

The bartender feigned a look of surprise, then pushed it back. "You know how many people come in here every day trying to get north? Algerians, Pakis, Ethiopians. It's a goddamn exodus, I tell you."

Slaton left the money where it was.

"But you don't look the type," the barman hedged.

Slaton took a long pull on his mug. The coffee wasn't bad, strong and hot. He produced two more twenties and laid them on the first.

"Maybe you are police," said the Maltese.

"Police?" Slaton replied. "Hardly. I have a passport, I have money. There's nothing illegal about buying passage in a cabin, is there?"

"The ferry across the harbor is easier. Always less trouble."

Slaton didn't reply.

The barkeep seemed to think about it, then tapped his index finger twice on the oak counter. Slaton pulled out two more bills, and the stack disappeared. The bartender turned away. He lifted three fresh mugs from a rack, filled them with beer, and slid the lot in front of Slaton. He nodded toward a corner table where three men were sitting.

Slaton sipped his coffee, studied them, and decided they were certainly officers. None of the three wore a uniform—always bad form in a bar—but their shoes had life in them and their shirts were clean, and their hair had been cut by someone other than a bunkmate with a number-two guide.

"Do you know what ship they're from?" Slaton asked.

"*Ionian Star*," the barman replied.

This told Slaton they were regulars. Greek most likely and, if he remembered correctly from his earlier survey of the docks, the ship was a bulk carrier. Coal or gypsum or salt. Three thousand tons of dry stores on a programmed run across the Med, with a regular stop in Valletta. A vessel that size suggested a complement of twenty officers and crew, more or less, all of it tethered loosely to a home office in Athens or Piraeus.

Slaton gathered the three steins and left an empty coffee mug on the bar. The oldest of the three men was talking as he approached, and all three gave a lusty laugh at a punch line—the two junior officers finding unquestioned humor in their captain's story. Slaton set the mugs on their table, pushing aside a set that were empty. Their laughter dropped like a buckshot-strewn quail.

"Can I join you for a moment?" Slaton said in English, pointing toward the empty seat on the fourth side of the square table.

The skipper regarded the beers, his men, and Slaton in turn. He nodded to the seat.

Knowing directness would be in his favor, Slaton got right to the point. "I'm looking for passage north. I can pay for a bunk and know how to stay out of the way."

The old Greek, more weathered up close but with clear brown eyes, studied him critically. Slaton reckoned he was drawing the same inferences the barman had—that he didn't look like the usual kind of refugee, and might be some kind of policeman. "I don't run a cruise ship," the skipper said. "That dock is across the harbor."

"I hear your food is better."

The captain looked at him evenly for a beat, then his furrowed face cracked and he broke out laughing. His lieutenants joined the chorus.

"Where is your next port?" Slaton asked.

"Marseille. But it doesn't matter. My shipping line has recently taken a hard stand against passengers. The insurance companies don't like it—too many complications. Go see the Turks in the corner. They are on their way to Istanbul. For the right price, they would deliver Jesus to the cross."

"But I want to go to Marseille."

One of the younger men, the larger of the two with curly black hair and a flat, crooked nose said, "The captain said no." He took a long draw on his free beer, wiped the foam from his lips with a sleeve, and said, "Now leave us alone."

Slaton didn't move. "Five thousand euros," he said.

The skipper's eyes narrowed. It was enough to buy ten legitimate round-trip tickets, either by sea or air.

"What kind of trouble are you in?" the skipper asked.

"Not the official kind. No immigration or police. I just want to leave Malta quietly. If your company has rules about paying passengers, they probably have them about stowaways too. Only the crew wouldn't be responsible for that. I'm sure people sneak aboard and get away with it now and again. Or maybe you're short a crewman and need to bring aboard a short-term replacement."

The big man stood, towering over the table. "The captain told you to—"

The skipper raised his hand and his minion went quiet.

Slaton ignored the second man's physical challenge.

He remained completely still, his eyes flat and expressionless.

The captain studied him, then stood and went to the bar where he had a prolonged conversation with the bartender. Slaton was encouraged. The captain returned, and asked, "You have papers?"

"Of course."

"Are they good?"

"Perfectly legitimate."

The captain leaned back in his chair and took a pull on his beer. "Eight thousand—cash."

Slaton made a point of frowning, but in fact had expected a five digit number. After an appropriate pause, he said, "Done."

"We sail at four tomorrow morning. Be at the gangway by three."

Slaton rose to leave.

"Oh," the captain added, "and send us another round, would you?"

# ELEVEN

Slaton arrived at the pier sharply at three. The old ship, which had appeared a weary shade of blue in yesterday's high afternoon, looked anemic under the yellow sulfuric haze of the nighttime loading dock. There was a bright glow of white from the bridge, but otherwise the ship appeared lifeless. Twin deck cranes poised like skeletal birds over the iron hull, all of it beaten and stained, and held together by rivets the color of old pennies. The wharf was quiet in the early morning, the only activity being a few long-shoremen who were hauling last-minute provisions aboard *Ionian Star* by hand cart. The more relevant load had already been poured into the holds, a few thousand tons of some dry-bulk cargo, and the ship rode noticeably lower on the water than when Slaton had first seen her.

He found the captain smoking a cigarette at the foot of the gangway, a curl of smoke rising into the black night. Without a word, he flicked his cigarette into the harbor and led Slaton up the metal incline. On the main deck they rounded the aft hold, its big hatches already secure, and at the base of the stern deck the skipper descended a steep metal staircase.

Slaton followed the Greek through a charmless maze of narrow passageways. The air below was stagnant, etched in grease and fuel oil, and a line of wire-framed bulbs snaked along the ceiling. Passing what were clearly crew's quarters, Slaton saw sea bags stacked on bunks and walls plastered with photographs—wives and kids, tear-out centerfolds of naked women, a few callous souls mixing the themes.

The captain stopped and opened the door to what looked like a closet. Slaton saw a rusted circular drain in the center of an eight-foot-square space. Brooms, buckets, and mops had been shoved to one side, making room for a single brown-stained, sheetless mattress.

The skipper held out his hand, and Slaton filled it with a thick envelope. The Greek didn't bother to look inside—there would be plenty of time for that later. He said, "It is good you are a man who travels light. We will make port in Marseille in three days. You may leave this room only to eat and to use the head. The mess hall is three cabins forward and the head is next to it. You eat after the crew. Any questions?"

"Customs in France?"

"Leave that to me."

Slaton didn't like the answer. The man had asked about his papers, yet hadn't bothered to inspect them. He *should* have looked.

The master of the vessel started to leave, but then turned. "If you have anything of value—there is a safe in my cabin. In spite of my best efforts, some of the crew can be . . . how should I say it . . . curious?"

"You've already taken everything I have."

The Greek studied Slaton's bulky jacket, then smiled.

"Then you are a man with no worries, my friend. Bon voyage."

The engine mechanics arrived in Santarém at dawn, the only passengers aboard a chartered Beechcraft-1900 from Guatemala City.

Umberto had been expecting them, and he greeted the two Guatemalans as soon as they stepped onto the tarmac. It turned into an awkward affair—even if his Portuguese welcome escaped the men, his smile should have sufficed, yet the two Spanish-speakers only walked past him ungraciously. They went straight to work, pulling their tools out of the cargo bay, and everyone clambered into the airport's truck. An undeterred Umberto took the wheel and steered toward the MD-10 on the far side of the airfield.

After helping the men unload in silence, Umberto left the mechanics to their business. He went to the operations office, built a cup of sweet light coffee, and stood under a mango tree as the Guatemalans set up camp under the big jet's wing. They opened toolboxes and uncrated expendables—altogether it was a heavy load, one that Umberto imagined must have stretched the little Beechcraft to its maximum gross weight.

After thirty minutes the men asked to borrow the largest work stand available, and Umberto complied. It turned out to be just tall enough, the service lift jack-knifing up to the midpoint of the starboard engine. From there they unlatched cowling panels and went to work. Umberto did not know what they were inspecting—oil levels or hydraulic fluid, he supposed, whatever was necessary to make a fifty-thousand-pound thrust engine spin in the designed manner.

Then, disturbingly, he saw the mechanics shake their heads and begin lowering the stand.

One of the Guatemalans stepped down to the ramp and approached a watchful Umberto.

"You have for bugs?" was what Umberto heard, the Portuguese-Spanish disconnect strong as ever.

"Bugs?"

The man made a swatting motion with his hands, then pantomimed holding something as he made the noise, "Ssshhh! Ssshhh!"

"Spray? Kill bugs?"

A big nod. "Yes, kill."

Umberto went into the operations office and began rummaging through cabinets. Twenty minutes and two cans of insecticide later the job was done. A massive nest of stinging insects, the likes of which he had never seen in the Amazon—not that he was any expert—fell from the starboard engine and splattered onto the tarmac like a rotten melon. The mechanics moved cautiously to the port engine, and apparently found no further infestations. One man climbed onto the spine of the aircraft and walked back to the tail section. He briefly inspected the third engine, which was centrally mounted and integrated into the vertical tail, and gave an enthusiastic thumbs-up.

The Guatemalans spent the balance of the morning on the starboard side until, with the torrid sun peaking and lunchtime near, they put down their tools, wiped their hands on a common rag, and asked Umberto, "Where is beer?"

This request passed without language barrier, and Umberto answered with a combination of words and hand gestures to guide them toward the second-nearest bar which was owned, not by chance, by his cousin Leonardo.

The two trod off, more duty than excitement in their strides, and Umberto wondered if they would be back today. He heaved a sigh. *With Central Americans you never knew.*

Slaton slept lightly through the morning and past noon. After waking, he stared at the ceiling with an arm bent behind his head. He heard the occasional crewman transit the hallway outside, and noted regular mechanical thumps from somewhere behind the walls. Sounds that were all to be expected, along with the steady drone of the ship's screws. Less predictable—his thoughts as he again tried to work out who was trying to kill him.

It all eventually tapered to one manageable question. Who knew that he'd taken up residence in Malta? In the end, he had a concise list of one. As far as he knew, only the former director of Mossad, Anton Bloch, was aware of the refuge he'd chosen. Indeed, only a handful of people knew that Slaton was still alive after surviving a mission gone wrong sixteen months ago on the western shores of Lake Geneva. Aside from Bloch, this included Yaniv Stein, whom he had already called into service, a certain retired Swedish policeman, and last and most ominously the new director of Mossad, Raymond Nurin.

Yet it was not so simple a net to cast. There were always other possibilities, most involving pure chance. A stray document or a slipped conversation at Mossad. An inadvertent paper trail. Or the most simple of all— an old enemy, visiting Malta, who had simply turned a corner at the wrong time and recognized a hardworking stonemason as something else.

Only too late did Slaton see the folly of his self-imposed exile. Disappearing had done nothing to keep his wife and son safe, and in fact had brought a severe handicap—today he was on one side of an ocean and his family the other. Christine and his son were exposed.

*His son . . .*

It struck Slaton like a hammer blow—he didn't even know his child's name.

He abruptly rolled off the mattress and stood, forcing his mind to matters at hand. He deleted the question of who was acting against him, and pushed aside his protective instincts for his family. With newfound clarity, he saw that he needed two things immediately—information and means. Both lay in Zurich, where his private banker kept a discreet office in the shadow of the Bahnhofstrasse giants. What happened later could not be considered. Not yet.

Zurich had to come first.

# TWELVE

It was midafternoon when Slaton emerged from his quarters, if a converted utility closet could be termed as such. In the mess hall he was given a bowl of brothy soup and a heel of French bread by the cook, a young Filipino, he guessed, who then began silently clearing dishes that had been strewn carelessly about the officer's table. The man didn't meet his eyes once, which Slaton took as an ominous sign.

He dipped his bread into the soup and chewed off a corner. "This food is good," he said.

The cook didn't reply. There was a chance he didn't speak English, but Slaton reckoned that if he knew any four words in the language it would be the ones he'd just said.

He tried a second time with the only phrase that might top it. "What's for dinner?"

"Menu in hall," the cook said.

"Have you been on this cruise long?"

"Just signed second two-year contract."

"Two years? I'll bet you've been a lot of places. Seen a lot of things."

No reply.

"How about the captain? It was good of him to let me come aboard. Is he a good skipper?"

Still nothing.

"You Filipino? I've been to the Philippines a couple of times. Once to Manila and another time—"

The cook disappeared into the kitchen.

"Nice talking to you," Slaton muttered into his bowl.

He found the cook's rebuff unaccountably frustrating. In his years with Mossad Slaton had often worked solo, loneliness his customary companion. Had Virginia changed that? During exile in Malta he'd found it increasingly difficult to distance himself from people: neighbors, shop owners, mail carriers. A ten-year-old named Kid. Now circumstances were driving him back into reclusion. The position of cook was among the most humble on any ship, and if anyone on board was going to talk to him it was the Filipino in the stained apron.

Like it or not, he was alone again.

Slaton put his empty bowl and spoon neatly on a tray, and shouldered out into the passageway. There was no one in sight, and he turned away from his room and walked down the corridor. He passed a door labeled ELECTRIC BUS 4, followed by staterooms where, if the stencils on the doors were accurate, the second officer and chief engineer were quartered. After these he came to an unmarked door, and Slaton nudged it open to find a storage closet that was filled from top to bottom. There were sea bags and suitcases, fishing poles and snow skis. Two folding bicycles leaned against an old surfboard. It was overflow storage, he supposed, a community repository where officers and crew could stow outsized items that didn't fit in their cramped berths.

Slaton heard footsteps and looked up just as a uniformed officer turned the corner. It was one of the men who'd been in the bar with the captain yesterday, the large man with the bent nose who'd been eager to back his skipper with his fists. His name tag and epaulets identified him as the ship's second officer.

"What are you doing?" he barked. "You are supposed to be in your quarters."

Slaton pulled the door of the storage room shut. "I was looking for a head that didn't smell so bad."

The man came closer and glared at Slaton with olive-black eyes. "There is only one—you know where it is."

The man was roughly six foot four, maybe two hundred forty pounds, which gave him a size advantage over Slaton. But only a slight one. He was clearly the kind of man who used his bulk to intimidate. His breath was rotten, something between sour milk and yesterday's fish, and Slaton weighed the merits of bringing this to his attention.

In the end, he said, "Yeah, I think I remember where it is."

Slaton turned down the passageway toward the head. He felt the black eyes follow him all the way.

The Guatemalans returned after a surprisingly short lunch, and if there had been beer involved Umberto saw no sign of it in their steady gaits.

They were joined by two new men who'd arrived on a scheduled midday flight. The second pair was from Lima—was there a Portuguese-speaking aircraft mechanic anywhere in the world?—and their first request was more conventional than the bug-slaying Guatemalans'. Umberto, under instructions from the city council to do whatever he could to help, used a utility tug to pull the airport's only ground power cart next to the big jet. The unit was twenty years old, a Cummins diesel on bald tires, purchased when the airport was in higher times and seeking ICAO certification. But the old cart cranked to life on the third try, and was soon feeding 400Hz AC power to the jet's distributive electrical busses.

While Santarém drank its afternoon coffee, the Peruvians removed boxes from the equipment bay, ran checks, and eventually wrote down a few part numbers. They gave their list to Umberto, who dutifully relayed it by way of the operations office fax machine to a number scribbled on top.

Everything seemed to be going well.

Two hours later the Guatemalans called for a fuel truck. The tanker was prompt, and they hooked up a high-pressure hose and began filling the main tanks. It was on the stroke of three that afternoon, under a steaming midday sun, that Umberto saw one of the mechanics rush to the fuel truck on a sprint and begin pounding on a red emergency shutoff switch. The switch worked, although not without a delay, and everyone watched in silence as two thousand gallons of Jet A fuel vented from a seam in the jet's wing, splattered to the tarmac, and coursed a river of amber into the surrounding rain forest.

"Is it a goner?" Christine asked.

"No, just a loose wire on the plug. I'll have it reconnected in no time. These garbage disposals are notorious for loose leads. It's because they vibrate so damned much."

She looked on gratefully. She had always considered herself a capable person, but when it came to electrical work she drew the line—that was better left to the professionals. Or at least to someone she trusted. In fact, the man underneath her sink was not an electrician but a neurosurgeon, undeniable overkill for a dodgy garbage disposal. She supposed having delicate hands on spinal columns didn't necessarily translate to fixing three-quarter horsepower InSinkErators. Still, Dr. Mike Gonzales she trusted.

"That should do it," he said, standing with a screwdriver in his hand. "Give her a try."

Christine flipped the switch and the motor whirred like an empty blender.

"You're a genius. What do I owe you?"

"Maybe a clean rag and a cup of coffee?"

Ten minutes later they were together on the couch while Davy navigated the room, alternately standing and falling on his diaper.

"You know, Christine, I think he's gotten bigger since you brought him into work last month. He's beginning to look a lot like you."

She smiled appreciatively, thinking, *He's his father reincarnate.*

"Hey, the Cleveland Orchestra is coming to town next week. I've heard it's a great show. Would you like to go?"

"Davy doesn't like loud noise."

The two exchanged an awkward look.

He said, "I'm not sure if Tchaikovsky would appreciate that. And you *could* get Annette to watch him."

Christine nearly replied, but instead began stacking bedtime books that had spilled from the pile on the coffee table. It wasn't the first time Mike had asked her out. He was a good-looking, once-divorced brain surgeon with a stellar sense of humor and a black Maserati. She'd turned him down every time.

"Christine, maybe I shouldn't be the one to say it, but it's been over a year. At some point you have to—"

"*I know* . . . I know what you're saying, Mike, and I appreciate the offer. It's just that I've got Davy to deal with, not to mention work. Life just seems too complicated right now."

Dr. Gonzales forced a nod. "Okay. I guess I'll have to call the escort service again."

She laughed. "Yeah, right. And thanks for understanding."

Two cups of coffee later, she gave Mike an appreciative hug and saw him to the front door. When it closed she felt blue, and not wanting to mope around the house, she soon had Davy bundled up and strapped into his car seat.

"Groceries and the gas station, buddy. Another rockin' night out with Mom."

She sat next to him, kissed him under the chin, and got a throaty chuckle in return. There almost seemed something familiar in his voice, but Christine knew that was ridiculous. She stared at her son, as she often did, and wondered how things might have been different if she'd had the good sense to fall in love with a schoolteacher or a sales rep. Even a neurosurgeon. It was her regular guilt trip, misgivings that still came every day. The last time she'd seen David he had been faced with an excruciating choice. If he didn't kill a particular man, he was told his family would never be safe. And what had she done? She'd made the situation impossible by adding her own ultimatum. *If you kill that man, don't ever come back to me.*

Up against that, David had gone into harm's way. She never saw him again. There was a memorial service in time, three weeks after "Edmund Deadmarsh" was officially declared deceased by the Commonwealth of Virginia. She'd stood in the church vestibule holding Davy, and Annette was there, along with a handful of neighbors, and a priest who talked fast because he had a noon flight from Dulles to reach an ecclesiastical conference in Florida. The day was dreary and the crowd sparse, probably all one could expect from God and the world when a Protestant minister gives final blessings to a Jew in a place the dearly departed had called home for barely a year. To his credit, the priest had tried to prepare, asking for details on David's good and kind life. Embarrassingly, Christine had fumbled for a response. *He killed a great many people, but would have been a terrific father if he'd survived his last assassination mission.* Hardly the stuff of a virtuous eulogy. Yet David *was* good—that much she knew and would keep in her heart forever. It was his situation, the realm in which he'd existed, that was hopelessly scored in sin.

Davy reached up from his car seat and put a finger to her face. Only when he touched the wetness on her cheek did she realize what had caught his eye and put a serious look on his face. She bent down and kissed him, again and again, until the throaty laugh returned. She gathered herself and took the driver's seat, and minutes later had the car moving slowly along the snow-edged street. Though Christine had no reason to chronicle the fact, it was the first time in a week she had left home with her son.

Less than a minute after she was gone, the garage door at Ed Moorehead's house opened. A dark Chevy backed out of the blackened garage, performed a neat turn in the road, and accelerated briskly in the same direction.

# THIRTEEN

Slaton reckoned that *Ionian Star* would bypass the Tyrrhenian Sea and skirt the southern edge of Sardinia, likely passing no more than a few miles from the coastline. He estimated this near-landfall to occur roughly two hours before sunrise, after which could be expected a full day of blue water, followed by a second night, before the lights of Marseille would materialize on the misty horizon. Uneasy with the reactions he'd been getting from the crew, Slaton had no intention of waiting that long.

He rose at five that morning by the alarm in his head, a long-hewn skill that was more reliable than he sometimes wished. He filled the pockets of his jacket with his remaining cash and passports, and then stuffed the folded jacket into a plastic bag taken from the trash can in the head. Listening at the door, he heard only a muffled conversation from one of the nearby berths. Slaton eased the door open and slipped into the hallway. He'd advanced no more than two steps when a door ahead opened.

The second officer stepped into the hall, his long arm blocking Slaton's progress down the passageway. He was clearly off duty, clad in sweatpants and a sleeveless T-shirt, and his black hair was matted on one side. "Where do you think you are going?" he asked.

Slaton stopped a few steps away. "Does it matter? I'm not bothering anyone at this hour."

"I'll be the judge of that." He looked pointedly at the bag under Slaton's arm. "What have you got there?"

Slaton opened the bag enough to show him. "It's my jacket. I got sick earlier and I made a mess of it. I need to find a washing machine."

The seaman grinned the way seamen did when land-lubbers lost their stomachs. His smile faded quickly. "It's been dead calm since we left Valletta. And five thirty in the morning is a funny time to do laundry."

Slaton didn't reply.

"Marco!" the officer barked.

There was an interval of silence, followed by shuf-fling, and the door immediately behind Slaton creaked open. The bleary-eyed chief engineer stepped out in his underwear—the other man he had bought a beer for in the bar in Valletta. The man had streaks of shaving cream on his face and a cheap disposable razor in his hand. He wasn't as big as the second of-ficer, but a blunt jawline and ham-hock fists gave him the look of a pugilist.

The second officer stared at Slaton's bag, furrows grooved into his thick brow. "I think we should have a look at that," he said. "It's my duty to be on the lookout for contraband."

In that instant a line was crossed, yet Slaton gave no sign of it. Quite the opposite, his expression soft-ened in an accommodating way and his body seemed to relax. Only the mineral-gray eyes might have sug-gested something else as they began to log new vari-ables, updating the changes of the last thirty seconds.

One sailor was standing behind him with a plastic razor in his right hand, another in front, the larger of the two. Both were casually dressed with little chance of a concealed weapon, yet the officer's right shoulder was flush to the cabin door, his arm out of sight and held in a distinctly unnatural set. If there *was* a weapon, that's where it would be.

With that Slaton's appraisal was complete, confirming an advantage that contradicted what might be assumed. In spite of the fact that these men had lived on *Ionian Star* for months, if not years, Slaton had home field advantage. If they had walked this passageway a thousand times, neither had ever weighed it in the manner he had over the course of the last twenty-four hours. They did not grasp that the corridor's narrow confines and thick-gauge steel walls could serve as weapons in themselves. They had never registered the delicate electrical junction overhead which, with one good pull, would create an electrical short to send the entire hall into pitch darkness. Neither man grasped the potential of the wall-mounted fire ax three meters away, the latch of which Slaton had discreetly loosened earlier, nor the thick fireman's hose and valve that with one turn would discharge a hundred gallons of seawater per minute under high pressure. In a frantic moment, they would not recall that the nearest watertight door, perfect to seal an escape, was ten paces away after a 90-degree right turn at the first connecting hallway.

*No*, Slaton thought without a trace of hubris, *these men see none of it because they don't live as I do.* Belying his confidence, Slaton stood with a passive air. He would not force the issue.

Inadvisably, the Greeks did.

Slaton saw a brief meeting of their eyes, and noticed the second officer's arm shift slightly behind the door. The sailor named Marco edged closer from behind. Almost imperceptibly, Slaton altered his stance, grounding the outside of his right foot firmly against the floor joint. He choreographed his first three movements, hoping these sailors were as thuggish and sleepy and simplistic as they appeared.

They were.

The door flew open.

Slaton focused absolutely on the big man's right hand, and the expected knife did not appear. Instead a thick iron bar came flying toward his head. He dropped low, and the bar clanked into the steel wall. From a crouch, and with one shoulder grounded against the wall, Slaton lashed a full-weighted kick to the bigger man's left knee. It ruined the knee, and consequently his balance. In the same plane of motion, Slaton pivoted and guided the falling officer's head into a wall of half-inch-thick steel. There was an audible crunch, and the iron bar clattered to the floor.

Slaton lunged backward just in time as the predicted right-handed haymaker whistled past his ear. He found the iron bar with one hand as he lunged toward the engineer, driving with his legs, and put a shoulder into the man's midsection that lifted him off his feet. The engineer hit the wall and spun a half turn before Slaton hammered the iron bar into the base of his skull. The man collapsed in a heap, the only sounds a lungful of expelling air and the rub of cotton over steel.

Twenty-four hours of planning. Six seconds of execution. The math of preparation.

Slaton stood stock-still. He watched and listened,

every sense on alert. There were no shafts of light under nearby doors, no shout of alarm or call to general quarters.

He moved quickly, and in thirty seconds had both men piled onto the mattress in his closet-berth. The engineer was groggy, and would recover to appreciate his pain. The second officer seemed to be breathing, but was otherwise motionless. Slaton had no time for, nor interest in, either man's prognosis. Outside the room he jammed the iron bar into the door handle, retrieved his jacket, and walked briskly down the corridor.

In the peaceful predawn hours that morning, with a dim glow footing the eastern sky, *Ionian Star* reached her nearest passage to the Sardinian coastline. Things were quiet on the ship's bridge as two sleep-deprived men, the watch officer and an ordinary seaman, swilled coffee to stay alert. Another pair of crewmen roamed the decks, an apprentice engineer who was there for a smoke, and a junior man ending his four hours of night-watch duty. None of them noticed the seven-foot surfboard that fluttered thirty feet down from the aft quarterdeck into a flat obsidian sea.

Equally unnoticed was a black-clad figure that dropped in a free fall seconds later.

# FOURTEEN

Hakim Ghazi stood on the bank of the Shatt Al Arab waterway with his head craned upward. His hands moved deftly to keep the reel of kite string taut. At his side stood two children, a boy and a girl, wonder in their eyes as they watched his every move.

Two hundred meters over their heads—perhaps a bit less as the upper wind was keeping the string at an angle—a bundle of forty helium-filled Mylar balloons stood clear in the cobalt morning sky over southern Iraq. Kites were more typical here, and it was perhaps the novelty of the balloons that held the children so enraptured. Ghazi had bought an entire case of the things a month ago from a shop in Al-Basrah, five kilometers north, explaining to the proprietor that he was planning a big birthday party for his three-year-old son. Ghazi, in fact, did not have a son. Not yet anyway. But perhaps someday.

"Can I do it yet, Mr. Ghazi?" asked the boy. He was holding a second reel of string that ran to the same bunch of balloons. Ghazi had given firm instructions to keep this line slack as the arrangement gained altitude.

"No, not yet. But it is almost time." Ghazi pushed his round-framed glasses higher on the bridge of his nose, and addressed the other child, the boy's older sister. She was twelve years old, and had been given the more demanding task. "Are you ready?"

The girl smiled and pointed Ghazi's smartphone toward the sky. She tapped the screen once and said, "Yes, we are recording."

"All right. Take in the slack."

The boy complied, winding up the professional-grade kite spool until the line was nearly taut.

Here Ghazi paused, taking a moment to check all around. They were two miles from the nearest house and it was still quite early. All the same, the local farmers occasionally wandered from their wintering fig and olive groves. Across the waterway, a mile distant, were the disquieting shores of Iran. Ghazi had never seen anyone there—useless wetlands predominated that side of the delta—but everyone in this part of Iraq kept a wary eye toward the east. The most regular problem was ship traffic, oil tankers and freighters riding the slow brown waters, merged from the Tigris and Euphrates Rivers, to the Persian Gulf and seas beyond. He saw nothing today in either direction along the waterway.

Ghazi double-checked the wind, an estimate taken from a small but accurate windsock he'd planted near the center of the berm they were standing on. The little cone hung nearly limp, indicating surface winds below 5 knots. Finally, he double-checked the reference mark on his string, ensuring it was at the two-hundred-meter point. Satisfied, he began a countdown that was quickly echoed by two high-pitched voices.

*Ten . . . nine . . . eight . . .*

He always tried to make it fun for the children.

When their count hit zero, the boy yanked hard on

the second string, and they all watched the plastic container beneath the balloons. It was fashioned from a five-gallon olive oil decanter, and when inverted by the pull of the string it dispensed its contents—a cloud of red liquid blossomed into the soft morning breeze.

"Follow it!" he said to the girl as the atomized liquid drifted toward the ground.

She tracked the red mist with the phone for a time, but then said, "I don't see it anymore."

It was all over in twenty seconds.

"That's all right," Ghazi said. He too had lost sight, just as in the other trials. He'd experimented with a number of different dyes before succumbing to the fact that a visible-light experiment was beyond the scope of his resources. It would have been useful in determining a precise measurement of fall rate. As it was . . . one did what one could.

The girl stopped filming and handed over the camera. Ghazi gave the primary reel to the boy.

The two children looked at him expectantly. "Can we do it now?" they asked in near unison.

Ghazi smiled. It was always their favorite part. "Yes, let's."

He pulled a switchblade from his pocket, flicked the release, and the razor-sharp blade snapped into place. Ghazi turned the knife in his hand and presented it to the girl, handle first. She took it and severed the string from the main spool. They watched the big raft of balloons, free of the liquid mass in the container and untethered, soar upward into a flawless sky.

"I wonder where it will end," said the boy.

"That is the joy, is it not?" Ghazi replied. "The wonder of what might be."

The balloons kept rising, and soon the happy bunch of silver dots became a less magical dark blob as it rode the upper level winds toward Iran. Ghazi had never calculated how high they might go, but he remembered the pilot, Tuncay, remarking that he had once spilled coffee in his lap when a large, brightly dressed bundle of silver had appeared unexpectedly in his windscreen at thirty-five-thousand feet. Mylar was a wondrous invention, with incredible tensile strength and excellent chemical stability. The kind of thing Ghazi himself might have invented had he ever been given the chance. Unfortunately, chemical engineers in Iraq found little opportunity to pursue inspiration with research.

"All right, off you go," he said. "And remember—if the wind is calm tomorrow, come at the same time."

The children trotted away, their sharp eyes still locked on the sky, mesmerized by what was now no more than a tiny dot. Wondering.

"Malika!" Ghazi called.

The girl forced her eyes downward, and Ghazi held out an empty hand. She smiled broadly and ran over with the still open switchblade. Ghazi took it and held it like a teacher directing a pointer at a student. "And remember, tell no one of our games. It is only for us."

"Of course, Mr. Ghazi!" She scurried away and took her brother by the elbow, and soon the two were running a winding path over the brown-grass berm in that carefree manner reserved for children.

Ghazi grinned with satisfaction. It would have been terribly difficult to conduct the trials on his own—yet he had found a way forward. Indeed, he doubted there were two more reliable assistants anywhere in Iraq.

He closed the knife and slid it into the backpack at his feet. Unzipping a second compartment, he withdrew a small box the size of a shoe, attached to which was a sensor on a coiled cord. He turned the machine on, performed a calibration sequence, then walked south along the levee. He angled toward the southern field where, given today's gentle winds, the liquid mist would have come back to earth. Two days earlier a westerly gust had arrived unexpectedly, ruining his measurements and sending an entire batch of his low-level source material across the Shatt Al Arab and into Iran. It ruined the morning's work, but there *was* a certain irony in it. *Back from whence it came.*

Just before reaching the hot zone, Ghazi made sure the children were gone, and he took a last look for any other wandering souls. The time of year helped. In summer, when the groves were busy and the harvest near, he would never have been able to use this place. The only options then for uninterrupted testing would be the surrounding marshes or the western desert. And the marshes, of course, were wholly incompatible with the design of his experiment.

Convinced he was alone, Ghazi took his one precaution. He pulled a disposable respirator from his pocket and placed it over his nose and mouth. Holding the sensor in front of him with both hands, he looked rather like a man divining for water. Which, in a wholly unapplied sense, was very near the truth.

For thirty minutes he walked back and forth over the levee. He stopped now and again to record readings that could later be plotted and compared to his previous data points. He was nearly finished when a truck appeared in the distance. Ghazi set aside his work and dropped quickly behind the levee. The vehicle was not military, but a large western-built pickup truck—most likely a contractor from one of the oil facilities in Rumaila. He never found out because the truck kept going.

Relieved, Ghazi went back to work. Ten minutes later he was walking back to the farmhouse. With the backpack on his shoulder he kept an easy pace, determined to enjoy the lovely morning. Ghazi was startled when a clutch of plovers scattered from the brush, and he paused to watch them wing skyward. *Asiaticus* or *alexandrinus*? he wondered. Whatever the case, he hoped they would fly far from here. The isotope he was using for his tests was not particularly high-level, but it was persistent enough. Ghazi pushed the idea from his head, lest his mood darken. If felt good to be working again, to have purpose to his day, and he resolved that when he reached the farmhouse he would brew a pot of the good English tea and pray.

Or perhaps just the tea.

Since leaving home, and the watchful eye of his devout mother, he had found himself increasingly distanced from Allah. If he was a Muslim now it was because he felt a need to be something. His transformation had begun at university, as was so often the case. There he'd discovered that he liked beer and dancing, and that he very much liked women. Ghazi still prayed on occasion, but blasphemed more often, and like most Iraqis he thought the country's clerics were cracked. Of course, the clerics themselves could afford the luxury of being pious—they had jobs and wives and no end of food on their blessed tables.

Upon reaching the farmhouse, Ghazi filled a pot with water and set it on the stove. As he waited for the boil, he unpacked his gear, taking particular care with the delicate scintillation counter. He glanced at his prayer rug, gave a short sigh, and left it untouched. Instead Ghazi went to the makeshift desk, and with warm sunlight streaming through the window he opened his notebook and began to correlate another morning's data.

# FIFTEEN

South of Porto Pino, on the southern shore of Sardinia, rests an errant horse-shaped peninsula known as Capo Teulada. It is a jagged and bleak place, accessible only by four-wheel-drive vehicles or seagoing watercraft, and then only useful in the more pleasant summer months when families gather for seaside lunches and young lovers ensconce themselves in quiet coves. There are no villages or townships and, if one discounts the small herds of bony goats, there is not a single permanent resident, this a consequence of the sandy, infertile soil, and an unfailingly rigorous topography.

Fittingly, Capo Teulada meets the surrounding Mediterranean in all her obstinacy with an imposing shoreline, ranging from vertical cliffs to bramble-encrusted coves. Tenacious birds nest in thorny plants, and the bitter winds of winter alternate with an iron summer sun. Yet for all Capo Teulada's shortcomings, none are apparent when viewed from the sea—particularly when one's vantage point rests a mere twelve inches above the surface.

It was some years ago in France, provisionally situated in a windswept safe house on the northern coast of Brittany, that David Slaton had taken up surfing.

For the first week of his residence he'd stood on the high hills watching waves that had built for a thousand miles reach in from the Celtic Sea, and he'd seen the clean point break raking the angled peninsula. So it was only natural, when he came across an old fiberglass twin-fin in a woodshed, that Slaton had put himself to the test. He by no means mastered the art in the following weeks, yet relished the physical challenge. He also found the waves a much needed diversion from his appointed mission—plotting the demise, by ballistic means, of a Hezbollah bombmaker ensconced in a villa some three kilometers south. The man was an oddity—a radical Shi'a demolition expert who actually survived to middle age, and who, suffering either a loss of religious zeal or a conversion to capitalism, had gone private, and earned enough handsome paydays to see him through his days in comfort. Unfortunately, as Slaton knew better than anyone, there were certain lines of work from which one could never retire, and in time the man's only earned pension came by way of a 168-grain boat tail round.

Now those swells of Brittany were a distant memory as Slaton paddled toward Sardinia on a dead-calm sea. On the waxed fiberglass surface in front of him was the double-wrapped trash bag containing his jacket and street clothes—which after an hour at sea might or might not be dry—along with his remaining money and identity documents. Effectively, all his worldly possessions encased in 4-mil plastic. The wetsuit he was wearing had come from the same storage closet as the surfboard, and while it was too large and leaked at the seams, the neoprene did enough to keep his core temperature at a safe level on the frigid February sea.

He smelled the briny air, and heard nothing more than the soft lap of waves against the board's rails. He estimated he'd jumped ship roughly six miles from land, a distance he hoped to negotiate in slightly over an hour. The muscles in his back ached, and twice he stopped to rest, the second time floating still on a silent sea as the sun breached the horizon. The radiant heat recharged him, and he felt warmer as the scalloped shoreline came near.

There were no signs of life along the desolate coast, and Slaton steered for a thin stretch of sandy cove. As the water became shallow, the gentle swells built into modest three-foot waves, but Slaton made no attempt to stand for the ride to shore. Even if there was no obvious peril involved, a life in the dark arts had taught him many lessons. Chief among them— style points were for dead men.

Keeping to his belly, Slaton skimmed ashore on a gentle roll of white water. He carried the board above the tide line, and in a dense stand of thicket exchanged his leaky wetsuit for nearly dry clothes. The wetsuit, surfboard, and plastic bag he buried in a depression, covering everything with sand and driftwood.

He hiked north until he found a road, and dawn had gone to morning when he reached the first town. It was a sleepy place called Sant'Anna Arresi, and by then his hair was dry and his pace quick—with the exception of the wound on his thigh, his injuries had largely mended. A hired cab took him to Iglesias, and there he waited thirty minutes for the train to Cagliari.

He spent time in front of a mirror in the station restroom washing salt from his face and finger-combing his hair, and he dumped half a pound of sand from his shoes into a trash bin. Slaton took a crusty roll with butter and a steaming cup of coffee as he waited in the platform café, and before noon that day he was at the Cagliari Airport, queuing up to the Alitalia counter.

He exchanged pleasantries with the ticket agent, a striking woman with black hair, olive skin, and inarguably Roman features.

"Your destination, sir?" she asked in the English he'd initiated.

Slaton took pause.

It was the all-important question, and the one that, ever since landing in a heap at the foot of the bastions of Mdina, he had imagined others were asking.

*Where would he go?*

Did his pursuers know about the banker in Zurich? Did they know about his family? Part of him wanted to rush to Virginia and build a fortress around his wife and child. But might doing so place them in the line of fire? He made his decision.

"Zurich, please."

"Business or coach?" queried the smiling woman.

"Business," Slaton said, thinking, *More euros, fewer questions*.

He handed over the credit card and passport in the name of Eric Risler, thankful for his foresight in establishing the credit account. It was difficult to go anywhere these days without a valid credit card— one of the curses of an increasingly Web-constrained world.

"You have spent time at our seaside?" she asked.

"I'm sorry?"

She held up his passport and Slaton saw it was

damp along one edge. "Oh, yes. There's probably some sand in it as well. The mark of a good holiday." He smiled, and so did the agent. It was hardly a concern. In truth, the imperfection gave the document greater authenticity. When she handed it back, along with a boarding pass, Slaton knew the legend of Eric Risler had held up perfectly—as a fifty-thousand-euro forgery should.

"Enjoy your flight, sir."

"Thank you."

Within an hour Slaton's circumstances had risen measurably. He was in a wide leather seat on the airplane and scanning his complimentary copy of *La Repubblica,* a second cup of coffee and cloth napkin on the tray in front of him. Nothing in the news drew his eye—always a relief, as the gray dealings of his life had more than once been reflected on the front page—and so Slaton folded the paper and pressed a switch, and the big seat contorted into a comfortable reclined position.

He closed his eyes and tried to sleep, but it was quite hopeless. He felt like a detective facing a baffling case, his few scraps of evidence misconnecting like stray shooting stars. The Pole he'd killed in the stairwell. Ben-Meir, a former Mossad operative. Who would assemble such a group? Men who administered money in Zurich? Others who administered death from Damascus or Gaza? Those in the latter factions certainly had motive, given Slaton's long and lethal past, yet neither the tribes of Palestine nor the madmen of Tehran would dispatch hired guns to Malta. They would use their own killers. Nothing seemed to correlate, and it left Slaton facing the most bleak question a man can ask.

*Who would benefit from a world without me?*

The most honest answer that came to mind was a bitter and disturbing one, and a revelation that did nothing to resolve his dilemma. The clearest beneficiaries were two innocents who were, at that moment, situated tenuously across an ocean to the west.

# SIXTEEN

Aircraft, like humans, deteriorate without exercise.

The mechanics had spent the previous evening troubleshooting the fuel problem. Under a flood of bright work lights, they'd sourced the spill to a dodgy wing tank check valve. The valve was nearing the end of its nominal service life, a high-cycle item on a high-cycle airframe, and fourteen months in the Amazon's baleful heat and humidity had only accelerated the inevitable. The only option was a replacement, and so the mechanics had given Umberto a purchase request for a new part, to be relayed by fax, before boxing up their tools and quitting for the night. While Umberto put the request through, the Guatemalans led the Peruvians, who smelled as though they'd bathed in jet fuel, to cousin Leonardo's for an evening of fun and refreshment. Umberto had gone home.

They were all back at dawn, the mechanics bleary-eyed yet determined, and a delivery truck arrived two hours later carrying an express shipment sent through a freight forwarding company in Belém. Umberto greeted the driver at the airfield access point and unlocked the gate. After the truck rumbled through, he secured the gate before inspecting the truck's open cargo bed. It was laden from front to back with crated spares and expendables, the most recognizable items being a pair of fifty-inch, thirty-two-ply main landing gear tires.

Like all Brazilians, Umberto was accustomed to a certain level of inefficiency, and so he was surprised by the speed at which these parts had arrived. Moving to the driver's-side window, he addressed the young man behind the wheel, who he'd already learned was a shaggy mulatto from Barcarena. Umberto was happy to finally have someone with whom he could converse.

"I will show you where to go," he said.

The young man looked across the ramp at an airplane that stood out like a skyscraper in a favela, but he said nothing as Umberto walked around and climbed into the passenger seat.

"This shipment came quickly," Umberto remarked.

The kid shifted into first gear. "Some of the parts arrived by air last night. Others we've had since last week."

"Last week? But we only sold the aircraft two days ago."

"Don't ask me. They load my truck, tell me to drive—I drive."

Umberto felt a worm of suspicion, sensing that the city fathers had been outsmarted. Signore Petrecca had clearly been planning this purchase for some time, which meant he would certainly have spent more to acquire his prize. "Do you know what is back there?" he asked, nodding to the cargo bed.

The young man handed over a load manifest.

Umberto looked it over. He was no mechanic, but having spent his entire life around aircraft, he saw many things that made sense: a twenty-two-cell nickel-cadmium battery, a start valve for a General Electric

CF6-50 engine, an engine-driven hydraulic pump, and a VHF radio module. Yet other items seemed unusual. Forty *cases* of engine oil, two suitcases, one red and one yellow, and twenty passenger seat cushions— this for an aircraft configured with only four seats, all in the cockpit. Most curious of all: six twenty-gallon cans of Sherwin-Williams acrylic urethane topcoat, in lusterless Matterhorn White, and an airless electric paint sprayer.

When the truck pulled up to the aircraft, the mechanics—there were three teams now, a second band of Guatemalans having appeared out of nowhere in the early morning hours—began unloading the truck. The driver, in typical Barcarenan fashion, settled back for a nap in the cab.

Umberto chipped in enthusiastically.

He hauled heavy boxes up the stairs and stacked them in the aircraft's massive cargo bay. On his third trip up the stairs he was surprised by the roar of the aircraft's auxiliary power unit spinning to life. This was another new development—it meant the jet could now source its own electrical power and conditioned air. The temperature inside the cargo bay dropped ten degrees—not cool, but a marked improvement over the unusually torrid morning outside.

With the truck unloaded, the mechanics began buzzing around the aircraft.

Umberto stood back and watched appreciatively. These men were making progress, and he supposed it was the way of a successful business. Perseus Air Cargo had signed a purchase agreement, and transferred more dollars to the Santarém city coffers than Umberto would see in his life. That being the case, they would not want their valuable asset rotting away on the banks of the Amazon. They would want it scything through blue sky and connecting to far-away airports. In short, they would want it making money.

The mechanics worked feverishly, as if facing a deadline to make CB68H airworthy. Umberto was there when the cockpit came to life in a mosaic of light, the warning systems blurting aural alerts and spinning through test cycles. Later two men mounted ladders and began spraying paint on the fuselage, and here, for the first time, Umberto thought the work seemed shoddy. There was no attempt made to cover static ports or vents, and the mechanic/painters only addressed the top half of the fuselage, leaving an awkward transition amidships to the original gray belly. He asked about this, only to be met by a shrug of disinterest. "This is primer. Pretty color comes later."

And so it went, six mechanics performing all manner of repairs. Umberto watched in fascination, and if he was truthful, with a trace of remorse. Nearing lunchtime one of the Peruvians came near, and unable to hold back any longer Umberto buttonholed the man and asked, "When do you think she will fly?"

The mechanic, a squat cinder-block type with deep furrows in his brow, scrunched his lips in a noncommittal way. "*Sabado. Domingo. Sólo Dios puede decir.*"

This much Umberto understood. Saturday. Sunday. Only God can say.

He was not a particularly religious man, and not an optimist by nature. All the same, as he regarded the buzzing machinery and flashing lights all around, Umberto thought they just might do it.

# SEVENTEEN

After a fifty-minute layover in Rome, Slaton caught a midday connecting flight and arrived at Zurich International Airport at three that afternoon.

He went straight to work, reasoning that there was enough left in the working day to make an approach, at least a cautious one, to his intended target. He hired a cab and settled in for a fifteen-minute ride to Bahnhofstrasse and downtown Zurich. He was struck by familiar sights as the cab climbed over the Limmat River and passed the Swiss National Museum, Gustav Gull's strained impression of a Renaissance chateau, before rounding the contrasting Hauptbahnhof in all its mechanized efficiency, the largest rail station in Switzerland gearing up for the evening rush.

Cold lay over the city like a stone, flurries spinning down to divide ancient basilicas from soulless monoliths of glass and steel. The cab veered onto Uraniastrasse, and the clock tower of St. Peters spired in the distance, a graceful contrast to the considerably less holy edifice of Credit Suisse. Nearing the offices of Krueger Asset Management, Bahnhofstrasse itself coursed before them, a once-busy thoroughfare given over to trams and a pedestrian boulevard.

"Slow down, would you?" he asked the driver. "I

haven't been here in a long time and I should take a few pictures to show my wife."

With the meter running, the driver shrugged and slowed.

Of all the earth's addresses, this was one Slaton had always known he would visit again. It was also a place where he might be expected. The operation on Bahn-hofstrasse had begun years ago, a brazen Mossad scheme in which a private banker, Walter Krueger, had been employed in the service of a brilliantly successful arms merchant named Benjamin Grossman. Krueger's part was simple, indeed the same as that of any banker: alleviate the concerns of the rich by making them more so. When Grossman met an untimely end, however, stricken by a sudden illness, things had quickly gone afield. In a move that surprised everyone, the luckless arms dealer bequeathed his worldly posses-sions, all 1.3 billion of them, to his lone Mossad conduit—David Slaton.

Herr Krueger, by Slaton's instructions, had subse-quently invested and—there was no more positive word—hidden the bulk of the estate. By Slaton's most recent accounting, one year ago, there existed for his benefit, if not in his name, well-rounded accounts in seven different countries. There was also a minor con-stellation of warehouses across the world brim-ming with the stock of Grossman's enterprise—bullets and guns and rocket-propelled grenades. These ar-maments Slaton had left in place, in part because he could think of no simple way to sell them, but more so because he knew there was no better end for such implements than to leave them rusting away in leak-prone buildings.

He wondered now if he had made the right choices. The small church-like building came into view on a gray side street, a modest affair surrounded by larger and more stable structures that housed larger and more stable institutions—a cornice-ridden stone amid the financial quarry that was Zurich. The snow-dusted sidewalks were busy, London Fog overcoats swaying over four-hundred-dollar shoes, gloved hands fumbling with smartphones. Slaton watched a man in business attire walk into the building while a young woman in a ski parka came out turning her collar up against the brittle air. A handful of businesses besides Krueger's leased space inside, and there was no way to tell which tenant was generating the traffic. Did Krueger Asset Management even remain as a going concern?

Once Krueger had established Slaton's dubious accounts, he could easily have managed them from home—and thereafter lived comfortably on the generous management fees. Yet he had expressed plans to keep the office, explaining that Switzerland's banking regulators were forcing greater transparency, and that to keep up pretenses he thought it wise to retain a handful of other clients, men and women with more reputable portfolios. Might that have changed in the last year?

Slaton turned his attention to the surrounding grounds, and beyond the building where his money resided he saw a modest open space, a park in another season whose green lawns had fallen to a lumpy carpet of white, and whose skeletal shrubs were tipped in new snow. He saw nothing out of place. No sturdy man eating gelato, no former Mossad operative sipping tea at a nearby café. Not that they would make it so easy.

He asked the driver to stop one block past the address, and there Slaton settled with the man and set out on the sidewalk at a measured pace. Near a trash can he picked up a small piece of cardboard from the ground. He tore it in half to make a triangle, folded it once, then twice, and shoved the wedge into his pocket. In the best Swiss tradition, he dropped the unused portion smartly back into the trash.

Approaching the building Slaton spotted a security system that had not existed on his last visit, a pair of closed-circuit cameras installed gracelessly under the ornate roofline. He kept his face turned down, a simple but effective countermeasure, and never stopped moving. It was the surveillance you didn't see that was dangerous. In the portico he was happy to find an unchanged letter-board directory, and in the last act of a six-hundred-mile day he approached the door with the familiar plaque: SUITE 4, KRUEGER ASSET MANAGEMENT.

To one side of the door was a frosted glass panel, and he clearly saw light inside. He tested the handle and found it unlocked. Slaton pushed the door open, reaching into his pocket as he did so and dropping the wedge of cardboard on the carpeted floor. He saw an empty reception desk—the domain of the ever-efficient Astrid—but noted a sweater on her chair and a large overcoat on the rack behind it. Slaton held the door open 90 degrees, and with a toe nudged his makeshift doorstop in place. With a clear avenue of escape established, he took a cautious step inside.

He listened keenly and sensed someone at the desk in the inner office—shuffling papers and the crinkle of leather under a heavy body. Krueger? He edged toward the door and was relieved to find the rotund banker alone, seated behind his desk.

"Hello, Walter."

Krueger looked up and went ashen, his eyes twin

orbs under his nearly bald crown. "Herr Mendelsohn! It's been . . . it's been a *very* long time."

Struggling for composure, the banker stood and snugged his tie to his neck, and the two shook hands across a monstrous mahogany desk.

"I didn't mean to startle you," Slaton said. "Astrid seems to have stepped out."

"Yes, she has gone for our afternoon coffee." Krueger was exactly as Slaton remembered, steady and officious, a man who each morning had one egg and one cup of tea in the same chair, and who could be counted on to do so in the face of market gyrations, foreign upheaval, or for that matter, nuclear winter.

A fast-recovering Krueger regarded the man he knew as Natan Mendelsohn, weighing him as he might a long-lost nephew. "How long has it been? Over a year, I think?"

"Sixteen months, October."

"Yes, yes. Well, you look very fit and tan. You must be loitering in the south."

Slaton said nothing, and an awkward pause ensued. The matter of his residence, like so much else, had always been emphatically avoided. Theirs was a delicate relationship, although in a rare departure Slaton had made sure that the man who controlled his billion-plus dollars knew full well what he was—an assassin.

Krueger shifted to the familiar. "I am happy to say that your accounts are performing well. The blind trusts have proved a particularly efficient strategy. I have to say, I'm surprised you haven't contacted me sooner. Have you been busy with . . ." Krueger's voice trailed off, until he finished with, "whatever you stay busy with."

"Busy enough," Slaton replied. "I've begun an initiative that will require a modest amount of cash."

"*Absolument,*" replied his banker in earnest, finding the ground increasingly firm. Krueger took a seat behind his desk, which was just as Slaton remembered: a phone with multiple lines, a computer on the L-shaped extension, and dead center the customary blotter, leather-edged and empty, waiting for important work. The banker referenced his computer.

"Please take a seat and I will call up your portfolio." As he typed, Krueger said, "I manage everything in a most secure manner. All trading is performed from this office, and each account requires a unique access code that I keep here." The Swiss turned in his chair and began spinning the tumbler on a heavy floor safe.

"Yes, I'm sure it's quite secure," Slaton said distractedly. The outer door was still wedged open, and he thought it a detriment now, particularly with Astrid soon to return. "I'll be back in a moment—I'm afraid I left your door open." Slaton crossed through the outer room and walked past the reception desk. He was kicking out his cardboard wedge when a flash of motion caught his eye.

# EIGHTEEN

It was no more than a glint, fleeting movement down the hallway to his right. Slaton studied the geometry and realized he'd seen a reflection from the window across the hall. As he eyed the main entrance doors, a sound followed, heavy boots skidding on loose snow. Then long seconds of silence and stillness.

Movement is an essential skill for an assassin, the ability to reach a position of advantage without being seen or heard or smelled. Not surprisingly, those who have painstakingly mastered such techniques are adept at spotting errors. Large cities, Slaton knew, were virtual forests of sensory static: cars, crowds, flashing lights. Yet aside from sporting events and playgrounds, the manifestation of full-speed human movement is a gross inconsistency, doubly so when it occurs at the entrance of a professional building.

Yet that was what he'd seen. That was what he'd heard. Someone had been running full tilt, and was now just outside the entrance. Silent. Waiting.

Slaton's reaction was both immediate and instinctive. He exited Krueger's office, closing a locked door behind him, and crossed the hall to Suite 3—if the sign on the door could be believed, a tax attorney's office. Slaton quickly pulled the door closed behind him. He saw a vacant reception desk and an office behind, a mirror arrangement of Krueger's suite. Behind the closed office door he heard muted voices and shuffling.

The door opened and a young girl appeared, pretty and slim. Her hair was askew and—Slaton could not avoid noticing—two buttons on her blouse were matched to the wrong holes.

"Herr Schimmler has no more appointments to-day," she stuttered.

Slaton gave a professional smile as his eyes by-passed the girl for the inner office. A story came to mind effortlessly. *Herr Schimmler is a specialist in estate planning and inheritance law, is he not? I must schedule an appointment regarding my mother's will.*

Slaton never had a chance to deliver the lie as hard footfalls came from the outer hall. Through the frosted glass he saw rapid movement. One silhouette, two. Then a third, and a crash as Krueger's office door gave way.

There were no shouted warnings of *Polizei!* Only the reckless haste of men ready to kill.

Slaton didn't have to ask the young woman if there was a back door—he had studied the building and knew there wasn't. But there *was* a window in the lawyer's office. He brushed past her and rushed inside.

"No!" she protested. "You mustn't go—"

He caught a glimpse of the lawyer, Schimmler, standing behind his desk, dumbstruck and with the tail of his shirt stuck in his fly. Slaton ignored him.

The window was there, the blind drawn for obvious reasons. Slaton pushed the slats aside, unlatched the window, and flung it open. The frigid air struck like a wall. Slaton straddled the frame, pausing long enough to shout, "Lock your doors and call the police! There are men with guns in Herr Krueger's office!"

He was already outside when he heard a door slam shut, five strides away when the woman screamed something unintelligible. Slaton struck out across the snow-dressed lawn on a flat-out sprint. He spotted a new threat instantly—parked at the building's entrance, a blue utility van with a plumber's logo that had not been there when he'd arrived.

He ran on a diagonal across the lawn, and skidded to a stop after rounding a building at the first corner. Slaton checked in every direction to make sure he wasn't being outflanked, and pulled the cheap tube-encased raincoat from his pocket, transforming his upper body in a moment from beige to bright yellow. Through the corner window of a second-tier art gallery, he studied the distant office where his banker was facing an assault team. What he saw was disquieting.

The three men from the streets of Mdina.

The twins were more alike than ever in workmen's overalls. Ben-Meir was there as well, seeming more familiar now that Slaton had a name to go with the face. They were hauling computers and files, dumping everything hurriedly into the van. The mere fact that they were working fast and in the open meant any pretense of disguise had been dropped. They knew what they were after, and seemed sure they could get it quickly. That sealed Walter Krueger's prospects—the banker was likely dead.

Had they followed him to Zurich? No—the van and overalls could never have been arranged so quickly. They had been lying in wait, just as in Mdina, knowing he would come to Krueger's office. Equally certain was that they would be gone within minutes, anticipating a police response, the exact window of opportunity already calculated. Eight minutes, ten perhaps? No, he decided. Here, in Zurich's main banking sector, the police could be counted on in no more than five minutes. If Slaton were running their op, he would have tested response times in advance by manufacturing a false alarm in a nearby building. Or perhaps they'd gone for a diversion, calling 112, the Swiss emergency number, minutes ago to report a crime four blocks away. An unarmed robbery or a crazed man with a knife—something requiring immediate response, but that would not necessitate reinforcements from the greater gendarmerie.

*Yes, that's how I'd have done it.*

Slaton began moving again, with more control. He crossed the street, keeping the building on his right shoulder while masking behind a row of ageless chestnut trees. The men were together at the back of the van. After exchanging a few words, all three headed back inside.

*Time for one more load.*

Just as they disappeared, Slaton saw something else—something that brought him crunching to a stop on the frozen sidewalk. Krueger's reliable assistant, Astrid, was striding up the sidewalk fifty meters from the entrance with a steaming cup of coffee in each hand. She was moving quickly against the cold, a flurry of practicality in her ankle-length skirt, heavy sweater, and no-nonsense flats. In less than a minute she would reach the entrance. Reach the blue van.

"Dammit!" Slaton muttered under his breath.

One of the twins came out with his arms loaded—a

laptop computer, wire dangling to the ground, and a stack of files—and dumped everything into the van. He took up a cover position between the vehicle and the entrance. The other two were still inside, taking too long, and Slaton wondered if he'd been wrong about Krueger. Might the banker still be alive? Or were they searching for the assassin who'd been there minutes earlier?

It didn't matter. If there was one person who had no part in any of this it was Astrid, now twenty steps away from a team of killers. Slaton cursed again under his breath, realizing that this entire disaster, at some level, was a thing of his making.

He broke into a run toward the building, angling for an approach with no line of sight to the entrance. Just as he put a shoulder to the cold brick outside Krueger's office, Slaton heard Astrid scream. He held steady.

Then her cultured receptionist's voice crumbling in anguish. "Walter! My God, Walter!"

A deep-toned response, reasonable and assuring, but edged with a hard accent. "There has been an accident. Please come inside—we need your help."

Astrid again. "That computer . . . it's Walter's. What are you doing?"

Slaton ventured a look around the corner. He saw a terrified Astrid looking through the doors into the hallway, backing away from the lone man outside. The man sidestepped in an arc, herding her toward the entrance.

Slaton had to act, but the geometry was damning— the man was facing him, leaving no element of surprise for a rush, and the bulge of a holstered weapon was clear under his coveralls. With no time to circle the building, Slaton looked all around. He saw only one weapon. Hoping to God Astrid recognized him, he stepped around the corner and stood in plain sight.

The guard saw him instantly and went for his gun, something heavy caliber and suppressed for sound.

"Astrid! Coffee!"

There was a terrible pause, a slow-motion moment in which three people with unique perspectives made quick decisions. Astrid lived up to his expectations— and then some. She popped the lids from the containers using her thumbs, and just as the handgun was leveling on Slaton's chest she flung two cups of steaming coffee into the guard's face.

He screamed and raised his arms, blinded by the boiling liquid, the gun now pointed at the sky. The indomitable Astrid finished the job, kicking him in the crotch with her no-nonsense flats.

The man grunted and doubled over, giving Slaton the two seconds he needed to close the gap. He led with a knee to the man's lowered head, which put him on the ground, but the guard kept his grip on the gun. It left Slaton no choice. He put two hands over his adversary's one, leveraged his weight, and brought the weapon close between their chests. He grounded the barrel in the man's gut, the long suppressor angled upward, and found the trigger with his thumb.

The weapon spat its lethal round. The guard shuddered and went still.

Slaton ripped the weapon free and scrambled to his feet. There was still no sign of the other two, nor the police.

He gripped Astrid firmly by the elbow. "Come on! We've got to get out of here!" He began dragging her away but she resisted. Slaton followed her shocked gaze and saw what was anchoring her. Walter Krueger lay just inside the building's portico, his body splayed awkwardly amid a spreading pool of red.

She looked pleadingly at Slaton. "We have to help Walter! We have to—"

Slaton jerked her away, forcing her eyes to his. "Walter is dead, Astrid!"

She looked at him, stunned and uncomprehending.

"Walter is dead," he repeated. "And if we don't leave this instant, we will be next."

# NINETEEN

"There's a patient in room 3 who says he needs to see you."

Christine hooked her lab coat on a peg in her office, and gave Lisa, her physician's assistant, a pained look. "I was supposed to be off an hour ago, Lisa. Brent can handle it."

"This guy specifically asked for you, says you saw him a few months ago. We couldn't find his records though."

"What's his problem?"

"He's got a bad leg, auto accident last year. Says it's giving him trouble. I took a look and he's got some serious damage. Rod replacement of the tibia, extensive grafting. He's had a lot of work."

"What's the name?"

Lisa handed over a new patient file with a handwritten name: Y. B. Stein.

"Never heard of him."

"He said you would remember the referring physician."

Christine opened the file and scrolled her eyes down the standard form. The name in the referring physician block caused her heart to stagger a beat. *Dr. Anton Bloch.* A name she knew, only not as a caregiver. Anton Bloch was a former director of Mossad—and the man responsible for recruiting David into that service so many years ago.

"You all right?" Lisa asked.

Christine took a long breath and gently closed the file. "Yeah, I'm fine. I'll see him."

She made her way down the hall to the door marked 3. Christine paused there, her hand hovering over the metal lever as if expecting it to be hot. She wondered what to expect. News about David? Had they finally recovered his body? Yes, she thought, this was exactly how Mossad would go about a notification—false names and pretenses. Part of her wanted to turn and run, but her damned practical nature prevailed. Whatever was inside, she would have to face it sooner or later.

Christine gripped the handle and pulled.

She stepped into the room only far enough to bring the door shut. He was sitting on the examination table, a good-looking man, in a craggy way, with a rough scar on one cheek and a mildly crooked nose. His black hair was coarse and cut short, and sharp eyes seized her with unflinching directness. That in itself, the iron gaze, was enough to put Christine off her game. Her heart misfired again as she realized who this man reminded her of.

"Who are you?" she asked, not in the tone of a caring physician.

"Yaniv Stein."

*Yaniv* Stein. Now the name clicked, a Mossad colleague David had once mentioned. But *that* Yaniv Stein had been killed during a botched mission in Iran. She looked more closely at him. He'd stripped off his trousers for Lisa's screening exam, and below his olive-drab boxers she saw the right leg. From the knee down there was indeed serious damage.

"Does that name mean anything to you?" he prompted.

"I'd say it's a common name in Israel. That *is* where you're from?"

He grinned and she saw a younger face, albeit with grooves deeper than they ought to be. Once again, painfully familiar. "Of course."

"Why are you here?"

Stein charged his lungs with a deep breath, as if about to exert himself physically. "Mossad sent me here to—"

"*Mossad?*" she interrupted, caution giving way to anger. "The same organization that betrayed my husband? That forced him into an impossible situation that got him killed? Get the *hell* out of my office!" she shouted.

The door opened and Lisa peered inside. "Everything okay in here?"

Christine took a deep breath. "Yes," she said. "Mr. Stein wants an open-ended prescription for pain meds, and I told him what I thought about it. He's leaving now."

Stein reached for his pants, stood, and began hiking them left and right up his legs. Lisa backed out and closed the door.

When Stein was done with his pants he sat back down on the examining table. "Give me five minutes, then I'll leave if you want. This is not an official visit, Christine. I don't work for Mossad—not anymore. As you can see, I have certain limitations. Anton sent me to see you."

"Why?"

"There's a problem."

Christine laughed derisively. "A problem. Do you guys take a course in that? Understatement 101?"

Stein ignored it. "Christine, we think you may be in danger."

"Danger? Why on earth would I be in danger?"

Stein took a moment to arrange his thoughts. "It goes back a long time. Many years ago David was involved in a Mossad mission targeting a particularly extreme offshoot of Hamas called al-Zahari. This organization knew no bounds. They undertook a terrible series of attacks directed at noncombatants—they intentionally went after women and children in the name of sensationalism. Mossad went all-out to identify who was responsible, and one al-Zahari cell came to light. Our government decided to hit back, and David was given the assignment. You know what his specialty was."

Christine didn't respond, but she knew all too well. David was an extraordinarily talented marksman.

"He killed four men that day," Stein continued, "all in a matter of seconds."

Christine folded her arms tightly across her chest. She'd always known there had been such missions, but David never spoke of them in detail—and she had never asked.

Stein continued, "The identity of Mossad operatives is kept strictly secret. Unfortunately, in this case we believe there was a breach. It's been many years, but recently we think David's name was tied to these deaths."

Christine had heard enough. "What does it matter? They can't take revenge against a dead man."

"Actually . . . you have to think about it from their point of view. The concept of Arab justice is rarely understood by Western minds. These people demand an eye for an eye, a system of tribal retribution that's been in place for a thousand generations. If they've discovered David was the shooter on that mission, and we believe that's the case, they won't miss a chance to send a message to Israel. Or more precisely, to the other *kidonim*. A message that says, 'Strike us, and we will go after you *and* your families.' "

Christine sat slowly in the room's only chair, a four-wheel roller that had never felt so unsteady. Room 3 was the practice's pediatric corner, and the walls were decked in whale stickers and fabric balloons. She felt the fight going out of her, and stared at a zoo-themed mobile while Stein continued.

"Al-Zahari will seek retribution—they have one man who specializes in it. He's very effective, and has more than once traveled abroad to kill."

"An assassin?" she found herself saying.

"Yes."

"And you're here to warn me about this? To tell me a killer is coming to hunt me down?"

"Actually," Stein said, "we think he may already be here. Last week we uncovered his false identity—unfortunately, the day after he arrived at Dulles."

Christine suddenly felt cold. She stood and put a shoulder to the door. Would it never end? David had existed in a world previously unknown to her, a place where lies were a dialect and death an occupational hazard. But now the tsunami of his past was rushing at her again. The difference this time—she would have to face it alone.

"You're saying this man could be near."

"Very possibly. And . . . it might not be limited to you."

Every muscle in her body tensed.

"You have a son now," he said. "David's son."

Christine's head began to swim. She tried to think of an argument, a way to tell this stranger who seemed so maddeningly familiar that it couldn't be true. It was hopeless, and she knew why. A mother's protective instinct.

She looked at him and whispered contemptuously, "You're bastards—all of you!"

Stein looked at her impassively, not arguing otherwise. Just as David would have done.

She sucked in a long, ragged breath. "What do I do about it?"

"Anton wants me to stay with you, give you protection."

She glanced at his now-covered leg.

"Don't worry," he said. "I'm capable enough. This is a defensive op, and when you play defense, knowledge and preparation are what's important. There are a lot of people looking for this guy, both your government and mine."

"My government? As in the FBI?"

Stein nodded.

"If they're involved, shouldn't they be the ones protecting me?"

"That's a bit delicate. Israel has shared this man's identity with U.S. authorities, told them how dangerous he is. But we can't mention David, or by extension you and your son. Not without raising uncomfortable questions for everyone."

"Will they find him?"

"Absolutely. Your intelligence services sometimes struggle abroad, but they're very good at finding people on their own turf. In a week, maybe two, they'll either have found him, or he'll have aborted his mission and gone home."

"So what . . . you want to follow me around, like a bodyguard or something?"

"Not follow—I can't protect you if you're moving. We go to your house. You, your son, and I. We stay there until this blows over."

"*What?* For a week or two? I can't do that, I've got a job. My colleagues here expect me to—"

"Get the flu," he suggested, "have a breakdown if necessary. I'll leave it up to you." Stein stood, looking considerably more robust than the cane in his hand suggested. "We'll pick up your son at your neighbor's house as soon as we get back."

Christine stiffened. By telling her that *he* knew where Davy was, he was telling her anybody could know. It re-stoked old anxieties, that precarious existence she'd known when David was in her life. Treat every stranger with suspicion, always know what's behind your back. Could she indoctrinate her infant son to such a repulsive existence?

*What choice do I have?*

"Look," he said, "you can say no. I'm here because I owe David. Mossad sent me behind enemy lines, and when things went bad they left me for dead. David pulled me out. Maybe you should ask yourself a question. What would *he* want you to do?"

It was a cruel hypothetical, but in the end effective. Christine relented and gave a nod.

"Grab your coat," he said. "We'll make a quick stop on the way to your house to pick up some food. In the meantime, I want you to start thinking about security. I need to know if you have an alarm, if there are any weapons in the house, which neighbors you can trust."

Dazed, she opened the door and Stein followed her to her office. There she took her coat off the hook, said something to Lisa—See you tomorrow?—and headed to the elevator with Stein in trail. She found herself watching the world with a terrible old mistrust. She ignored a wave from the new dermatologist outside Suite 9, and gave a wide berth to a young man on crutches waiting for the elevator. Tom, the roving security guard in the parking garage, seemed more frail than she remembered. Her car was parked poorly in a dark and isolated corner.

Everything had changed in a moment, reverting to what it had been in the bleakest days of her life. With each step, the question she'd asked herself hammered again and again in her mind.

*What choice do I have?*

# TWENTY

Thirty minutes after leaving Bahnhofstrasse, Slaton had Krueger's able assistant sitting quietly in the corner booth of a pub on Theaterplatz in Baden. Astrid had wanted to go to her apartment, a perfectly natural reaction. Also perfectly predictable, which was why Slaton had steered her here.

It would be a delicate task to revive Astrid Lund to what she had been an hour earlier—or as close as she would ever be. In Slaton's regrettably vast experience, people unaccustomed to violent death rarely faced it well on first exposure. To the positive, on the steps of Krueger's office Astrid had been steel in the moment of truth, giving Slaton the vital seconds he'd needed to gain an advantage.

Her hands were wrapped around a cup of coffee she hadn't touched, and only too late Slaton realized his beverage order had been characteristically insensitive—the very liquid she'd just used to scald a killer's face.

"I was late for work today," she said in a toneless voice. "I haven't been late in fifteen years."

Slaton said nothing. He wanted her to talk.

"Walter's injuries were terrible," she said, "but might he have survived?"

Slaton considered how to best phrase the answer, and perhaps taking the easy way out, he pointed to a wall-mounted television on the far side of the room. There was no sound, but the BREAKING NEWS caption might as well have been in flashing neon: PRIVATE BANKER DEAD IN BAHNHOFSTRASSE SHOOTING. POLICE SEARCH FOR SUSPECTS.

A reporter was interviewing an eyewitness, the lawyer from Suite 3, Herr Schimmler. He'd removed his shirttail from his zipper. Slaton considered asking for the volume to be raised, but the risk seemed to outweigh any benefit. The lawyer had likely bunkered up in his office during the attack, which meant he would never have seen the assailants. The only stranger Schimmler had encountered was Slaton, who was presently carrying a Glock 9mm that could easily prove to be the murder weapon, notwithstanding the fact that he'd discarded the awkward, custom-fit silencer in a back-alley Dumpster.

She said, "I've worked for Walt . . . Herr Krueger, for nearly twenty years. He had his faults, but he was a decent man."

"He was," Slaton said, not knowing or caring if it was true.

She looked around the place as if registering her surroundings for the first time—a positive sign—and said, "We should go back. The police will want to talk to us. They'll wonder where I am."

He nodded, having expected the subject. The police represented order, and the Swiss, in all their militant neutrality, craved order. Astrid finally addressed her coffee, and when she took the first sip her face fell to a grimace.

"Acchh!" She reached across the table for the cream

and sugar—the kind of thing that falls appreciably in one's hierarchy of needs in times of high stress. Another sliver of normalcy returning.

*"Why?"* she wondered aloud. "Why would three men come to Walter's office and murder him?"

Something clicked deep in Slaton's brain, like a mechanical unmeshing of gears. Unable to correlate the warning, he said, "I don't know why. But I can tell you I've seen those men before."

Astrid stared incredulously. Until now she had viewed Slaton as some blend of client, knight in shining armor, and grief counselor.

"You've seen them? Where?"

"They tried to kill me three days ago, in a place far from here. I think I might have led them to Zurich. Not intentionally, mind you—I don't know how they followed me."

Slaton could see her thoughts organizing, see her blue eyes sharpen.

"So . . . they came because they were looking for you?"

"Possibly."

"I remember the last time you were here, Monsieur Mendelsohn. It was just over a year ago." A pensive look, then, "Is that really your name? Mendelsohn?"

"Call me David." Astrid did not look surprised, and it occurred to Slaton that he was probably not the first of Walter Krueger's clients to use an alias. "I assume you are aware of the work he performed on my behalf?"

"In a general way."

He waited.

"All right, yes. I know a good deal about Walter's business dealings. There can be no other way when one works for a man for so many years. He was good to me, and in return I took my duty of discretion very seriously."

"I'm sure you did. But you know my accounts are sizable, and that I gave Walter wide latitude in managing them."

Astrid nodded. She was in her late fifties, he guessed, an attractive woman who was aging well, tall and slim, with shoulder-length blond hair fading to gray. Nothing had faded however in a pair of blue eyes as clear and vivid as any he'd ever seen.

"Do you think this is why these men came?" she asked. "A raid on your accounts?"

"I don't know. All I can tell you is that they're professionals."

"What sort of professionals?"

"I think that's obvious enough."

Astrid seemed freshly unnerved, and Slaton sensed a mistake.

"We must call the police," she said. "You could give them a description of those men, anonymously if necessary. They have to be held accountable."

He paused, reckoning how best to steer the conversation to the course he wanted. He needed Astrid's help—but the decision had to be hers. "That may not be so easy. They followed me across a continent. They killed Walter, raided his office, and two have escaped cleanly. This is no random burglary."

"Are you suggesting we *shouldn't* talk to the police?"

"I'm telling you that I've dealt with people like this before. There's a chance they didn't find what they were looking for, which means they could come after us. If so, the first place they'll look is the local gendarmerie. If we go to the police now they'll spend days asking us questions, but they won't keep us safe. The assailants might even have contacts inside the police force."

Her expression remained guarded, but he could see her considering it. After a long hesitation, she said, "I know what you are."

"Is that in my favor?"

"Walter told me things about you. He said you were dangerous. He said you dealt in arms . . . and perhaps worse."

"I've never dealt in arms."

"You just killed a man."

Slaton could think of no good response. "Years ago Walter had a client named Benjamin Grossman who *was* an arms merchant. Did you know him?"

"He came to the office a few times, yes. I know that he died two summers ago from a sudden illness, and that his estate was put in your care."

"All true. I authorized Walter to continue managing everything, and I've had no contact with him since. I have no idea what's become of Grossman's legacy. There were no quarterly statements, no annual meetings. As to your suggestion—yes, I've done things I'm not proud of."

A long silence ran and Slaton discreetly checked all around.

"Why do you do that?" she asked.

"Do what?"

"Your eyes never stop moving. Here, on the street, in the cab earlier."

He didn't answer, suspecting too much truth would not be in his favor.

"The way you killed that man today—have there been others?"

"Yes."

Her eyes sank to the table.

"Astrid, I intend to leave Zurich tonight. I will do so as quickly and quietly as possible. You can come with me if you like, but you must find a safe place."

She searched his eyes, obviously uncertain.

"It's completely up to you," he added. Slaton looked pointedly at her left hand. There was no ring on the second finger. "Do you live alone?"

"Yes, but what—"

"Is there a place you can go for a few days, somewhere out of town?"

"I have a sister in Vienna."

"No, no relatives."

She seemed to descend again, fear taking reign.

"Astrid, I know this is difficult. But you *must* find a safe place. You won't be able to convince the authorities to protect you—not the kind of protection you'll need. A week, maybe two, and things will settle. Then go to the police and tell them everything."

"Even about you? What you did to that man?"

"If that's what you want."

Astrid looked at him anxiously, nearing the place he wanted. She said, "The men who killed Walter— they have to be held accountable."

"Agreed. The question is how. The police aren't going to find them. On the other hand . . . I might be able to."

"You?"

The old ways were beginning to flow. *Use the truth to your advantage.* "They took Walter's computer. People do that because they want records. If I could see Walter's files, study them, I might be able to determine what their motive is. And by extension, who they are."

"And if you can? What then?"

"Then we decide what to do about it—together."

He watched closely, and was thankful for what she didn't say. *The records? The records are gone now.* He said, "Walter's files are backed up, aren't they?"

"Yes."

"Where?"

"There is a chalet in Klosters. He spends weekends there working. He encrypts the files and transfers them between his office and a computer there."

"Do you have a key to this chalet?"

She let loose a long sigh. "No. But I think I know where to get one."


Ben-Meir made his second bad-news call in as many days. "The *kidon* killed Stanev."

There was a pause, though only in part due to the distances involved. The faraway voice replied, "The computer?"

"We have it, as well as the codes."

"And the rest?"

"The banker is dead," said Ben-Meir, leaving the other unsaid.

"Well?" Irritation.

"We made plenty of noise. The *kidon* escaped."

Relief seemed to flow through the phone. "Thank God you didn't screw that up."

Ben-Meir bristled, but could only say, "The problem arose when he returned to rescue the secretary."

"What came of her?"

"I don't know—she got away as well."

"That could be a problem. I think you've forgotten how good he is."

"I will prove you wrong very soon."

"Let's hope. Only be sure you wait the full twenty-four hours. Not a minute less."

Ben-Meir opened his mouth to speak, but the line only clicked and went dead in his ear.

# TWENTY-ONE

Tuncay was waiting when his copilot arrived at Santarém airport.

Walid Arslan looked weary as he stepped from the small Embraer jet onto the steaming tarmac. He was thirty-five years old, thin-boned, and had a long sallow face that reminded Tuncay of a dog in a kennel. The face was presently covered in a beard—not the long, righteous testimony of an engaged Muslim, but more a badge of indifference. A man who had abandoned, among other things, the standards of his profession.

"Welcome to Brazil," Tuncay said.

Walid shook his hand—an embrace was not yet appropriate, as the two had only met twice before. Walid regarded the surrounding jungle. "So this is the Amazon," he remarked.

"I am told there is much more, but if I never see it I will die a happy man. It rains every day, and when it is not raining one can swim through the air."

Walid nodded.

"Come. I know you are tired after your flights, but we must get straight to work."

Tuncay led through the tiny terminal, outside, and

ten minutes later they arrived at the big jet. Walid's first impression was predictable.

"It is very big."

Tuncay knew the last time Walid had seen the bottom of an aircraft was several years earlier, and from the last perspective any pilot would ever wish—floating beneath a parachute while his Su-25 Frogfoot attack aircraft fell to the earth in a tumbling fireball.

Walid had told him the story on their first meeting. To say he'd been recruited into the Syrian military was less than accurate. *Supplied* was a better word, offered up by a well-to-do Druze family who'd fared undeniably well under the Assad regime. Walid had been granted an officer's commission and aviation training, and after two years he earned his wings in the Syrian Air Force. Things had gone nicely for a time, as they generally did for well-connected sons, until the outbreak of the war. The hostilities were into their twentieth month when a Stinger missile shot down not only his jet, but life as Walid knew it.

He'd been able to eject from the aircraft, and only the grace of a divine wind had pushed him out to sea on that final day of his service, away from a group of agitated and nearly deaf rebels who after months of bombings would have reacted with predictable passion had one of their tormentors dropped from the sky as a gift from Allah. Instead, Walid had been plucked from the Mediterranean by an old man, a onetime fisherman whose nets had burned to ash on the docks, set off by someone's mortar round, yet whose ancient trawler refused to sink. Ever a practical sort, the old man had gravitated to a new and surprisingly lucrative line of work—retrieving overboard sailors, drowning refugees, cowards in sinking dhows, and repatriating them to families who were happy to pay for his services. Walid settled with the old man using a wad of wet dollars from his pocket—there for just such a contingency—and walked up the dock into Tripoli, Lebanon.

It was here that Walid's life took a turn. Stranded in Lebanon, and seeing little future in returning to his squadron, he spent the balance of the war cooking soup and bread in a kitchen, likely feeding the very soldiers who had shot him down. As the war began to ebb, he learned that his family had scattered, the wealth and ties from the old days long spent and gone. For a time he tried to find work as a commercial pilot. Unfortunately, to be a former bomb-dropper, unemployed because his aircraft had been shot down, followed by desertion, hardly made a competitive resume for an aspiring airline pilot.

Tuncay learned of Walid Arslan through a cousin, and sensed a perfect fit for his needs—a man who was both trained and desperate. When Ben-Meir tracked him down he was working in an epicurean hovel in Byblos, sweating and cursing and roasting kebabs over an open pit. On that day last August, Walid had been a widower, insolvent, and frustrated by his faint prospects. Ben-Meir countered with a dream—one last flight that, if successful, would forever repair two of Walid's three shortcomings. A new wife, he was told, was strictly his affair. Walid had been an easy recruit. But then, there were millions of such men in the Middle East today—educated, military-trained, drifting aimlessly through economies racked by sectarian violence, corruption, and religious intolerance.

Tuncay had doubts about the peculiar cast assembled by Ben-Meir, but he had to admit they were so far proving effective. The very idea that this disparate group of exiles was working for an Israeli master was perhaps a reflection of the new Middle East. Then again, the number of zeros in the payday gave reflections of its own. As with mercenaries through the ages, men rarely quibbled over religion or politics when the money was right.

Tuncay saw his copilot studying the modification on the belly of the airplane. The Turk wiped a bead of sweat from his temple. If humidity kept an address, he thought, it had to be here.

"Will it fly?" Walid asked, his white shirt already seeming glued to his back.

"With a little luck, the mechanics say tomorrow she will be ready. I expect some systems will fail, but most are not critical. Redundancy is the hallmark of modern airliners. Anyway, there are other mechanics where we are going."

"So you have no worries?" said the ever-cautious Druze.

"I always have worries. What kind of captain would I be otherwise? But once we get off the ground, I calculate we could lose an engine and still reach our destination."

Walid looked at him solemnly. "You realize I haven't flown in a very long time."

"Can you raise a landing gear handle?"

The copilot grinned. "The big knob shaped like a wheel?"

"See? I knew I chose you for a reason."

Walid nodded toward the belly. "Do you think the system is still operable?"

"How would I know? I've never seen anything like it."

"Perhaps we should try to activate it once we get airborne."

"I think it looks simple. What could go wrong?" Tuncay gave a half-smile of his own, having asked the classic question pilots prodded one another with. "Now go upstairs, get familiar with the instruments. I am going to work on our flight plan."

Walid's apprehension was clearly not allayed, yet Tuncay suspected it had nothing to do with the airplane. Finally the younger man said, "Do you think this will work? All of it?"

Tuncay gave a thoughtful pause. "I wouldn't be here otherwise." He then added, "And neither would you."

# TWENTY-TWO

From Zurich they rode the A3 autobahn south and east, rounding the length of Walensee, the alpine lake that had inspired Liszt to compose his most subdued and lyrical piano piece. In the cast of a high moon, the Churfirsten mountains loomed ominously behind smooth waters, two-thousand-meter peaks lined like soldiers in neat parade formation.

Slaton fought a running battle with the car, a rattletrap Peugeot whose manual transmission, tiny engine, and bald tires were wholly unsuited to climbing mountains in winter. It was a small consolation that his left leg had duty on the stiff clutch pedal, as his right thigh was still sore. Astrid herself had never owned a car, but a longtime friend, Crystal, who lived in Lachen on the south shore of Lake Zurich, had a husband who moonlighted doing automotive repair work. The man unfailingly kept a project or two stashed in his side yard, and when Astrid had asked for a loaner for the weekend, Crystal happily provided a key. Slaton had kept out of sight during the visit so Astrid wouldn't have to explain the presence of a strange younger man.

The Peugeot was shabby but serviceable, and in Slaton's mind the ideal means of transportation—

virtually impossible to trace to either him or Astrid. She'd been mostly quiet during the journey, and Slaton did nothing to intervene. He knew she'd need time to come to terms with what had happened to Walter Krueger. Slaton was equally sure that she was watching him, and he imagined her internal argument. *Have I done the right thing, running away with a man I barely know? One who hours ago killed another man in cold blood?*

He was mildly surprised Astrid had not insisted on going to the police. He wouldn't stop her if she tried. Perhaps it was this very message, presented through his calm demeanor, that caused her to stay. To some degree, Astrid trusted him. Trusted that he could protect her. And perhaps in some dark corner of her mind, hoping the killer she'd befriended might eventually impart justice for what had happened.

Reaching the village of Landquart, Slaton steered carefully from the motorway. Another hour on a snow-covered secondary road, spanning the Prättigau Valley, put them in Klosters. Astrid, increasingly steady, gave directions to a yellow-lit A-frame building surrounded by thick evergreen trees whose branches were bent low by snow.

She said, "This office manages all the chalets on the street. Walter picks up his key here. I've come with him a number of times, so they'll know me."

He cast a sideways look. "Well enough to give you a key?"

"I think so. Once before, I arrived early and Walter was detained. In the end he couldn't come, and he arranged for me to pick up the key at the desk. At least two of the clerks would recognize me—I'm sure of it."

Slaton pulled to a stop in front of a small lobby.

"All right," he said. "I'll stay here and keep the car running. If anything feels wrong come back right away. We can find another way to get into the chalet."

Without comment she went inside. Astrid returned nine minutes later with a look on her face Slaton couldn't quite place. "What happened?" he asked as she slid in beside him.

"There was a new man behind the desk. I didn't recognize him."

"So you didn't get it?"

Astrid held up a keycard, and her deadpan expression went to a slight grin. "I told him I was Walter's wife. I said I'd left Zurich in a furor, forgetting my identification, because I'd just found out he was cheating on me. I called him a bastard and said I planned to take him for every penny."

"He gave you a key based on that?"

"I was very distressed. He looked up Walter's file, of course, and asked a few questions that I answered easily. Their address in Zurich, her maiden name. I might also have mentioned to the man that he had unusually nice blue eyes."

Slaton cocked his head, only then noticing that the top two buttons on Astrid's blouse—prim and proper Astrid—were newly unhooked and showing a surprisingly deep display of cleavage. Not for the first time, he reminded himself that spies were not the only ones capable of subterfuge.

"Second street on the right," she said.

Without comment, Slaton accelerated and made the turn.

Minutes later they reached the chalet, two stories of timber-framed gingerbread set amid a row of the same, the whole street outlined in the luminous spill of faux carriage lamps. A wilderness of style amid a forest of money. Smoke wafted from nearby chimneys, lazy strings of soot disappearing into a lusterless black sky, and the rooflines between them were caked in two feet of snow. At the height of the season, lights burned in windows and steam swirled from deck-mounted hot tubs. Hours ago the sidewalks would have been busy, skiers trudging awkwardly in heavy boots, skis and poles slung over their shoulders. Now, against the chilled evening air, après-ski activities prevailed in lodges and nightclubs.

Slaton pulled the car to a stop in front of a single-stall garage. "Can you open it?" he asked.

Astrid got out, walked cautiously over the icy pavement, and entered a combination into a security keypad. The door rose, and minutes later they were inside Krueger's chalet.

# TWENTY-THREE

Slaton stoked a fire to cut the chill, and then went about his usual safe house walk-through. He found two bedrooms, two baths, and a back door that led to a spruce balcony where a snow-encased hot tub commanded a stunning view of the mountain. While Astrid was in the bathroom, he discreetly checked the closet shelf, desk drawers, and nightstand—the three most likely places for a civilian to keep a weapon. Finding none, the Glock 9mm he'd acquired this morning was ever more a comfort in his waistband. He made one discovery of note—a rack of clothing on one side of the closet that he estimated to be very near Astrid's fit and style. He'd already concluded that she was Krueger's mistress, yet Slaton never passed judgment on the indiscretions of others—not given the body of sins he had accrued over the years.

"How long will we be here?" she asked on returning to the main room. Her voice was freshly unsettled, and he imagined her having taken a long hard look in the bathroom mirror.

"That depends on what we find." He turned on the computer, it whirred to life, and he soon saw a security screen. "Do you have Walter's password?" he asked.

A pause. "Yes. But let me do it."

She typed quickly, with a secretary's aptitude. Slaton registered her keystrokes with the corresponding talents of a spy: SEXYASTRID. Would he ever have guessed such a password from a staid banker and his well-organized assistant? Probably so, which was cold comment on his late financial manager's cyber-security measures.

"These are the files you want," she said, helping him navigate. He saw eleven, each electronic folder sided by a padlock symbol. "Seven of the trusts are strictly financial and comprise the bulk of your holdings—bonds, equities, cash, precious metals. The other four represent real estate and . . . well, what Walter referred to as 'inventory.' "

"I imagine he was more specific."

Astrid sighed. "The late Monsieur Grossman was a dealer of arms—guns, ammunition, explosives. Walter said there were warehouses, long owned through a series of shell companies. He did nothing to alter those arrangements. Apparently Grossman had no desire to answer to landlords regarding his inventory."

"What about security?" Slaton asked.

"Grossman had made arrangements in each location—he paid handsomely for private guards who would not ask questions. Walter kept to these contracts as best he could, but I remember there were issues at one or two of the warehouses. It's not the kind of thing he knew much about—after all, he was only a banker."

It made sense to Slaton. He looked at the eleven files and saw ambiguous names, albeit with loose commonalities. TriStar Holdings. TriStar Trust Management. TS Management Group. He suspected there were other telltale associations. If publicly registered, even in different countries, any supercomputer could link these accounts without breaking a cyber-sweat. Again, security was lacking.

"These files are encrypted?" he asked.

"Yes, Walter managed things either from here or his office, never at home. There are codes to manage the encryption scheme between the two computers."

"He kept them in his office safe in Zurich?"

"Yes."

"We have to assume the men we encountered to-day have them. What about here at the chalet?"

This question was met with silence.

He spun the chair a half-turn and met her eyes. "Astrid, none of this is any good to Walter now—he's gone. But if we can see these accounts it will help us understand what's going on. Not to mention the fact that I *am* their rightful owner."

She nodded and disappeared into the master bed-room. Slaton made no attempt to follow her. There was no safe or lockbox—he had already concluded that much—so the critical codes were likely tucked into a sock or written on the bottom of a tissue box. He turned back to the screen and rubbed a hand under his whisker-encrusted chin. It made a sound like sandpaper. He felt weariness seeping in, and tried mightily to keep his focus.

Astrid returned with a small notecard that had been creased by multiple folds. "Here," she said.

Slaton took it and saw eleven alphanumeric character sets correlated to the file names. It could not have been more simple. He typed in the first, and as they waited for results, Astrid said, "Those men who came—do you think they were after your money? Or perhaps what's in the warehouses?"

"A very good question," he replied. "Possibly both.

Let's just hope they've been too busy running to take control of the accounts and lock us out."

Fifteen seconds later the first financial file blossomed to the screen. "The funds in this one are still in place," he said. "Nothing has moved."

"Could it mean they don't have the codes after all?"

"Possibly." Slaton called up the remaining financial files, one by one, and each was the same. He was staring at the last one when a message in the corner of the screen caught his eye. ADMINISTRATIVE SETTINGS UPDATED. This was followed by a date and time. "Wait a minute—somebody altered the account settings three hours ago."

"So they *do* have access."

"Apparently." He navigated to the administrative page, and the recent change was annotated on the bottom. The old trustee, a Bahamian law firm, was out, and the new guardian's name was listed in red—a name that stood out like a bolt of lightning in the night sky.

"What the hell?" he murmured.

"David?" Astrid said, peering over his shoulder to read the screen. "Is that you? David Slaton?"

He saw no point in denying it. "They made me the new administrator of the account."

"But *why*?" she said, her voice laced in consternation. "These men *killed* to gain access to the accounts. They were yours to begin with—all they've done is uncloud the ownership and put them directly in your name."

Slaton was silent, contemplating a more basic question. *How do they even know my name?*

He checked the other accounts and saw the same thing. In the last hours his name had been placed on each account. Stymied, he moved on to one of the arms warehouses, and was about to type in an encryption code when he paused. To the side of the files was a date and time—a record of when each had last been accessed. All the financial accounts had been opened today. Yet of the property holdings, only one of the four had been accessed. He elected to view the three that had not been touched, reasoning it was the best way to recognize what was different about the fourth.

Astrid pored over the screens with him. "Where are these warehouses?" she asked as he scrolled through pages of deadly inventory.

"Kinshasa, Cali, and Jakarta. According to the files all three remain intact."

"Do you think that's true?"

"No way to tell—not without physically going to each location and busting down the doors to see what's inside. It's possible they've been raided. Grossman had a low-tech, high-volume business model. Thousands of AK-47s, millions of rounds of ammunition, crate after crate of rocket-propelled grenades. There were a few more exotic items, things like plastic explosives and night optics. Altogether it's enough to start a good-sized war. Enough to finish a small one."

"If everything *is* still there—what will you do with it?"

He heaved a sigh. "I never gave it much thought—but I should have. The best thing would be to destroy it all, but that's not as easy as it sounds. Arson is out of the question, too many explosives. Maybe scuttle everything in the deep end of the ocean."

They both stared at the last remaining file.

"What about that one?" she asked.

"Let's take a look."

He opened the eleventh file and, if the information

was correct, it could not have been more different. There were no weapons caches, indeed no inventory of any kind. Aside from the administrative page, the Beirut file consisted of no more than a lone street address that meant nothing to Slaton. Was it an abandoned cache? A warehouse Grossman had put in place but never stocked?

He let go a long breath and rubbed his hands over his face. He was bone-tired. "I can't think straight. I have to get some sleep."

"Yes, I'm exhausted as well."

"Why don't you take the main bedroom."

"All right. And in the morning?"

"To begin, we check the accounts again."

"You have access now. Why not take control and freeze these people out?"

"No," he said, "definitely not."

"Why?"

"Two reasons. First, they probably think they have the only code set. If we interfere they'll know we're watching."

"And second?"

"I don't give a damn about the money."

She gave him an odd look, as if he'd just told her the sun would rise in the west.

"The money in these accounts was never mine to begin with. It's as dirty as money gets, bloody from warlords and drug smugglers and terrorists. It's almost certainly the reason you and I are here hiding out in this chalet. I've killed two people this week, and took a new piece of shrapnel in my leg. Walter is dead, his wife a widow, and his kids have no father—all because of that money. So if it disappears today, I won't miss a dime."

"Yes, I see your point."

"We'll wait and watch. So far these people have done nothing but put the accounts in my name—for reasons I don't understand. But I still think the money will move."

"And if it doesn't?"

Slaton thought about it. "Then I'd *really* be worried. It would mean these people are ignoring nearly a billion dollars in liquid assets for something else. It would mean they're after something even more valuable."

# TWENTY-FOUR

Anna Sorensen was changing into workout clothes, her sweatpants on her boyish hips but only a sports bra on top, when her office door burst open.

Jack Kelly, her assigned protégé, bustled in with a ream of paper in his hand. Quickly realizing his error, he turned away and said, "Sorry, boss."

Sorensen slid a T-shirt over her head, and then on a whim slingshotted the 34C bra she'd just removed at Kelly. It ringed his neck and came to rest over one shoulder.

"You know," he said, "in today's CIA that could be construed as sexual harassment."

"You're damned right it is. It's seven o'clock on a Friday night—shouldn't you be at the Brew Pub with Ciarra by now?"

"What about you?" he countered. "This is your idea of a hot Friday night? Hooking up with a treadmill?"

When Jack turned around the ever-present smile was there on his face. He was a good sort, only two years out of Cornell, and still full of—whatever they filled kids up with there. He was tall and good-looking, and had a girlfriend who liked that he worked for the CIA, but not that his boss was blond, pretty, and single, notwithstanding the fact that Sorensen was ten years older.

"We're having some luck with that NSA alert we were given last week," said Kelly.

"What alert?"

"The Iranian forgery mill they hacked into—some guy selling passports out of a dentist's office."

"Oh, right," she said, remembering. The NSA, in the course of its daily analysis of terabytes of data scooped out of Iran, had discovered a computer in a small dental office in Ahvaz that curiously kept on its hard drive a comprehensive sampling of passport images from countries around the world. Further inspection revealed that the office filled few cavities, and was quite possibly an arm of MISIRI, the Ministry of Intelligence and Security of the Islamic Republic of Iran.

MISIRI, commonly pronounced "misery" in these halls, had in recent years succumbed to the fact that it suffered a crippling technological deficit in relation to its Western enemies. In light of this, the ministry had taken to divesting certain clandestine functions across the Islamic Republic. Limousines for the country's elite were dispatched through a shadow taxi network in Tehran; signal intercepts from the southern border were logged and studied in an abandoned library in Isfahan; and the photographs that appeared in each day's *Tehran Times* could be found, one day prior to publication, on the computer of an ersatz wedding photography business in Vanak, a concern registered in the name of an old man who walked with a cane, did not own a camera, and who by one reliable account was quite blind.

As cyber defenses went, it was a marginally effective countermeasure. A few undertakings were undoubtedly hidden, but those exposed were easily laid bare. In the case of the forger-dentist, the NSA was able to unearth and analyze a raft of counterfeit identity documents, and deemed them to be of unusually high quality. At that point things faltered. Given that Ahvaz was near the Al-Faw Peninsula—where Iran, Iraq, and Kuwait were divided by no more than ten miles—agency analysts laid even odds that they'd stumbled on nothing more than a criminal smuggling operation, and with bigger digital fish to fry, they had washed their hands of the matter by forwarding their findings to the CIA's Office of Terrorism Analysis, or OTA, eventually ending in Sorensen's in-box.

She asked, "Is there any word whether this scheme is government run?"

"Still nothing on that, but we got one hit right away." Kelly slid a printed message in front of her.

"Malta?" she remarked.

"Seems there was a running gun battle in the streets of Mdina three days ago. One guy ended up dead. He wasn't carrying any ID when they found him, but the locals did some good detective work and tracked him to the hotel where he'd stayed the night before. Using the name he checked in under, they cross-checked arrivals at the airport and found him in a video standing in the immigration line. The Maltese tied him to a passport, but they hit a stop there and uploaded the data looking for help. We ran the passport and it matched one from our dentist office in Ahvaz." Kelly was clearly excited.

"Okay, so we found one. But a running gun battle? That screams to me this whole thing is drug-related, which in turn suggests our dentist's office is a private operation after all and not MISIRI."

"I thought that too—until we got the second hit."

He dropped another message in front of her. "This came in thirty minutes ago."

Sorensen began to read. "A second death? And now we're in Zurich?"

"Actually, two morts this time. A banker was killed in his office, and a second man outside the building. It happened just off Bahnhofstrasse, so the Swiss police are taking it pretty seriously. The second man was on our list. He was actually carrying a passport from the Ahvaz operation."

"Okay, two in two days. But these are pretty far apart. What makes you think they're related?"

"Two things. First, the NSA alert said that from this list of false identities they uncovered, seven were bundled."

"Bundled?"

"They were paid for from the same account, all at once, and then delivered to an address in Haifa."

"Haifa? Now we're in Israel?"

"Yep. I've already looked up the address. It was a private postal box—sure to be a dead end."

"Okay," Sorensen allowed, eyeing her star pupil critically. "What's the second thing?"

Kelly set two photographs on her desk. "Like I said, the police in Zurich are pulling out all the stops. They just put out this picture from a CCTV capture."

He tapped the photograph near Sorensen's left hand, a grainy color image, and one she suspected had limited possibilities for enhancement. Her eyes went to the second photo.

"That one's from Malta," he said. "He ran past the entrance of a souvenir shop that was wired for video."

The second image was black-and-white, a profile, and had even worse resolution. Still, she saw the resemblance. "Are you trying to tell me that—"

"You see it, don't you? It's the same guy, Anna!"

Her eyes narrowed as she looked hard at the photos. "Responsible for two killings in two days? A thousand miles apart?"

"Eight hundred and fifty-six," said a now-smiling Kelly. He was a cocky bastard—one of the things Sorensen liked about him.

"All right, Sherlock, what do you propose?"

"We push this up the chain, get the Southern Europe and Iran desks involved. People are getting killed and there has to be a reason."

"No. This is way too thin."

"It's the *same guy,*" he implored, tapping the desk between the photographs.

"Even if you're right, so what? We don't blow resources without a demonstrated threat to national security. You're not giving me anything I can sell upstairs."

With that, Kelly's boyish face collapsed—he looked like the kid who'd been benched from the big ball game.

"All right," she said. "See if you can get valid identities on the victims. And take the other passport names from your Group of Seven and run them by our in-house data miners. Maybe they'll all turn up dead and we can close the book on it."

Kelly straightened on his half-victory. "I'm on it."

When he left the room, Sorensen began folding her work clothes, but the pictures were still on her desk—right where Kelly had left them. He *would* go far, she thought.

*Farther than I ever will.*

Sorensen had been with the Company for twelve roller-coaster years. She'd had big successes, but her last posting to the Far East hadn't gone well. She'd been placed under a desk queen who felt threatened by a fresh sharpshooter from Langley, and office politics being what they were, the woman had done her damnedest to shunt Sorensen to the organizational curb. So she'd called in favors and gotten reassigned to Langley's newly formed DC&A, Data Collections and Analysis Office, arriving professionally bruised but ready for a fresh start.

She felt like her career was at a crossroads. Stay in for the duration and fight the good fight, or leave and . . . and what? That was always the problem. There wasn't much of an aftermarket for depleted intelligence operatives.

Sorensen stared at the pictures, and like Jack Kelly found herself wondering if the deaths, including the banker in Zurich, could be related.

*No,* she thought as she slipped on her Nikes. *Nobody leaves a trail of bodies like that.*

# TWENTY-FIVE

Not all the world's silence is of the same character. A calm ocean differs from a windless prairie. A vacant office is not the same as a child's bedroom. Manifestation aside, there is but one certainty: silence is never so elusive as when it is sought.

These were Ghazi's thoughts as he regarded the four walls around him. The original owner had been trying to sell the tiny farmhouse and barn, situated on a decidedly infertile twenty acres outside Basrah, since the end of the first Gulf War. According to legend, the place had been attacked on at least three occasions during that conflict by pairs of A-10 Warthogs whose crazed pilots must have thought the barn an ideal place for Saddam Hussein to conceal Scud missile launchers. True or not, the rumors were well ingrained in local lore, and did little to enhance the property's resale value. So when Hakim Ghazi made a reasonable offer, six weeks earlier, the owner had little stomach for bargaining.

In a troubling case of buyer's remorse, Ghazi *had* noted a repair to the roof of the barn, a refrigerator-sized patch that indeed could have been the result of a bomb falling through. Of course, the patch was likely something less dramatic. A worker stepping through during a routine repair, or a rotted section of wood giving way in a storm. Still, Ghazi had gone over the floor of the place more than once looking for unnatural impressions or recently turned plots of earth, anything to suggest an unexpended American bomb waiting to detonate. He never found anything, and in the end, as a man of science, Ghazi reasoned that even if there *was* a bomb buried under the barn's floor, nothing would likely happen. Chemical stability was a matter of science, and science was gloriously dependable—on this point he was an expert.

Ghazi's precious silence was broken by the sound of a truck pulling up outside the farmhouse. He checked his watch: it was just after four o'clock in the morning. He tensed slightly, then heard the familiar grinding of gears as Sam backed into place. Ghazi went outside and walked to the barn in the predawn darkness. His lone employee was there, standing next to the Toyota pickup, a smiling Indonesian man barely five feet tall, and who weighed little more than the children Ghazi recruited to aid his experiments. Sam's given name was Supermanputra Alatos Minungkabau, but on arriving in Iraq to work the oil fields three years ago he had sensibly simplified things.

"How many?" Ghazi asked.

"Five drums," replied the little Indonesian. "There is also another two-thousand-gallon water bladder, a pile of gray metal bricks, and the two heaviest sheets of drywall I have ever lifted. I thought the truck would buckle on its way here."

Ghazi heaved a tired sigh at the thought of transferring another load. "I went to school for a very long time with one aim in mind, Sam. I wanted to never do work like this again."

"And I traveled thousands of miles to do this work every day," said the tireless young man.

Ghazi could not deny it—he was a good worker. He'd hired Sam from Tamooz Street in Al-Basrah, a quiet corner where undocumented workers who'd overstayed their visas congregated each morning. Sam knew how to drive a truck, showed up when and where Ghazi asked him to, and disappeared with equal dependability. He had never once inquired what the supplies were for, nor why he was asked to collect them in the middle of the night from a small barge in the marshes. The only time he'd ever stopped smiling was on the day, one week ago, when Ghazi had inadvertently shorted him twenty dollars.

That was easily fixed.

"Come," said Ghazi. "We must finish before dawn."

Together they lifted planks to the tailgate of the truck, and by a combination of pushing, prying, and gravity, they rolled the rust-red drums into a corner and lined them in a neat row. Thankfully, the equipment inside the drums tonight was not particularly heavy. The rest of the load was more challenging, and when they were done thirty minutes later, sweating in the cool night air, the two stood to regard their work.

Sam asked, "How many more loads will there be?"

"This is the last they will send," replied Ghazi breathlessly. He had never been told who *they* were, although it seemed obvious enough. He'd gone along on the first trip, Sam steering the dilapidated Toyota to a rendezvous deep in the Haziweh marshes. As with every meeting since, they had materialized at roughly two in the morning, a boat full of muscular Shiites dressed unconvincingly as marsh Arabs. All around them on the flat boat were crates and oil drums and lead brick. The Shiites helped transfer the load, but none said a word, and on that first night he and Sam had stood in silence watching the empty barge motor back east toward Iran.

Ghazi never made the trip again, insisting he was too busy here, and letting Sam think it was because he abhorred manual labor. In truth it was the Shiites who worried him—the few he'd known were so unpredictable. Indeed, that first night had caused him to wonder about the greater plan. Iran was undeniably involved, something that hadn't been made clear during his recruitment. There was no way to tell if that involvement led all the way to Tehran, or if it was perhaps sourced elsewhere. A well-connected individual? An ambitious sect? A mullah acting out some holy mandate based on his private discussions with Allah? In the Islamic Republic such things were rarely evident, and Ghazi supposed he would never know. He simply relented to the idea that if everything went to plan, it would be a success for all involved.

Sam performed clean-up duty, putting the planks back in the Toyota's bed and backing it into the barn. That done, he came for his due. "Same time tomorrow?" he asked.

"I'll need you the next day—we have a different chore. Come around noon." Ghazi handed over the day's wage, plus a little extra. "Go have a good time tonight."

"Yes, mister, I will be happy to do that!" Smiling as ever, Sam stepped outside, and pushed the barn door neatly closed.

Ghazi heard his steps recede, and when they disappeared completely he went to one of the drums and lifted the lid. The cover detached easily, and inside he found hoses, clamps, and a pair of industrial pumps.

He pulled everything out, piece by piece, and began checking every component. Nothing could be left to chance. It felt good to be nearing an end after so many months of planning. Yet it was also discomforting. When the final call came he and Sam would have one last job: load everything they'd acquired over the last weeks for delivery to the airport, then cover their tracks as best they could. It was this last thought that gave Ghazi a pang of remorse.

It was too bad about Sam—he'd truly come to like the little Indonesian. For that reason, he hoped in earnest one of the others would take the task of putting a bullet in the back of his head.

Slaton split accommodations with Astrid: she took the bed in the master bedroom just after midnight, he opted for the couch in the main living area. There was a second bedroom with two sets of bunk beds, but Slaton preferred keeping a line of sight to all the chalet's access points and having his back to a solid outer wall.

He stirred at seven the next morning according to the clock on the microwave. Astrid was in the kitchen, and with columns of morning light leaning on the windows, he ignored the smell of fresh coffee and went straight to the computer. He called up the accounts, and as the connection ran its course a merciful Astrid delivered a freshly brewed cup, which he took appreciatively and black.

"Anything?" she asked.

After stepping through all seven financial files, he sipped from the mug and said, "Everything is still in place, they haven't taken a dime. But they have been busy."

"In what way?"

He tapped the portfolio on the screen. "Someone has been executing trades."

"What kind of trades?"

Slaton scanned multiple pages before answering. "They're selling investments Walter made and buying others. Energy mostly. Oil futures, refineries and drilling, petroleum multinationals—mostly in Nigeria and Venezuela. They're also buying gold."

"Gold?"

"What's called vaulted gold, physical bars and coins stored in secure facilities. So far they're splitting that between two institutions, one in the U.S. and another in Dubai. But it's all still in my name."

"This becomes more strange every time we look. These people kill Walter and take control of the accounts, only to put them in your real name. Now they alter the investment mix but still take nothing? It makes no sense."

"Oh, it does. We're just not seeing it yet. We have to be patient."

Astrid looked at him with consternation, probably wondering how anyone could watch idly while strangers manipulated their ten-digit portfolio.

One account changed as they watched, twenty thousand shares of Siemens sold, and a follow-on order placed for fifty gold kilobars. He was sure that if they watched all morning it would be more of the same.

*But what's the endgame?*

Slaton concentrated on a single account and went back through its history, carefully scanning the trades Krueger had made. Buys and sells, bonds and equities. Until yesterday, all the transactions appeared straightforward, the conduct of a more or less reputable Swiss money manager. He went back to the previous year's transactions and saw more of the same, and the year before that.

His eyes grew tired, and Astrid brought more coffee. He went back another year to view Grossman's dealings, paying particular attention to the months just before he had died. The records would have been a treasure trove to a good investigator. There was constant activity, flows of money and counterflows of illicit arms. A handful of transactions Slaton recognized, movements of arms and money that he, under the alias Natan Mendelsohn, had brokered on Israel's behalf. Uzis to the police force of the moderate Palestinian Authority in the West Bank, the lesser of evils, from Israel's point of view, when compared to Hamas. Explosives sent to Jundallah, the Sunni wrench in Iran's Shiite machine. There were any number of uses for a man like Grossman, and Mossad had taken full advantage, Slaton acting as conduit.

The second pot of coffee Astrid simply brought to the desk. Slaton trudged onward, studying wire transfers, shipping documents, and accounts receivable. It was on the third page of the sixth file that he hit a dead stop. The dollar amount of the transaction was insubstantial, at least by Grossman's standards. In mid-July, nearly two years prior, and roughly a month before Benjamin Grossman had succumbed to cancer, Slaton saw a lone transaction: *$50,000 U.S. as 10% payment*.

This much was easily extrapolated: half a million U.S. dollars was to be paid for . . . something. Yet that wasn't what anchored his eyes to the screen. It was the address where the money had been sent. An address he had seen in another of Krueger's files—the last warehouse that had been curiously empty. Now, in the payment notation, Slaton had a name to go with the Beirut address.

He committed both to memory, which wasn't hard to do.

The address was 26 Geitawi Boulevard.

The name was Moses.

# TWENTY-SIX

Umberto was standing in a corner of the operations building, near the converted closet he referred to as his office. Across the room Captain Petrecca was filing his flight plan on the telephone. Umberto marveled at the man's confidence—even talking on the phone he exuded authority. Umberto had grown up near the airport, and he remembered as a child standing for countless hours near the runway—there had been no fences back then—to marvel at the big Douglas and Lockheed aircraft rumbling skyward to points across the globe. If things had been different, he might have been an airplane captain. Umberto, however, was nothing if not pragmatic, and he knew he'd long ago passed the point in life when truth overtook dreams.

The captain hung up the phone and headed for the door, seeming done with his preparation. Umberto made his move. "Would you like to see the weather forecast?" he asked, holding up a ream of papers he'd printed out.

"No, I have already done that. Besides, there are only two kinds of weather here—heat and rain. The only forecast I need for that is a window."

The captain walked outside into the gathering morning light.

Undeterred, Umberto followed him, trotting to keep up with the man's brisk pace across the tarmac. "How long will you be airborne?" he asked.

"At least two hours are necessary for a full systems flight check. Engines, avionics, pressurization. To certify airworthiness everything must operate properly."

"Very well," said Umberto. "I will make sure Miguel is ready with the stairs when you return." He was pleased, thinking he'd put that well—an oblique suggestion that he himself had no pressing duties. The captain only walked faster.

Sensing his opportunity slipping away, Umberto relented to the direct approach. "Will you take a passenger?"

The captain drew to an abrupt stop. "*What?* Certainly not! We have work to do and you would only be in the way." He turned and strode away.

Umberto was crestfallen. He stood dumbstruck for a moment, but then scurried after the man. When they arrived at the airplane the copilot was waiting at the foot of the boarding stairs.

"He wants to come with us," the captain said, "but I told him it would be impossible."

Umberto looked plaintively at the second pilot. He had spoken to the man only once, and on that occasion found him to be abrupt, bordering on rude. Umberto was equally put off by the man's unprofessional appearance—he kept a ragged beard and his shirt was old and tattered, certainly not appropriate for the second-in-command of such a magnificent aircraft. All the same, the copilot eyed him now with a degree of empathy.

"Surely you can understand," Umberto pressed, his

gaze fixed on the younger man, "there is little excitement here in Santarém. To ride in such an aircraft, it would be the thrill of my life. I think I could guarantee you free beer tonight at my cousin's bar—all you can drink."

The copilot smiled, first at Umberto and then at his superior. "Actually, Captain, I think we might have room for one more. Remember the sidewall seat in the cargo area. I was originally thinking one of the mechanics might come along to help conduct systems tests in the cargo bay, but perhaps Umberto would do. He's been a great service to us, and clearly he is a capable man."

Umberto watched as the two exchanged a look. The captain, though appearing unmoved, gave a grudging nod and climbed the stairs without another word.

When he was gone, a buoyant Umberto embraced the copilot. "Thank you! Thank you! I promise I will be useful!"

Behind the black mask of his beard, the copilot smiled back. "I'm sure you will."

The big jet began moving less than an hour later.

The preflight checks went well, as far as Umberto could tell, and soon he was belted into a webbed seat along the sidewall of the forward cargo area. Looking aft he saw the tunnel of the fuselage—other than the big tank between the wings, the bay was completely empty, which made the aircraft seem more cavernous than ever. The big jet's engines rose to a crescendo, and the takeoff acceleration pushed him sideways into the nylon webbing.

Soon they were airborne, and Umberto gripped the

rails of his seat as the ride became bumpy. The cockpit door was open, yet from where Umberto sat neither pilot was in view. He could, however, see a sliver of sky in the forward windscreen, and through the circular portal in the entry door across from him wisps of white cloud skimmed past at terrific speed. His senses were overloaded by the sights and sounds—it was every bit as exhilarating as he'd imagined.

They'd been in the air no more than ten minutes when the captain called out from the front. "It will be turbulent for a time! Keep your seat belt fastened!"

Umberto shouted that he would, quietly hoping that things eventually settled enough to allow what he truly wanted—to see the cockpit during flight. *What a sight that would be!*

Soon blue sky filled the port window, and the turbulence improved considerably. The big jet droned smoothly, and Umberto waited with all the patience he could muster. After what must have been half an hour, he could take it no more. He called out in a loud voice, "Sir, must I still remain in my seat?"

His words seemed lost in the big tube, muted by the hiss of rushing air. He wondered what caused that noise. The wind outside? Or was it the pressurization system? He had so many questions.

"Can I come up with you?" he called out.

No reply.

Could the pilots hear him? He had no idea, but he sensed his chance slipping away. For the second time that day, Umberto acted on impulse. He unbuckled and stepped cautiously toward the cockpit door. Rounding a bulkhead he saw the flight deck, bright sun streaming through the windshield, and it took a moment for his eyes to adjust. When they did, what he saw concerned him. The captain was there, half-turned in his seat. The man was completely ignoring his instruments, his gaze fixed on Umberto. Even more disturbingly, the copilot's seat was quite empty.

The little Brazilian stood still, confused. "But where is—"

It was a question Umberto Donato never finished.

# TWENTY-SEVEN

The worst news of the day came just after noon.

*9847 Old Cedar Lane.*

Slaton stared at the address for a very long time. He stepped through the accounts and saw it in each one, a second administrative alteration: not only was ownership being tied to his name, but it now reflected the address of a certain suburban Virginia residence. The house where his wife and his son were likely eating breakfast at this moment.

Had someone realized he was watching? Was it some kind of threat?

Struck by an urge for fresh air, he picked up his half-full mug and went to the window. Very carefully, Slaton surveyed the nearby chalets, cars, and sidewalks before venturing onto the balcony. He leaned on the rail and a sharp breeze bit his exposed skin, countered intermittently by rays of warmth as the sun battled broken cloud layers. He should have appreciated the spectacular scenery, the steep mountainside and conifer forest, all dressed in white and accented by crisscrossing dots of color that were skiers carving their way downhill.

Slaton saw none of it.

*The men from Malta once again. But who were they?*

Soldiers. That much was clear, notwithstanding the fact that the original squad of four was now down to two. Ben-Meir was Israeli, the one he'd downed in Mdina Polish. The others certainly had military backgrounds—until service in the name of honor and country had been replaced by a calling of greater liquidity. Yet whatever scheme Slaton was caught up in, it was not authored by a group of hired commandos. He sensed logistics and support, someone who could recruit soldiers and sign paychecks. An unseen planner and quartermaster.

Slaton watched a skier in a red jacket at the top of the mountain. It was a woman, he was sure, moving fast but with control. She floated left and right down the mountain, carving past the slower dots effortlessly like an alpine snowflake on a breezeless day. He envied her freedom, and appreciated the single-mindedness with which she went about her task. Watching the red jacket curve downhill Slaton was mesmerized, and soon one word settled in his mind.

*How?*

*How did they track me to Zurich?*

He had escaped the assault in Mdina by the thinnest of threads, then disappeared into the alleys of Valletta. He'd quietly arranged passage on a tramp steamer, and from there jumped into the cold Mediterranean. Finally, he'd traveled hundreds of miles under identity documents he knew to be pristine. Yet there they had been, lying in wait near the steps of Krueger's office within an hour of his landing at Zurich International.

*How?*

The red jacket reached the bottom and was lost in a sea of brightly colored parkas. Slaton paced across the balcony, and as he looked out across mountains glistening in the sun, he deconstructed the attack in Zurich. He recalled every detail as best he could, hoping to spur something new, something useful. And it did come.

The plumber's van.

He envisioned it parked in front of Krueger's office, and recalled the name and logo emblazoned on the side: LASZLO INSTALLATIONEN. And below that: SINCE 1940.

Slaton hurried back inside and typed the name into the computer's search engine, along with "Zurich." The answer came immediately. Laszlo Installationen was nowhere to be seen, not today, and certainly not in 1940. Which meant the van was a well-devised cover. Fictitious companies were always preferable. To steal a legitimate plumber's van guaranteed police involvement, not to mention the chance of surprise requests for warranty work from neighbors, or that another employee might spot the vehicle and recognize a fictitious work crew. Well-planned lies were always preferable. The only catch—they took time to manufacture.

Taking things further, Slaton knew it defied probability that Ben-Meir and his crew had planned a break-in of Krueger's office, and that he had simply stumbled in at the wrong moment. The timing was too perfect. Which left but one option—a preplanned hit on Krueger's office, the timing of which was based on his arrival. They had tracked him to Zurich. Once again, *how?* He was confident in the efficacy of his false identity, and from the airport he had gone directly to Bahnhofstrasse.

He was missing something.

He shifted in the seat, and a stab of pain caused him to glance down at his thigh. Slaton noted steam venting under the door of the master bathroom, Astrid in the shower. He went to the second half-bath and closed the door. Easing off his trousers, he pulled away the bandage and gauged his wound under the brilliant Hollywood lights. The gash was still there, and underneath the inch-long cut was a large lump. A foreign body lodged in the muscle tissue. Slaton had assumed it was a chip of stone or wood, or in the worst case, a deformed slug from a low-velocity ricochet.

*Or?*

An old thought echoed in his head, one that had first settled three days ago in a battered rooming house in Valletta. *Given such a team—experienced and heavily armed, with a well-designed plan, and facing an unarmed and surprised target—how on earth am I still alive?*

He then remembered the words he'd heard the crew-cut man utter into his microphone: *"No contact. Do we pull back yet?"*

*Yet.* As if a retreat was planned. As if their objective had already been met.

Slaton put it all together, and suddenly saw everything in a new light—a light that shone with disquieting clarity. There *was* a way to prove the theory.

The question was how to go about it.

# TWENTY-EIGHT

The distress call came one hour after takeoff, or as eventually noted by investigators, 10:21 a.m. Brasília Standard Time.

*"Mayday! Mayday!"*

Lucas Da Silva bolted upright in his chair. An air traffic controller for five years, he had heard those words on only one other occasion, a breathless plea from a student pilot who'd wandered too near a thunderstorm. The ever-steady Da Silva had managed to calm the young man and guide him to safety that afternoon, earning a plaque of commendation, and more meaningfully, a case of quality rum from the pilot. In spite of that favorable outcome, Da Silva had never forgotten the tone he'd heard on the radio that day—the naked, visceral helplessness of a man staring fate in the eye. Now he was hearing it again, only this time from a big jet, undoubtedly piloted by an experienced, professional crew.

A bolt of adrenaline shot down his well-caffeinated spine, and Da Silva replied, "This is Atlántico Center. Say call sign and nature of your difficulty."

An extended silence followed, and soon both questions were answered by his radar screen. Two hundred miles northeast, at the edge of the Atlántico Flight Information Region, Perseus Flight 10 was falling like a stone.

The terrified voice crackled again over the radio. "Perseus Ten! We have structural damage! We are—" Static interrupted the transmission. "We are in an uncontrolled descent and going down. Mark position!"

"Roger, Perseus Ten! Your position is noted. What further assistance can I give to you?"

The next transmission was garbled and completely unintelligible.

"Perseus Ten, say the number of souls and fuel on board."

Da Silva waited. He watched the altitude readout sink through ten thousand feet. Soon after, it went blank. He keyed his microphone. "Perseus Ten, the nearest emergency field is Val de Cans, one hundred and ninety miles on a course of one-niner-five degrees."

Silence.

"Perseus Ten, this is Atlántico Center, how do you hear?"

Da Silva repeated the question twice more, and on the second try he realized his supervisor was looking over his shoulder. The two exchanged a head shake. As was his duty, and with a trembling hand, the supervisor initiated the crash response.

A Brazilian Air Force helicopter, diverted from a training mission, was the first on scene ninety minutes later. The aircraft homed in on an emergency beacon and discovered a partially inflated life raft that was otherwise empty. With only enough fuel to remain on station for a matter of minutes, the crew came to a hover over water nearly eight thousand feet deep and carefully plotted the coordinates of a modest debris field.

It took the Brazilian Navy another hour to reach the drifting crash site. A Marinheiro class corvette, V19, arrived on scene, and without waiting for orders the nine-hundred-ton patrol vessel used its high-tech navigation suite and motivated crew to begin a search for survivors. They found the empty life raft, and also seat cushions, a yellow suitcase, insulation, and a dissipating oil slick that covered roughly a hundred yards. Everyone kept looking. The first casualty was spotted by a sharp-eyed lookout, a traumatized body that was quickly and respectfully recovered.

In those critical first hours little else was found, and soon an Air Force meteorologist gave bad news to those commanding the rescue operation. An unusually severe weather system was developing off the northern coast of Brazil, and forecast to churn unabated for a full three days. Sensing scant hope and measureable risk, the governing authorities made the safe call and, in a decision that would soon be revisited, ordered all search teams to stand down. Ships set new courses for home port, and aircraft returned to their bases as the search for survivors from Perseus Flight 10 was put on indefinite hold.

Though no one knew it at the time, it would take less than twenty-four hours to identify the recovered body as being that of the caretaker of Santarém–Maestro Wilson Fonseca Airport, a middle-aged man by the name of Umberto Donato who had reportedly hitched a ride on what was meant to be a maintenance test flight.

Less apparent, particularly in those frenetic first hours, was the significance of his untimely end.


Slaton walked with a pronounced limp, and was leaning on Astrid when they entered the only clinic in Klosters.

"I've had an accident," he said to the receiving nurse in French.

"I can see that," she replied as she brought up a wheelchair.

Slaton dropped into the chair with exaggerated heaviness.

He and Astrid were both wearing ski gear, complete with boots, jackets, snow pants, and goggles around their necks, all taken from the equipment closet of Krueger's chalet. Slaton's ensemble was oversized, but the poor fit was indistinguishable in such typically bulky outerwear. They'd gone to great lengths to build their appearances. Their ski boots were covered in snow, and clots of white peppered Slaton's hair. A chunk of ice was jammed into the cracked amber goggles hanging around his neck, and his right hand was missing a glove. The final prop, carried by Astrid, was a bent ski pole with a broken tip—the last inch was snapped off cleanly, an effect that had taken Slaton three attempts in levering the late Walter Krueger's poles into the gaps of his wooden deck.

The paperwork was minimal—unbridled tort law having yet to take hold in Switzerland's winter playground—before the nurse wheeled him into an examination room and poised over a clipboard. "Where are your injuries?"

"Where are they not?" he replied with a good-natured grimace. "I was going too fast on the east run and went over a ledge. I'm sore everywhere, but my leg is the worst." He pointed to a tear in his pants that was oozing blood, this manufactured by reopening the original wound, and necessary in any event to erase four days of healing. "I tangled with my pole—the tip jabbed me in the leg and broke off. I can feel something in my thigh."

"Let's have a look."

Together they gingerly removed Slaton's pants and thermal undergarment, also sized for Walter Krueger's ample frame, and a doctor soon arrived. He was a gentle old man with silver hair, and wore a turtleneck sweater under a loose lab coat. With one look he declared an X-ray was in order, and it was undertaken with predictable efficiency. The results were telling.

"There are no broken bones," he declared, "but you do have an object lodged in your thigh." The doctor held the ghostlike picture for all to see, his pen pointing to something that might well have been the tip of a broken ski pole. For his part, Slaton was happy the X-ray image had a narrow field of view, as there were other bits of shrapnel lodged in other recesses of his body that defied simple explanation.

After some back and forth, it was agreed the best course of action would be to remove whatever it was on the spot. The procedure was straightforward, beginning with a local anesthetic and ending with six stitches.

"The wound will be sore for a few days," said the doctor. "I can give you a prescription for pain medication." Slaton had no intention of taking opiates, yet for appearance's sake he gratefully pocketed the prescription.

The extracted object ended up in a small metal

bowl, and the doctor took it to a sink and rinsed it off. He seemed to study it for a time, then brought it to Slaton held by the surgeon's equivalent of tweezers.

"This doesn't look like the tip of a ski pole," said a man who would certainly know. "At least not any I've ever seen. I'm not sure what you've run across." He held it out to Slaton. "A souvenir, perhaps?"

"Why not?"

The doctor dropped the extracted object into Slaton's open palm.

Slaton had originally imagined a chip of stone, or perhaps a mangled bullet. What he saw was in fact similar in shape to the tip of a ski pole, a cylinder half an inch long, tapering to a point on one end. Almost a bullet, yet thinner, with what looked like a fabric thread trailing the back end. Slaton had never seen anything like it. Not exactly.

But he knew what he was looking at.

And it answered a great many questions.

# TWENTY-NINE

"We have to leave Klosters," Slaton said as they walked out of the clinic.

He took Astrid by the arm and they strode quickly past a pharmacy, then a cemetery full of neatly plotted graves, proof that even death did not obviate the Swiss compulsion for order.

"Leave?" she asked. "Why?"

"Because I know how those men tracked me to Zurich." He took the metal slug from his pocket. "This isn't a bullet or an accidental piece of shrapnel. It's a flechette transmitter."

"A what?"

"A tracking device, a special ballistic round that can be fired from a standard nine-millimeter weapon. I used something similar once, probably an earlier generation—my shot was from eighty meters, one round into the backpack of a Hamas motorcycle messenger. This one is different, more miniaturized, but the idea is the same. Once embedded it can be tracked from a drone or a satellite. Possibly a dedicated receiver that's useful out to a kilometer or two."

"They used this device to follow you?"

"It makes sense. The men who attacked me in Malta were professionals, and I couldn't understand how they'd missed taking me out. Now it's obvious—they weren't trying to. They were only flushing me, making me lead them to Walter."

Astrid said nothing. She looked utterly confused.

Slaton continued working things out aloud. "I think someone knew these accounts existed in Zurich, but didn't know exactly where."

"So . . . you unknowingly led them to Walter?"

"I was careless. Once I arrived in Zurich, they followed me using that transmitter, watched me walk into his office, and then made their move."

Astrid came to a stop on the sidewalk. As she stared at him a stray gust swirled a cyclone of snow around them.

"You met with Walter yesterday?"

Slaton beckoned her to keep moving, and Astrid complied. "Yes, briefly."

"You never told me that."

"Didn't I? We talked for a few minutes. Then I stepped out to the hallway while Walter was calling up my accounts. I spotted them coming."

"What did you do?"

"I went into the lawyer's office across the hall and told them to call the police. Then I escaped through a back window."

She went silent, and Slaton realized what she was thinking.

"I would have helped him if I could, Astrid. They came fast, and there was no time to warn Walter. They had weapons, I didn't. I also miscalculated—I assumed they were after me."

"But you came back."

"I saw you heading for the office . . . I felt like I had to do something."

She looked at him critically, trying to piece everything together—this from a woman who lived in a realm of spreadsheets and conference calls, not tactical assault and deception.

Slaton surveyed the streets and passing cars with renewed alertness—the tracking device in his pocket might or might not still be emitting a signal. They crossed Landstrasse, in the center of town, the streets alive with trams and cars, groups of weary skiers hauling their gear down from the mountain. As they passed a travel agency whose window held an improbable display of a plastic palm tree basking under a heat lamp, Slaton reached into his pocket and touched the tiny transmitter that had less than an hour ago been inside him. He was sure it was his imagination, but the device seemed warm and inordinately heavy—like a beacon in his pocket.

Slaton noted a delivery truck ahead on the curb, an advertisement on the sidewall tying it to a distributor of medical supplies in Liechtenstein. As they came near he watched the driver step down from the truck's rear loading door carrying a clipboard. The man disappeared inside a building, clearly ready to seal his paperwork with a signature.

Without breaking stride, Slaton tossed the transmitter into the half-empty cargo bay.

Astrid looked back over her shoulder, but Slaton ushered her forward.

"I think you're right," she said, "we should leave. But where can we go?"

Slaton had already considered the question and come up with two options. His first instinct had been to put the device in the chalet and take up a position nearby with the Glock. If the two men who killed Krueger arrived, he could extract payback, and possibly get information about the greater plan. It would be a bit of well-earned justice, and satisfying to a degree. Yet he saw problems with that scenario. Given how the previous two engagements had gone, there was a good chance Ben-Meir would bring reinforcements. On top of that, Slaton gave better than even chances that no one would come at all. If his thinking was right, the assassins of Zurich and Mdina already had what they wanted.

Which left only one choice.

"We have to find a place to stay," he said, "one that's far from here. The chalet is compromised—it's no longer safe."

"You think we are in danger?"

"I don't know, but we have to assume the worst. The car is still the safest way for us to move. I'll approach the garage carefully, and if anything looks suspicious we'll find another way."

Astrid, having grown increasingly steady since yesterday, seemed to waver. She opened her mouth, and he expected her to suggest once more that they call the police. What she said was, "If we can't go back to the chalet, I should go buy a few things. Some food and toiletries."

Slaton's attention broke from the street, and he pulled her gently to a stop and met her gaze. After a moment, he said, "All right."

"Where should I meet you?"

"The ski shuttle parking lot. Be in the departure line one hour from now."

"One hour." She turned to go.

"Astrid—wait."

She turned back.

Slaton moved closer and reached a hand under the waist of her unzipped jacket. To anyone watching, they would appear as lovers engaged in a parting embrace. Astrid tensed visibly as his hand curled around her beltline and found the gun. He'd made her take it when they left the chalet—that X-ray image he could never have explained. He discreetly pulled the Glock clear and slid it under his own jacket. "I might need this."

She pulled back and smiled nervously.

"One hour," he repeated.

She nodded and turned away, crunching over a sidewalk paved in clouded ice. Astrid turned a corner and disappeared.

Slaton began a mental clock, setting thirty seconds as his minimum interval. In that time he analyzed the variables around him. He spun a casual half-turn, paused for a moment, then did it again—to turn 360 degrees on a sidewalk invariably looked peculiar. He saw the usual crowds of a fading afternoon. Otherwise, having already walked these streets twice today, the field of play was familiar. Nearing the thirty-second mark, Slaton amended his first estimate and allowed ten more seconds.

He then set out purposefully and followed Astrid.

# THIRTY

The doorbell rang, and Christine found a Dominos delivery driver on her front porch. He was probably twenty years old, with fading acne and a barbell in his nose, wearing a shirt with the pizza chain's logo. The kid slid a flat box out of an insulated container.

"Large veggie?" he asked.

"Yeah, thanks. I wasn't in a mood to cook. What's the damage?"

The kid told her, and as she reached into her pocket for a wadded twenty Christine noticed Stein near the curb. He was leaning on his cane near an old Honda that had a plastic DOMINOS sign strapped to the roof. He was watching intently. Feeling uncomfortable, Christine settled with the driver, who thanked her for a good tip before ambling away. When he passed Stein on the sidewalk the two exchanged an amiable nod.

The Israeli waited until the car was out of sight before moving with surprising quickness to the front steps. "What the hell was that?" he demanded.

"What do you mean?" she replied, trying to sound surprised. Stein had gone outside to get the lay of the local area, but not before giving strict instructions to allow no one in the house.

He brushed past her, and with a lukewarm pizza in her hand Christine closed the door against the chill wind.

"Did we not talk about this?" he said sternly. "You cannot allow *anyone* near."

"It was a pizza delivery kid—I called in the order."

"Did you know him?"

She set the pizza on the kitchen table. "Of course not. But—"

"But he had a shirt? A car with a sign? He was carrying a pizza box?"

She gave no reply.

"Listen," Stein said, "I don't *have* to be here! I'm doing this as a favor to Anton, and because I owe David my life. When you make mistakes like that, you put all of us at risk, and I'll be damned if I'm going to get shot by somebody with an MP7 in a pizza container!"

Christine turned away and sighed deeply. "It's been a long time since I've had to think like that."

"I understand. But we need to be clear right now—if you want me to stay, you do things my way."

She bit her lower lip. Did she want him to stay? Not really, not given what he represented. Then a distant voice interceded, David's onetime reflection on his relationship with Mossad. *They didn't need me often. But when they did, they needed me badly.* As much as she hated it, if Stein's information *was* true she needed his help. Needed it badly. "All right," she relented. "It won't happen again."

Seeming satisfied, Stein went to the pizza box and opened it. "Veggies? My life is on the line for peppers and onions?"

"I should have known better. Next time, the carnivore's special." She watched him drop a slice on a paper plate, and asked, "So did you learn anything out there?"

"Like you said, there's only one road in. But at the cul-de-sac there's a footpath through the woods that leads to a park."

"I could have told you that."

"You should have."

Her face knitted into a frown.

"The path is in bad shape," he said, "deep snow, and there's a downed tree across the middle."

"You went back into the trees?"

"Far enough. And there are a few things you should know. I disabled your garage door opener and did some rewiring. We're not planning on driving anywhere, but if you want to raise the garage door you'll need to do it manually. Do you know how to do that?"

Christine nodded. "And what does that do for us?"

He pulled her garage remote control from his pocket. "I can light up the backyard with one click. Good for taking a look at night, and a distraction to anyone we see nosing around. Oh, and I put your trash can in the garage."

"Why? You expect someone to hide inside and wait for me to empty the diaper pail?"

He gave her a severe look. "Garbage outside attracts animals, and the last thing we need is a pack of raccoons nosing around in the middle of the night. The idea is to be proactive. By eliminating complications, we give ourselves every advantage."

"Proactive. Does that mean you at least shoveled my sidewalk?"

"Not a chance. Snow is good—nobody can approach the house without leaving prints. I also found a small padlock in the garage and used it to secure your electrical box."

"The lock on the workbench? That one's no good. I've been meaning to throw it out because I lost the key."

"Doesn't matter. I'll cut it off before I leave."

He busied himself installing fresh batteries in her flashlights. They had scoured the house earlier and found six flashlights, but only two that actually worked. Stein wanted to get them all up to speed and put one at the entrance to each room. Since arriving yesterday he'd been in constant motion, studying and watching and preparing. There was a relentlessness about the man, perhaps tinged with a dash of paranoia. Traits she recognized only too well.

Davy squealed from his playpen. She lifted him out, put him in his high chair, and began spooning mashed peas. "What about the house across the street?" she asked. She had told him there was a new neighbor.

"I took a good look, even got around the backside once. The blinds are all drawn, but I did see one light upstairs, the window facing the street. There was no mail in the box and the fireplace is cold. The tracks in the driveway suggest the car went out once, then came back, probably yesterday."

"You checked the mailbox? Isn't that illegal?"

Stein give her a curious look, and said, "I'll keep an eye on the place, Christine, but I didn't see anything worrisome."

She sighed. Davy's bib was covered in green, and she took the next spoonful not from the jar but from his chin. "Yaniv—"

He looked up from unscrewing the lens of a flashlight.

"If I seem doubtful or cynical, please don't take it for a lack of appreciation."

He smiled. "I know—it's okay." He watched Davy take the scrapings of the jar, and said, "You know, he really does look like—" The thought stopped there, and he shot her an awkward look before gathering an armload of flashlights and getting back to his mission.

Christine watched him go with an odd feeling. It wasn't what Stein had left unsaid, but something else. And it wasn't the first time she'd felt it.

One hour later, Slaton arrived at the shuttle parking lot dead on schedule.

Astrid was waiting, and he steered the little Peugeot through deep puddles to reach the loading curb. She spotted him right away.

"I'm glad to see you, it was getting cold out there," she said, sliding into the tattered passenger seat.

"I try to be punctual."

"I've been thinking about where we could go now."

"And?"

"I have another friend who lives in Wangen, where I grew up. She said she would be happy to have us for a few days."

"You've already talked to this friend?"

"Yes. I borrowed a phone and told her I was on holiday with my new fiancé." Astrid supplemented this with a coy smile.

"You're beginning to think like a spy. All right, Wangen is on the road back to Zurich, isn't it?"

"Yes, on the south side of the lake. It should take roughly an hour. My friend said she was on her way home from work and would have dinner waiting when we arrived."

"A home-cooked dinner," Slaton said, putting the car into gear. "How could I possibly say no to that?"

# THIRTY-ONE

"You're not gonna believe this," said Jack Kelly.

He said something else, but the words were drowned out. Sorensen pressed her phone against her ear, struggling to hear against a symphony of barking. "What?"

"Where are you?" Kelly asked.

"I'm at the Humane Society."

"Friday nights you work out, and Saturdays with stray dogs? Boss, we need to talk."

"No, we don't. Since I started this Langley posting I'm not traveling much, and I thought I might rescue a mutt. It's not easy for a woman to find a trustworthy companion these days."

Getting no reply, Sorensen stepped out from the kennel and into an empty exercise courtyard. "What have you got, Jack?"

"Two more hits on the Group of Seven."

"Wait, let me guess—an assassination in the Hague this time?"

"Even better. An airplane crash off the coast of Brazil."

"Seriously?"

"It was an MD-10, a big airliner. It disappeared from radar over the Atlantic. The names of the crew haven't been publicly released, but we have an agreement with

208 | WARD LARSEN

Brazil to immediately share the crew and passenger manifests of any air crash—a fallout from 9–11. When we ran the names, both the pilot and copilot were matches from the list I showed you last night. Both men arrived in Brazil on papers from our Iranian forgery operation, that same bundle of seven."

"Jesus," Sorensen said. "How many passengers were on board?"

"That's the good news—only one. This was a cargo jet that was on some kind of maintenance acceptance flight. The only other person on board was a Brazilian national, some local guy who worked at the airport. His name is definitely not on our list."

"All right, but . . . are you sure about this?"

"I double-checked everything. Four of the seven people on that MISIRI list have died this week, all under suspicious circumstances."

"Suspicious? People getting shot on the streets is one thing, but what's suspicious about an airplane crash?"

"Well," Kelly hedged, "nothing yet. But I definitely think we should look into it."

As he waited for her to make the call, a chorus of baying erupted from the kennels. Sorensen frowned. "Okay, I'll be there in twenty minutes. Let's try to find out what these pilots were doing down in Brazil."

"Any idea how we do that?"

Sorensen was about to say no when she had an epiphany. "Actually, yeah. I think I know just the man for the job."


Slaton kept a good pace in the Peugeot, and they arrived on the outskirts of Wangen at ten minutes before six.

"We are running late," she said.

"Are we? I'm sure your friend will hold dinner."

"The street is Dorfplatz. She said there would be a church on the corner."

"You haven't been to her house before?"

"No, she recently moved." Astrid straightened in her seat. "There, it's just ahead. After the turn stop at the fourth house on the right."

Slaton saw the church, and the street labeled DORF-PLATZ. He drove straight past them.

"What are you doing? That was the turn."

His eyes kept to the road. In silence another two streets passed before Slaton drew to a stop along the curb in front of a used car sales lot. He left the engine running and unlatched his seat belt. He pulled the Glock from his pocket and held it in his left hand.

Astrid stared at the gun. "You won't need that when we arrive at—"

"I need it right now," he interrupted.

Her face went to stone. "What do you mean?"

"I think you know." He let this sink in for a moment. "How much, Astrid?"

"What?"

"How much did they pay you?"

She sat very still.

He said, "I followed you this morning, back in Klosters. You didn't borrow a phone—you bought one." Slaton reached into the inside pocket of her jacket and pulled out a cheap prepaid phone. "You sat on a bench and made a call. I know because I watched you from the post office across the street. I couldn't hear what you were saying, but I didn't need to. It's easy to tell when someone is taking instructions because the flow of communications is very one-way, the receiver mostly nodding and saying 'yes' and 'all right.' That's what you did."

"But—"

He angled the barrel of the gun until it was pointed at her chest. "And there was something else. Just after Walter was killed, when we were talking at the pub in Baden—you asked why 'three men' would do that to Walter. Something about it bothered me at the time, but I couldn't place it. I made the connection today— you were never in a position to see more than one of them, yet you knew there were three men. Then, when we discussed going to the police right away, you gave up far too easily. My mistake for not seeing it."

She said nothing.

"There is no friend in Wangen, is there?"

Astrid deflated, her expression shot with guilt. One of her hands was near the door handle, but there was no tension in the musculature, no inching toward the cool silver handle.

"You made a bad choice, Astrid. I need to know— who are they?"

He sensed a hesitation, but not long enough for an amateur to fabricate a solid lie. "A man came to see me a few months ago. Walter was out for the day, so I was in the office alone. There were two other men with him, but they stayed in the hall and I never saw their faces. He said he represented Israel, and that they were the rightful owner of your accounts. He said you, Grossman, and Walter had stolen all of it. He said Israel preferred to settle things quietly, and gave two options. If I provided the encryption codes, he would pay me two hundred thousand U.S. dollars. Otherwise he would go to the police."

"What did you do?"

"I told him I didn't have the codes."

"But you knew where they were."

She nodded. "They knew I could get them. I was given time to think, and after two days I called a number I'd been given and agreed to their terms."

"You and Walter were having an affair."

She recoiled slightly, then nodded again.

For five minutes Astrid recounted the bitter details of a time-honed progression: late-night working sessions, a business trip to Paris followed by dinner to celebrate a profitable new account. From *cochon Basque* at Le Cinq, and a wine-soaked stroll along the Left Bank of the seventh arrondissement, there was but one possible destination.

"Our relationship had been going on for three years. Walter said he was going to leave his wife, but there was always an excuse, always another delay. I finally realized it was never going to happen. I confronted Walter. He blamed her, of course. He said she would ruin him if he ever left her. Our relationship became strained, and it was difficult for us to work together. I wanted to leave, but I needed the job."

"So you saw this offer as a chance to get back at Walter."

"Yes. But I swear by all that is holy, I never imagined what happened yesterday. I didn't care if they ruined Walter financially—perhaps I even hoped it. But it never crossed my mind that he would be physically harmed."

"And once that happened, you realized you were implicated. The police might uncover the affair, uncover your relationship with the killers. You could be charged as an accomplice to murder."

"Yes."

Slaton amended his earlier assumption. The tracking transmitter had not been shot into his leg to lead them to Walter Krueger. They'd already recruited Astrid, and she could give them the codes. The flechette seemed to have only one purpose—to pinpoint his movements, in particular his arrival at Krueger's office. But why?

Astrid gave the final hint. "There was also a surveillance system. After I agreed to help, the same man came one day and installed a camera in the office while Walter was out. It connected wirelessly to the computer at my desk."

Slaton recalled the team's approach to the building. It had been loud and sloppy, giving him a chance to get clear. The truth slowly dawned. The flechette, the surveillance system, the timing of their strike, his convenient escape. It was all part of a screenplay. "They were trying to set me up for Walter's death. They would have known when I arrived at the airport, what cab I took, and had a record of my arrival at his office. All of it could be fed to the police afterward."

Astrid looked at him blankly, clearly mystified.

"I end up being hunted and on the run, accused of killing Walter. Probably accused of killing you as well."

"*What?*"

"Did they tell you they were coming yesterday?"

"No. Last week I gave them the combination to the safe in Walter's office. I hadn't heard from them since, and I assumed they would come late one night."

"Only they came in broad daylight. Then two things happened they couldn't have predicted. First you went out for coffee."

"The other?"

"I came back to help you."

Slaton scanned the street and surrounding buildings as he carried his theory forward. After he'd escaped from Krueger's office, the accounts were placed in his name—more evidence. He was being set up for a gigantic fall. But what was the motive? Why would they ignore such a massive financial windfall only to put him on the run?

"This man who came to see you—what did he look like?"

"I don't know," she said, a tear running down one cheek. "Average height, thin. Short black hair and a dark complexion. He had an accent." Her head bent down and her chest convulsed.

Slaton had been expecting Ben-Meir, or one of the others he'd seen in Malta. None matched her description. "Could you place the accent?"

"Not really . . . perhaps Middle Eastern. He looked like so many of the new immigrants who've come to Europe. He made me nervous, and there was something odd about him. He seemed . . . how do they say it . . . unbalanced."

"I'm sure that was an act—he was trying to frighten you. You didn't see this man yesterday?"

"No. I only saw the one who threatened me outside the building . . . the one you killed." She wiped her cheek with the heel of a hand. "When you offered to guide me clear it seemed my only choice."

"It was, Astrid, I promise you. Only today you doubted me again. Why?"

"When you said you had seen Walter yesterday, it occurred to me that it could have been you who . . . who did that to him."

Slaton looked up and down the street. The evening was fading to gray, and passing cars sprayed slush from street-side puddles. "I didn't kill him, Astrid. Think about it—you saw the transmitter pulled from my leg. You know they lured me to Zurich. You helped them set up a video feed to record me in the office right before Walter was killed. If you hadn't gone out, there would have been two bodies in that office."

She closed her eyes tightly.

He said, "You used the phone you bought today to call them, didn't you?"

Astrid nodded. "I talked to the man who first came, and he said my doubts were correct—he said *you* had killed Walter."

"Did you mention the tracking device?"

"Yes, I said you'd found it. He told me Mossad had to track you because you were dangerous."

Slaton recognized this for what it was—a half-truth to support the greater lie. "Mossad is responsible to a government, Astrid. If Israel wanted to recover stolen money, this isn't how they'd go about it."

She looked more confused than ever. "He kept telling me how dangerous you were. He said they were working with the police, and that I should bring you here so they could arrest you."

She looked at the gun resting on his leg.

"Who do you believe?" he asked.

She crossed her arms over her chest. "I don't know . . . I only want this to end. Walter is dead because of me!"

Earlier, watching her make the phone call in Klosters, Slaton hadn't known how deeply Astrid was involved. He wasn't sure if she was a spurned woman lashing out or something more threatening. Now he had his answer. He also knew she was confused and unreliable at the moment, and didn't completely trust him. Without that he was helpless to protect her.

"Let me go!" she pleaded. "I just want this to be over!"

Slaton had no choice. He slid the gun back under the seat. "All right, I won't stop you." He reached into his pocket and pulled out a handful of twenty-euro notes. "Take the train back to Zurich. As soon as you get there call the police. Tell them everything, including your own part in this. The only way to get your life back is to face what you've done—*please* trust me on that."

He held out the cash and watched her think through life or death decisions like none she'd ever faced. Slaton recalled watching someone else wrestle with a similar dilemma not so long ago—a beautiful auburn-haired woman who'd sat confused and terrified in his passenger seat, wondering where safety lay. Christine had stayed with him that day. Astrid would leave, that much he knew. But where would she go?

She took the money, opened the door, and got out. Slaton made no attempt to stop her. He pressed a button to lower the passenger-side window, and she hesitated on the sidewalk for a long moment, a tentative figure in a world gone mad. Again she reminded him of Christine—a capable person whose world of routine had imploded. *Where do I go? Who can I trust?* That's what Astrid was thinking as she stood statue-like in a chill wind.

Finally, she made her choice.

She half-turned and walked briskly away, looking once over her shoulder to gauge his reaction. Astrid was ten steps gone, accelerating down the sidewalk, when Slaton was surprised by the trill of a phone. He looked down at the prepaid device she'd bought in Klosters—the one he had confiscated and set on the console between the seats.

The sound struck like a Klaxon, each unanswered ring seeming to rise in pitch as Slaton realized only one person in the world knew this number. And why call now? *Because they think she's still carrying it.* It was a trick he had once used himself, with lethal results—when a mobile phone rings, people pause to extract their handset and answer.

He slammed the shift lever into gear and gunned the engine. The little car caught up in seconds. "Astrid!" he screamed.

The roar of the engine froze her on the sidewalk, and she took a defensive step back.

"Get in!" he shouted. "Get in, now!" He reached across and threw open the passenger door.

She stood paralyzed with indecision. It proved fatal.

Slaton heard nothing more than a pair of muffled thumps, sounds he recognized all too well—the lethal signature of high-velocity rounds striking center of mass in a human body. Her tall figure snapped forward and she crumpled to the ground.

Slaton instantly knew three things.

Astrid was dead.

There were two shooters.

And he was next.

# THIRTY-TWO

Slaton lowered his head just as the driver's side window exploded in a storm of glass. The passenger window blew out at almost the same time. Caught in a crossfire, he pressed his face to the center console, stomped the accelerator to the floor, and popped the clutch.

Movement was his only defense.

He grabbed the wheel above his left hip and steered in the blind, trying to remember if a car had been parked on the curb ahead. Unsure, he veered left into the traffic lane. A horn blared immediately, followed by a jolt and a metallic crunch as the Peugeot sideswiped a car in the opposing lane. Bullets raked the dashboard and roof, semiauto rounds hurtling in as fast as two men could pull two triggers.

His headrest burst into a cloud of insulation and faux leather, but the car responded, its tiny engine clipping the redline in first gear. Slaton chanced a glance forward and saw his path angling toward the oncoming lane and a massive truck. A horn bellowed, and he swerved right as the rear window shattered.

*Rear window*. One shooter was falling behind.

He ventured another look while shifting into second, and straightened his path down the street. The steering seemed heavy and unresponsive. They'd taken out at least one tire. It didn't matter. He needed a mile, two at the most, and even on fully deflated tires he could outpace a man carrying a rifle.

Then a flash of motion—a man rushing into the street ahead. He stood squarely in the middle of the road, a hundred yards distant, a weapon pressed to his shoulder. The gun was thick and compact, a complete mismatch in firepower compared to the Glock under Slaton's seat. There was no way to turn around—the car was drifting as it was, and a hard corner might cause the ruptured tire to separate completely.

Slaton shifted into third and put his head down. Bullets rained in, full automatic now, pinging off the metal roof and the engine firewall in front of him, destroying what was left of the windshield and launching chunks of spidered safety glass. Then a pause in the assault, and with the car's engine screaming, Slaton ventured one last glance. The man was standing calmly—the only way to shoot straight and true—and switching magazines for a final, point-blank barrage. Slaton recognized him as the second swarthy twin from Malta. In seconds he would pass on the left side and empty a full magazine into the driver's compartment.

There was only one option.

Slaton counted two beats, then leaned his head out the side window. He peered over the side-view mirror, spotted his target, and whipped the wheel left. The man shifted aim, but in that same instant he recognized the car's new vector. He jumped, but too late, and the Peugeot struck a direct blow.

Slaton felt the impact, and in a blur the man bounded onto the hood and flew back, his body jackknifing across the forward edge of the windowless roof. His MP7 flailed by its carrying strap, and the writhing assailant flung out a hand, trying to reach his weapon. Slaton was quicker. In a smooth, mechanical movement, he swept the Glock from under his seat and dispatched the killer with a double-tap to the head.

His problem half solved, Slaton sat higher and steered the car with one hand while yanking the limp body into the passenger seat. He ventured a look back and saw the other shooter far behind, his weapon at his side. He simply stood and stared, and for a brief moment Slaton felt a contrarian sense of fellowship. In the immediate moments after a gunfight, nobody cares about caliber or tactics or rounds fired, or even whose objectives were achieved. All that matters is who's still standing. In this case there were two survivors. Slaton recognized the other as Ben-Meir. With an image of Astrid in his mind, he turned away and made a promise to himself he had never before made.

On two bad tires and with the engine overheating, he negotiated another two miles before steering the remains of the Peugeot onto a quiet side street. Slaton parked as tightly as he could between a Dumpster and a brownstone wall, and made a cursory search of the body next to him. In the dead man's hip pocket was a wallet with cash but no identity documents. He had more success in the inside jacket pocket—a passport with a slip of paper tucked inside. Hearing a siren in the distance, he pocketed the passport and left the man where he was, no consideration for last rites or prayers—just as would have been the case in the reverse outcome.

Slaton got out of the car and ran.

For six minutes he sprinted over ice-encrusted sidewalks, keeping to shadows where he could as dusk fell to night, and following signs to the Siebnen Bahn-hofplatz.

He paused outside the station to drop his weapon, folded neatly into a discarded flyer for the Swiss Peace Foundation, into a curbside trash bin, and was glad to have done it when he saw a pair of police officers searching a man near the entrance. One officer was male, the other female. Both seemed agitated. After sending their subject on his way, the woman took a call on her mobile. Her responses were much like Astrid's this morning.

*Yes. All right.* Taking instructions.

Guardedly watching the police contingent, Slaton veered to another entrance. Once inside he purchased a ticket from a machine and stood on the southbound platform where a train was just arriving. He stood patiently, his eyes quietly sweeping the station. A northbound train was parked behind him, and when an automated female voice announced the last call for boarding, he crossed quickly to that train and stepped aboard, the doors closing immediately behind him. Slaton saw no one else mirror his move.

At a glance he saw fewer passengers to the rear, and so he moved in that direction, walking slowly to facilitate his seat selection process. Roughly half the car was occupied, and he found the situation he wanted near the back. A set of two unoccupied seats facing another set of two, one of these occupied by a fiftyish woman. She was professionally dressed, slender, and well-groomed. Her hair was cut short, the way women did when style gave way to a packed daily calendar. There was a leather satchel on the seat next to her with a lone manila folder edging out. She was talking on a mobile phone.

Slaton met her eyes and nodded politely as he took a seat, and through the station-side window he checked the platforms again. No police in sight. That would change in another ten minutes. The train began moving, and the panorama in the window altered from well-lit tidiness to snow-encrusted steel girders and walls of graffiti. Discarded on the seat next to him was a route map for the rail line, and he picked it up and studied the connecting options ahead—Zug, Luzern, Zurich. From any of those stations he could disappear easily into the grid of efficiency that was Swiss Rail.

The papers he'd taken from the body in the Peugeot weighed heavily in his pocket, but Slaton decided to wait for a more private setting to examine them. He checked the printed ticket in his hand, and saw on the bottom the time of his purchase: 6:32 p.m. This prompted a calculation, followed by a decision, neither of which was a surprise. It was something he'd been wanting to do for precisely seventy-eight hours.

The woman four feet away was still talking on her phone. In a low, resonating tone that might be characterized as a bedroom voice, she was negotiating the disposition of a last will and testament. So she was a lawyer. He reached into the pocket of his ski jacket, thankful he'd had the presence of mind to retrieve Astrid's phone when he bolted from the Peugeot. He had already discarded the idea of dialing the last incoming number to talk to Zan Ben-Meir—in spite of being recently purchased, the number had to be considered compromised, and consequently the handset traceable if he powered it up. But it still had utility.

With the woman distracted by her call, Slaton

palmed the phone as he removed it from his pocket and placed it facedown on the hard plastic edge of his seat. Under the guise of shifting his weight, he leaned until he heard the telltale crack.

Then he waited.

# THIRTY-THREE

Slaton made his move ten minutes outside Wädenswil.

"Lovely evening," he said in American-accented English.

The lawyer, having ended her call, gave a polite nod. "Yes, isn't it."

"Does this train carry through to Zurich?"

"No, there is construction. You will have to switch in Thalwil."

"I see, thank you. I have a flight back to the States tomorrow."

"You are in Switzerland on holiday?" she asked.

"I'm afraid not. I have relatives here, and my uncle summoned me for a meeting to discuss financial matters. In truth, it wasn't much fun—I'm going through a messy divorce and my ex has her eyes on the family business. In the last week my uncle has fired every one of my attorneys and accountants. Very stressful—the kind of thing I usually try to avoid. If nothing else, it was wonderful to see his estate in the winter. I typically come in the summer months." Slaton dispensed his most engaging smile before letting his eyes drift to the window.

"Estate you say?" queried the lawyer. "What is his name?"

Slaton turned back. "Hoffman—Walter Hoffman."

The lawyer blinked. "Hoffman," she repeated, "the pharmaceutical magnate?"

"Yes, I suppose so. My name is James—James Hoffman."

They shook hands across the aisle.

"You are not involved in the family business?"

"Me? Good Lord, no—I'd have run it under years ago. I'm a language professor at a small college."

They chatted for another five minutes—three more than he'd planned—by which point she made known that she was an estate lawyer herself, resided in a lovely suburb of Baden, and by the way, had recently suffered her own divorce.

With her business card in hand and the outskirts of Wädenswil in the window, Slaton pulled the broken prepaid phone from his pocket, and said, "It's a shame I wasn't able to say good-bye to Uncle Walter. These damned expendable phones are so poorly built."

Esther Straumann, senior associate of the firm Fischer, Lenz & Frey, smiled with all that was good and kind, and said, "Here, Mr. Hoffman, please use mine."

Stein watched the garbage man through the kitchen window. The man was retreating to his truck empty-handed because the cans were in the garage.

His phone vibrated, and he checked the number on the screen but didn't recognize it. After a pause he answered.

"Hello."

"Hello, Uncle Walter. I'm sorry I didn't get a chance to say good-bye. Is everything going as planned?"

Stein grinned. "Things are good here, no sign of trouble."

"Glad to hear it."

"And you? Are you getting any closer to discovering—" Stein was cut short by a squeal. He looked over his shoulder to see Davy toddle into the kitchen with Christine right behind.

She scooped him up, admonishing, "Will you never stay where I put you?" She then locked eyes with Stein, a questioning look that asked, *Who are you talking to?*

Stein gave an easy wave, then broke from her visual grip and strolled to the far side of the room. When Christine disappeared, he asked, "Are you making any progress?"

"Progress? Probably not the right word. Let's say there have been developments. How is Christine holding up?"

"She's good."

"No issues having you as a houseguest?"

"She's doing what she has to do."

"Yeah, she's good at that. Did you find out anything about our mutual friend?"

"Ben-Meir? I made a few calls. Apparently Mossad did let him go a couple of years ago after a botched mission—something to do with an arms dealer in Switzerland."

"Grossman?" Slaton asked. "Was that the name?"

"Might have been. And I heard Ben-Meir went out recruiting last summer. He was offering a big payday for a few committed individuals. No word on what they were planning. Have you had any more run-ins with him?"

"Yes, but things dropped my way."

Stein chuckled. "You make it sound like a tennis match."

"Look, I shouldn't talk long, I've borrowed this phone from a lovely lady."

These words came in a more deliberate voice than the rest, and Stein grinned knowingly.

Slaton said, "I'm not sure when I'll be able to call again. Use the old number if you need to get in touch."

"The message board?"

"Right."

"Okay," Stein said, checking to make sure he was still alone. "But tell me one thing. What's the plan when you're done? Will you be coming home?"

An extended pause. "I hadn't thought that far ahead. We'll talk soon."

The call ended, and a reflective Stein stared out the kitchen window.

Far across an ocean, a gracious traveler returned a phone to his seatmate and bid her a pleasant evening, adding a promise to call if he needed legal help, or perhaps even to arrange a more casual engagement during his next visit to Switzerland. The two exchanged broad smiles and a lingering handshake before Slaton stepped off the train.

He made his way to the ticket counter and immediately purchased a northbound billet on the Deutsch Bahn, a route that would take him deep into the heart of Germany. His actual point of disembarkation would be a decision for later. With thirty minutes to wait, he went to the restroom and splashed water from the basin on his face, and used a clutch of paper towels to wipe it dry. All alone in the room, he backed up to a wall and squeezed his eyes shut, his head hard against the cold tiles.

Esther Straumann and Yaniv Stein were nowhere in his thoughts. Even Christine and poor Astrid had been relegated. There was only one person in Slaton's mind, and even if the visual image remained as much a blank as ever, he now had a sound. A tiny shriek.

For the first time ever, he had heard the voice of his son.

# THIRTY-FOUR

The crash of Perseus Flight 10 generated little interest.

Had the disaster involved a passenger aircraft with hundreds of fatalities, front page coverage and a lead run on television news networks would have been a given. Had the flight crew at least had the good form to crash on land, offering a spectacular fireball and smoking wreckage, amateur video might have gone viral. As it was, in an increasingly visual world, grieving families and talking-head speculators were insufficient—no tragedy was newsworthy until presented in a properly pixelated format.

So with only a trickle of debris scooped from one of the Atlantic's deepest basins, and a few banal comments from a tight-lipped and decidedly unphotogenic Ministry of Transportation spokesman, the crash found no more than a single paragraph in the next day's newspapers. Subsequent developments—of these there were few—could be mined only from websites and blogs devoted exclusively to aviation safety. Even conspiracy theorists tweeted a collective yawn.

Jurisdiction over air accidents is governed by the Chicago Convention; the location of the event, residence of the aircraft operator, and airspace governance all play a part in who assumes control of a crash site. In the case of CB68H—a derelict cargo jet with opaque registration, lost over international waters—it became more a matter of push than pull. Nobody wanted the chore, and in the end it was Brazil that drew the short straw by virtue of geographic proximity, the fact that its Coast Guard and air traffic controllers were already involved, and a persistent rumor that a mysterious registration application for the downed jet existed somewhere in the Brazilian Ministry of Transportation.

The Aeronautical Accidents Investigation and Prevention Center, formally a unit of the Brazilian Air Force, is the lead organization for aviation accidents in Brazil. Headquartered in Brasília, the agency has a reputation for issuing results in a less than meteoric fashion, often taking years to determine causes, and even longer to file safety recommendations. Its well-meaning investigators are regularly hamstrung by bureaucratic roadblocks, judicial interference, and laughable funding with which to undertake their far-reaching mandate. That being the case, Brazil routinely welcomes help from abroad.

The inquiry into the loss of Perseus Flight 10 came centered in Belém, the nearest large city to the crash site. Situated at the mouth of the Amazon, it is the second largest city in northern Brazil, renowned for river cruises, mango trees, and the pleasingly contemporary Val de Cães International Airport. It was here, in a little used hangar on the west side of the airfield, that a beleaguered Colonel Roberto Cruz sat behind a very clean desk.

Cruz, a career Air Force officer, was not a happy man. Only three months from retirement, he had been issued the most awkward of assignments—

overseeing an investigation whose final report would arrive years in trail of his first pension check.

Cruz had situated his desk centrally in the main hangar, hoping to keep the best possible grasp on things. Space was not yet an issue—the entire accumulation of wreckage so far took up a slab of concrete no larger than a double bed—and so his investigative team was scattered widely about the place. There were three officers from his "Go Team," and a half-dozen others representing interested parties, ranging from a lawyer for the air traffic controllers' union to a General Electric engine man. As soon as the crash registered, less than twenty-four hours ago, everyone had rushed to Belém on a moment's notice, only to find that there was little to do. Search and rescue was the important thing at this stage, but the weather wasn't cooperating, and since the technical analyses of accidents typically took years, the people around Cruz were merely settling in, diddling on mobile phones and reading magazines.

Cruz' mind wandered as well. He ignored the weather reports on his desk, instead reflecting on how his hardwood desk could have been made in Cuba and his cigar sourced from Brazil. That was how his day was going—indeed, how the end of his career was going. Vacillating between the pointless and the absurd. He picked up his smartphone, intending to mark his retirement date on the calendar with a happy emoticon, when the metal door at the far end of the hangar burst open.

The door slammed back against the wall—if Cruz hadn't known better, he might have thought it was breached by a battering ram—and the colonel stared slack-jawed, as did everyone else, at what walked in. A massive figure with broad shoulders and thick limbs, a face cut from a block of granite. His thick-booted stride echoed across the nearly empty hangar. The man's hair was cut short, military fashion, and when he locked eyes on Cruz there was no doubt where he was heading.

One word percolated in the colonel's mind: *American.*

He'd been told they were sending someone. Indeed, having worked with the United States' NTSB on other crashes, Cruz was expecting a good-sized team. Brazil's vexing neighbors to the north rarely saw value in economy. *Perhaps,* he thought, *this is the advance man.* Whoever he was, he came to a stop in front of Cruz' desk like a bull in search of a red cape.

"My name's Davis, NTSB. Are you Cruz?"

The colonel stood. At five foot eleven he was not a small man, yet Cruz found himself looking up at a brute who was a head taller.

"Yes, I am Colonel Roberto Cruz." The colonel shook a hand the size of a dinner plate. "I was told your office was sending a liaison."

"Liaison? Okay, you can call me that. What have you got?"

Cruz was familiar with American directness, and while he thought it crass, colonels did not become colonels without knowing when to address business. He briefed the NTSB man on the details that had so far been established by his nascent inquiry, covered easily in the sixty seconds it took them to walk to the far side of the hangar where the wreckage lay.

"This is what we have recovered," said Cruz, pointing to his little pile.

There were fifteen passenger seat cushions, some loose insulation, two empty suitcases, a piece of plastic trim, and a deflated Mae West–style life jacket. A yellow life raft sat deflated, crumpled and dispirited. Separated to one side was a smaller collection consisting of a fishing float, two plastic bags, a painter's respirator, and a half-dozen empty water bottles—two of these encrusted in barnacles.

"The oceans aren't as clean as they used to be," Cruz remarked. "But of course we retain everything found until we are certain it has no relevance."

"*Everything?*" Davis repeated. "This is all you have?"

"There was also a body."

"One of the pilots?"

"No, he was positively identified as a local man who worked at the airfield. According to a witness, he had gone along on the flight as an observer. The remains are being held at a hospital nearby, and we already have a preliminary report from the medical examiner."

The American said nothing. He only stared at the little clump of debris with his hands on his hips.

Colonel Cruz rolled his shoulders back, which better put on display his rank insignia and a chest full of medals. "Our investigation is ongoing. Much more physical evidence will be recovered, of course, once the weather improves and the primary wreckage field is located."

Cruz watched his guest put a toe to one of the hard-shell suitcases. "Is this how you found it?" the American asked.

"What do you mean?"

"I mean both latches are undone on this suitcase." Davis leaned down and lifted the top half open. "And it's empty."

"Yes . . ." replied a hesitant Cruz. "I'm sure it was

forced open on impact and the contents scattered to the sea."

"The sea," the American repeated. He bent down and examined the life jacket. "Was the mort wearing this?"

"The who?" Cruz asked, the slang defeating his schoolhouse English.

"The dead guy—was he wearing this?"

"No."

"The $CO_2$ cartridge has been activated. Why would anybody do that *before* they strapped it on?"

"I couldn't say." Sensing things slipping, Cruz offered, "We also have photographs taken by the search crews." He led to a nearby table and pointed to a few reports, including the preliminary autopsy, and a short stack of aerial photos. There wasn't enough yet to bother with a filing system.

The American flipped through it all, spending considerable time on the medical examiner's report. In the end, he held up a single photograph—an empty stretch of ocean marred by a free-form, rainbow-colored sheen. "This is a fuel slick," he said.

"Of course."

"Did you recover any?" Davis asked.

"Sorry?"

"The fuel in this picture—did somebody collect a sample for analysis?"

In a proud moment, Colonel Cruz fished through the short stack of papers on the table. "Yes, here it is. The Coast Guard retrieved a sample and we performed an analysis in our laboratory." He handed over the report.

The American looked it over, and his square features seemed to bend. "Engine oil?"

"Yes, already identified as the brand and grade used in these engines. The General Electric man confirmed it." Cruz pointed to a disinterested, fair-skinned man across the hangar who was thoroughly engrossed in an issue of *The Economist*.

The big American dropped the paper and photos onto the evidence table. "The MD-10 Dash-30 has a usable jet fuel capacity of thirty-six thousand gallons, contained in large and relatively thin-skinned tanks. It holds twenty-four gallons of high-grade engine oil tightly encased in the most dense parts of the accessory drive box."

Cruz stared blankly at the man.

"Does it not strike you as odd that all you found out there was *engine* oil?"

"Our investigation is in its early days . . . the search continues."

"Early days," the American repeated. It was an annoying mannerism, yet trivial compared to what came next. Davis turned and walked away. "Happy hunting," he called over his shoulder.

"But . . . where are you going?"

"Home."

"What? You were sent here to help us!"

On his exit there was no mistaking it—the boorish American opened the door with a good swift kick.

Cruz, a full colonel, was not accustomed to disrespect. Never was he simply ignored. On the other hand, from what he'd seen so far, he wasn't unhappy to let this man go. He went back to his Cuban desk, put a Brazilian cigar between his teeth, and addressed his mobile phone. He bypassed the contact list where his commanding general's number was listed, as well as that of the Brazilian Minister of Transportation.

Instead he navigated to the calendar and began calculating the number of days to his retirement.

The passenger terminal was nearly two miles away, but Jammer Davis had no intention of waiting for a cab at a remote outbuilding in the gathering equatorial heat. He set out along the service road that connected the hangar to the airport proper, a rutted gravel track threatened on either side by an encroaching jungle. Davis pulled out his phone as he walked and initiated a call.

The phone was a satellite device, and thankfully the connection held on the first try. The signal was received and decrypted in the Washington, D.C., area, although not at L'Enfant Plaza where the National Transportation Safety Board was headquartered, the United States' recognized body for investigating aeronautical misfortune. Instead, the satellite link reached one of the many antennae on the roof of a large and well-known building in Langley, Virginia.

"What have you got, Jammer?" Sorensen asked.

"An investigation that's going nowhere. I'm not going to find out anything useful about your two pilots—not anytime soon."

"You're sure?"

This mistake Davis met with silence.

"All right," she said. "You can file a report when you get back tomorrow. That was all I needed to know."

"No," Davis said. "You need to know a lot more."

"What do you mean?"

"You need to look into this. I did a little research of my own."

"What, on a computer? You can do that?"

Trudging over gravel in the Amazon heat, Davis flashed a grin. He really liked Sorensen, spook or not. Their relationship had sputtered over long distances, and when they did find themselves in a common time zone their interactions ranged from intimacy to combativeness to amusement. But never boredom. So when Anna had called yesterday, for the first time in a month, he'd been glad. Even more so when she'd asked for his help.

"I didn't like what I found," he said. "I need to take a detour on the way home and look into something. If I'm right, you and I need to meet with the director tomorrow."

"Stop right there, Major! You are not in the military anymore, which means you don't give orders. You are a retired Air Force pilot who does a little consulting on the side. And consultants don't demand meetings with the director of the CIA."

"This one does. And here's why." It took Davis less than a minute to capsulize his suspicions.

"Are you sure about this?"

"I wish you'd stop asking me that. Look, Anna, give me one day to get my ducks in a row. In the meantime, you do the same. Find out everything you can about the people involved in this—in particular, who runs the company that bought this airplane."

There was silence as Sorensen processed the order. "Where are you going?" she asked.

"Oregon. They have lots of ducks out there. If it turns out I'm wrong, I promise to call right away."

There was no response.

"And if I'm right?" Davis prompted.

"Yeah . . . I'll get you that meeting."

# THIRTY-FIVE

The truck clattered roughly over the old gravel road, kicking up a rooster-tail of dust that blossomed into the midday sky. Sam was driving, and Ghazi in the passenger seat—neither man had experience driving such a heavy vehicle, but Ghazi reasoned that the little Indonesian would draw less attention if they were stopped and questioned.

There was nothing incriminating about the truck, particularly since the tank was empty. Even when they drove in the opposite direction tomorrow, toward the airport, their load would be perfectly harmless. The vehicle was a tanker, a fifty-five-hundred-gallon water-hauler they'd bought from an American subcontractor that worked the oil fields. The Americans had a reputation for discarding serviceable equipment before its time, and while the truck had seen better days, Ghazi was sure it would run for another thirty miles. That was all he needed. One trip to the farm to take on its load, and then a return leg back to the airport. The remainder of their equipment would be transferred using the Toyota, the exception being the heavy bricks which they planned to distribute around the tanker, including the passenger-side floor where his feet now rested.

Ghazi rolled down his window, the unseasonably warm day taking its grip as the small clutch of buildings came into view.

"Are you sure the pump is working properly?" Sam asked.

"I am confident," Ghazi replied. When they had purchased the truck the main transfer pump was inoperable, but the Americans had made good on their promise—an able mechanic had it working before they left the parking lot. The pump was rated at one thousand gallons per minute, but it was old and leaky, and Ghazi knew that number wouldn't hold. It didn't matter—even half such a rate would suffice. "I watched very carefully how he primed it, and which valves he used. I will have no trouble repeating the process."

"That's good, because otherwise we would have to do the transfer by hand. Five thousand gallons—that is a lot of water to move."

"Don't worry, I have a backup pump at the farmhouse if necessary. This contract is important, so I've planned for every contingency."

Sam looked at him. "What exactly does your company do?"

Ghazi had long expected the question. "We have a contract with the Ministry of Oil to study cleanup methods should there ever be a major spill. We must perform an important test tomorrow."

Sam nodded thoughtfully, and Ghazi sensed a degree of suspicion. He was hardly surprised. For three years the Indonesian had had his boots on the ground in the epicenter of Iraqi oil production, and so he knew the level of concern here for the environment. It struck Ghazi that Sam had never asked more obvious questions. Why had they set up shop in such a remote location? Why did they perform most of their work in the middle of the night? He decided it was to Sam's credit that he'd never asked. Ghazi reached into his pocket and withdrew Sam's daily wage. As ever, the Indonesian took it with a smile that absolved any reservations.

When they arrived at the farmhouse, Ghazi scouted all around: the levees, the waterway, the walking paths. There was no one in sight. Sam opened the barn door and Ghazi backed the tanker truck in—it fit, but only just—and together they shut the big door.

The next hour was spent hauling lead brick, and lead-lined glass and plywood. Three empty two-thousand-gallon bladders, each folded to the size of a small table, Ghazi secured to the side of the tanker with rope. The remaining equipment, all extracted from the rusted oil drums in which it had been delivered, they loaded into the Toyota's bed and covered with a tarp. In the end, the little convoy would appear to be just what it was—a pair of industrial vehicles hauling equipment. The only difference from a hundred others that would travel the road to town tomorrow was the nature of their job.

"Seven tomorrow evening," Ghazi said firmly. "You must be on time."

"Sure thing, boss," said Sam, his smile giving way to a more circumspect look. "Boss . . . how long is this contract going to last?"

"Why do you ask?"

"My friend, he tells me they are hiring riggers in Rumaila."

"How much do they pay?"

Sam shrugged noncommittally. "Pretty good, they say."

"As good as half again what I'm paying you?"

The kid looked at him in amazement. "Really? You give me that kind of raise?"

Ghazi put a hand on his shoulder. "I can depend on you, Sam. Stay with me, and I promise you'll never need another job in Iraq."

Sam's broad smile returned.

When Slaton woke he was hundreds of miles removed from Wangen, Switzerland. The alarm clock by his bed claimed it was noon. He went to the window of his quaint bed-and-breakfast room and looked out over the streets of Sachsenhausen. A German winter had arrived in full force, three inches of new snow and a sharp wind snapping the black, red, and yellow standards flying from shop fronts down the street. The sky had all but disappeared, curtains of snow and sleet texturing the iron-clad gray above, and his window was edged in a fresh crystalline frame.

He had traveled through the night to reach the main rail station in Frankfurt, and arrived in Sachsenhausen just as the beer halls were closing and the last revelers weaving home. He took a room in the first place he found whose lights were on, and slept uninterrupted until the noon bells of three downtown churches rang in cumbersome disharmony.

To complete his restoration he took an omelet and juice in his room, in the company of *Die Welt*, and later a hot shower down the hall, and by one that afternoon he felt back among the living. In his room Slaton set back to work by taking his first good look at the passport and visa he'd retrieved from the body in Wangen. Slaton knew a good forgery when he saw one, and this passport was excellent. A Lebanese business visa was current, which made two useful points: the men tracking him were soon headed to Lebanon, and they'd been planning it for some time. He studied the slip of paper that had been folded into the passport. On it was an eight-digit character string, letters and numbers, preceded by the capital letters *LH*. Slaton thought he knew what it was, and there was a simple way to find out.

He collected his worldly possessions—a ski jacket to go over the stolen clothes on his back, a solid forged passport, and a still sizable wad of cash—and was soon out the door. He stopped at an electronics retailer and purchased a cheap tablet computer, paying cash, and ten minutes later, with his hair dusted in snow, he ducked into a café that advertised free Wi-Fi. At the counter he ordered a tall café Americano, and soon was seated at a table with an open-network connection—there was a time for security and a time for speed. This was definitely the latter.

With everything up and running, he navigated to the website for Lufthansa Airlines—LH. He typed in the name on the passport and the reference number, and within seconds saw that the man had been booked the previous evening, under his certainly fictitious name, on a direct flight from Munich to Beirut. A second passenger was also listed in the same booking reference—another name that meant nothing to Slaton, but he was sure it was Ben-Meir. It was poor operational security to group multiple operatives on a single reservation. Doing so left a paper trail, albeit in this case an electronic one. It suggested Ben-Meir was getting rushed, probably in response to the trouble Slaton had been giving him.

In any event, he had made his first mistake.

From his pocket Slaton retrieved the encryption

codes for his financial accounts and logged in to each one. He found that he remained—in his true name, David Slaton—a very wealthy petro-investor. Yet there was one significant change. A single transfer to a bank in Beirut. Slaton saw no name listed for the receiver, only an account number. Even so, he knew where the money had gone. It was the amount that gave it away. Four hundred and fifty thousand U.S. dollars, the balance due on a transaction that had begun nearly two years earlier.

Moses.

Twenty-six Geitawi Boulevard.

Slaton leaned back and sipped his coffee. *What to do about it?*

He felt certain Ben-Meir was on his way to Lebanon. Astrid's fate also remained heavy in his mind. She'd been a classic recruit—a scorned woman, financially needy, and with access to vital information. All the same, Slaton could never have kept his sanity over the years without clinging to one precept, a very private and firm ethical rule. Noncombatants were never to be targeted. They might be pressured or manipulated, but the killing was reserved for those who had earned it. He now held Ben-Meir in breach of that rule.

He was sure there were others involved, and they remained a threat: not only to him, but to Christine and his son. For the first time, however, Slaton had a vector, so there was no decision to be made. It was time to take the initiative. It was time to become the hunter.

He left the café and threaded south between the bars and brasseries of Schweizer Strasse, ducking his head against a sharp wind that scored through leafless trees. At the Südbahnhof tram stop he dropped the powered-up tablet computer in a deep puddle, cursed for the sake of anyone watching, and moments later sent it into a trash bin wrapped in a discarded newspaper. The capabilities of electronic surveillance were advancing every day, and he had no wish to be tracked again.

The question of where to go next was straightforward. He did not possess, and had no hope of obtaining, a Lebanese entry visa. He did, however, have the acquaintance of a most unprincipled Nicosian fisherman.

# THIRTY-SIX

Jammer Davis arrived at Portland International Airport that same afternoon. He rented a car at the first counter he came to, Avis, which was probably the most expensive. Sorensen had promised to cover it, and time *was* of the essence.

Two hours later he was outside Bend, Oregon, winding through the forests of pine and fir that were endemic to the Pacific Northwest. Indeed, in an indirect way, it was those forests that brought him here. Because winter was at its peak, there were no trucks hauling loads of timber, yet the telltale signs of Oregon's biggest industry were everywhere. Roadside diners with expansive dirt parking lots, tall garages to shelter heavy equipment, mills sided by wood-pulp mountains that were covered in snow. This was logging country.

Davis found his destination using the car's GPS device, although it was hardly necessary. Bend Municipal Airport was very well marked. He could not have arrived by commercial air, the field having no passenger terminal, no parking lot, and not a single scheduled flight. Bend Municipal's focus was support aviation, and like everything else here it centered on the timber industry.

Davis found a perimeter road—virtually all airports had them—and within five minutes he saw the building he wanted. Outside were five helicopters tied down for the season, distinctive skeletal frames that were among the most powerful vertical-lift aircraft on earth. They were used for two very distinct missions. The first involved hauling logs out of deep forest, places where roads and trucks were impractical. It was the second mission, however, that brought Davis here, in particular to a company called Pendleton Aviation.

He parked in front of the largest hangar on the airfield, and as he got out of his car Davis studied the place. The hangar door was cracked open and he saw an aircraft inside, something big and fixed-wing, with propellers and a red number 21 painted on the side. The runway was caked in snow and looked like it hadn't been plowed all winter. Davis guessed it would stay that way until spring. There was no one in sight, but he did see a light burning in an office attached to the hangar.

He pushed open the door to find an empty reception desk, then heard a voice from a room behind. He kneed past a small swinging gate, and at the first doorway he saw a man with a phone shouldered to his ear. His heels were crossed on a cabinet, and he was gesticulating toward the rear wall. The desk behind him was piled high with paper and knick-knacks, and there was a brass nameplate front and center: RAYMOND STEVENSON, PRESIDENT.

"Excuse me," Davis said.

The man turned around and held up a finger to suggest that Davis should wait. He did, very politely, and in the two minutes it took for the phone to find its cradle he studied the office. Nothing surprised him. There were photographs of aircraft, plastic models of aircraft, and three bookcases full of technical manuals on aircraft.

"Hi, I'm Ray Stevenson," the man finally said.

"Jammer Davis."

Davis shook hands with a midsized man, fiftyish, with open-air features and collar-length brown hair that had found its first gray highlights. He watched Stevenson pause to consider the name Jammer—everybody did—before asking, "What can I do for you?"

It was the obvious first question, and Davis had been contemplating his response since leaving Brazil. He could have told a version of the truth—that he was an accident investigator looking into the crash of an MD-10, an aircraft that had recently been modified in the hangar fifty feet away. But that would put the man on the defensive, and Davis didn't have time for that.

"I'm here on behalf of an Australian concern. We're studying the feasibility of modifying a large aircraft."

"What kind of mod?"

Davis told him.

Stevenson beamed. "Absolutely. What kind of airframe are we talking about?"

"An MD-10," Davis said. "I understand you've done one before."

"Four years ago."

Stevenson reached behind his desk for a scale model of an MD-10 painted with Pendleton Aviation's logo. He handed it over, and Davis held it over his head like a kid with a new toy. He looked near the tail and saw the aircraft registration number hand-painted with pride—CB68H. He studied the under-side and saw a modification along the belly where a pair of large doors had been mounted along the lon-gitudinal axis. "Pretty impressive. I'll bet it does the job."

"Like you wouldn't believe."

Stevenson dug into his file cabinet and pulled out a sheet listing the technical specifications of the modified heavy jet. Davis gave it a cursory look, but he knew he had to get more before heading back to D.C.—he'd already booked a red-eye flight for to-night.

"It might be helpful to talk to the current owner. Can you tell me who operates her now?"

Stevenson hesitated, which told Davis he'd heard about the crash. When he did answer, it came in care-fully measured words. "We did the modification for DGR Aviation—at the time they had a contract with the U.S. Department of the Interior. But things didn't work out. After a couple of slow seasons, the jet was put in storage. Maybe a year later it was bought by a leasing company. I'm not sure what came of her after that."

Davis doubted this last point, but he said nothing.

"Let me show you the video," Stevenson offered.

Davis watched a two-minute marketing clip on Ste-venson's desktop computer. It *was* impressive. After that he spent twenty minutes asking logical questions, covering things like reliability and performance. Then he made his last request.

"This all sounds good. I think my principals might be interested. Do you by any chance have an extra copy of the technical manuals—in particular the modification specs? Our engineering staff would need to look those over."

Davis felt like a modern-day Medusa as the man looking at him turned to stone. "What company did you say you were with?" Stevenson asked.

"I didn't say."

The mood in the room descended. Stevenson stood, which was a protest of sorts, but the effect probably wasn't what he was after. Davis towered over most men, and in this particular case his physique, suited perfectly for rugby, only accentuated the disparity.

Stevenson said, "I don't know who you are, maybe a lawyer or an insurance goon, but I think you should leave right now."

"I'll say it again," Davis replied, as if not hearing Stevenson, "I'd *really* like to see the tech manuals for your modified MD-10."

"Go to hell!"

Davis backed away one step, but he didn't turn toward the door. During the two minutes Stevenson had been yakking on the phone, he'd spotted what he was after. Second bookcase on the right, third shelf: *MD-10 VLAT Aircraft Reference Manual, MD-10 VLAT Maintenance Procedures Manual.* Davis pulled them from the shelf, two manuals, each fully four inches thick.

Ray Stevenson, incandescent with rage, responded by opening a drawer on his desk. Davis knew what would be inside. It was Stevenson's last mistake of the day.

Ten minutes later Davis was steering his Avis rental past the timber-railed airfield entrance, back to the main road with its opposing walls of hardwood forest. The shoulders were curbed with mountains of plowed snow, and as he backtracked his way to Portland International, Davis drove cautiously. The two thick manuals on the passenger seat would make for heavy reading later, particularly given the all-night nature of his flight. But Davis had what he'd come for.

By the time he got to D.C., eight hours from now, he would know exactly what they were up against.

Jack Kelly found Sorensen in the employee cafeteria.

"We've found another one," he said.

She didn't have to ask—he was referring to their Group of Seven. "Is this one alive, at least?" She'd meant it as a joke, but a solemn look came over Kelly's face. "Tell me you're kidding."

"Wangen, Switzerland, another gunfight. There was a second casualty as well, a woman who's been identified as the executive assistant to the banker who was killed two days ago in Zurich—the Swiss police had been looking for her."

Sorensen leaned back and put a hand to her forehead, the way people did when they needed an aspirin.

"The Swiss are all over this," said Kelly. "The woman was killed by a sniper after getting out of a car. The driver got away by running down the shooter with the car and then executing him at close range."

"And this driver?" she asked tentatively.

Kelly nodded. "A witness saw him ditching the car, and her description matched perfectly. It's our man from Malta."

She blew out a long breath. "That's three down. But at least he can't take credit for the death of the two pilots in Brazil."

Kelly gave her a plaintive look.

She said what he was thinking. "Yeah, I know. The good news is . . . there's only two more names left on the list."

# THIRTY-SEVEN

The quickest route from Frankfurt to Cyprus involved British Airways. Unfortunately for Slaton, the Sunday afternoon schedule forced him to first travel westbound to be subjected, for twelve hours, to the debatable charms of London's Heathrow Airport before making his connecting flight. He arrived at Larnaca International Airport at three minutes before noon on Monday.

Slaton was dressed like the other tourists escaping an unusually harsh European winter—khaki slacks, loose cotton shirt, wraparound sunglasses—and he breezed through immigration before navigating the steel-and-glass arches of the new Larnaca terminal. He hired a cab into town, and the driver had little to say to yet another boorish visitor from the West who would gawk out the window and tip poorly. This was the standing relationship between Cypriots and Europeans, established some eight hundred years earlier when Richard the Lionhearted, cast into a fit of rage when a ship carrying his future bride had not been welcomed ashore, summarily sacked the island. Soon after, and with his point well made, Richard sold the island to the Knights Templar for a token sum of gold Byzantines.

Slaton kept the tradition alive, adding a lamentable tip to his fare when he was dropped along the palm-lined beaches of Foinikoudes. The beach was as ever, a copper-tan playground at the crest of high season, the attendant cafés and hotels riotously busy. Slaton moved cautiously amid the crowds, even though he was increasingly confident the killers of Zurich were no longer tracking him. And if the scope and intent of their operation remained a mystery, he was reasonably sure of one thing—Ben-Meir had gone to Beirut seeking an address in the northern suburbs. Seeking a man named Moses.

He turned toward the city, and two streets removed from the beach he found a secondhand clothing store where he bought what he needed and a canvas bag to carry it in, and took a smile from an old woman behind the cash drawer who didn't care what he was buying or why he was buying it when a twenty-euro note slid across the counter. From the central district he walked east to the harbor's main pier where grand yachts, invariably flying the flags of nations with favorable tax laws, lay moored in wait for their well-heeled owners, professional crews polishing rails and sanding teak. A northerly turn at the water's edge brought a more humble nautical district, row after row of locally owned pleasure boats ready for a day's sail on the Eastern Mediterranean. He heard halyards tapping masts, and the occasional deep-throated rumble of a diesel springing to life. Beyond these tidy docks, past the protective breakwater, Slaton reached his end.

The quay here was far different. Gone were the thick precast seawalls, replaced by piles of concrete riprap that had been bulldozed to the shoreline. Foot-long steel cleats were absent, as were the broad finger piers planked in pressure-treated timber. In their place were makeshift wooden wharves that might have been assembled by a storm, a collision of wooden pallets and planks and old mooring lines. Some were kept afloat by oil drums, others strapped to derelict boat hulls, all of it joined together with a seeming aversion to right angles.

The vessels berthed here—there had to be fifty— were equally rough-hewn, their decks stained with rust and seabird droppings, and when they rolled on the swells their undersides evidenced a hidden battle beneath, barnacles fighting algae for parasitic dominance. Some of the craft were powered by sail, but most had some manner of diesel propulsion, and the smell of fuel oil hung heavy on the air. The few seamen Slaton saw reflected the fleet, not professionals in their prime suited in crisp white liveries, but leathered old men and young boys whose uniforms were shredded T-shirts and worn sandals, and who moved with a sun-infused languor. It was all just as he remembered.

He found the boat he wanted moored close to shore. *Kosmos* was forty feet of warped wood and chipped paint, a stout and wide-beamed bitch whose diesel exhaust stack was black with soot and whose worn rigging sagged in the warm afternoon air. Old, tired, and fitted for longline fishing—these days a second cousin to far more efficient purse seines—she was a model to economic ruin. Here, however, traditions were not taken lightly, and the Nicosian people, like few others, knew how to endure.

On her main deck a young man, bronze skin and clear eyes, was tending to a winch. The kid pinned a wary gaze on the fair-haired man who drew to a stop at the warped plank that was *Kosmos'* gangway.

Only two types of foreigners came onto these docks, and Slaton stood with a firmness that proved he was not a tourist gone adrift. Knowing better than to step aboard, he called across the divide, "I'm looking for Demitriou." Slaton said it in English—Greek was more widely used, but if there was any vestige of cranky King Richard's invasion it was his language.

The breeze shifted, mixing the odor of drying fish with the oily scent of bilge water. The young man stared a little longer, then nodded down the pier. Slaton looked and saw the man he wanted.

He had last seen George Demitriou eight years ago, during a time when Mossad was engaged in one of its routine skirmishes with Hezbollah. The scheme that day had been the maritime insertion of a team from the northwest sea, a direction in which the watchful eyes of Hezbollah were rarely turned, and from there the destruction of an unusually large arms cache. To make their approach, Mossad needed good local knowledge, and they'd hired Demitriou based on his reputation, his lack of scruples, and because the longline tuna catch was in the middle of a ten-year free fall. The raid was a qualified success, and Slaton had paid the man in full and not seen him since.

Demitriou was a big man with a heavy gut and thick forearms, and coarse black hair carpeted every bit of exposed flesh. His gait up the dock was less a stride than a roll, a wheeling slab of momentum. Slaton remembered the man's gruff demeanor, and also his opaque eyes, scored by decades of sun and salt—eyes that recognized him eight years later from a hundred paces. Nearing the boat Demitriou tipped his head sharply to one side, and the young man aboard *Kosmos* stepped ashore and disappeared into a clapboard shack at the top of the pier that served, as Slaton recalled, as the community lavatory, bar, clinic, and administration building.

"It's been a long time," Demitriou growled, stopping a few steps away. Neither man bothered with the façade of a handshake. "To what do I owe this pleasure?"

"I'm sure you can guess."

"Mossad has lost its nautical charts again?"

Slaton did not hesitate to build on Demitriou's mistaken assumption. "We still have them. But charts in these waters can be notoriously inaccurate. It's almost as if governments intentionally leave things off the surveys."

"You don't have to tell me. My brother lost his first boat to a damned cable trap you people put three hundred yards off the shore of Nahariya."

"Maybe he shouldn't have been so close."

The big Nicosian chuckled brusquely. "You know how it is. One must go where the big fish are."

Demitriou had once made a living as a fisherman, Slaton knew. He was also the kind of man whose leanings to less reputable sidelines was not wholly tied to the decline of longlining for tuna. Slaton had met many such operators in his years of clandestine work. He'd seen truck drivers and helicopter drivers, police captains and bell captains. There was no one common thread, but a fabric of the usual inspirations—adventure, vengeance, sex, religion. George Demitriou, brigand and smuggler, operated on the most common principle.

"Five thousand euros up front, five on the back end."

"To go where?" asked a cautious Demitriou.

"All the way north, to Aarida."

Demitriou scowled. "How many?"

"Only me. An early morning arrival."

"How close?"

"Close enough to swim."

"You are crazy! That is practically the Syrian border. The Lebanese are as nervous about the north these days as they are the south. They have new patrol boats, faster and with better radar. They'll have no trouble running down my old bathtub. As for the Syrians—only God knows what runs in those waters these days!"

Slaton waited. Unlike the bar in Valletta, there would be no price negotiation. He had made a generous offer for a night's work.

The Nicosian wavered. "You have it now?"

Slaton pulled a thick envelope from his pocket. The Cypriot reached out his hand, but Slaton left it empty. "There's one condition."

The smuggler's gaze narrowed.

"We leave now."

"*What?* Tonight?"

"Not tonight. Now, this minute."

"But my mate has gone home. And I don't have enough fuel to—"

Slaton cut him off by stepping onto a boat he had first boarded years ago. He went to the wheelhouse, and turned on the battery. The fuel quantity gauges sprang to life, indicating three-quarters full.

True to his nature, Demitriou only laughed, displaying a shockingly rotted set of yellow teeth. "The gauges, they are working again? Imagine that!"

Slaton smiled. The man was as treacherous as the waters he plowed, but it was an open, even expected duplicity, cementing all his relationships in mutual suspicion. Slaton found it oddly comforting. He set the cash on the helm. "I'll get the docking lines."

Demitriou hesitated, then said, "All right, we will go now. But I cannot keep the money on board. If the patrols board me in Lebanese waters I can talk my way to freedom. But if they find that," he gestured to the stack of bills, "I will never see it again. You can't expect me to go to such trouble for nothing."

It was Slaton's turn to pause. He had pushed the man hard, and the Nicosian made a valid point. "All right. Find a safe place for it." He tossed the envelope across to the dock and the fisherman caught it surely. Slaton watched carefully as Demitriou walked to the shack at the head of the pier. He stayed inside precisely eighty seconds. Longer than it would have taken to simply lock the money in a safe. Not long enough to have counted it.

Fifteen minutes later *Kosmos* was clearing the breakwater, and the playground of Larnaca faded as the boat's crooked pulpit settled to an easterly course. One hundred miles ahead lay one of the most embattled regions on earth, and home to Israel's most vitriolic enemies. Skirmishes between the countries dated to the day of Israeli independence, in 1948, and had continued on various levels ever since. In recent years, the government to the north had begun avoiding direct conflict, preferring the role of serial facilitator: harboring, funding, and encouraging every brand of anti-Semite known to exist. For a former Mossad assassin, Lebanon was the viper's pit itself.

To complicate matters further, Slaton knew that by appearance or speech he could never pass as Lebanese. He was operating with no external help, no supporting assault team or emergency extraction plan. He had but one advantage: motivation. He was fighting for the safety of his family.

So with Demitriou at the wheel and the compass steady, Slaton went below to prepare.

# THIRTY-EIGHT

Frank "Jammer" Davis was not an official employee of the CIA. For that reason, he was met at a secondary security station by Anna Sorensen.

"Hello, Jammer."

Davis stopped two steps away from Sorensen, a judicious distance he supposed. It only made him realize how unprepared he was. He'd thought she was off his emotional books, but as she stood in front of him now, blond and blue-eyed against the sterile hallway, Sorensen took his breath away. She looked better than ever, perhaps a few new pounds, but in a good, curving way, and her eyes were as ever: made for drowning. They stood parted in an awkward moment, and he wondered what thoughts she was having.

*To hell with it*, he decided. Davis reached out and put a hand to her cheek. It was soft and warm, and she leaned into it.

"It's good to see you," he said.

Sorensen smiled, and said, "You too."

They might have said more, might even have embraced, but with two uniformed guards hovering, she handed over a visitor's pass on a lanyard. Davis hung it on his neck, then walked through a scanner while one of the security men inspected the heavy binders he was carrying.

"You look great," he said after running the gauntlet.

"And you don't look tired," she mused. "You've been all over the hemisphere in the last two days—you should be exhausted."

He shrugged. "In Arctic survival training I built an ice cave and slept like a baby. So a Delta red-eye in business class, with a lie-flat seat? No problem."

"Business class?"

"It'll all be in the expense report."

Sorensen shook her head. "You'll never change, will you?"

"Not likely. Is that a bad thing?"

"No—I suppose that's what I like about you, Jammer. Utter predictability."

He smiled broadly as she led them down the hallway.

"The director is waiting for us."

"What's he like?"

"How should I know—I'm only a minion." She made a point of looking him up and down. "Is that your best suit?"

"It's my only suit. I stopped at Goodwill on my way from the airport."

Sorensen looked to see if he was serious. The jacket's fit told her he was. "I got a call from a sheriff's office in Oregon last night." The discomfort in her voice was clear.

"Really?"

"They were running an investigation—some poor deputy went through a half-dozen agencies before he reached me, and by then he was pretty steamed. Apparently somebody roughed up the owner of a flight operation out in Oregon. A janitor found the guy out behind a hangar—he was hog-tied and left in the passenger cabin of a mothballed helicopter."

"What kind of lunatic would do something like that?"

"The poor guy almost froze to death. He gave a description of his assailant, which narrowed things down pretty well. Lone male, six foot eight, built like a truck. It seems the guy had been asking about modifications to a large aircraft. The sheriff found a security video, and he was able to identify the license plate of a rental car. Eventually they tracked it to us."

"I thought the CIA was supposed to be good at keeping secrets."

"We're a government agency, so we cooperate with other government agencies. Honestly, Jammer . . . concealment is not one of your strengths."

"You mean I'd never get a full-time job here?"

"Unlikely."

They hit another security podium, this one staffed by a pair of guards that looked more serious. Davis figured they had to be getting close. "You know, I never asked," he said. "How did you end up working here?"

"I met a recruiter at Dartmouth. He asked me if I had any language skills, military training, or if I was a genius with computers. I said no, no, and not a chance."

"So what did they see in you?"

"I told him I took a profile test in freshman psychology that proved I was certifiably paranoid. He made me an offer on the spot."

Davis smiled.

They reached the director's office, and the receptionist asked them to wait.

Sorensen pulled back a step and studied him.

one of the security men inspected the heavy binders he was carrying.

"You look great," he said after running the gauntlet.

"And you don't look tired," she mused. "You've been all over the hemisphere in the last two days—you should be exhausted."

He shrugged. "In Arctic survival training I built an ice cave and slept like a baby. So a Delta red-eye in business class, with a lie-flat seat? No problem."

"Business class?"

"It'll all be in the expense report."

Sorensen shook her head. "You'll never change, will you?"

"Not likely. Is that a bad thing?"

"No—I suppose that's what I like about you, Jammer. Utter predictability."

He smiled broadly as she led them down the hallway.

"The director is waiting for us."

"What's he like?"

"How should I know—I'm only a minion." She made a point of looking him up and down. "Is that your best suit?"

"It's my only suit. I stopped at Goodwill on my way from the airport."

Sorensen looked to see if he was serious. The jacket's fit told her he was. "I got a call from a sheriff's office in Oregon last night." The discomfort in her voice was clear.

"Really?"

"They were running an investigation—some poor deputy went through a half-dozen agencies before he reached me, and by then he was pretty steamed. Apparently somebody roughed up the owner of a flight operation out in Oregon. A janitor found the guy out spent mostly in the halls of Langley. Davis shook hands with a tall man in his early sixties who was aging well, the kind of well-groomed silver fox who'd look right at home in a Cialis commercial. He also sensed a certain weather in his gaze, suggesting a man for whom life held few remaining surprises.

Coltrane greeted them enthusiastically, no undercurrent to say, *My time is precious so this had better be good.* He did, however, get right to the point. "I understand this involves an airplane crash."

"Yes, sir," said Sorensen, naturally taking the lead, "an MD-10 crash off the coast of Brazil." She glanced at Davis. "I should advise you from the outset that Mr. Davis, while he is a former Air Force officer, doesn't have an active security clearance."

Coltrane spun his hand in the air to tell Sorensen her ass was covered, and that she should get on with it.

"Last week we received an alert from NSA regarding seven names they'd mined from a targeted computer in Iran. They were convinced, and my department concurs, that they'd uncovered a high-end identity forgery operation."

"Official or freelance?" the director asked.

"At this point, we can't say. But right after we started looking, people on this list started turning up dead." Sorensen covered the shootings in Malta and Switzerland, all of which was as much news to Davis as it was to Coltrane. "As we began to look more closely, two more names popped up from the NSA's list—both of the pilots from this crash in Brazil."

Coltrane shifted in his seat. Having spent a career chasing small coincidences, such a spectacular correlation naturally piqued his interest. Davis was less enthralled—he was learning things he should have been told from the outset.

"My assistant and I focused more closely," Sorensen continued. "As you know, since the September 11 attacks our Office of Terrorism Analysis has quietly undertaken a program to track the ownership of civilian airliners across the globe. There are over ten thousand, but it's not as big a job as it might seem. The vast majority are owned and operated by reputable airlines in First World countries. OTA monitors leasing and sales, retirements and long-term storage, with particular attention to wide-body aircraft. Only a handful of big jets change hands each year in a way that gets our attention.

"As it turns out, this MD-10 in Brazil was already on OTA's radar. It was an old jet nearing the end of its service life, and had been grounded in a legal battle. For the last year it was parked at a small airfield in the central Amazon basin. Then just recently a company we've never heard of, Perseus Air Cargo, purchased the airframe. The deal went through quickly, and Perseus wasted no time. They brought in mechanics to get the aircraft in shape, and early Saturday it took off on what was supposed to be a maintenance test flight. The jet had been airborne for about two hours when it disappeared over the Atlantic. There was one distress call, but no indication of what went wrong. No survivors were found, but the Brazilian Coast Guard did find wreckage, along with one body."

Coltrane said, "Yes, I think I heard something about it."

"OTA put a small mention in your daily brief yesterday. Anyway, when I discovered that both pilots were tied to our forgery-mill list, I thought we should take a closer look. That's where Mr. Davis comes in. He's a former Air Force pilot, and also an accident investigator. Technically he's an NTSB contractor, but he has worked with us in the past."

"Yes, something over in Sudan, as I remember. I'd like to hear your version of that event someday, Mr. Davis."

"It'll cost you a beer," Davis replied. "And call me Jammer."

The director raised one eyebrow, but deferred comment. *Clearly a martini man,* Davis thought before saying, "I left for Brazil Saturday night, and arrived yesterday, the day after the incident. Miss Sorensen tasked me with three objectives. First she wanted any information I could find regarding the identities of those who purchased and operated the aircraft. She wanted to know if the jet was carrying anything suspicious. Finally, she asked for my opinion on what caused this jet to go down. On the first question, I didn't find much. The captain's name, real or not, was Gianni Petrecca. He negotiated the purchase of the airplane."

"Isn't that unusual," Coltrane queried. "A pilot acting as a buyer?"

"Not necessarily. We don't know much about Perseus, but it's clearly a small operation. For all we know this man could be a part owner of the company or a chief pilot. The only other Perseus employee we could identify was the copilot who showed up on the day of the flight."

Coltrane said, "Miss Sorensen said something about a body being recovered. Was it one of these men?"

"No," said Davis. "The flight plan listed only the two pilots on board, but there *was* a passenger—it's been verified by witnesses. The Brazilians positively identified the recovered body as that passenger. He was the local airport caretaker. Apparently he'd been helping the Perseus crew get the airplane ready, and they took him along for the ride."

"As sort of a favor?" Coltrane asked.

"Could be. As to whether the jet was carrying any cargo, I saw no indication of it. On a maintenance test flight it would typically be empty."

"All right," Coltrane said. "Any ideas about the cause of the crash?"

"That's why I'm here. To begin, when I arrived in Brazil I expected the investigation team to have already interviewed the mechanics who'd been working on the jet. Unfortunately, nobody's talked to a single one."

"Why is that?" the director asked.

"Because no one can find them."

"How could that be?" Sorensen said, this being news to her as well.

"They were foreign contractors, and apparently all have left Brazil. That didn't sit right with me in a number of ways. When you run a maintenance test flight on a jet that hasn't flown in a long time, you expect gripes after landing."

"Gripes?"

"Maintenance write-ups, things that don't work. Bad oil pumps, a radar that needs calibrating. Leave a jet in the Amazon for a year, and systems *will* go south. It's not uncommon on a flight like this for one of the wrench-turners to go along on the flight just to keep a running list of what needs to be fixed. At the very least, these mechanics should have been there when the jet landed. Three teams had been brought in from two different contractors in Guatemala and Peru. They showed up as soon as Perseus got approval to work on the airplane, and they got the jet airborne fast. Then . . . they just went home."

"The airplane crashed. Maybe they were worried about being held responsible."

"I considered that too, so before I left Santarém I stopped at the airfield office and asked around. Apparently the mechanics all departed on two charter flights that left right after our MD-10 got up in the air."

"What do you make of it?" the director asked.

"Let me tell you the rest." Davis covered how the wrong kind of oil slick had been found, and that radar data showed an airplane in a four-hundred-knot dive when contact was lost. "When a jet hits the ocean at that speed it's like hitting a brick wall. Only there wasn't a single piece of airframe wreckage recovered. No fuel tank remnants, no honeycomb composite from a horizontal stabilizer—the kinds of things that would usually break clear and float. I also saw the medical examiner's preliminary report on the body that was recovered. There was evidence of one crushing blow to the posterior skull, and the extremities all had broken bones. Otherwise the body was in decent shape."

"Isn't that what you'd expect in an air crash?"

"Not one like this. According to the radio calls and radar data, this jet was going down like a greased brick. A high-speed impact like that—it's catastrophic. Explosions and fire, lots of jagged metal. The body that was recovered had different injuries, the kind you might get from jumping off a bridge."

Davis paused and gave Coltrane a moment.

"So you're saying the evidence on this crash is contradictory, that it doesn't make sense?"

"Actually, just the opposite. This crash makes perfect sense. In fact, it might be the easiest accident I've ever investigated."

The director raised an eyebrow to ask the question.

"Because there *was* no crash," Davis said. "None at all."

# THIRTY-NINE

Director Coltrane sat stunned. "How can you be sure?"

"Sure?" Davis said. "That's a strong word. I can't use it yet. But if I'm right, you need to find this airplane fast."

"You think it's a threat?"

"I do, and in a way we've never seen before."

Davis took one of the binders he'd brought and dropped it on Coltrane's desk. It landed with a thud, and the director and Sorensen stared at it. The title was *MD-10 VLAT*. Curiously, there was a dime-sized hole just off-center on the front cover.

Coltrane lifted it, turned the manual sideways, and leafed through pages until a flattened slug of metal fell onto his desk.

"Is that what I think it is?" Sorensen asked.

Davis shrugged. "Let's just say I'm glad I wasn't looking into a Cessna crash—those manuals are a hell of a lot thinner."

Sorensen said, "Now I know why that guy in Oregon had such a cold night."

Coltrane asked what that meant, and Sorensen, realizing her mistake, was forced to fill him in on Davis' indiscretions. An indifferent director set the binder back on his desk. "VLAT," he said, looking at the manual's title. "What does that mean?"

"Very large air tanker. It's designed as a firebomber, a unique airframe that's been modified to drop five thousand liquid gallons in a matter of seconds—enough to cover a football field. It's effective in dealing with forest fires, although the idea never exactly took off. MD-10s are expensive to operate, and they have operational limitations, things like how low and slow you can drop. It's all right there in the manual."

"What else could you use it for?" the director asked warily.

"A good question. Maybe anthrax or plague . . . if you've got the right agents and could put them in solution. Drop it high enough, you could cover a whole city, even a small country. I'm sure there are people in this building who could come up with some pretty frightening scenarios. We're talking about a highly specialized airplane—only a handful like it exist. Now, out of the blue, somebody goes to a lot of trouble to buy one and make it airworthy. Then they want everyone to think it crashed."

"But it didn't," said the director.

"That's how I see it. She's out there somewhere, maybe on a quiet airfield in some small, out-of-the-way country. Those drop tanks could be getting charged right now with something that will make September 11 look like child's play."

The director's well-groomed façade vanished. Davis had given Sorensen hints to his concerns, but even she was speechless. The two stared at the bullet-shot binder as if it were the devil's playbook.

"If I were you," Davis prompted, "I'd drop everything and find out where the hell this airplane went." He stood and reached out a hand to the director as if expecting a shake. "So that's my report. I'm sure you both have work to do."

Director Coltrane remained frozen. He finally said, "I appreciate your help on this, Mr. Davis. Will you stay on a little longer? We could use your expertise."

Davis paused. "I did have a rugby match this afternoon, but I suppose I could put it aside . . . in the name of national security, and all. But there's also the matter of dinner with my daughter tonight. She's a student down at Duke and has to head back to school tomorrow."

Coltrane rubbed a finger over the hole in the binder on his desk. "This trouble you had out west—I'm not sure exactly what happened, but it looks somewhat serious. If you were to help us find this aircraft . . . I'm sure we could make any repercussions go away."

Davis leaned forward and hovered over the director of the CIA's nameplate—much as he'd done the previous day over another nameplate, one whose owner spent the night hog-tied and freezing inside a scrapped helicopter. "With all due respect, Director, if I miss dinner with my daughter there's going to be trouble in the east."

"Jammer," Sorensen intervened in a tight voice, "I think what the director is trying to say is that—"

Davis held up a hand to silence her. He waited for Coltrane.

The director grinned. He was a man not used to being challenged, here of all places. But no one reached the seat he was sitting in without understanding the art of negotiation. "All right. Perhaps I should put it differently. I'll make certain this trouble from Oregon gets lost. No strings attached. But I'm scheduling a briefing on this matter for three this afternoon. I'd very much like it if you'd be in attendance."

Davis smiled. "Well, since you put it like that—how could I say no? In the meantime, sir, you *really* need to start a search for this airplane. SIGINT, HUMINT, CYBER. Whatever it takes."

"Any suggestions where to look?" Coltrane asked.

Davis looked up as if calculating. "We can take out some time for refueling, but they've had roughly a forty-hour head start. At five hundred miles an hour—the average cruise speed of a jet like that—your search radius is close to twenty thousand nautical miles. Which, of course, is nearly the circumference of the earth. Meaning—"

"Meaning," Sorensen said, breaking in, "it could be anywhere in the world."

The aircraft they were looking for was, at that moment, six thousand miles southeast and six miles up. It was going nowhere with the greatest possible precision.

There are two hundred million square miles of sky above the earth, and while certain air corridors see continuous traffic, wide swathes of airspace remain effectively a void. These are the black holes, areas where radar coverage is minimal or nonexistent, and where aircraft are not watched, tracked, scanned, or monitored. As a consequence, pilots rarely venture into these frontiers unless absolutely necessary, and then at their own risk. Government oversight is dubious—where there is any government at all.

The tropical air thirty-four-thousand feet over the west African nation of Gabon is just such a place. Surrounded by the likes of Equatorial Guinea, Congo, and Angola, the federation's very name is derived from *gabão*, the Portuguese word for cloak. Gabon wears its name well, resting on the equator in a seasonless languor, blanketed year round by heat, humidity, and an unrelenting sun.

CB68H had been there for the best part of thirty-six hours, boring holes through blue sky and thunderstorms, night and day, clinging to the dense air at its best endurance airspeed—a ponderously slow 230 knots, this being the aerodynamic sweet spot at which its massive wings and engines merged to the point of maximum efficiency. The jet had so far made four landings at Leon M'Ba Airport in Libreville, each time remaining on the ground only long enough to take on fuel and oil, and to meet briefly with a mechanic who'd been contracted in advance to address technical discrepancies. So far, fortunately, there had been few.

By way of a satellite link, Tuncay was in regular contact with the chemist, Ghazi, who would provide the coded signal to send them to their next destination. Ghazi also gave updates on the reports of their demise; so far, there was nothing in the news to suggest that their staged crash off the coast of Brazil had been debunked. But then, they assumed that if the ruse had been discovered, it would not be made public knowledge—particularly if anyone realized the significance of the airframe they'd stolen. If that happened, the hunt would be on.

The critical thing was keeping the airplane out of sight for as long as possible. Unfortunately, to conceal a wide-body airliner from the world's finest surveillance assets was no easy trick. After considerable debate in the planning stages, it was Tuncay who had made the case, to good effect, that the best place to hide an airplane was in the sky.

He was staring bleary-eyed at the fuel gauges, which had become a clock of sorts, when Walid came forward from the cockpit bunk. The Druze stretched his arms over his head and yawned. "When do we land?" he asked.

"Ninety minutes. Come take a shift, I am getting tired."

Walid sank heavily into the copilot's seat. "I think I have logged more flying time in the last two days than in four years of flying for the Syrian Air Force."

"Perhaps so—but I wouldn't bother putting the hours in your logbook. Once this is done, neither of us will ever fly for hire again."

Walid chucked wearily. "True. But in two days, if we want to fly again, either of us could buy a private jet."

Tuncay might have smiled if he'd had the energy. He punched a button on the center instrument console. "The controls on this navigation selector are worthless."

"I'm sorry," replied a contrite Walid, apologizing for the third time. He had earlier toppled a can of Coke he'd set on the console, and despite a ten-minute blotting session with a package of napkins, the control head for the number-two VHF navigation receiver remained a sticky mess. The rest of the cockpit was hardly better: food wrappers and magazines tossed on the floor, an uneaten sandwich moldering behind one rudder pedal. It was the kind of housekeeping one would expect from owners who had no financial stake in their home. Or in this case, owners who knew their home was on the brink of condemnation.

Tuncay added, "The number-two autopilot has tripped off twice, but it seems to reset. And your radar altimeter is useless."

"Do we need it?" Walid asked.

Tuncay swept his hand in the air as if sweeping the question aside. "Of course not. We are limping along, but none of that matters. If we can keep two of the three engines running and lower the landing gear a few more times, our mission will get done."

"When do we go north?"

"If all goes to plan, one more fuel stop, and then we will make our dash. Hopefully the chemist and the Israeli will have everything complete on their end."

"I'm not sure I trust them, the chemist in particular. You think such a man will be able to carry through on his part?"

Tuncay stood and took his turn to stretch. "Will any of us?"

The two pilots, who had met only months earlier, exchanged an awkward look. "He is Sunni," said Tuncay, trying to lighten the mood. "Have you ever known a Sunni who was not trustworthy?"

Walid could not contain a smile. His captain went to the bunk, and for amusement he typed the coordinates of their next destination into the flight computer. Two thousand, nine hundred and seventeen nautical miles on a zero-six-one degree bearing. Six hours of flying time, more or less. After that they would have only two more flights in the old jet, each shorter than the previous.

And each progressively more perilous.

He was erasing the coordinates when an alarm suddenly sounded. A wide-eyed Walid stiffened in his seat, but then relaxed when he realized it was only the autopilot disconnect warning. The big jet drifted lazily to port, a shallow bank that Walid easily countered using the control wheel. Manual flight was always available as a backup, but tedious and rarely used in the age of automation. He reengaged the autopilot and it came online smoothly. The big ship righted, once again flying herself.

Minor crisis averted, Walid pushed his seat rearward. He put his heels up on the instrument rail, reclined his seat, and did his very best to keep his eyes open.

# FORTY

When it comes to building assassins, Mossad leaves no stone unturned. Slaton remembered the signals intelligence training block well. It had lasted two weeks, and of that, three tedious days were spent on hardware. He could still envision the engineer who'd come to their classroom on the second day, an unreservedly nerdish sort who had droned for eight hours about effective radiated power, atmospheric attenuation, and antennae directivity. The prospective assassins in Slaton's group—there were five to begin—gave the bookish little man no end of hard stares, making the point that they would rather be out on the tactical ranges shooting something.

As it turned out, the engineer's painfully arid briefing had been deliberately orchestrated. The next day the commander of the training detachment was the first to enter the room, followed closely by the engineer. He explained that those who'd kept focus the previous day would be glad they had. The engineer gave a hard stare of his own, or the best he could manage, as the practical exam was issued, along with a promise that a passing grade was mandatory for anyone wishing to continue along the road to becoming a *kidon*.

278 | WARD LARSEN

The aspiring killers were given a detailed list—twenty-five varied types of antennas—along with a smartphone. The engineer who'd been so rudely treated the day before was allowed to issue the time hack, and off everyone went. The trainees had seven hours in which to photograph a specimen of each of the twenty-five aerials. Slaton would later reflect on how well-designed the exercise was, requiring not only recognition of the various transmitters, towers, and dishes, but also a working knowledge of where each might be found. It also told the instructors who had been paying attention on the dullest of days, a subtly vital skill, and served as a practical exam in field photo-surveillance. Most importantly, the seven-hour limit added an element of pressure.

When the day was done and the results graded, only two trainees remained. Two had failed to locate all the required types of antennae, and another was let go when he was arrested outside an Israeli Air Force base—a military policeman on regular rounds had spotted the man taking pictures. David Slaton was a survivor, and now, years later, he found himself still using what he had learned.

His survey of *Kosmos* had begun on the dock in Larnaca. Certain electronic devices could be tied to the shape of their antennae—the distinctive whip of a marine VHF radio, or the rotating bar of an open array radar. What Slaton did not see was more relevant—no white dome to signify satellite connectivity, which was presumably beyond the means of a tuna-chasing smuggler.

Less apparent, and more worrisome to Slaton, was the possibility of handheld devices. Demitriou probably did not have a satellite phone, again for economic reasons, but a mobile phone was a near certainty.

Given that *Kosmos* was presently forty miles from the nearest shoreline, they were beyond the coverage of any cell tower—typically ten to fifteen miles from shore for voice, slightly more for text. That isolation would end in the early morning hours as they approached the treacherous coast of Lebanon.

Standing at the washbasin by *Kosmos'* foul-smelling head, Slaton ignored the cracked mirror in front of him. Mossad had also given lessons on changing appearance, a segment far more entertaining than the engineer's and taught by a woman who for twenty years had spackled some of the most famous faces in Hollywood. That training was useless tonight. He was fair-haired and, in spite of his Maltese tan, relatively light-skinned, with gray eyes and Nordic features that spoke far more of the Baltic than the Mediterranean. Even with professional makeup, contacts, and hair dye, he would need a very dark evening indeed to pass as Lebanese. A generation ago he might have resorted to a full *jellabah* to mask his appearance, but these days in Beirut one saw more Nike and knockoff Vuitton than traditional robes and sandals. Fortunately, in an ode to globalization, Slaton could present himself for very near what he was.

Since the end of the July War with Israel in 2006, Lebanon had rebuilt much of its tourist infrastructure. Seaside hotels were back in business, their swimming pools clogged with well-heeled European families. Farther inland, rooftop nightclubs and hookah dens shared equally in the profits of peace. Best of all—February was always a high month.

During his brief excursion into the shops and salons of Foinikoudes Beach, Slaton had purchased a dark Ralph Lauren shirt and Zanella trousers, and a pair of comfortable Bruno Magli loafers. These tags of quality, if lost on his pelagic captain, would openly support the image of a well-to-do European reveling in the charms of western Lebanon. Slaton completed his ensemble with a light jacket of more egalitarian taste, in the pocket of which was a set of wraparound sunglasses and a knit watch cap. The brown jacket also had a blue zip-out liner with a hood. In sum, he would look like any of a thousand tourists, yet could change his appearance in seconds with a half-dozen permutations.

He checked that his pockets were zipped and secure, and before going on deck Slaton coiled his last acquisition, from a Larnaca hardware store, into his back pocket. In stagnant air that reminded him of an automotive garage, he stood still and listened carefully. He heard an empty gin bottle rolling back and forth on a railed shelf, keeping time to the seas outside, and the steady hum of *Kosmos'* old diesel. From the wheelhouse above came the tin-echo blare of pop music on AM radio—a receive-only device that was not a concern.

Slaton's magic number was twelve—the distance from the coastline, in nautical miles, where they became vulnerable. It was the internationally recognized territorial boundary, and while "innocent passage" was permitted within, this came at the price of occasional boarding inspections by Lebanese coastal patrols. Outside twelve, *Kosmos* was safe. Inside, even a Cypriot-flagged fishing scow was fair game.

He went above and found Demitriou at the helm.

"How close are we?" he asked.

"Thirty miles," the skipper answered.

Slaton scanned ahead, and could just make out faint lights on the highest hills. He moved next to Demitriou to study the horizon, and also the VHF radio controls near the helm. There was a bulbous microphone with a thumb-lever for transmitting. The radio was powered up, but the volume dial was turned to zero. Demitriou had both hands very deliberately on the wheel.

"We will reach the coast off Aarida by three, well before sunrise."

"You'll be back in port for lunch."

"Sunset," the big man corrected. "I must catch dinner on the way home. If I return to port empty-handed, there might be questions."

"Questions about where you've been? Or about your proficiency as a fisherman?"

"Neither one serves me, so I will put both to rest." Demitriou looked him up and down. "You think you can pass for Lebanese looking like that?"

"Hardly."

"How will you swim ashore in such clothing?"

Slaton responded with a circumspect look and said, "You haven't asked about the second half of your fee."

To his credit, the smuggler answered quickly. "I assumed it would be the same arrangement as last time. After your safe delivery, one of your friends will find me at the docks."

Slaton thought, but did not say, *Only you've realized that I don't have any friends this time.*

He saw a moving map display on the main console. The boat was old, but Demitriou, like all fishermen these days, could not rely completely on the old ways. Slaton reached for the display controls, and the skipper watched closely but didn't protest. He expanded the map until the coast of Lebanon was fully visible at the right edge. "I've changed my mind," he announced. "Put me ashore here." He pointed to a stretch of coastline midway between Tripoli and Beirut.

"*What?* No—we have an agreement. The patrols are too heavy in that area."

"The course is one-three-zero degrees, Captain. Steer it."

Slaton watched the rising lights in the distance, now a string of flickering jewels above the coal-black sea. He waited for a protest, but the old whiskey compass near the ceiling began to swing. Then he saw something more troubling. Demitriou's far hand was on the VHF microphone—he wasn't holding it, but his knuckles were discreetly pressing the transmit button.

It was just as Slaton had feared. He knew where he'd made his mistake. He'd had the Nicosian isolated at the dock, but then allowed him to take the money to the harbor shack. Eighty seconds. *Longer than it would have taken to simply lock the money in a safe. Not long enough to have counted it.* Slaton doubted there had been time to call anyone, so Demitriou had probably told a friend, perhaps the young deckhand. Told him where they were heading and when they would arrive. He'd probably scribbled down a VHF channel—with the transmit button pressed, as it was now, the radio would serve as a homing beacon.

Slaton could only speculate on the rest of the betrayal. The information had likely been forwarded to a contact in Lebanon—smugglers in these waters could ill afford to take sides, so Demitriou would have contacts on both shores. There were people in Lebanon who would pay far more than five thousand for an infiltrating Israeli commando, a bounty guaranteed by the fact that a state of war had existed between the nations since 1973. In that moment, staring through a salt-encrusted windshield, Slaton's view of his situation hardened, and he knew there was but one option. For the second time in his life, mutiny.

Demitriou seemed to read his thoughts. He made a subtle move, his far hand snaking into a storage bin.

Slaton did not hesitate.

With concise movements, he half-turned away from Demitriou, then rotated back to deliver a vicious elbow to the shorter man's temple. The big fisherman hit the deck like a dropped anchor, conscious but stunned to inaction. Slaton rolled him facedown, put a knee in his back, and from his back pocket extracted a handful of plastic zip ties. He'd bought the heaviest gauge available, half-inch bands with enough tensile strength to keep the ship's engine on its mounts. Demitriou mumbled incoherently as Slaton bound his wrists behind his back and looped the ties through an unused belt loop. Finally, he secured the captain against a stanchion.

Slaton returned to the helm, and in the storage bin he discovered an old six-shot .45 revolver. It was big and clumsy, an elephant-pistol whose black steel had gone green, and whose barrel-mounted sight was severely bent. Still, it might have worked. Slaton had expected something like it—no smuggler worked these waters without protection, and it was also just the thing for taking potshots at nuisance sharks that might threaten a nearly boated prize bluefin.

He emptied the cylinder of four bullets, threw them overboard, and put the gun back in the storage bin. Slaton checked the compass and set a new course, then pushed up the throttle until the tachometer hit the red line.

What Slaton could not know was at that very moment, one hundred and ninety-six miles over his head, an image of *Kosmos* was being logged by a satellite of the United States' National Reconnaissance Office. It was called BASALT, a synthetic aperture radar bird nearing its perigee, the point at which an orbiting body is closest to the earth.

Within seconds that image was devoured by computers at the NRO, which automatically scrubbed through a list of prioritizations. *Kosmos* was quickly identified—her length and beam and rigging were distinguishing enough, and she had long been on file as one of the thousand or so fishing boats that frequented these waters. The fact that she was approaching Lebanese waters caused barely a ripple. The NRO's assets had very recently been tweaked with new commands, and in the next minutes along her elliptical path BASALT would scour every airfield in Lebanon, Syria, and Jordan for a mysterious MD-10. Longline tuna boats, regardless of the waters in which they sailed, had fallen precipitously on the list of priorities.

BASALT was not alone.

For the last four hours America's most advanced satellites and drones had been scouring the earth. They downloaded images using every manner of sensor, the variances in their products essentially a matter of spectrum: electro-optical, infrared, radar, laser. These results were pored over at first by computers, with the most promising results, along with those that remained ambiguous, forwarded to legions of interpreters at the CIA and NRO.

It had already been ascertained that no fewer than two thousand airports existed across the world with a runway big enough to handle an MD-10. At that moment, 92 percent of them had been scanned by one method or another. The only airfields ignored were a handful of landing strips below 75 degrees south latitude—an arena that lacked regular satellite coverage for anything except ice sheets, and whose few airports harbored more flightless birds than aircraft.

As a subtheme, analysts determined that there were one hundred and twenty-two hangars on earth capable of swallowing an MD-10, thus potentially rendering their target invisible. The vast majority of these were owned by either airlines or maintenance repair and overhaul companies, legitimate and responsible businesses who one-by-one confirmed what was on hand in their shelters. There were loose ends, of course, and these were dealt with on a case-by-case basis. A shadow at an airfield in Sudan was eventually written off as a canvas decoy, the newly independent South Sudan trying to impress their tormentors to the north. An airframe on a taxiway in eastern Kenya raised hopes, but the aircraft was eventually identified as a derelict Russian model of similar size and silhouette.

Across the globe, CIA field operatives were dispatched to take pictures of some sixteen large aircraft hangars, and friendly intelligence services were tasked to quietly scout another dozen. A U.S. Navy drone was diverted to fly past the open door of an aircraft paint barn in southern Iran, and an Antarctic geological team—a professor and two graduate students from the Scripps Institution of Oceanography who were preparing for a mission funded by NOAA, and whose communication suite was first rate—were quietly asked to peek into a cavernous maintenance facility that had been abandoned in southern Chile.

By seven that evening, Eastern Langley Time, the count was down to thirty-six airfields, all in decidedly nether regions of the world, whose tarmacs had not been thoroughly canvassed. Nine hangars also remained whose contents were unaccounted for. Of these, four were in North Korea—and as such were under constant watch anyway—along with three in China and a pair in Siberia. None seemed likely prospects.

In bunkers all around Washington, D.C., teams of image analysts descended into a collective gloom as they fired blanks in a rare full-court press. Some began to express doubts that the airplane they were searching for even existed, whispering that it perhaps had crashed in the waters off Brazil after all, and that a certain air accident investigator was off his rocker. The crash inquiry in Brazil was monitored from afar, but there were no new developments.

The meager results were fed up the chain of command, rumors swirling that it rose all the way to the White House. All anyone could say for sure was that within thirty minutes of the day's last progress report being sent up, a second order came down.

Everyone was to stay the night and keep looking.

# FORTY-ONE

The crane ratcheted to a noisy stop at the side of a dirt path, shattering what had been a still and silent night in the western foothills of the Lebanon Mountains. Smoke hissed from its stubby exhaust, creating an eerie shroud in the shine of headlights from the dump truck following behind.

Mohammed Jalil stepped down from his crane to meet the man who had hired him. Jalil's eldest son, who was driving the dump truck, stayed respectfully in place.

"All right," Mohammed said, "we are ready."

His employer for the evening, who'd been standing in the dark waiting, looked at him with concern. "You are late," he said.

"There was a minor technical issue," Mohammed replied. "Everything is working now."

"Can you still have the job done one hour before sunrise?" The man was old and Christian, and therefore doubly cantankerous, but Mohammed was in no mood to argue. The old man was the leader of the Hamat village council, while Mohammed hailed from Batroun, four kilometers south. There had been divisions between the villages for a thousand years, but none of their fathers' squabbles mattered tonight.

Mohammed was a simple man in a simple business, and when people paid cash in advance he easily put aside that he was an occasional Muslim.

"Of course," he replied. "Six hours is more than enough. Do you care what I do with the scrap?"

The man seemed to consider it. "Do what you will. The only stipulation is that you carry it at least three kilometers from here."

"Three kilometers?"

"Is that a problem?" asked the village elder.

"Not at all," said Mohammed. "But it is an unusual request. I can only wonder why the people of Hamat are being so particular. This thing has been rotting away here for twenty years. Now it must be dealt with under the cover of darkness, and the remains taken far away?"

"These restrictions were not dictated by the people of my village. We both know this airplane was left here long ago by the government. It has been forgotten since your son was a boy, and the liars in Beirut—they would leave it here until Jesus rises again. No one cares that it is an eyesore, or that our children have been hurt trying to climb inside. Twice we have sealed the doors and windows shut . . . but time has its way."

Both men regarded the massive jet that loomed like a mountain in the darkness before them. Something of a local legend, the aircraft had arrived on an equally black night decades ago—the exact year was the subject of some debate—and had not turned a wheel since. Back then the place was called Wujah Al Hajar Air Base, an outpost of hope and security before the troubles had begun anew. The buildings were nearly gone now, their wooden walls and planked roofs defeated by age and the elements, the remains long ago scavenged for cooking fires. Aside from a handful of cobblestone foundations, the only structure remaining was a single ancient shed with a warped roof, the door long missing. When the Air Force pulled out, the place had been designated hopefully as an international airport, but without funding or flights everything had gone to seed, even the runway deteriorating to the point that the rich kids from the coast had given up using it to drag race their European cars. Only one thing remained to suggest this place had ever been a thriving airfield: the shell of a single old airplane.

It was an American machine, Mohammed knew, something called a Tri-Star. Its engines had long ago been salvaged, and one wing drooped as if the bones inside were cracked. All the low-hanging aluminum panels that could be pried free had been pilfered long ago by scrap hounds. The wheels were no more than rusted steel hubs, these surrounded by piles of vulcanized rubber nuggets. Birds nested in any number of openings, leaving their offerings to accent the chipped off-white paint, and the cockpit windows had long ago been smashed out by stone-throwing boys. Adding insult to the once proud jet's injuries, a black mark on the tail evidenced a lightning strike that had occurred some ten years ago, God having his own say on the matter.

"This thing should have been dealt with long ago," Mohammed agreed, surveying the old carcass. "Why now?"

"Because someone has given us the money to do it."

"But not the government, you say?"

The old man spit on the ground. "The government does nothing. A man has paid us in advance."

"Who is he?"

"I don't know, and I don't care. He came to us weeks ago and gave us a good wage to do the job in a certain way. 'On this exact night,' he tells me, 'take the pieces at least three kilometers away, and have it done one hour before sunrise.'" The old man shrugged. "Maybe he is one of the princes from the coast, with a castle and a blue swimming pool. Or perhaps he owns land nearby and wants to build a resort, and this beast is blocking his view. Why should I care if he wants it done quietly in the middle of the night? All that matters is that it will finally be done."

Mohammed nodded. "So be it."

He went back to the cab of his crane and fired up the diesel. Turning on his work lights, he looked upon his task with a measure of anticipation. He routinely destroyed condemned buildings and razed crumbling barns, yet tonight's job would require a degree of artistry. To knock things down and tear them apart was often disparaged, seen as little more than a brute's work. But to do it well, with skill and efficiency— that was something else. Mohammed knew because he had been demolishing things all his life, beginning with a sledgehammer and a wheelbarrow, and graduating over the years to full-blown mechanization. If you took something down the wrong way, he knew, you could damage your equipment, even put your life at risk. At the very least, a proper teardown hastened completion and minimized cleanup, which in turn got you home or to the next job that much more quickly.

The dump truck pulled near and Mohammed lowered his cable. The special attachment, carried in the bed of the truck, was an improvisation—a slab of steel two-inches thick and four meters square. He had taken it from the hull of a merchant ship he'd scrapped years ago, and it had long served in Mohammed's yard to bridge a gulley in the lot where he parked his equipment. He'd always thought it might prove more useful—and therein lay the artistry. Mohammed needed something special for this job, and a two-ton steel plate seemed just the thing.

When his son had the cable attached, he gave a thumbs-up, and Mohammed raised the boom to its maximum height and rotated everything into place. He started at the left wing, the one that drooped, and waited for the plate, which was spinning slightly, to reach the desired angle. When it looked just right, Mohammed pulled the release lever. The massive steel sheet scythed down cleanly and did its job, a five-meter section of the left wing crashing to the ground.

Mohammed smiled with profound satisfaction. He then maneuvered to his left, raised the metal plate high, and again poised his hand over the release lever.

# FORTY-TWO

CB68H landed at Basrah International Airport in Iraq during the wee hours of that same morning. The control tower had been unmanned since ten o'clock the previous night, but as was common, the airfield remained open in a proceed-at-your-own-risk type of operation. In the black of night, the big jet taxied clear of the runway, and on the receiving taxiway a small Toyota pickup flashed its lights, and then pulled in front of the behemoth in the classic manner of an airfield "Follow Me" truck.

The MD-10 did exactly that, and the odd convoy came to a stop minutes later on a remote corner of the airfield. Two fuel trucks were waiting, along with a trailered set of loading stairs, and nearby were a forklift, two pallets of gear, and a tanker truck carrying water. Three people waited to greet the pilots: a grizzled Iraqi who would manage the refueling, a slight Indonesian here to drive the forklift, and a second Iraqi, slightly built and much younger than the first, who appeared to be in charge.

Everyone worked quickly, and thirty-six minutes after touching Iraqi soil the jet was fully refueled and its cargo loaded. During that time the aircrew was also busy. The copilot mounted a ladder to service the port engine with oil. The captain did his best to hammer shut an access door on the lower fuselage, first using the side of his fist, and then a large rock. The panel, normally used by maintenance to access an unpressurized electronics bay, could simply not be latched in place, and in the end the captain used nearly an entire roll of duct tape to seal it shut.

At the forty-minute point, the copilot went to the flight deck and ran through the preflight checklist. The younger Iraqi also climbed on board, while the captain met with the refueler and the Indonesian at the Toyota.

Fifty-eight minutes after touchdown, CB68H was again lifting into the sky with its crew of two, one passenger, and a peculiar load consisting primarily of water and lead which, even though low in volume, summed a respectable fifty-six thousand pounds. The copilot activated the flight plan by radio, and a generic white blip blossomed on an air traffic control radar screen in the Iraq Civil Aviation Authority's southern sector. The copilot claimed to be flying a Challenger 600, an aircraft with similar speed and climb performance to an MD-10. According to the filed paperwork, the aircraft was registered to a corporation in Iran, and the destination was listed as Al-Qusayr Airfield in Syria, a former military facility notched near the northeastern corner of Lebanon.

The air traffic controller was familiar with such missions. There had been a constant flow in recent years, humanitarian relief flights from the Middle East and beyond to aid the beleaguered victims of the war. The Challenger was a regular customer, and while Iranian-registered jets usually rounded Iraqi airspace on their goodwill missions, a few paused for technical stops at the airfield in Basrah, a rare instance of cooperation between cranky Mesopotamian neighbors. Indeed, the controller had seen a Challenger arrive at Al-Basrah earlier that evening at the beginning of his seven-hour shift, and so the man only yawned as he passed the flight strip over to the controller working the adjacent sector.

It was roughly at this time, with the blip solidly in radar contact and having been cleared on direct routing, that the navigation lights on CB68H suddenly extinguished. Because the aircraft was twenty-two thousand feet above open desert, no one noticed.

Along the same lines, during the brief time CB68H had been on the ground there was but one person at Basrah International Airport who might have witnessed her stay. His name was Zaid, and he was the night security man. Yet because he was only responsible for what lay inside the terminal building, and because he was in the middle of a flaming row with his girlfriend and busy texting on his phone, Zaid never noticed the big jet's arrival or departure. Nor did he see, roughly one hour later, a small Challenger business jet that quietly taxied, took off, and made a gentle easterly turn in the general direction of Iran.

Also unknown to Zaid, although he would soon be questioned thoroughly, was the matter of two bodies a mile away that were resting in the bed of a Toyota pickup, freshly executed and fast coming to one with the cool desert night.

It was two hours before dawn when the Lebanese Navy AMP-145 patrol boat, *Saida,* caught up with the shadow it had been chasing all night. They intercepted the Cypriot-flagged tuna boat, *Kosmos,* to find it trailing a wandering arc eight miles offshore and running at full throttle, this evident by a stream of black soot belching from her exhaust and explosions of white spray at her bow, all highlighted in reflections of drawn moonlight.

*Saida* paralleled the fishing boat's irregular course for ten minutes. She sounded her siren and followed established protocol by issuing verbal warnings using both radio and bullhorn, all while her searchlight danced a galloping pattern over the longliner's old wooden hull.

There was no response, and *Saida*'s skipper, Commander Armin Gemayel, watched in amazement as *Kosmos'* crew ignored their warnings and continued an erratic course. The little ship battered mercilessly through a rising southwestern swell, sheets of spray flying over her decks. With the twelve-mile limit looming, and *Saida* herself taking a beating, Gemayel lost his patience and gave an order that surprised everyone. The patrol boat moved closer to issue a final radio warning, and when nothing happened the forward deck gun crew opened fire.

In a testament to either the crew's marksmanship or good fortune, the second round issued struck a fatal blow to *Kosmos'* engine. The steady stream of black from her funnel became a torrent, and soon the old ship was bobbing listlessly on a choppy sea.

The boarding process was quick and efficient, and when the all-clear was given after ten minutes, Commander Gemayel followed his advance party aboard. By that time a woozy George Demitriou had been cut free of his bindings and was sitting with his back against a side wall. The Lebanese officer hovered over him.

"Where is this Israeli spy you promised me?"

Rubbing his reddened wrists, Demitriou jabbed a

thumb toward the bow. The commander made his way forward, and on the starboard foredeck he saw an empty clamshell container the size of a barrel. It was orange and white in color—and quite empty.

An angry Gemayel stormed back to the wheel-house. "He went ashore in your life raft?"

Demitriou gestured to his swollen temple. A large knot had risen and blood matted his thinning hair. "What could I do? The man is dangerous—he took me by surprise."

"Where did he go ashore?"

"South of Tripoli . . . Batroun perhaps. I can't say for sure. When I got my senses back *Kosmos* was running seaward."

Gemayel was livid. At this point he had few options. He could tow *Kosmos* into the naval base, but a Cypriot tuna scow and her bruised skipper were hardly a prize. Worse yet, if he turned Demitriou in to the thugs of GDGS, Lebanon's ruthless intelligence service, they would interrogate him properly. Under duress Demitriou would certainly divulge the insertion of an Israeli spy into their country, not to mention the relationship he kept with a certain midgrade naval officer who was fresh into his new command, and who had effectively allowed the Israeli to slip through after being forewarned.

One of Gemayel's men came from below and spoke quietly into his ear. More bad news. Not only had Demitriou botched the rendezvous, but he wasn't even carrying anything worth appropriating. No drugs, no guns, no money. Unable to hold back, Gemayel kicked the toe of his boot into Demitriou's good temple.

"Your father and mine knew how to do business," he snarled. "During Chamoun and the insurrection, they knew how to make a profit while keeping out of trouble. Clearly you did not inherit this gene. Don't ever come near my waters again without the tax!"

The boarding party loaded into their inflatables and crossed back to *Saida*.

George Demitriou stood slowly, his stance wavering, more from his spinning head than the rough seas. He watched the naval boat churn away, and when it was a hundred yards distant, he reared back and spit a mouthful of blood toward the ship and her mother country.

Just as his father had done so many years ago.

# FORTY-THREE

"Maybe this airplane really *did* crash," said an analyst to Sorensen as they went over the latest reports.

Davis, who was officially part of the hunt now, had staked out a comfortable leather armchair for the night. He said, "There was no crash. We're just not looking in the right place."

The air in the room was heavy and scented in coffee—not the boutique aroma of a five-dollar-a-cup blend, but the burnt-bean odor of a cheap diner.

"What about camouflage?" Davis asked. "You know, like tarps or netting. The Russians and Cubans used to do that kind of thing, right?"

"The Cold War was a long time ago," Sorensen responded.

"Are you calling me a dinosaur?"

She smiled good-naturedly. "I'm saying that kind of deception works with visible imagery, but it's pointless against radar."

"And everybody has radar sats these days," said another analyst.

Davis watched a bank of monitors where technicians were scrolling through images. Airport after airport flipped by in God's-eye views, a few warranting a pause and magnification before being discarded.

"It's a big world," said Sorensen from behind his shoulder.

Without looking at her, he replied, "Yeah, but it's also a big airplane. And you're not going to find it at CDG."

"Where?"

Davis pointed to the image currently on the central monitor—a tremendous airport with four parallel runways. "That's Paris Charles de Gaulle. Someone went to a lot of trouble to steal this airplane. They simulated a crash, for Christ's sake, so they're not going to turn around and fly it into a major European hub. We need to narrow things down, which means putting ourselves in their position."

"All right," Sorensen prodded. "How would you hide a wide-body airplane?"

"First let's assume this scheme is not being run by a country. I think we can rule out the Chinas and Russias of the world. Of course, Iran or North Korea are always possibilities, but even they'd use a surrogate—no country would want its fingerprints on something like this."

"So we can stop looking in Iran and the PRK?"

"I would. This jet has to be in some out-of-the-way place." Davis stared silently at the screens as images snapped past. He finally broke out in a smile. "But you know where I'd hide it?"

Sorensen looked at him, and the photo-surveillance slideshow paused as an entire bank of analysts who'd been listening turned around. Davis told everyone his idea, and within minutes the battery of screens went blank as a new search was prepared.


Slaton paddled onto the beach in darkness and immediately dragged the emergency life raft into the dunes above the high-tide line. He stabbed the raft with a knife from its own survival kit, and buried the rubber remnants in a sand swale.

He set out on a course perpendicular to the sea, knowing it would eventually intersect the coastal north-south highway. Slaton moved as quickly as the terrain and predawn darkness allowed—he doubted an all-out manhunt was underway, but he suspected someone in Lebanon was aware of his arrival. An hour earlier he'd seen a Lebanese Navy patrol boat heading in the direction of *Kosmos,* and he thought it might be Demitriou's doing, perhaps a junior naval officer whose career would benefit greatly from single-handedly apprehending an Israeli spy. If so, Slaton was in the clear, because no self-promoting officer would document failure in his nightly watch report. A remorseful Demitriou would be chastised and sent packing, bringing the whole matter to a close.

As he moved east, it struck Slaton how different this insertion was from the last one he'd done. That mission had been bold even by Mossad's standards, a plan to assassinate a top Hezbollah captain. Their target, a man more deserving than most of an accelerated journey to the afterlife, was scheduled to appear at a rally in the Ras Beirut district. The intelligence was solid, and the mission drawn with care. Slaton's team had planned and trained for over a month, while Mossad's facilitators, the best on earth, had provided faultless passports and visas, and virtually unlimited funding. Transportation, a safe house, even groceries were put in place by an advance team. Easy in, take the shot, easy out. And if anything went wrong, Slaton had an army behind him—quite literally if necessary.

Everything had gone smoothly, and when the moment of truth came he had been situated under a concrete beam in a construction site six hundred yards from where the target was to appear—a simple shot on the firing range, but considerably more complex when perched on loose gravel in light rain at dusk, and when your bullet was to fly over a busy market square with smoke wafting from meat carts and people shouting and car horns blaring. Slaton never got a shot that day. As was too often the case, their solid intelligence proved wrong. The target had simply never shown, and Slaton and his support element vaporized into the lingering late-September heat. Weeks of training, men put at risk—all for nothing.

He hoped his assumptions for this mission were more accurate.

After two miles Slaton found the old coast highway, which was little used since a more modern motorway had been built years earlier to the east. At the shoulder he turned south and assumed a modest pace. He paused near a grove of olive trees, and pulled out a flashlight and a nautical chart he'd found in *Kosmos'* wheelhouse. The map was twenty years old, laminated against the sea and bent with folds by a skipper who still plotted courses on paper and measured distances with a pencil and mileage scale. But the chart depicted the coast in good detail, and as expected he was near a place called Baachta, forty kilometers north of Beirut.

Slaton began moving again.


It was well before daybreak when Slaton encountered a gas station along the southbound shoulder, and as he approached it a small delivery truck pulled off the road and parked in front of the diesel pump. A man got out of the driver's seat and stretched.

Slaton mussed his hair, more than what the Mediterranean and a sleepless night had already done, and made his approach.

"Hello there."

The man looked up, and in the yellow cast of a floodlight Slaton saw that he was quite young. A good sign, furthered when he replied in English, "Good morning."

"Is there coffee inside?" Slaton asked.

"Always. Boutros runs his place all night, and he needs it to keep his eyes open." The man appeared casual. Paradoxically, he would likely have been more cautious if Slaton had been Lebanese. An out-of-sorts European here was a curiosity, but hardly a threat. It was the displaced Syrians and the asylum-seeking refugees who would cut your throat for a few dollars.

"I've had a tough night," Slaton said. "Drank a bit too much. As best I can remember, two very pretty girls took me for a long drive. Where the hell am I?"

"Near Baachta," the young man said, not without sympathy, as he opened the truck's fueling door and removed the cap. "And they left you here?"

"I'm afraid so." Slaton pulled out his wallet and opened it just wide enough to show a ripple of cash. "Say, can you tell me if there's a bus nearby that runs to Beirut?"

It took another five minutes. Slaton paid for a full tank of diesel, two cups of coffee, and soon after found himself in the truck's passenger seat listening to the driver's take on the new Lebanese prime minister who was, in his opinion, no better than the old one. Slaton was receptive at first, but soon slumped drowsily against the window. He needed the rest, and at any rate, a degree of lethargy was perfectly in character.

The driver soon gave up, and through heavy eyes

Slaton looked out across the sea. The coastline was still dark, a black-velvet canvas flecked by clusters of lights. The forty kilometers to Beirut would pass quickly now, and with little physical effort. Ever so lightly, he slept.


The dump truck received its last load from the once-sleek skeleton at Wujah Al Hajar Air Base at twenty past five that morning. The city elder from Hamat had long ago departed—by now either asleep in his warm bed or being harangued by his querulous wife—leaving Mohammed and his son to finish things.

In the cast of the truck's headlights they made one last check of the asphalt pad where the jet had been parked. They'd already picked up every bit of scrap they could find—screws, rivets, shards of plastic and sheet metal. When that was done Mohammed undertook the contract's last and most peculiar directive. With a flashlight in hand, he walked the entire length of the nine-thousand-foot runway, kicking aside plastic bottles, an old car tire, and at the far end the remains of a dead goat that had probably had been done in by jackals that very night.

Once finished, Mohammed checked his watch. It was 5:42.

He drove his crane past the old airfield gate, which had not been closed in years, and the headlights faithfully showed the way home. Not wanting to disturb his neighbors, Mohammed slowed when he reached his property. The engine noise was just ratcheting down when he saw a peculiar sight over the shadowed hills. In the matte-black sky, a brilliant light seemed to be hovering to the north.

Mohammed pulled his crane to a stop in order to

look more closely, and he in fact distinguished not one light, but a tight group of three, all dazzling white against the ebony night. He thought it might be an airplane, but the signature red and green lights were not evident. It was hard to tell just how far away the object was, but soon the lights sank low and disappeared behind the hill he'd just crested.

A number of thoughts came to mind, but one took hold. A silly idea, really, and one that defied all logic. Mohammed shook his head as if to dislodge the notion. Weary after a long night's work, he put the machine back in gear and it crawled the last hundred meters, ending parked next to the already empty dump truck. His son, as usual, had beaten him to bed.

Mohammed dismounted, and as he walked the dirt path toward his house he took one last look over his shoulder. Seeing and hearing nothing, he chuckled.

"No," he mumbled to no one in particular, "it *couldn't* have been that."

# FORTY-FOUR

The city of Beirut, having been established some five thousand years ago, was not prone to fleeting change. So it was, when Slaton looked out over the Central District from the back of a cab early that morning, he did so with a loose sense of familiarity.

The driver kept his window open, and the scents of the city cascaded inside, garbage on one gust, saffron and cinnamon the next. As ever, Slaton saw a place divided deeply by culture and religion, yet curiously homogenous in appearance. There were Christians and Shiites, Bedouin and Sunni, labels largely indistinguishable as Slaton surveyed the crowded sidewalks. The only obvious misfits were the Westerners, men and women inclined to casual clothes and aimless strides, and who tethered themselves unfailingly to the logos of McDonald's and Starbucks. To pose as one of that lot, he thought encouragingly, would be simplicity itself.

Slaton exited the cab in the district of Saray, near Government Palace, and within sight of the Lebanese Parliament building where some of the world's most ill-at-ease politicians resided. He struck out north on foot, and before reaching the harbor turned right, away from Boulevard Charles Helou. The seats of national power were no more than a mile behind him when things began to deteriorate.

The roads were the first thing he noticed, curbs crumbling where there were any at all, and suspension-rattling potholes dotting the asphalt. The architecture was forlorn, bent sandstone buildings that seemed to lean on one another, rooftops and balconies blending like some kind of time-hewn geological strata. Laundry lines were racked with designer dresses, and rusted rooftop aerials supported new dish antennae. Young men lacking both jobs and hope—a jihadist recruiter's dream—stood slouched against walls with slow-burning cigarettes in their hands. Slaton found himself checking over his shoulder, although not as a matter of tradecraft. It was just that kind of neighborhood.

By the time he reached Geitawi Boulevard the roads had fallen to a maze, not straight lines designed for automobiles, but ageless paths that predated any kind of municipal planning. After three wrong turns, he finally found number twenty-six. It was not what he expected.

Instead of a sturdy warehouse, he was looking at a group of apartments, three stories of stone and glass with a relatively modern visage. At the base of the building was a concrete block parking garage set into a steep hillside. In sum, 26 Geitawi Boulevard, while by no means opulent, seemed a respectable residential address. The obvious problem—this was not where any arms dealer would keep a valuable cache of weapons.

Slaton crossed the street to the entrance, as he did so trying to map the floor plan of the units above. All three floors appeared to be of the same layout, windows and balconies arranged in uniform mirror images. Each floor had four units—A, B, C, and D?—which he estimated to be two-bedroom affairs. There was an iron gate at the portico, and he paused to check a much-altered directory of tenants. Right away he saw two possibilities: in 3B, M. Nassoor, and in 2A, M. Habib. *Could either be Moses?* he wondered. The name Habib looked like a recent entry, sharp ink on fresh paper. Nassoor had seen sunlight and the elements—of the two, the only one likely to have been in place two summers ago.

It wasn't much to go on.

Slaton looked up and down the quiet street. One block away loomed the silhouette of Geitawi Hospital, among the largest in the city, and he supposed many of these apartments were occupied by professionals who worked there. At this time of day, some would be occupied. Wives or husbands, nurses who worked the graveyard shift. Reaching the gate, Slaton got his best break of the day—someone had wedged a brick between the gate and its frame to keep the lock from engaging.

He passed through without hesitation, and bypassed the elevator for the staircase. As predicted, he found four doors on the top floor, the nearest marked 3B, which was M. Nassoor. The door looked relatively new but its frame appeared feeble, certain to give way to a stout kick. Was that the best approach? In a perfect world he would fall back and watch the place for a few days, perhaps identify M. Nassoor. He could log the patterns of all the residents, and choose a clean method of entry and multiple paths of egress. Unfortunately, time was not on his side. Ben-Meir had likely already come and gone, which put Slaton further behind each minute. He was studying the lock, and wishing he wore a more substantial heel than what Bruno Magli built, when he heard a voice from inside. A woman speaking Arabic, giving instructions. Then the squeal of children.

Everything felt wrong. It wasn't the feral kind of doubt that preceded imminent harm, but a sense that he'd somehow miscalculated. Could there be another 26 Geitawi Boulevard? Was he in the wrong district? What kind of armaments would anyone keep in a two-bedroom apartment full of women and children?

The door handle rattled.

Slaton bolted back to the stairs, the door of 3B creaking open just as he cleared the first landing. In the street he rushed around a man on a bicycle before disappearing into the recesses of a nearby courtyard.

*What am I missing?*

He watched the entrance and saw a woman emerge. She wore Western clothing, and seemed to be struggling with something as she backed out. Then he saw what it was. Two young children—a girl of perhaps five and a boy in a wheelchair. The boy's age was hard to gauge; he looked limp, and his limbs were malformed. His head lolled to one side, and his body rocked as the chair negotiated ruts in the sidewalk. They set out at a relaxed pace in the direction of the hospital, the girl skipping alongside while her mother dutifully pushed the chair.

Slaton wasn't sure what to make of it. He waited until they were out of sight, then moved back to the iron gate and found it still blocked open. At the foot of the stairs he hesitated, still sensing he'd gotten something wrong. Straight in front of him was the parking garage—it looked like a fortress, heavy block walls and iron bars across the openings. He moved closer and saw assigned parking spaces, including one marked 3B. And next to that . . .

A seed planted in his mind.

Each parking spot had a corresponding storage room stenciled with the apartment number. The door of the closet marked 3B looked sturdy, just like the others, yet the owner had added a secondary lock with a thick hasp of tempered steel.

Slaton scanned the garage: three cars, one scooter, one motorcycle. There was no one in sight. He went to the nearest car and found it locked. The second, an old Citroen, was a convertible whose canvas top was already torn near the rear window. Slaton reached inside, unlocked the driver's door, and seconds later had the trunk unlatched. He retrieved the lug wrench from the spare-tire well and went to the door marked 3B. He ignored the sturdy lock, which would have entailed serious work, and instead simply pried the door from its hinges. Seconds later he pulled the door clear. Slaton stared at an empty closet.

His hope faded again, only to rekindle when he took a step inside. In the three-meter-square space, the first thing he noticed was a pattern on the floor. The groomed concrete was covered with dust—like every surface in Lebanon that wasn't regularly swept— and he could see marks where something had been kept. *No, where something had been removed.*

Slaton leaned in closer and saw dozens of round outlines that might have been made by gallon-size paint cans or jugs of bleach. Or if he were a pessimist? Binary, chemical-laden artillery shells? He stood with his hands on his hips. Were these outlines a signature of what Grossman had tried to buy for five hundred thousand U.S. dollars? Could anything so valuable have been kept in a parking garage storage closet?

His eye then caught on a tiny plastic case on the

shelf in front of him. It was the size of a matchbox, almost invisible in the unlit storage closet. Slaton took the case in hand, and before he could study it he noticed a second one up higher, on a louvered vent near the ceiling. It was held in place with two strips of tape, and Slaton used the crowbar to reach up and flick it down. He searched carefully and found a third above the door frame, again secured with tape. He scanned from wall to wall but found no others.

Slaton stepped back into the garage and studied the three cases in good light. They were identical, each half the size of a credit card and formed as a thin plastic box with a cover that could be rotated open. The covers were each affixed with a tiny printed label. He snapped open the first case and found six distinct surfaces inside: each shone like unexposed film and was stamped with numbers.

All at once, Slaton realized what he was looking at.

It was a thoroughly discomforting conclusion, yet it answered the most difficult question. What could have been kept in this closet that was so valuable? What was worth the death and destruction that had tracked Slaton across a continent?

Now he knew.

He snapped the plastic case shut, and studied the label on the cover. All three devices were imprinted with the logo of Geitawi Hospital. Underneath that was a name. Indeed, a name he had seen before.

Moses.

Or more completely, Dr. Moses Nassoor.

# FORTY-FIVE

"His name is Osman Tuncay."

Sorensen was briefing Director Coltrane in a conference room at the CIA's Counterterrorism Center. All around Coltrane were the heads of working groups, including Near East, South Asia, Information Analysis, and Terrorism Analysis. Jammer Davis sat quietly in a corner.

Everyone was weary after a long night poring over satellite imagery. They'd so far found no sign of the MD-10, so Sorensen had begun tackling the problem from alternate angles. A driver's license–quality photo filled the wall-mounted screen behind her.

"He's one of the pilots from the alleged crash in Brazil," she continued. "We began with his passport, then immigration authorities pulled a good shot from closed-circuit cameras in the arrivals concourse at Brasília International. Our computers fed all of it into facial recognition software, which hit on this picture. The confidence level is very high. He's Turkish by birth. The photo you're looking at is from the employee database of an airline called Arabian Air. Tuncay flew there for eighteen years, but he was recently let go in a downsizing. His employment history with the airline checks out against his European pilot certificate, medical records, and training logs."

"So he really *is* a pilot?" Coltrane asked.

"It seems so. From there we used ONYX."

The director nodded and said, "I'm familiar with it, but others here might not be."

Sorensen explained. "ONYX is an experimental software program designed to crosshatch varied inputs—it compares our own files to police reports, news links, and intel briefs from sister services. The idea is to find quick connections amid all the raw data.

"Once Tuncay's identity was nailed down, we redirected ONYX to the other six names from our Iranian forgery mill. We uncovered images of the second pilot, but the quality was marginal and we still can't confirm his identity. We had more luck with the shooting victims I mentioned in the last briefing. The fatality in Malta was a man named Stanislaus Kieras—former GROM, Polish Special Forces. After leaving the military he took a series of private security jobs in the Middle East, then last year he fell off the grid. The victim in Zurich was Gregor Stanev, a former Bulgarian army sergeant. He also had Special Forces training, and did some recent private security work for the Afghan government."

"So we're talking about mercenaries?" Davis prompted.

"Essentially. Another from the list was confirmed as being gunned down in Wangen, Switzerland. So far, we don't have any leads on his identity."

"It seems pretty unhealthy to be a part of this little Group of Seven," Davis remarked.

"Yes. And there's one other intriguing connection." The wall behind Sorensen went to a map of Europe with three highlighted circles: Malta, Zurich, and Wangen. "These are the locations of the three shootings. We're following the investigations closely, and in each case, by either witness statements or surveillance video, there is a rough description of the shooter. We're almost certainly talking about the same man in all three events."

Coltrane's eyes narrowed. "You're saying one man has killed three of the people on your list—in three different European cities?"

"All in five days."

"Any idea who he is?"

"This began in Malta, and the man police have zeroed in on there was reasonably well-known. He'd been living there for about a year, working as a stonemason. By all accounts he lived a very quiet life until last week."

"A stonemason," the director repeated.

"That's what they say. He was actually on a job when three or four men—clearly from our Group of Seven—came after him with guns blazing."

"And he's been involved in two more shootings since then," Coltrane surmised, "but nobody can find him?"

"It's not for lack of trying. Police and security agencies all across Europe are looking for this man, and we're doing our best to help."

"Maybe we shouldn't be," interjected Davis. All eyes in the room went to him. "We're busting our butts looking for an airplane that could be used as a weapon of mass destruction. One by one, the seven people who stole it are becoming an endangered species. Seems simple enough to me."

"You think this man, whoever he is, is on our side?" Coltrane asked.

"I wouldn't go that far. But clearly there are some parallel interests. Maybe he'll finish the job for us. At the rate he's going—what, one every couple of days?—he'll be done by the end of the week."

Davis couldn't quite read Coltrane's expression, but he thought there might have been an underlying smile.

The director said, "As intriguing as all this is, none of it changes our immediate focus. How goes the search for our missing airplane?"

Sorensen said, "I'll let Jammer cover that."

Davis made his way to the head of the table. "We haven't found our jet, but I think I know why, so I've suggested some refinements to our search. We've been scouring airports big and small, and our assets are stretched thin. We should concentrate on smaller airfields in backwater countries, but watch them more closely."

"More closely?" Coltrane asked. "What good will that do us?"

"Here's my logic. This crash ruse was never going to hold for long. A few days, maybe a week at best. So whatever these people are planning, they've got a narrow window—it's going to happen soon. Once I factored that in, I realized where the ideal place is to hide a big airplane—you keep it in the sky."

"Is that possible?"

"To a point. We suspect there are two pilots, so they could alternate flying and resting. If it was me, I'd navigate to some quiet corner of the world, a place with lousy radar coverage, maybe near an ocean. Make up a holding pattern, fly at max endurance airspeed, and you could stay up ten, maybe twelve hours between fuel stops. That's the only limitation. They could land twice a day, spend thirty minutes getting refueled and maybe adding some engine oil, then go right back up in the sky where they're more or less invisible."

"How long could this go on?"

"I see only two limitations: something vital on the airplane breaks, or the pilots lose their sanity. A few days would be easy. Maybe a week. But not indefinitely."

Coltrane nodded as if the idea made sense.

"So," Davis reasoned, "the way to find them is to narrow things down. You look for long runways in out-of-the-way places, an airport that's not busy but has the infrastructure to refuel a big jet with thirty thousand gallons of kerosene."

"Kerosene?" Sorensen repeated.

"That's essentially what jet fuel is. Of course, you could go to all these places and ask questions. You could talk to fuel contractors and air traffic controllers. But that would take time. Satellites are still our best bet. Wherever we have coverage, we should take pictures of these airfields on a thirty minute cycle—with any luck, we can catch the airplane on the ground."

"That's still a lot to cover, isn't it? How many airports are we talking about?"

Sorensen responded, "My team estimates we're still talking about a thousand airstrips, and we can't cover them all on Jammer's thirty-minute cycle. But we *have* figured out a way to narrow the search further."

This was news to Davis, who'd been planted behind a computer for hours. He listened with renewed interest as Sorensen said, "We found an image of our targeted aircraft—it was captured two months ago at the airport in Santarém. This airplane has a unique appearance on satellite, a dark blue paint scheme on the upper fuselage in a pattern that's distinguishable on most imagery wavelengths. We've started filtering for the same scheme."

Coltrane was about to speak when Davis cut in with, "You didn't tell me this."

Sorensen, clearly taken aback by his accusative tone, managed, "Well . . . it's something we only came across a few hours ago. You were busy."

"So busy that you didn't bother to—" He stopped right there, knowing what he was about to say would do no good for either the investigation or his relationship with Anna Sorensen. Apart from that, a new angle began brewing in his head. Davis got up to leave.

"Where are you going?" Coltrane asked.

"I need to make a phone call."

# FORTY-SIX

In a disturbing new habit, Christine found herself fingering back slats on the blinds of her second-floor window whenever she was alone. She was under strict orders not to do so—according to Stein, the inherent risk was too great. Her inherent fear was more compelling.

She scanned the lawns and sidewalks all around, but invariably her eyes settled on Ed Moorehead's place. From her upper bedroom window Christine saw the house on a diagonal, framed perfectly between a pair of leafless maples. The light in the central upper window was always illuminated. Other lights in the house came on intermittently, but the second-floor window was constant, day and night. She'd once seen movement behind the slatted window covering, and on another occasion, for a fleeting moment, she swore she saw someone peering back at her.

"What are you doing?"

She let the slat drop, and saw Stein standing in the doorway. She felt like a teen caught smoking a cigarette in the attic.

"I think that's obvious."

"Please stay away from the windows."

She didn't reply.

Stein shifted to a more conciliatory tone. "Did something alert you?"

"What do you mean?"

"You live here—you'd probably sense something out of the ordinary before I would."

"No, everything is fine." Davy coughed twice. She'd moved his playpen to her room, and he was there now, sleeping softly under a circus-art mobile, clowns and horses drifting over his head. "I heard your phone go off a while ago," she said. "Anything I should know about?"

Stein began wandering the room. "No, just a call from a friend, nothing to do with my being here." He paused at her closet and looked inside. "I should have asked earlier, but did David keep any weapons in the house?"

She answered without hesitation. "When he moved in I asked him not to. And before you ask, I've never owned a weapon in my life. Wouldn't know what to do with one."

Davy stirred in his slumber, and Stein nodded toward the door. They headed downstairs, and in the living room she began picking up toys. "Have you seen anything of my new neighbor across the street?" she asked.

Stein stopped at the dinette and opened his laptop computer. "No, I've been keeping a close eye on the place. There's definitely somebody there, but it seems quiet."

"The light upstairs is always on."

"Is that suspicious?"

"I don't know. I guess it's the timing that bothers me. He only moved in a week ago, right before . . .

before all this started. And I've still never seen the guy."

"How do you know it's a guy?"

"My neighbor saw him."

Stein began helping with the cleanup. He tossed a plastic truck into the toy box. "You never told me that. Which neighbor?"

"Annette next door, the one who watches Davy when I'm at work."

"Did she get a good look at him?"

"I don't think so. She saw him in the garage, but it was dark."

"Too bad. With a good description we might be able to rule him out as our man."

Christine stood with a stuffed bear in her hand. "I could call and have her come over. You could ask her about it."

"No, too many complications. Our story is that you're sick, and her seeing me here would only raise questions. Like I said, I've been watching the house—whoever's inside hasn't left."

"Isn't that odd?"

"Not really. Honestly—the guy we're worried about wouldn't rent a house and watch his target for a week or two. The al-Zahari sect is far more direct."

"Is that supposed to comfort me?" she said sarcastically.

"Relax, Christine. Pretty soon this will all be over. I'll be out of your life and you can get back to what you were doing last week."

"Until it happens again?"

Stein walked over and put a hand on her shoulder, an effort to ease her tension. The moment turned awkward, and Christine sensed something wrong.

The realization came slowly, like a late-winter sunrise. Something was missing. And she knew what it was.

The other kind of tension.

Christine Palmer was no narcissist. She was also not a fool. She was a decent-looking woman—not in the bold way of a runway model, but a more simple, austere attractiveness. For better or worse—and she'd visited both camps—men found her attractive. It was a part of her life that had largely gone off-radar, suppressed by a tumultuous year in which she'd gained a child and lost a husband. There was still the occasional offer, most recently from Dr. Mike Gonzales, which implied she hadn't completely gone to pot.

Yet from Yaniv Stein there had been nothing.

Stein was unmarried, that much she'd learned. She was the widow of a comrade in arms. They were two vibrant young people at the crest of life, even if those lives had been battered by a common menace—the Israeli intelligence machine. Discounting the chance of homosexuality on his part—something she strongly doubted—Stein had shown not the slightest trace of attraction. No glimmer of an inquiry, no mildly leading question about their respective futures. Not once had she felt his eyes linger on her nightdress. He never asked if her clogged sink needed fixing. As far as Christine could remember, the steady hand now on her shoulder was the first time he had touched her. She looked at him quizzically, and when the answer came her thoughts stilled like a stopped metronome.

Christine tried to bury the idea, but it only surged back. If she were honest, an idea that had been delivering glancing blows since Stein's surprise arrival in her life. *No,* she thought, *even before that.* It had been born over the last year, conceived by an endless series of unanswered questions.

*Was it possible?*

Christine stepped back and her gaze came sharp. She saw concern in Stein's expression.

*"My God!"* she whispered.

"What is it?"

She didn't answer at first, not knowing how to say the unsayable.

*"What?"* he implored.

"He's alive, isn't he?"

Stein only stared in reply, her shock seeming to transfer to him. Which was an answer in itself.

"David is alive," she said accusingly. "He's the one who sent you here."

# FORTY-SEVEN

Slaton needed to establish exactly what had been in the storage closet. He could think of only one way.

He walked to Geitawi Hospital, and at the main entrance encountered a reception desk staffed by a pair of young women, one of whom was talking on a phone. Slaton approached the other, and said, "I'm looking for Dr. Nassoor."

The woman replied in the English he'd started, "I'm sorry? Who did you say?" Her accent was heavy, but at least he wouldn't have to suffer through Arabic.

"Dr. Nassoor," he repeated. "Can you tell me where to find him?"

"There is no doctor here by that name." When the second woman hung up the phone, she asked her, "Do you know of a Dr. Nassoor?"

A blank stare, and then, "You mean Moses?"

"Yes, that's right," Slaton said.

"I rarely hear him referred to as a doctor, but I suppose that's what he is. Do you have an appointment?"

"He's expecting me later this week, but I was forced to move up my schedule."

"Of course. Basement level, you'll find his office on the right."

"Thank you."

He took the elevator down, turned right, and when he reached the correct door Slaton saw why his question had so confused the women. The name and title were placarded in bold block lettering: MOSES NASSOOR, PHD., HEALTH PHYSICIST. Nassoor was not a medical doctor, but a physicist. Slaton noted radiation warning symbols on the thick walls, and nearby were two treatment rooms fronted by massively heavy doors. If the signs on the doors were accurate, one sheltered a linear accelerator, and the other something called a gamma knife. It was situated here, Slaton imagined, because the machines likely weighed tons, and because the building's foundation and surrounding bedrock would serve to shield stray emissions of radiation.

He was standing directly in front of Nassoor's office door when it opened abruptly. A lab coat nearly ran him down, in it a smiling midsized man with shaggy black hair and thick glasses.

"Pardon," they said at the same time, one in Arabic and one in English.

Slaton edged aside, but caught the name on the man's hospital ID badge as he passed. Slaton continued down the corridor and turned into a restroom, holding the door ajar with his shoulder once he was out of sight. He waited. Seconds later the elevator chimed, and Slaton heard the door slide open. When it rattled shut, he walked briskly to the stairs and followed Dr. Moses Nassoor.

They all watched the broom handles snap like twigs.

"You see?" said Tuncay. "I told you it wouldn't work. We must use something stronger."

"I am a chemist," replied an irritated Ghazi, "not a mechanical engineer."

They were standing in the MD-10's cargo bay, staring down into the empty holding tank. Ghazi had rigged the clamshell doors so that when they opened the gap would be restricted by three wooden dowels they'd sectioned from a broom handle. The idea was to limit the doors to less than an inch of travel instead of the full five-foot chasm they were designed to provide, thereby metering the dispersal of the solution. The broom handle modification was a complete failure.

"You should have considered this more thoroughly," Tuncay said, his annoyance bristling through.

Ghazi nearly snapped back, but then relented—he knew there was a degree of truth in the accusation. Directly behind them was the lead castle, a four-foot stack of brick shielding that would protect him when he opened the canisters. Reaching out of that was the pump and hose assembly meant to transfer the primary solution to the main tank. Ghazi had given extensive thought to safeguards, solubility, and agitators, not to mention the dispersal experiments he'd undertaken with the children. Clearly he had not given enough thought to the matter of re-rigging the doors.

It was always the simplest problems that gave the most trouble.

Ghazi circled around the three big bladders in the cargo bay, now filled to capacity with water, and at the forward entry door he descended the ordinary painter's ladder that took the place of boarding stairs. Tuncay followed him down, and together they padded across the chipped concrete ramp to view the problem from underneath. As they walked toward

the airplane's midsection, both men eyed their surroundings cautiously. They had landed just before
sunrise, and Tuncay parked the jet where the other old
relic had been only hours before. *Exactly* where it had
been, in fact, its tires within inches of the same place-
ment, and the jet's nose pointed to within one degree
of the correct compass orientation—Ben-Meir had
taken pictures of the old Tri-Star when he'd come to
arrange its demolition, and even gone as far as to paint
reference marks on the tarmac. It seemed a mad idea,
to cut up and remove an old hulk in the middle of the
night and park CB68H in its place, yet they had gone
about it meticulously.

So far it seemed to be working.

"I don't like it here," Tuncay said. "It feels too open.
I climbed up on the wing at first light and saw a road
in the distance. Anyone traveling it can see us as well."

"We need only one day," said Ghazi, although not
with conviction. "Ben-Meir is certain we will be safe
until nightfall."

"Ben-Meir . . . and where *is* our illustrious field
commander?"

"I haven't seen him in an hour. He and Walid took
up positions in the hills, watching for anyone who
shows too much curiosity."

"Ben-Meir—he might scare someone away. But
Walid?"

"They have weapons," Ghazi said. He looked
squarely at the pilot, and for a moment the two seemed
to share something. Of all those involved, the Turk
was the one he felt most in line with, a thoughtful man
with a practical nature. Ghazi let loose a long breath.
"What have we gotten into, my friend? Three have
died, yet here we are still."

Tuncay only shrugged. "The job is nearly done. A

few more hours, and we can go our respective ways. Live quietly and in peace."

Ghazi tried to catch Tuncay's eyes, to see if he truly believed it, but the pilot's gaze was riveted to the ground.

Tuncay bent down and picked up a piece of sheet metal the size of a shoe. "You see this? Foreign objects—they are everywhere on this tarmac. Our number-five main tire is nearly flat, punctured by a bolt we must have rolled over in the dark."

"What do you expect? Last night an entire airplane, as big as this one, was demolished on this very spot." Ghazi moved directly under the belly doors. "Is the tire a problem?"

Tuncay tossed the metal scrap far into the brush. "No, I don't think so. One tire out of ten shouldn't matter—not unless it disintegrates during takeoff and damages the others. Then again, how would I know? It's not something I've dealt with before. In the past, if I had a flat tire I called a mechanic and had it fixed."

Both men craned their necks upward and studied the doors. With his hands on his hips, Ghazi said, "We need something stronger, with greater tensile strength." He scanned all around, but saw nothing useful. Low hills surrounded the old abandoned airfield, and the few buildings that had once existed were little more than foundations. There was probably not a hardware store within fifty miles. His gaze settled on the truck Ben-Meir had arrived in. It was a jeep of some sort, a bastardized stretch model whose second row of seats had been ripped out to allow a larger carrying bed—that was where the canisters were now, secured under a tarp. The jeep was rigged for off-road travel, a heavy-duty jack and jerry can strapped to the tailgate. Ghazi's bespectacled gaze honed in on the front bumper where a sturdy winch was mounted.

"Do we have a drill?" he asked.

"Yes, I think so," the captain replied.

"Go get it."

"It's true," Stein admitted, "David is alive."

Christine eased unsteadily onto the couch and stared at the distant wall. For how long had she cried and grieved, been consoled by others for her terrible, untimely loss? David had been legally declared dead, albeit under the false identity of Edmund Deadmarsh. *And how perfect was that?* Yet his body had never been found, and there was little hard evidence of what happened to him on that fateful night on a bridge in Geneva. The official report declared that he'd been shot multiple times—as evidenced by three witnesses, one of whom was a police officer—before his body went over a rail and into the Rhone River.

But there it had ended.

David was dead because the caretakers of Mossad proclaimed it so. They might have believed it. Or maybe they only wanted to.

But in the depths of her soul, Christine Palmer had never been convinced. She hadn't mourned unnecessarily on their anniversary, hadn't fallen to tears on the day she found the birthday card David had bought her but never delivered. And of course, the closet still waited to be cleaned out. Annette routinely chastised her for not letting go. *You need to see other people, dear. You need to get on with your life.* Christine had brushed it off every time.

Somehow she'd known.

"Where is he?" she asked.

"I don't know."

"Can you call him?"

"No, he only has my number. It's not safe for him to carry a phone right now."

An odd thing, she mused, not to have a phone in this day and age. Odd for anyone else. "Tell me, Yaniv . . . why did he send you?"

"That much is legitimate. He thinks you need protection."

"Why didn't he come himself?"

His hesitation was too long, and in the end he only shrugged to say he didn't know.

One last question. "Is David ever coming back?"

Stein didn't know that either.

# FORTY-EIGHT

Nassoor weaved through a maze of corridors. Slaton followed at a distance, trying to look purposeful.

Hospitals were a tricky setting for tradecraft. There were mirrors mounted on every corner and hallways with double doors, not to mention numerous corridors labeled NO ADMITTANCE that created barriers. And the greatest challenge of all—hospitals were rife with thick-skinned nurses accustomed to challenging anyone who invaded their turf.

Fortunately, Moses Nassoor's trail turned out to be a short one. He ended up outside in a large courtyard where picnic tables were set in the shade of mature cedars. A children's playground was situated at the far end of the yard, and there Slaton saw Nassoor's reason for coming—the family he'd seen leaving 26 Geitawi Boulevard. Nassoor waved as he approached them all. The girl, certainly his daughter, was pumping on a swing, his wife behind her giving the occasional push. He greeted them both, a cheek-kiss for his wife, and a swat to his daughter's leg as she flew past that generated a squeal of glee. Nassoor then went to the nearby wheelchair and kissed his son.

There were a half-dozen wooden tables, most

occupied by hospital staff who sat smoking cigarettes and drinking tea from small cups. Slaton took a seat at a free table, because to stand would have looked odd, and he watched Nassoor interact with his family while contemplating how best to approach the physicist. For the first time in memory, he came up with nothing.

He watched Nassoor lift the boy from the wheelchair and carry him to a large glider swing, the kind often seen on hospital playgrounds, even those in Lebanon. Nassoor sat with the boy in his lap and pushed rhythmically with his feet. The swing gathered momentum, rising and falling, and from thirty yards away Slaton heard the boy's throaty laugh. He was eight years old, perhaps ten—it was hard to say given his crimped limbs, and a spine that was bent and likely years underdeveloped. But there was nothing underdeveloped in the infectious laugh that echoed across the courtyard. It made everyone smile, the tea drinkers at the other tables, the whole Nassoor family.

Slaton felt a peculiar discomfort as he watched the pastoral scene, and it took some time to realize what it was. Envy. *What must it be like for a father to hold his son?*

He looked down at his hands and saw them shaking ever so slightly. Hands once reputed to be the steadiest in all Israel. He flexed his fists and shut his eyes. He ignored Nassoor and his family, ignored his entire tactical situation. It was a loss of focus like none he'd ever suffered. *But why?*

Then, behind tightly closed eyes, a disconcerting picture came to mind—Christine and their son on a playground, and in the distance, sitting at a picnic table, an assassin in wait. The image was drawn in his likeness.

Was that what he had become? Had he fallen so far as to hunt down loving husbands and fathers? He knew the unspeakable answer. Slaton had killed many men, and on balance they were a deserving bunch. Yet even the most hardened terrorists had lives and loves. It was a necessary act of moral theater—and one in which he regularly took comfort—to imagine every target as evil incarnate. Today, however, watching a man with positive qualities so nakedly on display, it was quite impossible. Nassoor had likely done something terrible, but here he was cradling his crippled son. Doing his damnedest to make a needy child happy.

And if Slaton injected himself into their lives at this moment? That was a scenario with only one foreseeable outcome.

He turned on the bench, putting his back to the Nassoors.

His missions for Mossad had been many, an almost formulaic process. The planning invariably opened with incriminating photos, which meant his first impression of every target began the process of demonization. A shadowed figure planting explosives or running from the scene of a shooting. A fingerprint lifted and matched from a tiny piece of shrapnel. If Slaton's involvement became necessary, it meant a trial of sorts had already been run, albeit without a table for the defense. Intelligence analysts acted as prosecutors, their evidence documented and presented in vivid color—red predominating. Spymaster judges delivered verdicts and passed sentences. Slaton? His part was simplest of all, that of an executioner who didn't need a black mask because he existed in a black world.

Now, sitting on a bench in Geitawi, Lebanon, Slaton

332 | WARD LARSEN

found a new appreciation for that approach. For years he had conducted his assignments without reservation, keeping faith that a process of justice—such as it was—had already been run.

*But now?*

He looked over his shoulder at the playground. Could he pass judgment on this man? Certainly Nassoor had done wrong. Certainly he had committed crimes. But the motives behind what he'd done were nowhere to be seen. Was the man a fanatic, bent on killing and maiming innocents in the name of Allah? Or was there reason and intelligence behind what he'd done? Could Slaton put this man at mortal risk in order to keep his own family safe?

The answer came immediately and could not have been more clear.

Slaton stood and walked away without so much as a glance over his shoulder.

He was back at the main building, reaching for the door, when someone called from behind.

"Excuse me!"

Slaton froze. He turned.

"What is it that you want?" asked Dr. Moses Nassoor.


Colonel Roberto Cruz was sound asleep at home when his mobile phone rang. He looked at the bedside clock: 10:22 in the morning. He'd been up most of the night preparing an afternoon briefing on his stalled investigation for the Brazilian transport minister. His phone's screen did not identify the caller, other than to tell him it was an international call.

He sighed a commander's sigh. Being in charge of

the inquiry, he had no choice but to answer. It could be news regarding vital evidence—of which so far there had been precious little. He picked up and said, "Colonel Cruz."

"What color was the airplane?"

Cruz blinked. He recognized the voice instantly—or perhaps it was the manner. "Is this—" Still in the grip of a sleep-induced fog, the American's name escaped him.

"Jammer Davis. What color was the airplane when it took off?"

"Color? You mean—"

"I mean last week the airplane was blue and gray. I'm sure you've interviewed witnesses by now, and somebody must have seen the jet take off. What color was it then?"

Cruz was suddenly wide awake: he wondered how the American had found out about this. "Well, yes . . . we did come across something in our interviews. The aircraft was originally, as you say, blue and gray. Last night a witness told us the aircraft was painted not long before it took off, and we confirmed this with a second reliable source. The top half of the fuselage was changed."

"Changed to what?"

"It was not white, not gray, they both agreed— something in between. One of the pilots said it was a primer coat that would be covered by a livery once a long-term lease was arranged. How did you know about this?"

"Respirator," said Davis.

"What?"

"The painter's mask in your little collection of wreckage."

Cruz only now made the connection.

"All right," said the brusque voice from overseas, "here's what I need you to do. First—"

"What I need to do is run my investigation!" Cruz barked. "I don't need rude Americans giving me orders in the middle of the night!" He heard his wife stir in the next room.

After a lengthy pause, Davis continued, "You haven't found any wreckage, have you?" His inflection made it more an accusation than a question. "You don't have any new witnesses. All you have is the same little collection of junk I saw two days ago." Another pause. "Colonel, help me with this and I'll have all your questions answered within twenty-four hours."

Cruz dropped his head on his pillow and heaved a sigh. "Tell me what you want."

The slightly built physicist looked at Slaton through heavy round spectacles, his eyes darting left and right. "What do you want?"

"Why do you think I want something?" Slaton replied.

"You followed me here from my office."

Slaton could have argued otherwise, or manufactured a swift and convincing lie. He let it go. "I shouldn't bother you," he said. "Not when you're with your family."

Nassoor's posture straightened, bucking up—the way any man did when flight was not an option. Just then, a group of three nurses vacated the nearest picnic table. It was the physicist who gestured toward it and nodded. Slaton glanced at Nassoor's family—they seemed oblivious.

At the table they took opposing seats.

"Who are you?" Nassoor asked.

Slaton's response was quick, and loosely based on the truth. "I'm Benjamin Grossman's representative."

Nassoor's steady demeanor disintegrated. "I have given you what you wanted!" he said in a harsh whisper. "Can't you leave me alone?" His English was almost without accent, and Slaton imagined he had studied abroad.

"I think you've made a mistake, Doctor."

"How so?"

Feeling he was on the right track, Slaton gambled with, "It has to do with the other man who came to see you—when was it, yesterday?"

The Lebanese nodded.

"That man never met Benjamin Grossman in his life."

Nassoor's face went ashen. "But if you are with Grossman and the other man was not . . ."

"Then you just sold something very dangerous to a complete stranger." Having already made a number of correct assumptions, Slaton took the final leap. "And when I say dangerous, let's be up-front. We are talking about nuclear material. A potential weapon of mass destruction."

A speechless Nassoor cast a glance at his family.

Slaton wished he had done this differently, but his hand was now forced. "You've dug a very, very deep hole for yourself, Moses. I should tell you that I represent a certain government to the south, one that Monsieur Grossman worked with closely." For a Lebanese, *south* had but one meaning. Nassoor did not appear surprised. "I think," Slaton said, "that both of us would benefit if you began by telling me everything you know."

Nassoor looked at him thoughtfully, yet Slaton couldn't read what he was thinking. It wasn't because he was dealing with a man trained in deception. Quite the opposite. He was dealing with an amateur, a man whose linear world had gone dreadfully askew.

For reasons Slaton would not understand until later, Nassoor relented. "It began two summers ago . . ."

# FORTY-NINE

Moses Nassoor found himself in very deep and dark water. To his credit, he recognized his dilemma and did not hold back.

"It began nearly two years ago. I had traveled to a clinic in Aadra in order to repair their X-ray machine. I am one of but two medical physicists in all of Lebanon. Our facilities here are not advanced, at least not by Western standards, yet the need is great. During my visit to the clinic I had a discussion with the doctor who ran the facility. He told me they were facing a strange epidemic, one that he could not place. Dozens of patients had arrived with gastrointestinal issues, ocular bleeding, kidney failure. The doctor was trained in infectious diseases, so that was naturally where his thoughts went. I immediately recognized these symptoms as radiation sickness."

"Did you tell him this?"

Nassoor paused. "I couldn't be certain, not without testing, so I asked him to let me see one of the more severely ill patients. He agreed, but didn't have the time to accompany me—he was a very busy man. The patient was a woman, perhaps fifty years old. At her bedside I used a scintillation counter to scan a burn on her arm. The results were conclusive for gamma radiation. A very high level."

Nassoor watched his family as he spoke. His wife glanced at him, but she didn't seem concerned, clearly thinking her husband was addressing hospital business.

The physicist pulled out a pack of Marlboros, more out of anxiety, Slaton guessed, than anything else. He bumped one out and offered it, but Slaton politely declined. After lighting up and taking a shaky draw, he said, "I should have told the doctor then that I knew what the problem was. But I was curious. I wanted to know where the contamination had come from. I asked a nurse for more information, and quickly learned that all the patients had come from the same neighborhood, and that many knew each other. I drove there and began asking questions. It didn't take long to discover what had happened. Some boys scavenging metal had come across a cache of cesium-137 chloride encased in canisters."

"Where would this have come from?"

"I can't say exactly, but it was probably manufactured in Russia—they run the largest production facility for cesium-137. It is a widely used isotope. Cancer treatment, food irradiation. The oil and construction industries use it in underground measurements. It's a high-energy gamma emitter with a relatively long half-life of thirty years. Due to the large quantity involved, I'd guess this particular shipment was meant for food irradiation—before the war it was common practice in Syria. Then came the uprising. Whoever controlled this tranche of source material clearly lost track of it, or perhaps it was diverted when the owner tried to transfer it to a safe haven. Whatever the case, the shipment ended up in the hands of people who had no idea what they were dealing with. I found it outside a work shed in Al Qutayfah—fifty-five canisters of cesium-137 chloride stacked like cordwood."

"Where exactly?"

"You mean the address?"

"Yes."

Nassoor's face crinkled as he racked his memory. "It was a dirt path off Route Five, south of town. I don't remember the street name or number—I'm not even sure there was one. It was the second house east of a railway track."

"All right. What else?"

"The material released on site did considerable damage, but that was only a fraction of a single container. I estimated the onsite contamination in Al Qutayfah to be roughly fifty terabecquerels—that's a measure of radiation."

"I'm no expert," Slaton said. "How much is that?"

Nassoor took another long draw on his Marlboro. "You recall the nuclear reactor explosion at Chernobyl?"

"Of course."

"Cesium-137 was the principal source of contamination in the aftermath. Eighty-five thousand terabecquerels were released. In Al Qutayfah, I estimated that roughly five thousand grams of cesium remained encased in the fifty-five canisters—that would equate to roughly sixteen thousand TBq."

"That's still a lot."

"It's a nightmare. Two decades after Chernobyl, cesium-137 still renders more than fifteen hundred square miles either uninhabitable or unfit for agriculture. Cesium chloride is unique in the threat it presents. It is a salt, and therefore easily soluble in water. In an explosion, as happened in Chernobyl, it can be aerosolized and carried on the wind. Once on the ground, it has a particular affinity for seeping into clay substrate."

"And so," Slaton surmised, "if someone wanted to use this as a terror weapon?"

"It would be devastating. Once introduced into the environment, cesium is very difficult to recapture. During a much smaller release in Goiânia, Brazil, hospitals were overwhelmed by over one hundred thousand panicked people when word of the contamination was made public. In wide areas topsoil had to be scraped away, and countless buildings and homes were demolished. It took years to clean up."

"What did you do when you realized what you'd found?" Slaton asked.

Nassoor hesitated mightily, his nerves crossbow tight. "Some would say I should have told the authorities. But you have to remember, during that time, in Syria—God only knows where this material would have ended up. I also had other considerations. Earlier that year a man had come to my home. He said he had a business opportunity for me. At the time my position at the hospital was in risk of being cut, so I listened."

"Was it Grossman?" Slaton asked.

Nassoor nodded. "Yes. He talked about the conflict in Syria, and the spill-over into Lebanon. He said there were a great many complications, and since I was one of the few specialists in the country who dealt with nuclear materials, there was a chance I would be approached at some point to give advice. People might come across things, have crazy ideas about what to do with them. Grossman said he had the backing of a country, a major power that wanted very much to recover any such materials. I assumed it was either the United States or Israel, but it made no difference to me. No scientist can function here without remaining apolitical. He made a convincing argument—if I came across any dangerous radiological material, it could be made safe, and in the course of this I would earn a significant 'finder's fee.' Those were the words he used."

To Slaton it all made perfect sense. "So the cache of material from Al Qutayfah?"

"It was sitting outside, completely unguarded. As long as the source material remained in canisters it was secure, and the release had so far been manageable. But sixteen thousand terabecquerels . . . something had to be done. The owner of the property and his wife were both dead, so I talked to their relatives. I said there was a small chance that chemicals in the canisters could be responsible for making everyone sick. I was careful to avoid any definite link, and never mentioned that nuclear material was involved. They begged me to take it away. So I did. I borrowed a truck from a friend and put the material in storage."

"In your parking garage?"

Nassoor stared harshly, and Slaton recognized his mistake.

"Yes," Slaton said, "I saw where you kept it. But what happened then? Why did Grossman not take it as planned?"

The Lebanese seemed on firmer footing, his voice increasingly charged with truth. "He sent an initial payment, ten percent."

This meshed with what Slaton had seen in the accounts—fifty thousand dollars paid on a commitment of five hundred thousand. A hefty amount for a midlevel man on a civil servant's salary. "But the rest never came," he surmised.

"No," said Nassoor. "I kept trying to contact Monsieur Grossman, through the autumn of that year, but he never responded."

"Because he died during the summer."

Nassoor now wore the look of surprise.

"It was cancer, all very sudden," Slaton explained.

The Lebanese seemed suddenly unnerved. "What kind of cancer?" he asked.

"I don't think the primary site was ever identified. I only know it advanced very rapidly, nothing to be done."

The physicist put his hands over his face.

"What?" Slaton asked.

"It was my fault."

"What—the cancer? How could you be responsible for—"

"It wasn't cancer . . . I sent him a sample."

"A sample?"

"Grossman was a cautious businessman. He sent the ten percent, but insisted that further payments were conditional on getting a sample of what he was securing."

"You're telling me you sent him radioactive cesium . . . through the mail?"

Nassoor nodded. "A very small amount, by overnight express. There was a chance it could have been discovered, but I am quite familiar with how our screening systems work here in Lebanon—in fact, I created them. The safeguards are rudimentary at best. There was no way to properly shield the material for transport. It would have weighed far too much and generated suspicion. I simply placed a sample of the powder in a tiny lead source container—we use them occasionally at the hospital—then inserted the container into one of the chocolates in a gift box. I sent Grossman an e-mail in advance explaining how to handle the package."

The two men stared at one another, both seeing what had happened. Grossman had gotten a box of chocolates, one containing radioactive cesium chloride, but the warning e-mail had gone lost in cyberspace. In his years of intelligence work Slaton had seen a good share of fiascos, but this broke new ground.

Nassoor ended the silence. "The symptoms and organs that would be affected, a rapid systemic deterioration—it could easily have been mistaken for advanced-stage cancer of some unknown origin."

"Or perhaps Grossman realized what had happened, knew his fate was sealed, and told everyone it was cancer for the sake of convenience."

Nassoor nodded. "Tell me—Grossman worked for Israel, did he not?" When Slaton didn't answer right away, Nassoor said, "As I told you earlier, I am not a political man. Israel keeps material like this in almost every hospital, and for a country with a hundred nuclear weapons . . . I know they could have no other intention than safekeeping."

"Only now it's not safe," Slaton argued. "But yes, Grossman was working with Israel. Tell me what happened when you realized your deal with him had fallen through."

Nassoor heaved a sigh. "What could I do? The material sat in my storage room like . . . like some kind of unexploded bomb. I contemplated getting rid of it, perhaps dropping it in the sea or burying it in the desert, but the risks seemed too high. Imagine being caught moving such a cache—I would be tortured and killed, probably my family as well. So I left it where it was, hoping for some escape. Then, two months ago, I received a phone call from a man who said he was aligned with Grossman. He told me he would come soon to collect the canisters and pay the balance of what I was owed."

"Two months ago, you say?"

"Roughly, yes. He said he would call again to arrange payment in cash. He also asked where I kept the material."

"And you told him?"

"No," Nassoor said, "of course not. I was frightened, but I also wanted to finish this whole affair. I took my family away and arranged for an absence from work. We stayed with family and friends."

"That was a good move."

"Was it?" Nassoor heaved a sigh. "Another call came a few days ago. They were ready to make the exchange. I was to personally hand over the cesium in exchange for the money. Only I couldn't do it . . . not like that. I simply told them where it was and said to leave the money in the closet. When I went home yesterday—"

"The storage closet had been emptied," Slaton finished.

Nassoor nodded. "There was no money, of course. But I was so relieved that the canisters were gone—I didn't even care."

Slaton remembered the transfer of four hundred and fifty thousand dollars to a Beirut bank. Money that was likely now in Ben-Meir's pocket. "You never saw who took the cannisters?"

"No, we only spoke by phone." Nassoor crushed the remains of his cigarette into the dirt with a toe. "What do you think will happen?"

"To the material? I think it will be weaponized.

You've already said it can be dispersed as an aerosol in an explosion."

"Yes, it would be frightfully easy. Or as I said, cesium chloride is a highly soluble salt. It could be used to contaminate a water supply, or . . . or God knows what."

Nassoor was visibly shaken, realizing his complicity in some impending catastrophe. One that could cost hundreds, even thousands of lives. "I was so relieved when I saw the empty closet," he said reflectively. "It was as if a great burden had been lifted. I brought my family home only this morning thinking the nightmare was over. Then I realized you were following me. I didn't know if you were here to give me four hundred and fifty thousand dollars, to arrest me, or . . . or worse. That is how it will always be. Tomorrow, the next day. Some of life's missteps follow a man to the grave."

Slaton said nothing.

With a half turn, Nassoor looked endearingly at his family. "My son, Ameer, he is a good boy. But he has many troubles. Very expensive troubles. In the West there is help for such things. But here . . ." He looked back at Slaton. "Would you have done differently?"

Slaton thought about this for some time. "I honestly don't know," he said. "I've never faced a choice like that."

"What will you do with what I've told you?" Nassoor asked with the weight of a confession.

Slaton was unable to give absolution. "I'm going to do whatever it takes to find that material. And the people who took it."

"Then I should tell you one more thing. Last night I spoke to one of my neighbors—she is a widow, a busybody who sees herself as the concierge of our building. She saw a black truck leave the garage yesterday—something rugged, for desert travel. Because it was not a resident's vehicle—she knows them all by heart—she tried to see who was driving. It was a man. Not young, not old. He had a trimmed beard and wore glasses."

Slaton nodded, quietly satisfied that he had tracked Ben-Meir so accurately. "Anything else? A license plate number? Writing on the truck?"

"Only one other thing," Nassoor said. "She said the truck turned north, onto Armenia Boulevard. The driver would only do that if he was heading north, away from the city."

"That's helpful," Slaton said, wishing for more.

"Do you think there is any chance the money will come?"

"I think you know the answer."

Nassoor nodded, and after a long hesitation he asked, "What will become of us?" The inclusion of his family in the question lent it a tragic quality.

Slaton remained silent. He stood to leave, but then paused and looked solemnly at the slight physicist. "I don't know, Moses. Really I don't. But I wish you the best of luck."

# FIFTY

The winch cable was a thing of beauty. Ghazi had cut two ten-foot sections, then interlaced the braided-steel cable through a series of holes that Tuncay had drilled along the rim of each door. In the end it looked akin to a pair of industrial-grade shoelaces drawing the bomb bay-like doors together. After adjusting the tension twice to manipulate the gap, everything looked ready.

"All right," Ghazi shouted. "Now!"

With a loud *clunk,* the uplocks released, and he watched the big doors droop ever so slightly. He quickly moved in and measured the gap at three intervals. "Yes, that is perfect. Less than two centimeters."

Tuncay came down from the flight deck, and Ben-Meir was already there—the ever-surly Israeli had left his guard station in the hillside scrub for an early afternoon progress report. In the closed position the doors kept a tight seal, important for keeping leakage to a minimum, and when the release mechanism was activated they parted less than half an inch. Ghazi wondered if this would vary in flight under low pressure generated by the passing slipstream. Or would dynamic pressure perhaps push the doors upward? Without flight testing, there was no way to tell. There was also the question of how everything would perform under a load. He desperately wanted to fill the tank once with water for a wet test, but, according to Ben-Meir, the nearest spigot was four miles away.

"Very impressive," said Tuncay.

"Yes, a wonder of modern engineering," added Ben-Meir sarcastically. "But why are the agitators still not in place?"

"The agitators are next," Ghazi replied.

"How long will it take to pump the water into the tank?"

"I estimate two hours. Then another hour to put the cesium into solution. That must be left until the very end, and once the process is complete no one can go near the drop tank."

Even the ever-stoic Ben-Meir appeared unnerved, and Ghazi smiled inwardly. There were two kinds of people—the relative few who understood and respected radiation, and the majority who feared it irrationally. But then, that was what they were all counting on.

"Do you have protective gear?" Ben-Meir asked.

"Of course," Ghazi replied, "and I have partially opened one of the canisters to validate my procedure."

"What about you?" Tuncay asked Ben-Meir. "Have you spotted any threats?"

"Two boys and a goat walking to a nearby well," he replied. "When they saw me coming with a gun they ran for the hills."

*Smart boys,* Ghazi thought. He said, "Everything will be ready by midnight."

"Good," said Ben-Meir. "Eight more hours—then you and I will have done our part. I'll have you at a club in Beirut before sunrise, with whiskey pouring down your throat like a river."

"You can have your whiskey," Ghazi replied, irritated as ever by Ben-Meir's goading. "Tomorrow morning I will be far from here. When the world becomes aware of our work, I want to be on the opposite side."

"Don't worry," said Ben-Meir, "we've made sure the blame will fall elsewhere." He strode away purposefully, ready to resume his watch over the hills.

Ghazi pulled one of the tank agitators from its crate—it looked like an anemic outboard motor with a flat-bladed propeller on one end. He sighed, and said to Tuncay, "When this began, I truly believed we could escape any consequences. None of us would have gotten involved otherwise. But now . . . I am not so sure."

"Why?" asked a cautious Tuncay.

"You heard Ben-Meir this morning. Three of his men are dead. One in Malta and two in Switzerland. This assassin he talks about . . . this *kidon* . . . he is formidable."

"I'm not so sure," Tuncay replied.

"Why?"

Tuncay cocked his head in a circumspect way. "We only have Ben-Meir's word. Does it not strike you as convenient that the only member of our tactical team to survive is the token Israeli?"

Ghazi set aside the agitator. "You think he is colluding with the *kidon*?"

Tuncay looked cautiously to where Ben-Meir had disappeared into the scrub. "You are good at math. The smaller the divisor, the greater the profit for those who remain. I say the assassin has had help. Never forget—they are both Jews. You and I talked about this once, the first time we met. We wondered if there could be more than seven in the group."

"You think he is the eighth? This *kidon*?"

The pilot shrugged. "Who can say? But on that first meeting I heard Ben-Meir take a phone call. He was outside on a balcony, thinking he was alone."

"What was said?"

"That is my point—I don't know because he was speaking Hebrew."

"*Hebrew?* You are sure?"

"I know enough to recognize it."

"He might have been talking to family, his banker, even a mistress."

"All I will say is this, my friend. When you drive south with Ben-Meir toward Beirut tonight, make sure you do not fall asleep. You might wake to find yourself in Tel Aviv—if you wake at all."

Ghazi shook his head. "No, you are wrong. If I know anything, it is that Israel has no part in this."

"How can you be sure?"

"Because the equipment you see here—the lead, the agitators, the special pumps—it all came from Iran."

A stunned Tuncay looked questioningly at the chemist.

"I was there," Ghazi said. "Nighttime deliveries in the marshes outside Basrah. I can't say exactly who is involved, but this equipment definitely came from Iran."

Neither man said anything for a time, and Ghazi went back to unpacking the machinery. In the silence his thoughts swirled. An Iraqi chemist, pilots from Turkey and Syria, an Israeli who hires thugs from eastern Europe—he didn't even know their nationality, may God have mercy on their souls. It was as disparate a group as could be imagined, which was probably why they'd so far gone undetected by Western intelligence agencies. But Iran? It had been in the back of his mind, ever since his first visit to the marshes of Haziweh. Could there be such a silent partner, one known only to Ben-Meir? He said in a half-whisper, "I don't know who has dreamed up this madness. All I can tell you is that it will end soon."

"Yes," Tuncay agreed, casting a wary eye toward the fifty-two canisters stacked nearby. "A few more hours. What could go wrong?"

Davis found Sorensen alone in a small conference room near the Operations Center. The look he got upon entering was not an endearing one.

"Look," he began, "I'm sorry."

"You made me look like a fool in front of the director! Coltrane thinks—"

"Stop right there, Anna! He's impressed with your work, but you sidestepped me. I can't help you if I don't know what's going on."

After the two exchanged a long stare, it was Sorensen who relented. "All right, we don't have time for this. I should have kept you up to speed."

"Yeah, well . . . I screwed up too."

"How?"

He told her about the respirator he'd seen in the wreckage. "I should have looked into it. I just talked again to the guy running the show in Brazil. They found empty paint buckets in a pile of trash, and a number of airport workers saw the jet getting repainted. It's no longer dark blue on top. It's an off-white now, like half the airplanes in the world— apparently light colored jets save money because they require less cooling on the ground. This is definitely going to make our search harder."

"But at least we'll be looking for the right color airplane."

"Assuming they haven't painted it again."

She frowned, but refrained from calling him a pessimist. "All right, I'll order the changes to our search parameters."

"You can forget about the registration number too."

"Registration number?"

"It used to be CB68H, but there was a small bucket of black paint in the same trash pile. I'm guessing they altered the tail number. It could be anything now."

# FIFTY-ONE

Slaton departed Geitawi Hospital and walked west-ward at a brisk pace, sweat gripping the back of his shirt. As he strode past mosques and churches, town-homes and tenements, Dr. Moses Nassoor dominated his thoughts. Physicist? Father? Terrorist? Perhaps a bit of all three. He was not a patently evil man, nor a virtuous one. Nassoor was part of the other 98 per-cent, the greater herd whose lives were so casually shredded by the Hezbollahs and Mossads of the world.

Slaton covered two miles before reaching an estab-lishment that would provide everything he needed. He walked into the Beirut Four Seasons Hotel, a predict-ably lavish property fronting the city's main yacht ba-sin. At the lobby entrance he paused at a pedestal and scanned the schedule of events taking place in the interior conference rooms: a meeting of Lebanese school headmasters, a free lunch-and-lecture sales pitch on how to invest in real estate in Lebanon, and, in perhaps the most damning compass of where the country was headed, a conference for representatives of Morgan Stanley Smith Barney, Wealth Management—Middle East Division. Slaton pressed ahead to search for an opening.

He found her sitting near Ballroom One: unnaturally blond hair and legs crossed stylishly, a shoe dangling off one heel. Her name tag said VANESSA. She was gatekeeping behind a table with the Morgan Stanley logo, arrayed on which were stacks of brochures, complimentary pens, and a small tablet computer. Above all that—an uncommonly engaging smile. Vanessa was thirty, well-coiffed, and impeccably dressed, trying hard to look attractive and for the most part succeeding.

If there was a discontinuity in Slaton's approach, it was that he wasn't wearing a business suit. Outside mission requirements, he rarely reflected upon matters of grooming or style. Christine had occasionally fought the good fight, suggesting he try a coordinated tie or a splash of cologne, and perhaps there was a part of him that wondered *what if?* If so, it was a very small part, and one he easily ignored. James Bond could have his tuxedos. Bona fide assassins were nothing if not pragmatic, dressing in every situation for utility. When their appearance became incompatible with an op, they fell back on their second most reliable attribute. They lied convincingly.

He said in French, "I hope you can rescue me."

"Certainly, monsieur," replied Vanessa through chemically whitened teeth. "What is the problem?"

"I've just arrived for the meeting. My flight was terribly late and the imbeciles have lost my luggage. I have no registration information—it was all on my computer. And to make the day complete, my mobile has gone dead."

The woman smiled sympathetically, and began referencing a printout of names in front of her, one that Slaton was already reading inverted—a silly parlor trick that came in surprisingly useful.

"The name is Winterbourne," he said.

"Of course." She placed a check next to the name. "You were actually scheduled to attend tomorrow's presentation."

"Was I? My assistant arranged everything. I'm lost without my phone."

"Aren't we all? There is space available if you'd rather attend today's seminar. The topic is most useful." She held up a brochure titled, *Loss Harvesting as a Tax Strategy*.

Slaton demurred, even if he was quietly struck by the chutzpah of a sales pitch promoting the tax advantages of losing money. "I'll wait for my scheduled session," he said.

The woman nodded deferentially, which, along with the three printed asterisks next to Winterbourne's name, suggested he'd chosen an associate whose clients held substantial portfolios. She handed over the usual canvas welcome bag and an identity lanyard in the name of Thomas Winterbourne. He looked inside the bag and saw pamphlets and prospectuses, along with a handful of notepads and pens emblazoned with the company logo. He smiled like the true Winterbourne would when he arrived tomorrow to instigate a brief period of confusion—no concern to Slaton, who would be long gone.

"Thank you," he said. He began to turn, but then stalled as if finding an afterthought. "Actually, there is one more thing you could help me with. I should check my e-mail from the office. One of my assistants has been organizing a very large account."

The woman named Vanessa smiled, and turned a small tablet computer to face him. "We're all on the same team, aren't we?"

"More than you could imagine."

She was conveniently distracted by a phone call, and in a pageantry of discretion Slaton pulled the tablet toward the end of the table. Within a minute he was looking at the online message board he had years earlier shared with Stein. It remained active, and he saw one new message: *Quiet here except C has figured it out. She knows you are still out there.*

As he stood leaning over the keyboard, the seminar broke, and the double doors behind him were breached by a flood of chattering, phone-checking Morgan Stanley reps who overwhelmed the atrium. Slaton tuned it all out. *Of course she figured it out.* Not only was Christine smart, but she knew him better than anyone. He inserted this new variable into his near-term planning, and decided it changed little. He had tracked Ben-Meir, the last identified threat, to Lebanon, so in the coming hours his wife and son were as safe as he could make them. But further ahead? A week or a month from now? He simply couldn't address that question—not until he finished what he'd come to do.

Ben-Meir was half a day in front of him. Unfortunately, Slaton had no idea where he was heading. North was the only tenuous clue, this based on the observations of one marginal witness. But it made sense. Slaton's fingers hovered over the keypad as he considered checking his financial accounts. He decided against it, concerned that merely accessing the accounts might highlight his position to Ben-Meir and his associates, or even police investigators in one of the countries where he'd recently left a body.

Vanessa ended her call. It was time to move.

Before returning the computer to its owner, Slaton cleared the record of his work, then momentarily accessed a common Web-based e-mail platform, followed by a stop at Morgan Stanley's public website.

It was an elementary cleanup that could easily be defeated, but if Vanessa ventured a casual look she would see nothing surprising.

"Thank you for your help," he said, placing the tablet back in front of her.

Vanessa smiled in a way that might or might not have been part of her job.

Slaton wished her a good day, and at the front entrance the bellman hailed him a cab.

"Dbaiyeh," he told the driver, "the convention center." As the cab pulled away from the Beirut Four Seasons, Slaton immersed himself in a brief internal debate. *The Dbaiyeh convention center*. Why had that address slipped out so naturally? It *was* north, and a logical destination for a Westerner originating at a high-end hotel and carrying a trinket bag from an investment bankers' conference. Yet that wasn't the real reason.

Slaton ignored the driver as the cobalt calm of Saint George Bay rolled past on his left. Two facts lay heavy in his mind: stolen radiological material, and bets made in his name involving oil. Disparate occurrences that shared no obvious common ground, yet whose union was a certainty. He had uncovered a terrorist threat of unknown manifestation. The only option, of course, was to stop it. Slaton didn't bother to rationalize his efforts as anything noble or righteous. These people had killed Krueger and Astrid. They had tried to kill him, and were undeniably a threat to his family.

That alone was enough.

Yet there Slaton hit a stop. Ben-Meir's trail was quickly going cold, and an attack involving radiological material could be imminent. Slaton relented—he needed help, and as distasteful as it was, there was only one logical place to get it. And there was the truth of the destination he'd given the driver.

He reached into his newly acquired canvas bag and began composing a message. Slaton settled on a bullet list, a format that emphasized directness. He had three objectives: establish his bona fides, generate urgent interest, and arrange contact on his terms.

Using a Morgan Stanley pen and stationery—a nice touch, he thought—Slaton wrote:

> *Mdina last Tuesday, 1 dead*
> *Zurich Friday, 2 dead*
> *Wangen Saturday, 2 dead*
> *1 each city to my credit*
> *Barclay's account 90202-002838-0*
> *I have time-critical info on WMD in Aadra*
> *Les Palmiers, Station Chief, 2 p.m. today*
> *No more than two in support*

He read it through once and was satisfied.

Two o'clock allowed roughly one hour. Plenty of time for them to verify his information and launch a search team toward Aadra. Just long enough to instill fear at the highest levels of the organization, yet not enough time to devise a countersurveillance mission, at least not one so deft he would have trouble spotting it. If they came to the shops and pubs along the coast road of Dbaiyeh, in a rush of good haircuts and laundered shirts, Slaton would spot them like so many moons in a night sky. It was good, he thought. Their only option was to play by his rules.

In one hour he would have what he needed: an audience with the CIA.

The journey to Dbaiyeh took fifteen minutes, and two blocks short of the convention center Slaton directed the driver's attention to a church, and said, "I've changed my mind. Drop me there."

The driver shrugged and did as asked. Slaton settled with the man from the curb, and the cab departed with a canvas bag full of financial brochures pushed deep under the driver's seat. He traversed a sun-swept courtyard, and rounded the administrative annex of the church to reach an ageless cathedral. It was a typical Armenian Catholic house with tall and narrow windows, and above everything rose a trinity of domes topped by crosses.

Slaton was here because he needed an emissary, and while it was always possible to hire beggars or prostitutes or street urchins, he had long been convinced that the most reliable secret agents were God's own.

With a dwindling stash of five hundred euros in his pocket, he passed under a limestone arch at the cathedral entrance, appreciating the symmetry, fit, and color of the curve-cut stonework. He pushed through heavy doors into the holy realm, and there, at the front of the long aisle and below a wooden depiction of Jesus on the cross, stood the man Slaton was looking for.

# FIFTY-TWO

With considerable fanfare, the United States of America established its first diplomatic outpost in Beirut in 1833. It has been neither a happy nor continuous presence. In 1917 all personnel were abruptly evacuated when relations with the Ottoman Empire soured. During World War II diplomatic services were suspended intermittently until the Battle of Beirut, in 1941, when the remaining Vichy French occupiers were evicted. In 1975, the Lebanese civil war brought a precautionary reduction in station staff and dependents. Soon after, as if to validate this forethought, the incoming ambassador, Francis Meloy, was kidnapped as he was being driven across the Green Line to present his credentials, his bullet-riddled body later recovered from a nearby beach. In 1983, a suicide bomber killed forty-nine embassy staff and injured dozens. In the name of security, a beleaguered U.S. State Department relocated the embassy to the safety of Awkar, north of Beirut, where it was bombed again a year later to the toll of eleven dead and dozens injured.

It is a telling fact that the embassy in Beirut, Lebanon, is the only U.S. diplomatic mission to keep a standing memorial honoring staff members killed in the line of duty. That the outpost endures today is nothing less than a monument to diplomatic tenacity.

And it remains as much a target as ever.

Father Vartan Bartakian approached the embassy with no small measure of caution. He knew he was being watched closely as he crossed the street, no allowance given for his black robe and collar, nor the benevolent smile etched on his face. He walked past a queue at the main entrance, where young men and women waited patiently for information about visas and study abroad opportunities, pausing twice to issue blessings along the way. After a sharp turn at the northern wall, he navigated a maze of concrete barriers with the agility of a slalom skier before coming to a stop in front of two United States Marines, the no-nonsense sentries of the iron-gated employee entrance.

One of the men—the thicker and burlier of the two—stepped forward and said, "Can I help you, Father?"

Bartakian's smile did not waver. "Yes, I do hope so. I am here without an appointment, but the ambassador sees me regularly. I have urgent information that must be brought to the attention of your chargé d'affaires."

The guard exchanged a look with his partner. "The chargé d'affaires," the big man repeated. "You're sure?"

It was plain knowledge within these thick walls—and apparently plain enough outside for local priests to be privy—that the resident chargé d'affaires was in fact the head of the CIA's Beirut station.

Bartakian held up a thin envelope. "I am to deliver this," he said. "I've been told it contains extremely vital information."

"Just a minute." The guard went to a hardwired phone in a nearby shack, and Bartakian used the pause to admire the new embassy. The architecture was impressive, a monument to wealth and grandeur that rivaled even his church. Also like the church, it reminded him of a grand ship—a place whose superstructure was there to be marveled at, but whose means of propulsion lay well below the waterline.

The grim-faced guard returned.

"Mr. Donnelly is busy, but he would like to see the envelope."

"I am under very strict instructions, my son. I must deliver it personally." The father smiled with what could only be taken as holy purpose. "I have been assured that to ignore this information would prove extremely embarrassing for all involved."

A second phone call ensued, and soon Father Bartakian was being ushered inside.

"We found the airplane in Iraq," Sorensen said guardedly.

"What's the bad news?" Davis asked, having been told that this too was coming when she'd found him in the break room.

"It's already gone. We did like you suggested, concentrated on the most likely airfields and took snapshots every thirty minutes. There was an MD-10 on the ground at Al-Basrah International just before three a.m. local last night. We got hits on two passes, but the jet definitely wasn't there thirty minutes before or after."

Davis broke away from his study of a vending machine. "Okay, that fits our profile. But how can you be sure it's the right airplane? Since it was night, we can't go by paint color."

"I'm ahead of you on that. We have a tech team that specializes in LTD."

"LTD?"

"Like-target discrimination."

Davis raised a questioning eyebrow. "What the hell is that?"

"It was developed with vehicles in mind. For example, say we come across a random Isuzu in the middle of the desert—it might be a sheep farmer, an opium smuggler, or a terrorist we've been after for years. We've developed a system for turning high-resolution radar data into what is essentially a fingerprint for a particular vehicle. It can match dents, antennas, gun mounts, broken door handles . . . even the amount of wear on the spare tire on the tailgate."

"I'm impressed," said Davis, "both by the technology and that someone had the foresight to develop it."

"It really works. If you look at any car or truck closely enough, especially one that travels off-road in the Middle East or Southern Asia, you'll find distinguishing marks."

"And you used this software to ID our airliner?"

"We drew a baseline from the picture taken when the airplane was parked in Brazil, then compared that profile to the airplane in Al-Basrah last night. It was a slam dunk." Sorensen smiled.

"Okay," he said, looking at his watch. "That puts us only ten hours behind. Not to strafe your kite, but that still leaves us with about a four-thousand-mile search radius."

Sorensen deflated, but only slightly. "It puts us in the ballpark, Jammer."

"True," he said supportively, "but it's a helluva big stadium."

"We have people swarming all over the airport."

"Have they found anything yet?"

"An empty fuel truck, some loading equipment. There was also a pickup truck in the desert nearby with two bodies in the cargo bed. Both male, both executed. One of them had on a uniform—we think he was the fuel truck driver."

Davis waited, but there was nothing else.

"Any idea where they might go next?" she asked.

He considered it. "This jet was on the ground less than an hour. Aside from taking on gas, they had time to kill two people, dump the bodies in a truck, and drive into the desert. I think you should look at the fuel truck logs. Jet fuel isn't cheap, even in Iraq, and the companies who sell it keep tight, gallon-by-gallon records. I'm guessing they took on less than a full fuel load. If you can prove that, it makes our circle a lot smaller."

"Right. That's good."

"No, that's bad," said Davis.

Sorensen heaved a sigh. "Why?"

"Think about it. A new load of cargo, a partial fuel load. We don't have much time here, Anna. Whatever these people are going to do . . . they're going to do it very soon."

# FIFTY-THREE

The United States embassy in Beirut, by virtue of its turbulent past, is operated under a unique staffing model by its attendant services.

Ambassadors to Lebanon are invariably career State Department employees, this a glaring exception to the custom wherein lead diplomatic posts are reserved as political appointments, presidents finding places for their deep-pocketed campaign donors, close friends, and Ivy League fraternity brothers. France, England, Sweden, and Brazil—these are the verdant gardens, the well-bought consular A-list. An ambassadorship to Lebanon, on the other hand, lies considerably further down the alphabet. With its magnetism for bombings, kidnappings, and religious-inspired mayhem, Beirut postings are invariably filled—on a strictly volunteer basis—by brave and long-tenured employees from Foggy Bottom.

The position of CIA station chief is filled using an altogether different approach. Langley maintains its usual embedded subsidiary in the U.S. house of Lebanon, and for the employees of the CIA, Beirut is ground zero. It is the place where careers are made and lost, a tinderbox in which young and indestructible case officers put their tradecraft on the line to engage razor-sharp bomb-makers and witless suicidal jihadists. Iran and Pakistan might be as combustive, Iraq a few years earlier. But with the Jews to the south, the Persians to the north, and nearly twenty state-recognized religious sects, there is no more unsettled country on earth than Lebanon.

And Larry Donnelly wouldn't have been anywhere else.

How a man of his checkered past had come to command a vital CIA outpost was a curiosity to his friends, an enigma to his subordinates, and a source of long-running consternation to Lebanon's internal security service. His third wife had left him five years ago, taking two kids, half his pension, and one thoroughly untrainable black Lab. With the arithmetic of his life in shreds, Donnelly had done what any red-blooded CIA officer would do—he sought out the most knife-edged posting he could find, and to his surprise was given Beirut. Nothing cured a midlife crisis like putting a target on your back, or so his thinking went, and the assignment had so far exceeded his expectations, as had the rooftop bars and hedonistic vacationers of Hamra. Donnelly rose most mornings with an aching head, on occasion next to a woman half his age, but always delighting in what the next day would bring.

Today, apparently, it was Armenian priests bearing cryptic messages.

Father Bartakian was shown into his office after a short wait, and the United States chargé d'affaires to Lebanon crossed the polished cedar floor to greet him. "Father Bartakian. How good to see you."

The priest smiled a smile of benevolence that could only have been learned in seminary. "Yes, but it has not been so long. I was here only last month for the ceremony to celebrate twenty years of freedom from the Green Line."

"Yes, I remember now. I suppose it was worth commemorating, but as you and I both know, lines are drawn on paper. Peace is far more elusive." Donnelly retreated to the furnished half of the room and said, "Please have a seat."

Bartakian did, and Donnelly played the good host, not hiding behind his desk but instead taking an adjoining twin chair. Soft leather crinkled equally under the men, notwithstanding their precipitously different weights in God's order.

Bartakian said, "A man came to see me today. He gave me a letter and asked me to deliver it to you personally." He pulled an envelope from a pocket in his robe and handed it across.

"Is this man an acquaintance? A parishioner perhaps?" Donnelly thought he might have heard a chuckle.

"Oh, no. I have never seen him before. Of that, I am certain."

"What did he look like?"

The priest considered it. "He was fair-haired, unusual gray eyes. A pleasant sort, really. I would say he has a background in stonework."

"Stonework?"

"He showed me a section of masonry in the southern nave where the mortar was failing. Something about a bad mix, but simple enough to repair, he assured me."

"Did this stonemason give a name?" Donnelly asked, setting the unopened envelope aside for the moment.

"Come to think of it, no. I don't believe he did."

"Nationality?"

"He never said . . ." The priest hesitated.

"But?"

"If I were to guess—I'd say he might be Israeli."

"What makes you say that?"

Donnelly again saw the patriarchal smile.

"I have been a priest for nearly forty years, Mr. Donnelly, and have lived my entire life in Lebanon. Do that," Bartakian said, "and even you could spot a Jew."

Donnelly kept his own smile in check. "But I wonder," he said, "if you've never met this man before—why would he ask *you* to deliver a letter for him?"

"I rather wondered that myself. But then, consider the obvious. I have long been a leader in the local religious community, and my church is a short walk up the street from the embassy. As you well know, I have been a guest here dozens of times for various functions. It seems a natural extension that I would keep acquaintances at the embassy. A searching mind might even imagine that I've been asked to report suspicious activities gathered from my pews or—God forbid—in confessional."

Donnelly crooked his head in amusement. "Well, it goes without saying, we live in a dangerous part of the world. There is *some* degree of obligation for the church to do what it can to keep the peace. As for your Israeli stonemason, if he worked things out as you say, then it strikes me that he might also be trained in . . . diplomatic work."

Bartakian shrugged noncommittally. "Friends and liars, Mr. Donnelly. It is not my duty to distinguish among them, but rather to serve all God's children equally."

Donnelly grinned and gave the envelope a pat.

"Anyway, Father, thank you for bringing this to our attention."

He rose and escorted the priest to the door. There Bartakian paused and put his hands together near his chest—had they been six inches higher the CIA man might have mistaken it for a prayer. "You know," Bartakian said, "this gentleman donated three hundred euros to our repair fund—the old domes in the chapel have been leaking for a year now. I thought it was quite generous given the small favor he asked in return. He also suggested that you . . . or should I say the United States of America . . . would very possibly make a matching contribution."

The spy frowned.

The priest smiled, adding, "We *are* approaching the rainy season."

"I'll see what I can do."

Bartakian turned to leave.

"You know, Father—"

The robe twirled to face him.

"Our skill sets are not as dissimilar as one might think. If you ever leave the church and need a job—give me a call."

"Oh, I will never leave the church, my son." The priest spread his arms wide, almost a benediction. "But I will pray for America tonight. On that you have my solemn word."

# FIFTY-FOUR

Less than thirty minutes later, Donnelly was quick-timing down the steps of Notre Dame University—the Louaize, Lebanon edition whose red-tiled roofs and sun-bleached dormitories would never be confused with those of its cousin institution in South Bend, Indiana. At the foot of the hill he referenced the map on his phone, and turned left on Zouk Mikael. The school was less than two miles north of the embassy, but in spite of the proximity it was not a neighborhood Donnelly frequented. After a twisting drive through hills that overlooked the Dog River Valley and the sea beyond, he had found himself on sidewalks teeming with students on the bright afternoon, and crossing streets overrun by scooters and bicycles. A very public place, and presumably why it had been chosen.

He found the café, Les Palmiers, at the first corner. Donnelly referenced his watch to see that he was nearly on time. He'd read the letter twice before leaving the embassy, then forwarded it to Langley, along with a message to say he was going to the meeting. There hadn't been time to wait for a reply. The whole affair might be a waste of time—he'd certainly been sent on his share of fool's errands since arriving in

Beirut—yet something in that list of details, so meticulously arranged on Morgan Stanley stationery, had convinced him otherwise.

Donnelly paused at the entrance, and his eyes stepped through the tables, beginning with those on the outer patio. There was no need for red carnations or folded newspapers. Practiced spies had no trouble spotting one another—at least, not when that was what they had in mind. His gaze settled on a light-haired man under a big Perrier umbrella whose eyes—unusual gray, according to Father Bartakian, although Donnelly couldn't say from this distance—momentarily made contact. The man was alone, or so it seemed, and well situated in the most tranquil corner of the place, an orphan table between the main traffic aisle and a waiter's stand.

Donnelly squared his shoulders and crossed the room. The man did not rise to greet him, and of the three remaining chairs Donnelly naturally picked the one opposite. Only after sitting did he realize that all the angles worth watching were at his back.

"I'm not alone," Donnelly said.

The man across the table showed no reaction.

"But I only brought two, as you requested. I ordered them to stay across the street. Four is the usual minimum for a man in my position."

"You should have brought them all. I would have."

"Maybe next time," Donnelly said. He looked around the busy café. "You know, this isn't a very good place for a private conversation."

"An even worse one for an abduction."

A waitress appeared, and Donnelly ordered a beer, his tablemate black coffee. He lit up a cigarette—half the patrons were smoking as it was, another reason he liked Lebanon. "You don't drink?"

"Not when I work."

"Is that what this is—work?"

No response. Donnelly felt an urge to lighten the mood. "It's always been my opinion that a little booze could solve most of the world's problems. I mean, consider the most screwed-up countries. What do they have in common? They're the ones that ban alcohol, dancing, and prostitution. If you ask me, the United States shouldn't waste so much money on jet fighters and aircraft carriers. Do you know how many strip clubs we could open on the Pentagon's budget?" He waited, but again got no reply. "All right," he said, "so who the hell are you?"

"I'm not going to give you a name. Not yet. Let's just say I'm former Mossad."

Donnelly smiled inwardly, remembering what Father Bartakian had said. *I'd say he might be Israeli.* The sandy hair and light eyes would throw most people off—and so it made that much more sense. "Former?" he queried. "You don't look old enough to be retired."

"I didn't retire. I quit."

"Why would—"

"Are you wearing a wire?" the Israeli broke in.

This put Donnelly off stride. "Of course not."

"Then you should go get one. I have a lot of information, and I want you to remember it precisely."

Donnelly broke eye contact and heaved a sigh. He looked around the room, and in a less than natural movement he loosened a button at the collar of his shirt and pulled a white wire free. It was no thicker than a fabric thread.

"Very nice," Slaton said. "Am I on live feed?"

A nod.

Their drinks came, and Donnelly took a heavy

draw on his beer that put foam across the width of his upper lip.

The Israeli said, "Let's not fence. I know who you work for. When I finish, you'll know enough about me to understand that we have mutual interests."

"All right. Convince me."

The Israeli began talking.

Donnelly listened closely to a man who had, by his own admission in the letter, killed three people this week. He knew a great deal about violent men, and in his experience the more tranquil the façade, the more dangerous they were. The man across from him was leaning back casually, his body languid throughout the presentation. Anyone watching might have thought he was strategizing an upcoming polo match. Over twenty minutes his manner neither quickened nor slowed, not when he explained how he'd killed three men, and not when he asserted that over a billion dollars was in play. Yet in spite of his easy manner, Donnelly heard precision in every word, an exactitude of thought that impressed, although did not please him. If this Israeli—if that's what he was— undertook such care in what he was saying, he would take equal care in what he was holding back. And by the end he was convinced—the man *was* holding something back.

Of this Larry Donnelly was sure.

"I once found an old golf club in the garage," Christine said, "with a mirror attached to the clubface."

Stein was sitting on the other side of the dining room table. He was cleaning his gun—she would have been astounded if he hadn't been armed—and listening politely.

"Isn't that something you would use to look under a car? To look for a bomb?"

Stein only shrugged.

"Whenever a new neighbor moved in David was always the first to greet them. Only it wasn't just a greeting. I could tell he was vetting them. Interrogating. Not like they were a threat, necessarily. He wanted to know who spent time on the road, who hunted, who worked odd shifts." She paused, and then said, "What was it like?"

"What was what like?"

"Working for Mossad," she clarified. "The things you did for them."

"You mean the things David did for them?"

"I suppose so. He never talked about it. I asked a few times, but he always changed the subject, or shrugged it off by saying something like, 'We were at war.'"

"First of all, you should understand that David and I weren't the same—not in Mossad's eyes. He was unique, both in what he was capable of and what he was asked to do. I worked with him a few times, yes, but most of my time was spent in the IDF. In the military we had rules of engagement, boundaries."

Her eyes were riveted.

"It *was* war—has been for as long as you and I have been on this earth. But you want specifics?"

"I want to understand. I've seen David stare for an hour at a painting in the National Gallery. I've seen him do stonework that's nearly a work of art. But I've glimpsed his other side too. When he's on a mission . . . there's something different about him. He's so focused and relentless, almost like a machine."

"That's how you have to be, at least if you want to survive."

"I've had that briefing. But I'd like you to go through one mission for me. Tell me what he did."

He drew a deep breath. "All right. I won't try to convince you how deserving our target was. If a mission reached David, any moral or ethical questions had been finalized. A *kidon* has to trust that, which in itself is no easy thing. There was one time David and I were assigned to go after a man who—"

"Did he have a name?"

Stein hesitated. "Jameel. If there was a first name I don't remember it."

She nodded.

"He was a guy who had good reason to think Mossad might be after him. Because of it, he was careful, and they had a hard time locating him. So Mossad came up with a scheme. They arranged a bit of legal mischief and Jameel's cousin, who was imprisoned and awaiting trial, was released, ostensibly by error, from Shikma Prison in Ashkelon. Mossad tracked him for weeks, and eventually he led them to a safe house in Mughazi, near Gaza. An advance team got a glimpse of Jameel, confirmed it with a photograph. He apparently had been staying there for some time, so David was given his orders."

Stein paused, but Christine did not ask what those orders were.

"He and I went in, along with a woman named Sonya. We set up shop, a one-room flat in a nearby building, three floors above the apartment we were watching. Remember—we're talking the Gaza Strip, which is strictly enemy territory. None of us left the room, and for six days we watched Jameel's apartment. There was one main window, and we saw him once or twice, but only for a moment—the blinds were almost always drawn. The only other thing we had was a marginal audio feed from a directional microphone. There was never a clear opportunity for David to shoot, but we did notice one thing—this safe house had a single bathroom. We had a good angle on that window, although there was a thin curtain that never moved. When anyone used the toilet, David could use a particular scope and site in clearly on the head of the person using it. We kept careful logs, because that's what you do in a surveillance op—track when everyone wakes up, eats, has intimate relations."

"And when they go to the bathroom."

"Exactly. Your target will be there sooner or later—unmoving and unworried. For six mornings in a row, between eight forty and nine fifteen, someone sat on that toilet, and stayed there for between six and eight minutes. Of course, all David saw through his scope was a silhouette—no way to be sure it was Jameel, but we were reasonably sure he was the only inhabitant who never left the apartment. There were between three and five other people inside at any given time, some rotating in and out as guards, others arriving occasionally for tea-and-strategy sessions. Some of them used the toilet sporadically, of course, but that one constant remained. Every morning. Same time. Same place."

"And on the seventh morning?"

"Before sunrise we were packed and had the room cleaned. Two cars were in place outside. Sonya and I were out by eight. At 9:02 David struck. He took one shot, broke down his gun, and we were all across the border fifteen minutes later."

"And was this mission a success?"

"Did we get Jameel? No, we didn't."

"David missed?"

Stein chuckled. "David doesn't miss. That same morning a second surveillance team was still tracking Jameel's cousin, the man we had released from prison. Turns out he'd gone to the safe house that morning—we eventually learned, to deliver a message from a rival militia he'd become affiliated with. We never saw the cousin go in because we couldn't see all the building's entrances, and the other team didn't report it until later—they had no idea we were across the street."

"And that's who David killed?"

Stein nodded. "It might have been random chance. Or it might have been that Jameel's people knew we were there. Maybe they thought the cousin had been turned as an informant. We could never say for sure how or why any of it ended the way it did. As it turned out, Jameel was killed three weeks later, ambushed by a rival faction in Gaza."

"More revenge?"

"Who knows?"

Stein began reassembling his weapon, his movements confident and familiar. It again reminded her of David, who seemed too sure of himself, she sometimes thought, as if he could never imagine a mistake. Never imagine losing. And he'd loved her in the same way.

Stein put the weapon in his backpack and hung it high on a coat hook, holding to their agreement to keep the gun out of Davy's reach. "I know you want to understand the world David lived in," he said, "but there *is* no understanding it. There are barbarians out there, Christine, people who are the personification of evil. When you fight them, there can never be a clean victory. You don't raise your flag on a hill or sign an armistice."

"But where does it end?"

"That's the problem—it never will. At least not for Israel. But I can tell you that my part is done. The only reason I'm here today is because I owe David. As far as Mossad goes, I'd never have anything to do with them again. Even if I *could* walk in a straight line."

"And David? When this is done, do you think he can put it all behind him?"

"For everyone's sake, let's hope so. The next time you see him, you should convince him of that. Tell him he has to leave the past where it is and move on."

# FIFTY-FIVE

Slaton watched Donnelly burn through three cigarettes while he covered everything from Malta to Beirut. The only thing he left unaddressed was his relationship to America—in particular, his wife and child. The CIA had facilitated his initial move to the United States, but it was a carefully crafted identity known to only a few individuals in the agency. That legend, in the name of Edmund Deadmarsh, had long ago been blown, the supporting documents sunk into a deep and dark body of water. To rekindle that relationship here, he knew, risked disclosing his true identity. Which in turn, created but one more path to his family.

Slaton ended his story at a storage room on Geitawi Boulevard.

"What did you find inside?" Donnelly asked.

"WMD."

The acronym instigated a pause, and Slaton watched the CIA man scan the room. He'd done so regularly since arriving, which Slaton took as damning evidence of a long career in the field. More positively, it suggested that Donnelly's security team was not in direct line of sight. "Weapons of mass destruction?

Your message said that was in Aadra—we have a team on the way there now."

"That's where the material was initially discovered, and there's still plenty of evidence—enough to convince you how serious this is."

"Where exactly do we look? And what kind of threat are we talking about?"

Slaton set on the table one of the three plastic-encased dosimeters he'd taken from the storage room. He had cut away the bottom lip, the identity strip where Dr. Moses Nassoor's name had been printed. In time he was sure the Americans would discover where it had come from. He was equally sure that Nassoor would face some manner of justice for what he'd done. That was out of Slaton's hands.

"I found three like this in the storage closet. Check the readings. The material is cesium-137. It was brought to Geitawi from a farm outside Al Qutayfah, Syria." Slaton added a description of the dirt path and rail tracks near Route 7. "Behind the main house your team will find a workshop, and all around it are traces of this isotope."

"Traces?"

"Clear evidence of a release. Cesium-137 has medical and industrial uses, but large quantities are commonly used to irradiate food. Its half-life is thirty years—your team should use protective gear. Twenty months ago there was an outbreak of ill health in Aadra caused by this material. The health system failed—it never made the correlation. As an aside, if I was the CIA I might consider some kind of training program. Primary-care physicians in this part of the world ought to be able to recognize radiation sickness."

"I'll put that in my after-action report," said Donnelly dryly. "What else?"

"First let's talk about what I want in return."

"I'm listening."

"I need information. And certain guarantees."

"Guarantees? You think you can just give a note to a Marine sentry and expect the CIA to jump through—"

"I am rescuing you," Slaton broke in, "from a *catastrophic* intelligence failure. I believe this material will be used in a radiological attack. Right now neither of us knows who we're dealing with or what their intentions are, but we have to assume that time is of the essence."

"Do you think this cesium will be used against Israel?"

"It's a possibility."

"So why didn't you go to Mossad with this? Even if you no longer work for them, I'm sure you have connections."

"I think this entire disaster was sourced from a series of Mossad screwups. I don't trust them right now. In truth, I haven't for a long time."

"So the CIA is your backup intelligence service?"

"We have common interests. This group has killed two innocent people, and established themselves as a threat to me personally. I think we're looking at a gray cell, an op that isn't state sponsored, at least not overtly. I tracked the last man I know about to Geitawi where he picked up this material, and I think he's transporting it as we speak. His name is Zan Ben-Meir, an Israeli national. I'm also certain there are others involved. I want you to find out who they are. I want you to tell me *where* they are."

Donnelly stabbed his fourth cigarette into an ashtray. His fingers tapped on the side of his mug. "You've got balls, I'll give you that. You think that if the CIA can verify what you're saying, if we can identify who's involved, that we'll serve them up to you on a platter?"

"If you want quick and quiet closure . . . yes."

Ever so slightly, Donnelly shifted in his seat.

Slaton said, "My offer is not open-ended. Give me good information, and I'll finish this. I expect a decision from Langley within one hour. Your acceptance of my terms will come by way of the CIA director's press release."

"What press release?"

"The one he's going to issue sixty minutes from now. It will include the phrase, 'We have an agreement in principle.' I don't care what the balance of the text reads—he can be announcing a new Far East initiative or a bid for office supplies. Use your imagination. I'll verify the issuance and subtext on the CIA website."

Donnelly frowned. "And if Langley agrees? How do we get in touch with you?"

"By calling your phone." He held out his hand.

With a weary sigh, Donnelly reached into his trouser pocket, pulled out a smartphone, and pushed it across the table.

"Password?" Slaton asked. Donnelly gave it to him, and he typed seven characters into the security screen. The phone was ready to work. He scanned the various icons. "Which is the tracking app?" he asked.

Donnelly showed him. Slaton tapped the symbol and within seconds had the signal disabled. He guessed this was the only beacon, but there was no way to ask and expect a truthful answer. On a more positive note, he saw an application that looked familiar and might be of great use later.

Donnelly said, "You realize that as long as it's powered up anybody can track it like a regular phone."

"Of course," Slaton said, turning the phone off. "Once I have confirmation that we're working together, I'll turn the phone back on. I expect to see a direct contact number for Langley. And I'll be expecting information."

An irritated Donnelly looked out across the street. "What if I told you I had ten agents outside ready to close in?"

"I'd say you're a liar. It would be like me telling you that I had a silenced Beretta under the table."

Donnelly looked at Slaton's half-hidden right arm. To his credit, he didn't flinch. He asked, "What exactly did you do for Mossad?"

Slaton got up from the seat with one hand still in his jacket pocket. He removed it to produce a ten-euro note, which he dropped on the table. "I think that's obvious enough."

"It's him," Sorensen said. "Mdina, Zurich, Wangen. Everything checks. This is definitely our Maltese stonemason." She was addressing Director Coltrane in his Langley office, Jack Kelly at her side as they went over the message from the Beirut station.

Kelly said, "I don't like the bit about, 'one each to my credit.' It's almost like he's bragging about killing these men."

Coltrane stood in rumination before a very hightech window that overlooked a sleeping forest of leafless elm and chestnut trees. He said, "No, he's giving us a character reference—such as it is."

The Operations Center had been humming with activity since the letter from Beirut arrived, and things accelerated after Donnelly's meeting with the Israeli.

"What about the Barclays account?" the director asked.

Sorensen said, "We have a good contact at the bank—or more accurately, MI-5 does. It's a large private account, roughly sixty million U.S. dollars. It was managed by Walter Krueger—the banker who was killed in Zurich last week. The funds have been in place for over a year with very little activity, but in the last few days there have been some changes."

"What kind of changes?" Coltrane asked distractedly, still facing the window.

"The money was cashed out of a diverse portfolio and reinvested much more narrowly—everything is now in oil. Refining, exploration, drilling leases. Somebody went all-in."

"Do we know who that 'somebody' is?"

"That was the other strange thing. The account was originally established as an offshore trust, but a few days ago the ownership was altered. Everything was put into the name of one individual." Sorensen referenced a printout to make sure she got it right. "The new owner of record is named David Slaton."

The director turned. Coltrane opened his mouth as if to speak, but then seemed to have second thoughts.

"Does that name mean something to you?" Sorensen asked.

"Yes." Nothing more came until Coltrane said, "You should both get back to work."

Sorensen and Kelly stood frozen for a moment, and exchanged a *What the hell is going on?* look.

They were heading for the door when Coltrane added, "This man who's contacted us in Beirut . . ."

Both turned.

"Give him anything he wants."

After the two analysts were gone, the director remained at the window with the name fixed in his head. David Slaton. Coltrane *had* heard it before, but only once, during a late-evening, martini-laden discussion with the outgoing director when he'd assumed command of the agency. It wasn't from any official record, or even an off-the-books operation. Closer to a legend, really.

*"There was a favor for Israel. We took in one of their operatives, a man who recently saved them great embarrassment. He's a killer, as pure and simple as they come, who ended up in a delicate situation. Mossad wanted him to disappear with a faultless identity. They were very concerned, so I offered our help. The name is David Slaton . . . or at least it was. I doubt you'll ever hear it again . . ."*

From his predecessor's words, one phrase looped again and again in Coltrane's head.

*He's a killer, as pure and simple as they come . . .*

# FIFTY-SIX

He thought he might get the CIA's help, but Slaton wasn't going to sit idly while they made up their minds. He'd taken a circuitous route after leaving Les Palmiers, patient countersurveillance measures on the sidewalks of Dbaiyeh. Among the details he had not shared with Langley was the observation of the self-appointed concierge, passed on by Nassoor. *The truck turned north, onto Armenia Boulevard. The driver would only do that if he was heading north, away from the city.*

It was the thinnest of trails. In northern Lebanon lay the seaport of Tripoli, and beyond that Syria, with its rudderless government and a populace reeling from civil war. Farther still were Iran and Iraq, always at odds with one another and each unpredictable in its own right. Then the most terrifying scenario—Turkey, a full member of the E.U., and thus the perfect geographic conduit for sending a load of gamma-laden terror anywhere in Europe.

Slaton considered that the initial turn north could be a false assumption, or even intended as misdirection. For all his grievances with Mossad and the government of Israel, he retained a strong kinship with the Jewish people and their homeland. Could Ben-Meir be heading there? He thought it unlikely. Unless Ben-Meir was working for Israel, which Slaton strongly doubted, that would mean crossing one of the most closely guarded borders on earth. A veritable brick wall.

He saw but one certainty—no one would undertake such a ruthless quest, killing to steal nuclear material, only to hand it over to authorities for safekeeping. He was watching the world's worst nightmare unfold, a radiological attack that could be unleashed at any time, against any number of targets. Contaminate a food or water supply, blanket a major city in radiation. Or perhaps irradiate a religious shrine—the Middle East was the cradle of civilization, littered with holy sites that could be defiled with foreseeable outrage. The kind of outrage over which wars were fought.

Slaton's only option at the moment was to pursue Ben-Meir. The man had a considerable head start, but he was transporting a heavy and valuable load which would require extreme caution. North was the most likely route, so Slaton would move in that direction, hoping that as he made up ground the CIA could more narrowly focus his search—help him zero in on a killer hauling fifty-two canisters of radiological hell.

First, however, Slaton had to prepare for his hunt to succeed. Ben-Meir had been alone in Geitawi, yet he was not operating solo. Nor would he be without firepower. So Slaton's immediate objective was clear. From Dbaiyeh he headed away from his quarry, boarding a city bus that would take him back to Beirut. There he would apply the most fundamental of an assassin's tenets.

Never go into a gunfight empty-handed.

Sorensen returned to the Operations Center to find Davis hunched over a computer display. She knew he'd been sweeping through satellite images for the better part of an hour, ever since they'd gotten word that a closetful of nuclear material had gone missing in Beirut.

"Anything?" she asked.

"No," he said distractedly, not altering his flow. "I've been over every active airfield in Lebanon, Syria, and Jordan. No sign of our jet."

"There had to be a connection. We've got a stolen aerial tanker that someone's been going to great lengths to keep out of sight, and a cache of hijacked nuclear material. It all fits too perfectly."

"Yep."

"What time frame are you using?" she asked.

"I allowed a ninety-minute flight from Basrah, and from there I'm right up against real-time stuff. That's about a nine-hour window. It narrows our search a lot—there aren't many airfields in the region with a runway long enough to support an MD-10."

"Could it have landed and gone straight into a hangar?" Sorensen asked.

"There are even fewer of those—maybe ten that are big enough, and most are already occupied."

"Could it still be in the air?"

"Doubtful. We've got two guided-missile cruisers and an aircraft carrier in the area, and all have top-of-the-line radar. It wouldn't even matter if they turned their transponder off. We can see everything in the air right now that doesn't have feathers—and a few targets that do. No, they've done something else." He broke away and sat straight in his chair. "I think we should look at abandoned airfields."

Sorensen frowned. "I don't think we target those for surveillance."

"But can you get images?"

Sorensen didn't know, so she collared a technician from a nearby workstation who provided the answer. "We have coverage of the entire area—that's no problem. But we don't store the coordinates of unused airfields."

"There must be dozens in the area," Davis said.

"There are," said the tech, "but we don't keep track of them. No reason to. If you give me coordinate sets, I can have images in a matter of minutes."

"How do we do that?" Sorensen asked.

When the technician didn't answer, Davis knew he had his work cut out for him. "The old-fashioned way. We get our hands on some aeronautical charts and start plotting. Do you have anything like that around here?"

Sorensen dispatched Kelly on the mission. "Lower level, where the archived documents are kept." He acknowledged the order and disappeared. She then gave Davis the latest from her meeting with the director.

"The Barclays account," he commented, "everything invested in oil. I think that's important."

"So do I. And there was something else about the account. The ownership had recently been altered. The new name on the account is David Slaton. Does that mean anything to you?"

"Nothing at all," Davis said.

"Well . . . it meant something to the director."

"What did he say?"

"He didn't want to talk about it."

"You know what your problem is around here?" he said. "You people keep too many secrets. In the military everything is right out there. The information might be good, or it might stink, but it's always available for everybody to see." Davis went back to his search as a woman arrived with a message for Sorensen. When she read it a look of pain washed across her face.

"What now?" he asked.

"It's from our team at the airport in Basrah. I told you they'd found two bodies in the desert nearby. Well, it seems there were also two shipping containers in the bed of that pickup truck. They were stenciled in Cyrillic, so it took some time to figure out what had been in them—apparently our friends loaded up a couple of Russian-manufactured industrial agitators."

Davis turned to face her again. "Agitators? Like . . . for mixing things?"

She nodded. "On a big scale, apparently."

"What's the status of that team you sent into Syria? Have they confirmed whether this threat is real?"

Sorensen checked her watch. "No word yet. But we should find out soon."


The Rapid Reaction Team lived up to its name.

Hurriedly dispatched from the U.S. Embassy in Beirut, an armored Chevy Suburban drove at breakneck speed toward the Syrian border while advance warning was forwarded through diplomatic channels: a Red Crescent medical facility outside Damascus was in dire need of emergency supplies. The lead guard at the border checkpoint might have gotten the word, because he waved them through, although not before inspecting a single passport in which the driver's photograph was obscured by a hundred-dollar bill.

The special embassy detail was comprised of two men and two women, and when they pulled to a stop at the tiny farmhouse outside Aadra thirty minutes later, all four doors of the specially equipped Suburban rocked open simultaneously. For any other CIA station in the world it would have been an astonishing response—four qualified personnel assembled within minutes, and sent across an unfriendly border with all the equipment and training needed to quantify a radiological threat. For the Beirut station it was a well-practiced drill.

The team trained endlessly, and during the last year had been scrambled on no fewer than four occasions, all reports of chemical weapons that had turned out to be spurious. Perhaps softened by these false alarms, the team's leader was casual as she stood regarding the house. It was a beaten-down affair, even by local standards, the roof warped and the square windows footed by broken glass. The front door was open, swinging aimlessly in the breeze, and there was not a trace of smoke from the stovepipe chimney on a chilly February afternoon. By all appearances the place was abandoned.

The leader spun an index finger in the air. Everyone knew what to do. One of the men, the best linguist, went to the house and began calling out in Arabic to ask if anyone was home. The other man stayed near the still-running vehicle—their best escape if it came to that. The second woman came to stand by the leader's side.

Getting no response to his calls, the linguist cautiously stepped inside. As the team leader waited, she studied the workshop in back, which had figured centrally in the briefing. The shack was sided by the biggest tree on the property, a leafless acacia that looked like a pencil sketch in the falling late-day light.

"Should I put on a suit?" the woman at her side asked.

The leader looked left and right. The nearest neighbor was five hundred meters away, but somebody might be watching. The last thing they wanted was to start a panic. "No, not yet."

"House is clear!" called the Arab-speaker from the open doorway.

The two women walked around the side of the house watchfully, steering toward the workshop. The second woman carried a radiation detector tuned to sense gamma emissions, a bulky handheld device. They were halfway between the workshop and the house when the team leader saw a fuzzy mound at the base of the acacia tree. "Is that what I think it is?"

"Yep," her second replied.

It was a carcass of some kind, the species indistinguishable—nothing remained but a pile of bones and a few shards of hide.

"Goat?" the leader asked.

"Or a big dog. And look over there."

In the distant field were two larger carcasses, either sheep or calves, judging by their mass.

"Anything on the meter?"

"Crap!" said the second woman. "I forgot to turn the damned thing on!" She activated the device, and both immediately heard a crackling electrical buzz. The needle on the gauge jumped straight into the red zone.

The two women instinctively took a step back, and the one in charge announced the obvious, "Yeah, Brenda, I think we'd better go put those suits on."

# FIFTY-SEVEN

Beirut is a place with a great many guns. The police and military have their share, and dozens of religious and ethnic sects keep extensive arsenals. After a long and bloody civil war, the perceived need for protection is universal. Unfortunately for Slaton, even in the midst of so much firepower, there was little chance of a weapon being cheerfully issued to an Israeli assassin.

He arrived at the Central Beirut bus station at 4:21 that afternoon. Near the ticket counter he found a brochure detailing the system schedule, and after buying a kebab from a grizzled sidewalk vendor, he sat on the steps of the old municipal hall and studied the map. He concentrated on routes that paralleled the Green Line—even today, few modes of public transportation crossed the demarcation zone, the city remaining split into a Christian east and Muslim west.

Along this line, the factions had dug in during the tenuous peace, like contemporary, urban variants of the trenches of the Somme and Ypres. The official cessation of hostilities had been over twenty years ago, yet truces here were a fluid concept. The more recent civil war in Syria had spilled into Lebanon, driving flare-ups and divisions among the belligerents that were smiled upon elsewhere. Israel, for one, was perfectly happy to sit back and watch ISIS tap swords with Hezbollah. So it was, all along Beirut's wavering Green Line, militias held their ground determinedly, flew their flags with swagger, and stockpiled weapons for the next battle. And during the intervening lull in action, as was typical of armies everywhere, the mood of the troops would be a lazy one.

Slaton boarded a bus for what turned out to be a short ride, finding what he wanted two hundred yards west of Martyr's Square, in a zone controlled by Sunni Arabs. He remained in his seat until the next stop, then exited and backtracked, and studied everything for a second time.

The building that had caught his eye was no more than a shell, the upper half wrecked by artillery barrages, and rubble piled high around the bullet-scarred foundation. The first two floors, however, appeared largely intact, and at the only viable entrance Slaton saw two armed men. One was tipped back in a chair with a shotgun in his lap. The other stood casually, his Kalashnikov resting against a nearby wall as he thumb-typed on the screen of a mobile phone. They were Sunni, certainly, evidenced by the blue scarves of the Future Movement, two men who'd been given guns and told to keep an eye out for nothing in particular. The building was a militia stronghold, proved by the banner hanging over the entrance, and by the fact that Slaton had not seen a policeman or a Lebanese Army soldier, in a city that crawled with them, within five blocks of the place.

There were two possibilities as to what lay inside. He might be looking at a command center, a place where senior officers met occasionally to strategize, and more frequently to drink strong coffee and discuss the latest rumors. The other option, and the one more to Slaton's liking, was that this was an armory. Given the condition of the building, and the fact that the only vehicles outside were two beaten trucks, he leaned toward the latter being the case. Like all armies, the militias of Lebanon positioned their arsenals thoughtfully, situated near enough to the front lines that arms could be brought to bear quickly, yet not so close that they could swiftly be overrun by an enemy.

Slaton was studying the place, trying to verify its purpose, when the answer was gifted to him. Two men emerged from the building, each cradling an armload of weapons. One after the other, they dropped an assortment of rifles, two with grenade launchers, presumably not loaded, into the bed of the lead truck, a dusty Isuzu pickup that was missing its tailgate.

He watched intently as the men went back inside. They soon returned with a second load—another armload of rifles for one, and the other struggling with a pair of metal ammo boxes. After depositing everything in the Isuzu, they bantered briefly with the guards, the sentry with the phone now done with his text.

Having worked with all variety of military units, Slaton thought he understood what was happening. There was an outside chance this cache of weaponry was being moved to a new location, but the far more likely answer aligned with the workings of an infantry unit, which was effectively what these militias were. No foot soldier was useful until he could shoot straight, and that required training. Target practice, however, was not an urban exercise—too many innocent bystanders, not to mention a watchful enemy two blocks away who might dangerously misinterpret a hundred-round barrage.

Slaton was convinced that the trucks he was watching would depart soon, probably heading east.

Sometime tonight, in a nameless sand swale some-where in the desolate Bekaa Valley, a rendezvous would take place. Squads of new recruits would be briefed by the equivalent of noncommissioned offi-cers. An old sergeant would hold up an older rifle and explain where to find the trigger, although not before emphasizing which end was to be kept pointed down-range at all times. When the talking was done, the rest was straightforward. Teenage boys and out-of-work waiters would spray bullets for an hour in the direc-tion of ill-lit paper targets and spent gin bottles. After a brief intermission, more advanced firepower would be demonstrated by the instructor cadre, and sometime before midnight two dozen weapons, hot-barreled and laced in the acid tang of spent gunpowder, would be dumped back into the truck for the return trip to the armory. Mission complete.

Slaton began moving along the relatively quiet side-walks of Independence Street—even years after the end of hostilities it remained a no-man's land. He crossed the street on an angle, masking behind a slow-moving produce truck. The four men chattered for a time, until one went to the cab of the Isuzu, which was now fully loaded, and pulled it twenty meters for-ward along the curb. Slaton adjusted his pace, antici-pating that the driver's partner would reposition the other truck, a Mitsubishi SUV, directly in front of the entrance.

That was exactly how it happened.

The rest was no more than timing. On reaching the adjacent sidewalk, Slaton governed his pace and con-centrated on the Isuzu. When the driver got out and headed back to the entrance, Slaton noticed what was not in his hand. He was ten steps from the truck when both men disappeared inside, leaving only the guards—one had gone back to his phone, and the other was watching Slaton, but not in an anxious way. Peace had a way of softening men.

Slaton glanced into the cab of the Isuzu and took inventory: windows open, doors unlocked, rearview mirror, shift lever of a manual transmission. Best of all—a set of keys hanging loose in the ignition. Slaton bolted toward the cab.

He had the motor cranking before the first shout. By the second Slaton had a hand on the wheel and another on the gearshift. Lying flat across the bench seat, he adjusted the mirror to see what was happening behind him. The guard who was standing had reacted first, and in the oblong reflection Slaton watched a Kalashnikov come level, followed by a hesitation while its operator fiddled with the fire selector. As Slaton popped the clutch the soldier got off one wild burst, more an alarm to the others than a threat. The truck lurched into motion, and the AK's barrel dropped when the guard realized what was happening—tires squealing, the Isuzu was coming straight at him in reverse.

Slaton spun the steering wheel and the back left tire bounded onto the curb. There was a flash in the mirror as the second guard, having clambered out of his chair, made the only sensible move—he dove for the safety of the entrance alcove. His partner was right behind him, the Kalashnikov clattering to the sidewalk. The truck gained speed, and Slaton spun the wheel hard right. In a perfect strike, the Isuzu's right rear quarter-panel smashed into the other truck. Slaton slammed the shift lever into first and floored the accelerator. Steering back into the road, he ventured a look back and saw the left front wheel of the Mitsubishi cocked at a hopeless angle.

The guards recovered and shots rang out, the rounds absorbed somewhere in the truck's light frame. Slaton looked up only once to gauge a turn onto the first side street. He misjudged slightly and the Isuzu clipped the curb, vaulting onto two wheels before the undercarriage crashed back to earth. With the guards' line of fire broken, Slaton sat up straight and drove for a mile like a Formula 1 madman. Another turn put him on a busy Yerevan thoroughfare, where he slowed to the pace of the local madmen.

Two miles later he found what he wanted—a large retail store, Swedish furniture apparently, with a loading dock at the rear. Slaton steered toward a spalled concrete platform where twin receiving doors were locked down tight. The truck wasn't handling well—something had given way in the chassis—and he clipped a Dumpster before grinding to a halt in a hiss of steam.

He got out, walked quickly to the Dumpster, and began foraging. An eight-foot-long box that had once held a floor lamp he discarded as too cumbersome, and a rectangular wooden crate he deemed too small. Slaton settled on a beach umbrella sleeved in a colorful four-foot nylon carrying bag. He removed the umbrella and found it in two sections, a lower pole meant to screw into the sand, and an umbrella that was damaged, its fabric detached from a floral of plastic ribs—no doubt the reason it was here. Slaton ripped the multicolored fabric from its frame, kept the nylon sleeve, and tossed the rest back into the Dumpster.

He eyed the truck's bed like a child at an ice cream counter. Rifles predominated, mostly AK-47s, but also a pair of Turkish-made Kalekalip sniper rifles. Slaton was reaching for one of these when he spotted a third type—a compact SVDS. The Russian-made marksman's weapon was common here, although this particular item had, quite literally, been through the wars. The SVDS was a respectable long gun, rugged and tight, and after a brief inspection he deemed the weapon serviceable. Better yet, it was topped by a night-vision scope—not a complex IR illuminator, but a more reliable starlight scope, a passive system designed to amplify low levels of ambient light. When Slaton uncovered a box of standard 7.62 millimeter cartridges in the first ammunition box, his decision was made.

He divided thirty loose rounds into four pockets, slipped the gun inside the umbrella fabric, and that into the nylon sleeve. Slaton drew the drawstring tight. The shape of the sheath was slightly altered, but hardly noticeable. He saw a beaten six-pack cooler in the cab of the truck, opened it, and found the remains of someone's lunch.

One minute later he was walking along General Chehab Street. He passed beneath the long shadow of the Lebanese Canadian Bank, and near an empty police car he discreetly dropped the Isuzu's keys into a poorly managed hedgerow. With one more right turn, Slaton was strolling a beachside path with an empty blue cooler in one hand and an umbrella in the other, a brick-red sun kissing the shimmering sea.

# FIFTY-EIGHT

There are three ways to mitigate exposure to radiation: time, distance, and shielding. With the first two implausible, Ghazi relied on the last. He used extreme caution with the first canister. He was forced to manipulate the transport casks by hand until they were nearly open—simple enough once you knew how the assembly operated, and with the right tool to key the retaining ring and initiate aperture rotation. That done, Ghazi began the most delicate part of the operation.

His work area was shielded by eighteen inches of lead brick, with a small viewing port constructed of lead-lined drywall and special glass that also contained lead. He worked with industrial tongs, and once the first container was open he moved it with great care toward a mixing chamber fashioned from one of the fifty-five-gallon drums. Inside the barrel, two agitators ran continuously to dissolve the cesium chloride, a readily soluble salt, into thirty gallons of water. Behind him on the amidships deck were the three two-thousand-gallon bladders, each filled with ordinary water and connected by a network of pumps to the hopper tank. Ghazi would initiate that transfer soon, before takeoff, but the drum laden with the slurry of radioactive material would be combined after takeoff using a remotely activated switch. Ghazi expected some leakage from the doors, and he thought it best to reserve as much radiation as possible for their target.

"Is it working?" called Tuncay from fifty feet away. Ghazi had told him to keep a distance once this stage was reached—in truth, more because he didn't want to be disturbed than any kind of safety hazard. Radiation had its benefits.

"Yes," shouted Ghazi. "Everything is fine."

"I will tell Ben-Meir and Walid you've begun the final stage. How long will it take?"

"Two hours," Ghazi called out. "No more."

The pilot disappeared down the painter's ladder.

The first canister took nine painstaking minutes. When it was done, Ghazi could not help but glance at the dosimeter attached to his shirt. So far so good— the reading was moderate. Once he got a rhythm, he was sure the others would go more quickly.

"One down, fifty-one to go," he muttered into a wall of lead.

An hour later Slaton was seated comfortably in the lounge of the five-star Phoenicia, enjoying a café au lait and, more importantly, a commanding view of the hotel entrance. He had quickly solved one of his problems, that of firepower, while waiting for actionable intelligence from Langley. Now he needed transportation.

Renting a car was out of the question, as he had not even entered the country legally. His dwindling supply of cash precluded purchasing a vehicle without papers, and while Donnelly and the CIA might eventually offer something from the embassy motor pool, that would come with strings attached and cost valuable time. As was his custom, Slaton opted for a more direct approach.

For twenty minutes he watched the valet parking stand outside the Phoenicia's entrance, where two young men in white uniforms were busy with the evening rush. Slaton saw a Porsche and a Mercedes arrive, and a Jaguar depart. He watched the flow of the operation, noting that it took four minutes for the attendants to make a round trip to their parking area on that ever-purposeful trot demonstrated by valets around the world.

The fourth car to arrive, an Audi sport sedan, drew his close interest. Or more precisely, its occupants did—a middle-aged Lebanese man and a well-dressed woman. Neither carried baggage, and after leaving the Audi in the care of the taller of the two valets, Slaton watched the man slip the claim ticket into the side pocket of his suit coat. The couple then headed straight toward him, the coat pocket passing within six inches of his shoulder before ending on the opposite side of the lounge where a large group of equally fashionable people were mingling.

Slaton repositioned to a different chair, bettering his view, and he ordered a Coke from a waiter, ignoring an urge to ask for ice—only Americans did that. The air was carved with expensive scotch and even more expensive perfume, the staccato clink of stemware a constant backdrop. He watched a twenty-dollar martini spill on a two-hundred-dollar tie, and saw a minor drug deal take place across the bar. But mostly, Slaton watched the suit coat.

ASSASSIN'S SILENCE | 403

He watched it for a full twelve minutes, at which point the driver removed his coat and draped it over the back of his chair. Slaton stood and circled to the far side of the room. He waited.

The man's date drifted to chat at a nearby table. Slaton edged closer.

A shapely waitress in a low-cut blouse approached with the man's starter martini.

Slaton picked up his pace. At the moment she bent over to deliver the drink, along with a considerable display of cleavage, Slaton brushed past the chair.

Ninety seconds later he presented the Audi's claim ticket to the smaller valet, a smiling young man named Andre. The ticket was wrapped in a twenty-dollar bill, and instead of mirroring the kid's smile, Slaton gave him a *be-careful-with-my-car-or-else* glare. With his partner off on a retrieval, a purposeful Andre trotted away flashing an index finger to a fresh queue of arrivals—an Aston Martin and a Ford—to tell them he would be right back. Things would be very busy for the next few minutes.

Which suited Slaton perfectly.

The Audi was small and quick. Slaton steered the car to a side entrance and parked near a pair of hotel courtesy busses, one of which had a flat tire and looked as though it had been out of service for months. With the Audi acting as a screen, he went to the derelict bus's rear luggage bay, which had until recently been empty and locked. He retrieved the umbrella-encased rifle and placed it on the Audi's rear floor.

Slaton soon had the car merging onto the coast road, and he set a quick pace to the north. The phone in his pocket weighed heavily, but he decided not to turn it on. Not yet. North of town he sped through Maameltein, and past the Casino du Liban, famous for its black ties and flush clientele. Soon the lights of Beirut went dim in his mirror.

He would be happy to never see them again.

# FIFTY-NINE

It struck Davis like a meteor out of the blue.

He was canvassing images of the long-abandoned Wujah Al Hajar Air Base, sixty kilometers north of Beirut, when he came across a thirteen-hour-old picture that piqued his interest. A second photo, taken ten minutes ago of the same two-acre plot of concrete, brought everything together.

"I've got it!" he said in a voice that reverberated across the CIA Operations Center.

Sorensen was the first to reach his side.

"Look at this frame from last night," he said.

Sorensen stared at the image. "What is it?"

"It's an airplane being scrapped—sectioned apart like a sliced vegetable."

"You think the jet we're looking for was flown in here and demolished?"

"No. Look here—" He tapped on what looked like a crane. "Now look at this same spot a few minutes ago."

Sorensen understood instantly. "In the middle of the night they removed a derelict jet and parked theirs in its place."

"Exactly. It wouldn't work for long . . . but they might not need much time."

"Where is this?"

"Once upon a time it was called Wujah Al Hajar Air Base—it's about an hour's drive north of Beirut."

"So our airplane is there right now."

"It was ten minutes ago."

Sorensen considered it. "The Israeli told us that the cache of cesium was taken out of Beirut in the last forty-eight hours. If so, then it's probably already loaded on that airplane."

"Almost certainly . . ." Davis said, his voice fading off as he studied the most recent image. "Only it won't be there for long."

"What makes you say that?" she asked guardedly.

Davis tapped on a white plume on the screen. "This is infrared—white means hot. The jet has its auxiliary power unit running."

"Which means?"

"I'd say they're getting ready to leave."


Sorensen met with Director Coltrane three minutes later. She explained their theory that the fifty-two canisters of radioactive cesium chloride they were searching for was at an abandoned airfield in central Lebanon, probably loaded onto an aircraft that could disperse the material anywhere within a five-thousand-mile radius.

The director looked uncharacteristically stunned. "Christ . . . all these years we've been worrying about sarin and VX."

"Do we get in touch with the Lebanese and have them intervene?" she asked.

The director snorted in exasperation. "Legally, I suppose we should. But that puts the most lethal radiological weapon we've ever seen in the hands of

Hezbollah. The government of Israel might have an issue with that."

"So what do we do?" Sorensen asked.

"There's not really much choice. We stop this ourselves."

"How?"

"Any damned way we can!"

Larry Donnelly, thinking his curious day was done, had gone back to pattern, which tonight involved a promising dinner with an attractive British Army liaison officer. The restaurant's lighting was low as the sommelier decanted a Bordeaux, and Major James was smiling her lascivious best when his new phone—a replacement for the one stolen earlier by an Israeli assassin—lit with a message. His attempt to ignore it was nullified when, at a glance, he saw a subject line the likes of which he had never before seen.

Priority Alpha recall and mobilization. The embassy equivalent of DEFCON 1.

"I'm sorry," he said, pushing back his chair and fumbling for words. "Something very important has come up."

The major, a stunning brunette who knew a lot about wine, smiled as if she understood. Or perhaps it was the prospect of having a hundred-dollar bottle of Chateau Malescot, 2005, all to herself. Donnelly's one surrender to propriety was to settle with the waiter, and sixty seconds later he was surrounded by his security detail and talking on the limo's secure phone.

Mostly he was listening.

"Wujah Al Hajar Air Base," said a voice from Virginia in an Alabama drawl. "It's fifty kliks north on the coast highway, near Selaata. Call up your tactical squad. Delta Force is being scrambled but they're at least four hours out. We may not have that much time."

"Delta Force?" Donnelly repeated. He didn't know what was happening, but he guessed it involved the Israeli he'd talked to earlier. More to the point, if Delta Force was involved, this was a career-maker. Or a career-breaker.

"Does this have to do with the inspection team we sent to Syria?"

"A full briefing package is waiting for you at the embassy."

"All right, I'll activate the tactical squad."

At the embassy Donnelly worked fast. He found the briefing in a sealed folder on his desk. He'd been right—the Rapid Reaction team dispatched to Syria had found incontrovertible evidence of cesium-137. Having met the Israeli, Donnelly wasn't surprised by the result. He was dumbstruck, however, by the acceleration of events and the forceful tone of Langley's reaction. His orders were to assemble the tactical squad and proceed at best speed to a long-abandoned airfield, fifty kilometers north, where the radioactive material was possibly being loaded onto an aircraft. He would carry out those instructions to the letter.

Much like the WMD team he had earlier dispatched to Al Qutayfah, all U.S. embassies kept a standing plan for mustering a tactical force. It was drawn from Marine guards, military cadre, and CIA staff, and could be assembled on a moment's notice for deployment anywhere in the host nation. The team trained for widespread contingencies: off-site hostage scenarios involving embassy staff members, perimeter protection in the face of uprisings, and a last-ditch extraction plan should a full-blown evacuation become necessary. Intervention in radiological attacks, Donnelly knew, had never made the manual, let alone been practiced, which meant some old-fashioned American ingenuity would be required. Inside twenty minutes a convoy of three vehicles, the heaviest armored limos on station, burst through the north gate and hurtled toward the Dbaiyeh highway.

From the back seat of the middle car, Donnelly looked out the window and tried to imagine what they could be facing. How many adversaries? What kind of weapons did they have? How much time was left to act? These were answers Donnelly desperately wanted. Yet as the group struck out north along the coast highway, the limo's satellite suite remained ominously silent. For now, they were running blind. Then there was the other complication.

The Israeli.

He was presumably on their side, but in this corner of the world, where allegiances shifted like the desert breeze, one never knew. He remembered the man's presentation at Les Palmiers, precise words and carefully constructed thoughts that could not have been bettered by Langley's legal department. So too, he remembered the gray eyes that never wavered, this from a man who was on the run, and who had ended three lives in as many days. Indeed, Donnelly had sensed something missing in the Israeli.

Was it remorse? Conscience?

No, he realized, it wasn't any of that. It was a complete lack of fear. He had seen it before in certain soldiers and field operatives. They were invariably hard men, braggarts and louts mostly, the occasional madman. But this Israeli was none of those things. He was capable, Donnelly was sure, yet he also sensed commitment—a very deep commitment—to something or someone. *That* was what made him different.

And at the moment, it was what made him essential.

# SIXTY

Slaton was halfway to Tripoli and passing through Byblos, held to be the oldest continuously inhabited city in the world, and a place whose name shared origins with that of the Bible, when he turned on the phone he'd seized from Donnelly. Finding an urgent message he returned the call.

"Where are you?" asked a female voice without introduction.

"I'm sure you'll have me triangulated soon," Slaton said. "I'm on the coast road northbound, heading through Byblos."

"Did you see our confirmation on the CIA website?"

"I didn't bother to look."

"That's pretty confident." A pause as if the spokesperson was expecting a reply, then, "All right, what we need you to do is—"

"Who is this?" Slaton interrupted.

"You're speaking to the National Counterterrorism Center. My name is Sorensen. The director is monitoring this call."

Slaton considered making her prove that point, but decided it wasn't necessary. "All right. I headed north out of Beirut because I suspected the material was taken in that direction. Do you have any intel on its location?"

Slaton waited through a long silence that implied the director was indeed listening in. He imagined Sorensen being briefed on what to share, and perhaps what to hold back. She came back on the line and talked for a full minute, explaining that a suspicious aircraft the CIA had been searching for had landed that morning at an abandoned field near Selaata.

"You think this aircraft is going to transport the material?" he asked.

"*Transport* is not the right word. This is a unique jet, a very large tanker that's designed to disperse large quantities of retardant on forest fires. Or in this case, we believe something far worse."

It was Slaton's turn to go silent. For days he had been focusing on his own predicament, his private war with Ben-Meir. Now a larger picture was presented, an unprecedented threat that could affect thousands. He remembered Nassoor suggesting that the cesium could hypothetically be aerosolized to carry on the wind. "So they're going to disperse it using this airplane," he said, his thoughts verbalizing.

"We believe so," said the voice from Langley. "We haven't identified a specific target, but we think deployment may be imminent. The group behind this has gone to great lengths to hide the aircraft. It last was seen in Basrah, Iraq, and we've confirmed that equipment was placed on board there that could be used to weaponize the material."

One word sank deep in Slaton's mind. *Target.* A

vague theory began to percolate, but didn't completely come together.

"We have your location now," said Langley. "You're fifteen kilometers south of Wujah Al Hajar Air Base. We need you to get there as quickly as possible."

"And then what?" Slaton prompted.

The longest pause yet. "Right now we need eyes on that aircraft. We have a Special Forces unit in transit, but they're still three hours out. Donnelly is thirty minutes behind you with a team from the embassy. We believe there's a chance the jet is being prepared for departure. If so, we may ask you to do what you can to . . . intervene."

"Intervene," Slaton repeated. "Do you have a head count? How many would I be up against?"

"So far only two confirmed at the aircraft, but there may be more. We have supporting intelligence that links this plot to a group of seven individuals . . . three of whom you've already eliminated. We think two of the remaining four are pilots, very possibly the individuals who are at the aircraft now. The other two may be in the area."

The phrase "supporting intelligence" reminded Slaton of reports he'd gotten from Mossad in the past. It did not instill confidence. All the same, it was the best information he had—as far as the CIA knew, he would be facing no more than four adversaries, two of whom were being tracked in real time.

"Are you armed?" Sorensen asked.

Slaton pulled the phone away from his ear and stared at it. Had the camera been enabled, it would have recorded a most incredulous expression. He ended the call and pocketed the handset. Turning his full attention to the road, he pressed the accelerator to the floor. The Audi's big engine answered.

Ghazi removed his work gloves and tossed them into the scrub behind the airplane. He returned to find a nervous Tuncay standing near the nosewheel.

"You are sure it is safe for Walid and I to be inside the aircraft?" the pilot asked.

"Yes," Ghazi replied with all the conviction he could muster. In truth, there *was* a measureable degree of risk. Ghazi had handled the material behind heavy shielding, but once removed from the shipping canisters some contamination was inevitable. "Go no farther aft than necessary, and when you abandon the aircraft after landing make sure you move forward, away from the fuselage. Everything aft of the tank will be hot by then, particularly underneath."

"Hot?"

"Not as in temperature, but—" Ghazi stumbled for a way to say it without inciting panic. There wasn't one. "Everything will be fine, truly. Your escape is arranged?"

Tuncay nodded. "There is a little-used airfield south of our target area. I purchased a small aircraft and secured it in a hangar. From there, Walid and I can reach the Rub' al Khali and Yemen in no more than three hours."

Ghazi nodded. He knew Rub' al Khali by its other name—the Empty Quarter, the largest sand desert in the world. He was surprised Tuncay was sharing his plan, and decided the Turk was probably anxious, seeking last-minute affirmation of the merits of the idea. "Yes, that is good," Ghazi said, trying to sound reassuring. "Yemen is a place known only to God."

Tuncay, looking little relieved, said, "It is time we finish this. Go to the hill and relieve Walid."

Ghazi frowned. "I'm a chemist. A gun is useless in my hands."

"You practiced earlier."

A silence ran as both men recalled the sad affair, when Ben-Meir had made Ghazi take target practice. Aiming at water bottles from ten meters, he'd missed with an entire magazine. Ben-Meir had doubled over, laughing.

"It doesn't matter that you can't shoot," Tuncay said. "Just keep your eyes open and use the radio if you see anything. If anyone approaches, point the rifle to frighten them away. Walid and I will have the jet airborne soon. Then you and Ben-Meir are free to make your escape."

Ghazi took little comfort in this, remembering what Tuncay had said earlier about Ben-Meir speaking Hebrew. "I will await my payment in Rome, I think. And you?"

"I plan to avoid civilization completely. By the time the world realizes what we have wrought, I will be lost in the darkness of Africa."

The two men exchanged an awkward look, both knowing the other was lying. Not that it mattered.

With a sigh, Ghazi looked reflectively at the massive jet. "So many years of school . . . this was not how I envisioned using my education."

The Turk chuckled. "Nor I. But it pays the bills, no? You have done your part, and soon Walid and I will finish things. Now, enough talk—go relieve my copilot, and tell him to hurry."

"Yes. The quicker we are done, the better." Ghazi donned a bulky jacket, zipped it high against the cool night air, and headed into the hills.

# SIXTY-ONE

When the map on the phone showed him to be at the nearest point to Wujah Al Hajar Air Base, Slaton left the highway for a tributary road. Three miles from where the cesium-laden aircraft was supposedly parked, the dirt road narrowed severely and came to an end at an outcropping of boulders. Out of habit, he drove the Audi into a stand of brush along the siding.

He retrieved the rifle and performed a final inspection, regretting that there was no time for a few calibration rounds. The gun's action was uneven, and a thick film of dirt covered the polymer stock. He also found substantial carbon residue in the firing chamber. Right then, Slaton would have paid a million dollars of his ill-inherited fortune for an ounce of good gun oil and a rag. He exercised the mechanism a few times and things smoothed out, and from his side pocket he removed ten rounds of ammunition and slotted them into the curved, double-stacked magazine. Slaton shouldered the gun and moved east into the foothills.

He felt oddly at ease with the terrain, the topography similar to the kibbutz where he had lived as a teenager. The place where he'd hunted small game amid stunted trees and brush. The dry breeze seemed fresh and clean after the urban staleness of Beirut. He came across an old farmhouse but kept a respectable distance away. A quarter moon walked its path above high clouds, offering little ambient light, and an evening dew dampened every sound—altogether, the best possible conditions for offense and movement.

When he estimated a mile remaining, he pulled Donnelly's phone from his pocket and powered it up. He knew his position would register instantly in Virginia—and God knows where else—but there was little choice. He needed to run the application he'd spotted earlier.

The powder-blue icon was drawn like a flashlight beam pointed downward, the top of the beam splitting two upper case letters: H and G. Slaton was familiar with Project HighGround. In recent years Israel and America had become increasingly intertwined in cyber-war and technology projects, the most spectacular success being the Stuxnet virus that temporarily crippled Iran's nuclear program. HighGround had been born in that same era, and one of Slaton's last workdays with Mossad, in collaboration with Unit 8200—Israel's NSA—had been to field test an early version of the software.

If any common need had arisen from the war in Afghanistan, the tumult in Gaza, and the chaos of Syria, it was that field commanders desperately needed better access to intelligence—in particular, real-time satellite and drone surveillance video. The HighGround concept had all the hallmarks of a successful technology project. It was devilishly simple, and relied, for the most part, on proven off-the-shelf technology. Any secure satellite phone, like the one he was holding, could be programmed to receive direct downlinks from surveillance assets in the sky. A celestial mapping tool, patterned after widely available satellite tracking software, was incorporated to inform the user which assets were overhead at any given moment.

Three years ago, on a frigid night in the Negev Desert, Slaton had held a similar phone to the sky and watched markers representing satellites and drones float across the display, all superimposed on the timeless backdrop of the heavens. He'd been genuinely impressed. The usefulness of such a system seemed immeasurable, although Slaton had been warned that, once operational, the system would be initially available only to the commanders of elite military units. The user network had clearly widened since then, with the CIA a card-carrying member. The intelligence community had a good argument. After the tragic overrun of the Libyan diplomatic mission in Benghazi in 2012, and attacks on the Egyptian and Yemeni embassies that same year, what station chief wouldn't covet the ability to see what was happening in the streets and neighborhoods outside their compound?

Now, not far from the Negev where he had first seen the software, Slaton held a phone to the sky and watched a celestial array blossom to the screen. He began scanning at a high inclination, left and right, before dropping the phone toward the western horizon. The majority of satellites not in geostationary orbit travel from west to east as viewed by observers on earth, so anything inbound in the next few minutes would appear in the western sky. Drones, of course, were another matter and could be lurking anywhere. Four options came highlighted on the screen: two were currently available, as evidenced by green tags, and a pair of amber-boxed birds would arrive within the next fifteen minutes. All were U.S. assets, cooperation with Israel having apparently reached its bounds. He also noted two hollow red tags in the margins which required "secondary clearance approval." A new level of bureaucracy for which Slaton had no time.

He dragged a cursor over the four solid tags, one by one, and was given detailed information on each source: satellite or drone, type of image, and whether the focal point could be slewed directly to his target as a function of user priority. These were high-cost assets, and to actually direct their operation was not without restrictions—the intelligence establishments of D.C. would never relinquish complete control.

Something called KL-7A12 seemed the best offer. Slaton could enter any coordinates within twenty kilometers of his present position, and in the time it took to brew a cup of coffee he would receive a series of multispectral images with enough resolution to distinguish between a handheld RPG and an AK-47. Slaton could only smile, thinking, *If this isn't the Holy Grail for a field commander, it's damned close.*

As he input his request, Slaton noted changes from the original software. The map now defaulted to his present position. All he had to do was pull the cursor a short distance to the east, and the old Wujah Al Hajar Air Base came clear in the screen. Slaton tinkered with the field of coverage, resolution requirements, and sent his request. The sat-phone initiated its electronic handshake before politely asking him to: STANDBY IMAGES.

Two minutes later he had what he needed. Timely, accurate pictures of what was happening over the next hill. The Holy Grail indeed. The images were stills, not a live feed, and Slaton supposed bandwidth remained a stumbling block. Or perhaps continuous-stream feeds were reserved for higher level users than CIA station chiefs.

He pushed and pinched the screen until he had what he needed. In shades of black and white, a large aircraft was parked near a runway. He saw a lone vehicle nearby—the one seen leaving Nassoor's garage?—whose thermal signature suggested a cold engine. Slaton discerned two people, twin white stalks with extremities who were standing on the nearby tarmac. Two of the four suspects, the same picture Langley had briefed. Two pilots? A mechanic perhaps? Might there be others inside the jet?

The most important question for Slaton remained—where was Ben-Meir?

He drew the cursor left and right, up and down across the phone's little screen. He ignored a herd of goats and an abandoned car, and found what he was looking for within sixty seconds—two guards, one east and one west of the adjacent valley, both roughly a kilometer from the aircraft and established in strong defensive positions. Slaton studied the images carefully before continuing his search. He found no other threats, concurring with the CIA's estimate: four. This was the remainder of Ben-Meir's team.

He again studied the guards at the highest resolution. Both carried long-barrel weapons, and in the captured image one appeared to be scanning, presumably with some variant of night-vision optic. This was a serious complication. If one guard was employing night gear, Slaton had to assume the other was as well. He also allowed a comm link between the two. He had his own night scope, of course, but in terms of magnification and field of view it was not a high-quality item.

It was a vexing tactical problem. Long shooting was a perishable skill and he had not practiced in some time, never with this weapon. Still, at a reasonable range he thought the SVDS would be accurate enough in his hands. It was not, however, sound suppressed. His first shot would alert the surviving guard, complicating a follow-up between widely spaced targets. Slaton studied the geometry of the terrain, and considered whether he could move to a position from which he could quickly take both men. With two, perhaps three hours to stalk, there might be a way. He didn't have that long. He also had to consider the pair near the aircraft. How would they react when they realized they were under attack?

Slaton made his decision. He pocketed the phone and began to move. He would mask behind the final hill and close to within a thousand yards of the nearest guard. From that point he'd use the phone to refresh his intel one last time.

And then?

Then he would have critical decisions to make.

# SIXTY-TWO

The MD-10 was under constant surveillance at Langley, multiple sources being monitored. A high-resolution satellite feed provided the next warning.

"Sir," said the lead analyst, "we've got activity."

Everyone watched in silence as one of the two men near the aircraft—the pilots who'd been on board since Brazil, everyone agreed—tugged a pair of large objects from underneath the landing gear.

"What's he doing?" Coltrane asked.

There was a brief silence before the lone pilot in the room spoke up. "Pulling the wheel chocks," Davis said. "They're getting ready to leave."

Everyone watched the white form climb the ladder, pull it up inside the jet, and shut the entry door.

Director Coltrane asked, "How long do we have here, Davis?"

"The engines aren't running. I'd say ten minutes if they're in a hurry. More likely twenty, even twenty-five if we're lucky. That ramp is torn to hell, so they'll taxi cautiously. Best of all, they seem casual, which implies they don't know we're watching."

"We can't allow them to take off," Sorensen said. "As long as that jet is on the ground our problem is contained."

"Where is Donnelly's team?" Coltrane barked.

The rightmost monitor switched views and a blue dot blinked on a map of the coast highway. "Twenty minutes out," a technician said, "maybe a little more."

"Even if they get there in time, how can they stop a jet that size?" Sorensen asked.

"By parking on the runway," Davis said. "There's only one stretch of concrete and that jet needs every inch of it. You'd be putting a few cars in jeopardy, but it would do the job. Problem is, if the pilots don't see them soon enough to successfully abort their take-off . . . you end up with a two-hundred-mile-an-hour fireball."

"A radioactive mess," Sorensen reasoned, "but at least it would be confined."

"At this point," Davis said, "it might be the best possible outcome." His eyes alternated between the images in front of him. "Unfortunately, I see a bigger problem with the idea."

"What?" Coltrane demanded.

Davis gestured toward the blue dot representing the embassy convoy. "On the map it looks to me like there are two ways to get to this airfield. One loops around south—the old airfield access road, I'm guessing. The other is more direct—that's how our Israeli friend made his approach, and your team is headed the same way. On a GPS map it looks good, and probably would have worked twenty years ago. But if you cross-check what the satellite is showing us— that road no longer connects to the runway."

All eyes in the room alternated between the competing images.

The director deflated in his chair. "You're right— the road weaves through the hills, but comes up two miles short at the closest point."

"Exactly," Davis said. "Your team is going the wrong way."

Donnelly's convoy was speeding up the coast highway when the secure data-link chirped to announce an incoming message.

"They're saying we took a wrong turn," said the Marine corporal in the passenger seat.

"*What?*" Donnelly exclaimed. He leaned forward and checked their position on the GPS map. "This is the shortest route, the one the Israeli took! Langley tracked the ping on his goddamned phone . . . on *my* goddamned phone!"

The corporal typed Donnelly's reply minus the expletives.

Seconds later the answer came.

ROAD YOU ARE APPROACHING DOES NOT REACH AIRFIELD. REQUIRES THREE MILES ON FOOT. MUST HAVE LIMOS ON AIRFIELD TO BLOCK RUNWAY. DOUBLE BACK AND APPROACH FROM EAST.

The corporal gave an estimate. "That puts us twenty-two minutes out."

Donnelly pounded his fist on the back of the front seat. "Do it! Go!"

The three limos broke formation and battered their way across the median in a weaving, uncoordinated dance. A massive cloud of dust enveloped them all, and in a flurry of headlights and reflections the trailing car clipped the fender of Donnelly's. A symphony of obscenities followed, first inside the cars and then on the tactical frequency, before the convoy began racing in the opposite direction.

"We're too late," Davis said.

Everyone looked at the screen. The MD-10's port engine was beginning to glow bright.

"Your embassy team isn't going to make it in time."

"What about the Israeli?" Sorensen said.

Coltrane answered, "He's not there yet, and whatever weapon he's carrying isn't enough to stop this jet. The only thing he could use to block the runway is the vehicle parked next to the airplane—he'd never reach it in time."

"So what the hell do we do?" Sorensen wondered aloud.

Davis stood and scanned the leftmost display at the head of the room, a map that covered a five-hundred-mile radius. "We need an airplane," he said.

"What? You mean a fighter to shoot this thing down?"

"No. At least not yet. Do you have a link to Air Force and Navy flight ops? I want to see everything we've got flying in the area right now."

A technician in the corner answered, "We don't have a standing DOD feed, but I can access air traffic control data from the region and then filter which returns are ours."

"Do it!" Davis barked.

Coltrane sent Davis a severe gaze, but apparently decided this wasn't the time for a power trip. "What are you after?" he asked.

"Anything that flies," Davis said. "Right now we probably have a hundred military aircraft flying over the Middle East—fighters, tankers, helicopters. If we can find one within ten, maybe fifteen minutes of that airfield, we can divert it to land on the runway and act as a roadblock."

The monitors at the front of the room blinked as they began building an air traffic controller's image of the airspace over and around Lebanon. "Give me ten, maybe twenty more seconds for the feed," the technician said.

"Let's not waste it," Davis said, glancing at Coltrane. "We need comm links set up to the Air Force and Navy, CENTCOM, whoever has operational control."

This time Coltrane added the emphasis. "Do it now!"

As those lines were being run, the data arrived, a God's-eye view of every United States military aircraft within five hundred miles of Lebanon. Within seconds every set of eyes in the Ops Center was fixed on one white square floating serenely over the Eastern Mediterranean.

The call sign was Reach 41.

# SIXTY-THREE

Slaton peered over the crest of the hill. The second set of HighGround images showed the guards still in place, neither having moved. The man on the western perimeter, the closer of the two, wore a heavy jacket and was backed into a rock outcropping, meaning he had a limited field of view. The man to the east was caught in the second image still looking through some kind of scope. In a minor venture of probability, Slaton decided the easternmost of the two white blobs was Zan Ben-Meir. He was about to power down the phone when a message blinked to the screen. The subject line read: CRITICAL.

He read the rest.

AIRCRAFT PREPARING TO TAKE OFF. DELAY IF POSSIBLE. INTERVENTION TEAM ON WAY TO AIR BASE. ETA 19 MINUTES.

He considered a reply, but they were asking the impossible. Delay a wide-body airliner from taking off? The only methods that came to mind did not fall in the category of delay. Explosives, rocket-propelled grenades—any of which would precipitate a radioactive catastrophe. Shoot out the tires? Not practical given the gun he was carrying at a range of a mile and a half—downright suicidal with two armed men ready to respond.

No. Slaton had to deal with Ben-Meir and the other guard first, two of the remaining four conspirators. If the aircraft managed to get airborne, the Americans would simply have to deal with it.

He sidestepped down behind the ridge, turned north, and moved quickly in the light of the low moon. The brambles were thick, but on a goat trail that ran below the ridgeline he made good time. Roughly three hundred meters from the western guard's position Slaton crawled once more to the crest. Through the green hue of his starlight scope he scanned the surrounding area.

It took thirty seconds, and no small amount of patience, to locate his target. He was sitting on a rock, his gun leaning against a tree five paces away. Slaton had guessed right. This was the amateur. For a full minute he searched the opposite hillside, but didn't see Ben-Meir.

He cursed under his breath, then settled the gun's reticle on the amateur. He was sitting still, his knees pulled up to his chest to retain warmth. From three hundred yards with a calibrated weapon, a simple shot. Even with the gun in hand, which he'd never fired, the probability of a kill was very high. His finger hovered over the trigger, but then came off. Once he took the shot, Ben-Meir would be alerted. Slaton lowered the barrel.

There *was* a better way.

Reach 41, a Mississippi Air National Guard C-17, was cruising smoothly at twenty-five thousand feet when a chime sounded on the secure sat-com. Lieutenant Colonel Gus Bryan stirred briefly in his bunk aft of the cockpit, but then quickly drifted off again.

"Skipper," came a vague voice.

Bryan's eyes blinked open. "Can't a man get no sleep 'round here?" he mumbled in his Deep South drawl.

They had taken off from Frankfurt six hours earlier, enroute to Riyadh, Saudi Arabia, with a brief logistics stop at Incirlik Air Base in Turkey. Nearing the end of a six-day run, and having traversed nine time zones, everyone was dead tired. The copilot, Captain Bob McFadden, was running the show in the right seat, and Staff Sergeant Roy Willis, the loadmaster, had crashed somewhere in back. McFadden brought up the message, read it once and said, "Skipper, you need to take a look at this."

Bryan ambled forward, banging his knee on the center console as he arrived. "Dang it!" He recovered and admonished McFadden, "I told you to quit with that *skipper* stuff. Do it one more time and I'm gonna give you a mop and make you swab the deck." McFadden was a former Marine, and a Connecticut Yankee to boot. But he was a damned good pilot, which was why the 183rd Airlift Squadron had hired him out of active duty last year.

"All right," Bryan said, "where's the fire?"

McFadden pointed to the message, and Bryan saw an amended tasking order: they were to divert to a new destination at maximum practical speed. He'd never seen anything like it. He'd also never heard of the airfield. "What the hell?"

"What do you make of it, sir?"

"No idea. I've diverted for bad weather or to deliver troops to a hot spot . . . but this is strange. That mission priority is one they talk about on checkrides, but outside nuclear war I never figured I'd see it. So where is—" he double-checked the message, "Wujah Al Hajar Air Base?"

The ever-efficient McFadden began scrolling through navigation charts, but came up empty. "I don't see it."

"Look here," Bryan said, pointing to the message, "they gave us a lat-long."

McFadden typed in the coordinates, and a manual waypoint symbol lit to the aircraft's map display. "Fifty-two nautical miles east," he said.

"*East?* You mean—"

"Yep," McFadden said, seeing the problem. "Smack in the middle of Lebanon."

Bryan, wide awake now, slid into the left seat. "I got the airplane. You start typing. Find out if this is for real or if one of our old bar buddies is yankin' our chain."

# SIXTY-FOUR

Tuncay watched Walid start the number three engine. A pneumatic starter spun the big fan, and when Walid raised the start lever to idle, fuel sprayed into the engine's combustion chamber. Nothing else happened.

"Something is wrong!" Walid said in a clipped voice. "Number three is not lighting off."

"Stop the start!" Tuncay commanded.

Walid moved switches and the big turbofan wound down, its signature hum lowering in pitch until silence reigned. "What now?" he asked.

Tuncay frowned severely.

"We need a mechanic," Walid said.

"Yes, I will call right away!" Tuncay replied sharply. "A power-plant specialist who is familiar with General Electric CF6 engines. That should be simple enough on a deserted Lebanese airfield in the middle of the night. Oh, and we must warn our mechanic not to go near the fuselage amidships because that's where the radiation is."

Walid went silent.

A fuming Tuncay pondered the problem. They were not excessively heavy—the aircraft had a minimum fuel load—so it was possible they could take off on two engines. Unfortunately, that would require a

432 | WARD LARSEN

great deal of runway, and their best chance of not crashing on takeoff to begin with was to use as little of the rutted concrete as possible. There was also the matter of the thrust asymmetry introduced by a dead but windmilling starboard engine. Would it be manageable? Would the craft yaw to one side and careen into the hills? There was no way to tell.

He was mulling it all when the increasingly useless Walid said, "Look! The circuit breaker for the number three engine ignition has popped."

Tuncay looked at the vertical panel above and behind his copilot where hundreds of circuit breakers were arrayed. Sure enough, the tiny round button through which power flowed to the number three engine ignition system had popped, removing DC current from the igniters.

Walid looked at Tuncay, who nodded. He turned in his seat and reset the breaker by pushing it in.

They went through the start sequence a second time, and both men held their breaths. The starboard engine lit off and spun to life perfectly.

Walid sat with a smile etched on his face.

Tuncay could have kissed him.


"NVGs?" Lieutenant Colonel Bryan said. "They want us to land at some place we've never been using night vision gear?"

"That's what the order says," said McFadden, who'd been exchanging a continuous stream of messages with CENTCOM. "They want our approach to be lights-out until just before landing. We're supposed to block the runway so an MD-10 that's parked there can't take off."

"Well now ain't that just fresh! Is there any kind

of instrument approach I can use to line up with this runway?"

"Uh . . . no, sir. I asked about that, and it seems the reason I couldn't find this airport in our nav database is because it's closed."

"*Closed?*" Bryan exclaimed.

"As far as I can tell, it shut down over twenty years ago."

Bryan gave his copilot a look that caused the ex-Marine to freeze. He rang the loadmaster on the intercom.

A sleepy voice answered, "What's up, Colonel?"

"Willis, tell me again what we're carryin' back there." After nearly a week of trash-hauling, the manifests had run together in Bryan's sleep-deprived brain.

"Only nine pallets, but it's heavy stuff. A couple of replacement engines for Seventh Corps armor, and a load of gear for a Special Forces unit—I'm not exactly sure what it is, but the hazmat log lists a thousand pounds of high explosives."

"We've been diverted and we'll be landing in ten minutes—be ready!"

"Ten mi—"

Bryan snapped the switch that removed Sergeant Willis' voice from the intercom. He checked the navigation display and saw they had thirty-nine miles to go. "A night diversion to land at a closed airport with NVGs . . . and I'm carrying half a ton of high explosives! Christ on a bike, can it get any better?"

At that moment, the Lebanese air traffic controller sounded on the radio. "*Reach Four-One, I show you off course. You are approaching Lebanese airspace! Turn right heading two two zero immediately!*"

The pilots stared at one another.

McFadden said, "If we don't say something they might try to intercept us."

"No, Lebanon doesn't have any fighters . . . at least, I don't think they do."

"They have surface-to-air missiles."

Bryan keyed his microphone, "Lebanon Control, Reach Four-One is declaring an emergency! We've lost two engines and require an immediate diversion!"

The air traffic controller started to say something, but Bryan took off his headset. From here on out, the radio would be nothing but a distraction. "Thirty-two miles. Get in the box and build me an approach as best you can to that runway."

"How do I know which way is into the wind?"

"To hell with the winds. Go with whichever side has the least terrain." McFadden started typing on the navigation computer. "When you're done, go and dig out the NVGs—and while you're at it, say a little prayer that the batteries are good."

There was no mistaking the sound of the engines.

Being an experienced soldier, Ben-Meir only glanced at the MD-10 as it prepared to move. From his position on a tree-shrouded promontory, and without the use of his optics, the aircraft was no more than a dim outline. The jet's navigation lights remained extinguished, which meant the only manufactured light was a pale white glow from the cockpit windows.

Ben-Meir turned away and surveyed the hills one last time. After months of planning and preparation, his part of the mission would be complete in a matter of minutes. It had not been easy—he'd lost three men, the entire assault force he'd recruited. The *kidon* had been better than he'd imagined. Or perhaps more fortunate. Their original intent had never been to eliminate Slaton. Indeed, quite the opposite. But then he'd lost Kieras in Malta, followed by Stanev in Zurich. By the time of the encounter in Wangen, all bets were off as far as he was concerned. Still the *kidon* had survived.

It hardly mattered. Ben-Meir pulled his collar up against the cool night air. *This time next week, I will be in a very warm and pleasant place.*

Through his optics he saw nothing to the east or south, his primary areas of responsibility. Of course, with Ghazi standing watch on the opposite hill, Ben-Meir knew he was effectively responsible for the full swing of the compass. He searched farther afield and saw a distant herd of goats, and in a wadi at the bottom of the valley the abandoned hulk of a car, its metal losing heat more quickly than the surrounding earth. He lowered his night scope, breathed a sigh of relief, and was trying to recall the check-in time for his morning flight out of Beirut when the report of a shot echoed through the hills.

Ben-Meir snatched up his optics and checked Ghazi's position. More shots rang out, one of them sounding a different pitch. A second weapon. He spotted two figures. One was unfamiliar, staggering and leaning on a tree. The outline of a hot-barreled rifle lay on the ground nearby. The second figure was moving, making awkward but steady progress toward the runway. Ben-Meir recognized Ghazi's bulky parka, marked with the IR reflective tape he had wrapped around each wrist.

Ben-Meir scrambled down the hill, stopping periodically to scan for other threats. The man in Ghazi's abandoned position had gone still, his back propped against a tree. Ben-Meir realized that Ghazi was heading directly for the aircraft. *Idiot.*

They didn't have a communication link set up— there had been no time to acquire the hardware, nor to train a chemist on the fundamentals of tactical communication. When he'd heard the first shot Ben-Meir feared he would see a strike force, a dozen or more commandos ghosting in from all directions. Yet things seemed quiet, no more shots, no darting movement through the hills. Someone had stumbled across Ghazi's position, he reasoned, and the nearsighted chemist had actually gotten the better of an armed shepherd or a smuggler—Mohammed, the demolition man he'd hired, had warned him the hills were thick with both.

Ben-Meir neared the man leaning against the tree trunk with his weapon trained. His senses were keen, sight and sound filtering for the slightest deviation. He saw only a shoulder at first, and then the side of a watch cap. The head inside the knit cap was rolling, like a man about to lose consciousness. Ben-Meir saw a weapon on the ground, an unusual make but vaguely familiar—a high-end marksman's rifle. Which meant he was looking at more than an errant goatherder or a black-market smuggler.

The man shifted against the tree, and Ben-Meir took no chances. From twenty meters he sent a round into the shoulder joint. A scream of pain, and the figure fell writhing to the ground. Both hands were in view now, comfortingly empty, and Ben-Meir lowered his gun to his hip over the last few steps. His target, facedown in the dirt, emitted a weak, liquid-filled groan. Ben-Meir rolled the man with his boot and saw a contorted face covered in blood and dirt. Saw the eyeglasses on the ground next to him.

His chest tightened, and all too late Ben-Meir realized his mistake.

He was looking at Ghazi.

He spun and lunged sideways in the same motion. It didn't save him.

The first bullet struck squarely in his upper chest, an explosion of pain like nothing he'd ever experienced. The second round hit lower, a gut shot, and put him on the ground. Ben-Meir tried to focus. His weapon was in the dirt, just out of reach, and he thought with an odd detachment, *So this is what it's like*. He had been on the other end of this exchange many times, and it was curiously illuminating to see things from the target's perspective. He straightened his back long enough to meet his executioner.

He was standing in Ghazi's jacket, the chemist's weapon poised in his hand. It was the *kidon,* of course, twenty meters away. *After a completely silent approach,* thought Ben-Meir appreciatively. The pain was excruciating and he hoped, in a mercy he had not always visited upon others, that the assassin would end things sooner rather than later.

It was Zan Ben-Meir's last thought of this world.

# SIXTY-FIVE

Five thousand miles away, twenty-three men and women sat motionless in the Langley Ops Center. For eight minutes they had watched in silence, mesmerized, as three pixelated images moved through the scrub-filled hills of central Lebanon. In an extraordinary game of cat and mouse, they saw the Israeli stalk one perimeter guard, disable him at close quarters, and then, for reasons no one could fathom at the time, trade clothing with his victim. Few in the command center held tactical experience on their resumes, and so the run of the ensuing sequence of events was unclear until the final, decisive shot. When the end came, as viewed from a satellite feed without sound or commentary, it was surreal. From half a world away, they had witnessed an assassin at work. A veritable theater of death.

It was an NSA imagery tech, on loan from Ft. Meade, who finally broke the silence. "I would say those are confirmed kills."

Sorensen related the math, "Of the seven on our list, he's now removed five."

Another voice asked the question on everyone's mind. "Who *is* this guy?"

Sorensen eyed the director, who nearly said something, but then demurred. She remembered the meeting in his office when he'd reacted to the name they had uncovered. *David Slaton*.

"Sir, the MD-10 is on the move," said the imagery tech.

On two adjacent screens, everyone watched the massive jet pull out of its parking spot.

"Where is that C-17?" Coltrane demanded.

"Fourteen miles out."

"Will it get there in time to block the runway?" Coltrane asked.

"It'll be close," said Davis, "but probably not."

The imagery tech said, "We may not need it."

All eyes went to the thermal image on the central monitor. The assassin was two kilometers from the runway. He was running fast with a rifle in his hand.


Tuncay steered the big jet carefully over the narrow taxiway, and decided that Wujah Al Hajar Air Base must have been built long ago—probably when propellers were used for propulsion, and certainly before aircraft had two-hundred-foot wingspans.

"I hope this taxiway is stressed for a half-million-pound aircraft."

As if to answer, he sensed the jet's main wheels begin to mire in the asphalt. Tuncay advanced the throttles to keep up momentum, but it felt as if they were taxiing through beach sand.

"The runway is concrete," Walid said. "Once we reach it we will be fine."

"Flaps twenty-five," Tuncay commanded.

"Twenty-five?" Walid questioned.

"It is a higher than normal setting, but allows us to use less runway and lift off at a lower speed."

Walid nodded at this logic, and moved the flap lever to the gate marked 25. The wing flaps obliged, both men watching the gauge to be sure they extended properly. The two pilots ran a pre-takeoff checklist, and on reaching the runway Tuncay pirouetted the MD-10, pointing its nose toward the far end.

"Landing lights?" Walid inquired.

"No, there is just enough moonlight. I can see the runway."

"But why not turn on the lights?"

"We don't want to draw attention, Walid. Our landing lights can be seen for thirty miles, and if anyone sees us taking off they might alert the authorities. Besides, we don't have to worry about other air traffic. This field hasn't been used in thirty years."

Tuncay pushed up the throttles, and the three General Electric engines surged to full thrust. Even with the dense load amidships, they were nowhere near the aircraft's maximum gross weight. Acceleration was brisk, the cool night air and sea level pressure drawing maximum performance from the turbofans.

Walid called out, "Eighty knots."

Tuncay made a brief cross-check of his own airspeed indicator. He had little trouble seeing the outline of the runway, the desert left and right discernable in the faint light. The big jet bounced and rattled over the beaten runway, and Tuncay prayed that none of the ten tires would fail. At 100 knots, Tuncay felt the controls stiffen in his hands as aerodynamic forces began to take hold. At 150, Walid called, "Rotate." Tuncay began firm back pressure on the control column, pulling two hundred and fifty tons of metal into the air. At 170 knots, he instructed, "Landing gear up."

Walid was reaching for the gear handle, the jet no

more than fifty feet in the air, when a light as brilliant as the sun appeared directly in front of them. It was absolutely blinding.

"Pull up!" Walid screamed.

On raw survival instinct, Tuncay did exactly that.


The disaster unfolded right in front of Slaton.

He had been barely a hundred meters from the runway, standing in a shallow wadi etched during the airfield's years of disuse, when his path reached the closest point to the lumbering jet on its takeoff run. He'd done his best to establish good footing and shoulder his weapon—he had hopefully retrieved the SVDS—but the futility was instantly clear. It was like pointing a BB gun at a two-hundred-mile-an-hour elephant.

Slaton had dropped the gun to his side and stood helplessly. He felt the ground shake under his feet, felt the reverberations of three giant turbofans violating the still air. And then—the most amazing thing happened.

The night sky came alive with light.

He watched the big jet lurch upward in an outrageous maneuver, heard its engines surge to a thunderous, more desperate pitch. The massive outline seemed to hover for a moment, illuminated like a snapshot in the blackened sky.

Only then did Slaton recognize the second jet.

Its landing lights were ablaze as it dove for the ground. Two behemoths traveling in opposite directions seemed to merge above the runway, and Slaton tensed for a momentous collision, expecting a fireball like a supernova.

Nothing happened.

The roar of turbines reached a crescendo, quite literally tearing apart the night air. The second aircraft passed just underneath the MD-10, and the prospect of cataclysm faded as quickly as it had arrived. The MD-10 nosed forward and faded into darkness. The second aircraft, almost as large, wasn't so lucky. It was destined for the ground, a crash imminent, until the nose rotated upward at the last instant. The murderous rate of descent eased, and the wheels slammed onto the runway in a storm of dust. The big jet bounced twenty feet into the air, more a carnival ride than a landing, but the wings remained level and its wheels met the earth again, this time with a degree of control.

In a flurry of dust and noise the thrust reversers deployed, and the new jet came to rest at the far end of the runway. Its silhouette, reflected in its own landing lights, was enough for Slaton to make an ID: dark gray paint, distinctive T-tail, and a subdued emblem on the rear empennage to settle any doubt. He was looking at a United States Air Force C-17.

Slaton ventured one last look skyward. He saw nothing but black. The aircraft carrying Moses Nassoor's cache of cesium was riding the wind.

# SIXTY-SIX

Slaton made his weapon safe and sprinted downhill, hurdling rocks and weaving through tangled under-growth. Twice he nearly fell, and on reaching the concrete runway he took up a dead sprint to the far end, slowing only when he approached the C-17.

The jet's four engines seemed to be shut down, but he recognized the high-pitched whine of an auxilliary power unit. The aircraft was eerily still, shrouded in a dissipating cloud of dust with its landing lights still on, illuminating the desert ahead like a massive flash-light.

Slaton was walking under the port wing when the crew entry door opened and a ladder extended. A lieu-tenant colonel in a flight suit came down the boarding steps, cussing a blue streak all the way to the ground. The man noticed Slaton, who still had a rifle in his hand, just as his feet hit the ramp.

"Are you with the embassy?" the pilot yelled.

Without hesitation, Slaton said, "Yeah."

"Well I don't know what's going on here, but this is bullshit! Somebody almost got me killed just now, and my jet is probably damaged." He strode back and began inspecting the C-17, paying particular attention to the landing gear. "The governor of Mississippi is *not* gonna be happy about this!"

A second pilot, this one a captain, descended to the tarmac, followed by an enlisted man who Slaton assumed was the loadmaster. Both looked pale and shaken. Slaton continued watching the door, expecting a Special Forces squad to follow. There was no one else.

The captain said, "Colonel, I just got off the line with command post. I told them we almost had a midair collision trying to land."

"What did they say?"

"They pushed me to another channel and said stand by for further orders."

"*Further* orders? I'll tell 'em exactly where they can put their further orders!" The livid aircraft commander strode to the boarding stairs, but halfway there he stopped and veered to a course that ended one step in front of Slaton. The light colonel was about to say something when he seemed to register for the first time that he was addressing a man with a gun. Together with the civilian clothes, it implied that he and this stranger were not necessarily part of the same organizational food chain.

With the good sense of an old soldier, the pilot—Lieutenant Colonel Gus Bryan, according to his name tag—ratcheted down.

"I will assume," Bryan began, "that the airplane we nearly met at two hundred feet was the one we were trying to keep on the ground?"

Slaton considered this. The CIA must have realized its intervention team wasn't going to arrive in time. "So that's what you were trying to do? Block the runway?"

The Mississippian nodded as his crewmen circled the aircraft for their own inspections.

"Too bad you didn't get here sixty seconds sooner," Slaton said. "It would have worked."

"So who the heck are you?"

"Not relevant."

"Would it be relevant to tell me what that airplane was doing here? They closed this airfield around the time I was partying at Ole Miss."

"I don't see much more than a strip of concrete, but apparently that still works. As for the airplane you almost ran into—it's carrying a load that's making a lot of people nervous."

Bryan eyed him seriously, probably because what Slaton said made sense. "What kind of load?"

"Radiological."

The lieutenant colonel's anger subsided.

The loadmaster and captain came back from their walk-around inspections of the jet. "It all looks in one piece," the loadmaster said. "The brakes are hot but they should be fine after maybe thirty minutes of cooling."

"Thirty minutes?" the colonel remarked. "They're gonna have a lot longer than that to cool. This runway is a mess." With a boot toe he turned over a chunk of loose concrete. "Potholes and cracks everywhere. Flying this jet out isn't going to happen until a team of civil engineers shows up and makes some serious repairs." He surveyed his airplane, then turned back toward the stranger. "Radiological you say?"

Slaton nodded.

"Who was flying it? Lebanese Air Force? Terrorists of some kind?"

"I'm not exactly sure. In this part of the world, things like that can be a little hard to nail down."

"Where is it headed?"

"I don't know that either. But I'm going to find out."

"How do you propose to do that?"

"Easy—I'm going to use your radios." Slaton shouldered his weapon and headed for the boarding stairs.


Davy had been crying for the best part of two hours. It was out of the ordinary, and when he began running a low temperature and sneezing Christine guessed he was coming down with a cold. Mercifully, he fell asleep in his crib just after dinner. She too was exhausted, having not had a good night's sleep in days.

She found Stein downstairs, standing with a sandwich in one hand and the television remote in the other. He was surfing through channels. "I'm going to try and get some sleep. I think Davy is coming down sick, and he probably won't sleep through the night."

"Okay. Anything I can do to help?"

"I suppose a run to the pharmacy for an antihistamine is out of the question?"

Stein shot her a disapproving look.

"Right." She hesitated, and he seemed to read her mind.

"No—I haven't heard from David."

Christine nodded and went upstairs, and spent a full five minutes watching Davy sleep. His breathing was steady, punctuated by the occasional sob after his earlier meltdown. *Has to be that,* she thought. *The nightmares don't come until later.*

She went to her room, and instead of undressing changed into a pair of comfortable jeans and a loose sweatshirt. Her running shoes went to the foot of the bed, which would please her not-so-dead husband. *Always be ready on a moment's notice.* Of course, that sage advice presumed one was on the run. Her situation was quite the opposite, bunkered up with a bodyguard in her home. Her eyes fell closed, and she easily ignored the sound of the television down the hall and a rattle of wind at the window.

Minutes later she was fast asleep.

At that same moment, across the street, the front door of the house on a right-hand diagonal swung slowly open. A large man dressed in layered clothing emerged. He moved with palpable caution, and from the travertine-wrapped porch, he looked left and right up the street before closing the door. He moved with an unnatural gait, this due to the heavy metal bar hidden in the recesses of his jacket, which partially immobilized his right side. So encumbered, the man set out at determined pace toward the snow-encrusted sidewalk, and on reaching it he veered slightly to his right. He crossed the street heading directly for Christine Palmer's house.

# SIXTY-SEVEN

The Middle East is a region unlike any other. In a geographic footprint that would fit within the state of Nevada lies a combustible merger of eight troubled nations: Israel, Iraq, Saudi Arabia, Syria, Jordan, Egypt, Lebanon, and Turkey. Starting from the center, in Lebanon, a typical jet aircraft might reach any of those borders within twenty minutes. Not by chance, each of these surrounding nations is capable of launching fighters to intercept intruding aircraft, or if a more direct approach is desired, to shoot them down using surface-to-air missiles. If this brew of weapons, mistrust, and cross-purposes is not perplexing enough, most of these eight countries are home to warring tribes and religious factions that keep some degree of autonomous military capability. Finally, as a coup de grâce to any hope for regional stability, the majority of shrines holy to the Christian, Muslim, and Jewish religions reside in this same unsettled outline. The birthplace of so many of the world's religions, in a somber paradox, is no better off for it.

Director Thomas Coltrane had a monumental problem on his hands.

Their efforts at containment had failed miserably,

which meant he and his Ops Center team were now little more than witnesses to a radiological bomb gliding through the world's most unfriendly skies. They knew precisely where the aircraft was, the U.S. Air Force having excellent radar coverage in the area, but without some idea of where it was going there was little hope of setting countermeasures in place. As far as they knew, the plot unfolding before them involved seven individuals, five of whom had already been dispatched by an assassin, a man not under Langley's control, yet who had proven brutally effective. Unfortunately, not *quite* effective enough.

"Our target is fifteen nautical miles from the Syrian border," said a front-row voice. "Heading is steady to the southeast." The specialists, on their own initiative, had already taken to calling it a target.

Sorensen said, "We need to get fighters in the air for an intercept."

The Ops Center's DOD liaison, already thinking along those lines, said, "We have the carrier *Reagan* in the eastern Med, roughly three hundred miles west. I'll find out how soon they can have Hornets in the air. CENTCOM is checking what else is available—the Air Force always has fighters deployed somewhere on the Saudi peninsula."

Everyone nodded agreement, and someone suggested that the neighboring U.S. consulates should be put on alert. Another voice observed that because the MD-10 was traveling southeast, it would soon be within range of Patriot surface-to-air missile batteries in both Israel and Saudi Arabia. Coltrane had already made notifications up the chain of command, a chart in which there were few boxes above his own. The director of national intelligence would soon brief the president on the impending disaster. Sidebar agencies had also been notified, but these were largely a distraction. In proof of this point, facing Coltrane's big leather chair was a communications suite whose blinking lights represented no fewer than six government entities waiting to speak to him.

"All right," he said, "I'm going to bring everyone in on a conference call and ask for help on this. Foggy Bottom can handle embassy notifications and dust off their response plan for a radiological attack. I want CENTCOM and the Joint Chiefs to coordinate—"

*"You don't need any of that crap!"* a voice boomed from the back. A room full of busy chatter went silent and everyone looked at Jammer Davis. "You need a pilot, a meteorologist, and a chaplain."

Davis was situated at the back of the room, planted in a chair far too small for his massive frame. He was chewing on a vending machine burrito.

Coltrane said, "Let me guess—you're the pilot?"

"I'll go out on a limb here and say I'm the only person in this room who's ever shot down an airplane."

"Mr. Davis, you've proven yourself useful, but I think the situation has progressed outside your area of expertise."

"I think it's outside *your* area of expertise. You've got a large airliner flying over foreign soil that's loaded with a radiological agent. There's a strong chance this material will be dispersed before it lands. The list of potential targets in this part of the world is overwhelming. You've got population centers, economic targets, military facilities, religious shrines. We need to get ahead of the curve and figure out where this jet is headed."

"Which is exactly why I need to bring others in."

Coltrane turned away, picked up his handset, and

initialized the first of his calls. He'd been talking for less than five seconds when a big hand swept in and cut off the call. A furious Coltrane looked up and saw Davis at his shoulder. "Do you realize you just hung up on the Secretary of State? *You are out of line, mister!*"

In a calm, low voice Davis said, "If you spend the next ten minutes on interagency coordination, your chance to stop this will be gone. You are facing a crisis, sir. But you've also got twenty good, capable people right here in this room. Use them!"

Coltrane's eyes swept out, and a sea of eager, competent faces stared back.

"Would you like to know where this jet is headed?" Davis asked.

"You can tell me?"

"No, I'd just be guessing. But there's no need for that. The pilots flying it have already told us where they're going—we just haven't been listening."

Coltrane's eyes narrowed severely, but his anger gave way to curiosity. He set down the handset. "What do you mean?"

Davis pointed to the white dot on the map. "Those pilots know perfectly well where they're operating. If they try to cross any border without a flight clearance, it's an invitation to be intercepted. So unless the captain is planning on staying in Lebanese airspace, which makes no sense, you'll find a flight plan on file with Lebanese air traffic control. The crew might have called it in by phone, or maybe filed it by computer. They might even have coordinated a clearance by radio after they got airborne. Of course, the paperwork isn't going to say they're flying an MD-10—they know we'll be looking for that. It'll say the aircraft is an Airbus or a business jet. That's what I would do. To the air traffic controllers there's no difference—they see nothing but a blip on a screen. But there *is* a flight plan in the system. Has to be."

After a brief pause, Coltrane pointed to a woman at the communications desk. Her fingers began racing over her keypad.

Coltrane said, "I'm not sure I buy into your theory. These people have gone to incredible lengths to hide what they're doing. They managed to chop up a derelict airliner in the middle of the night, remove the pieces, and park another jet in its place without anyone noticing. You think they'll just publish a route to their target for the world to see?"

"No—it won't be that simple. It won't be a straight line. If this is truly the strike mission, they'll plan a feint, an ordinary flight path that takes them *near* their target but not directly to it. When the time is right, they make a hard turn and push up the throttles. Three minutes, maybe five, and they'll be right where they want to be before anyone can react."

Coltrane sat rail-still in his seat. "What else?"

"We're talking about the aerial dispersal of a contaminant. Your typical firebomber will drop its load all at once, from maybe five hundred feet. That covers a linear mile, more or less. If they fly lower, down in the dirt like a crop duster, the footprint becomes smaller and the radiation more dense. In that case, we could be talking about an area the size of a football field. However, either of those cases present one problem. Flying a wide-body airliner at five hundred feet is tricky at night—it would require special equipment and some training."

"Which leaves us where?"

"The nightmare scenario." Davis waited, but no one asked. "Drop five kilos of cesium from thirty thousand feet, and you can rain gamma emissions over a whole city, maybe even a country. Not as dangerous, obviously, from the standpoint of radiation density or the threat to a population. But as a terror weapon?"

Coltrane nodded. "It would be devastating."

"It would be Chernobyl with wings." Davis took another bite of his burrito. "The flight plan will include a cruise altitude. Put the two together, and it might help you predict the target. Once you know *that,* you can decide how to handle it. Next, any response is going to require accurate information on the winds aloft at every altitude. Like I said, you need a meteorologist."

Coltrane set a woman to that task.

Davis picked up. "Miss Sorensen is correct—you need fighters in the air as soon as possible to shadow this jet. You *could* use the Air Force of one of the neighboring countries. Israel and Jordan are reliable, and probably Saudi Arabia. Their pilots are well-trained, and disciplined enough to not screw this up by getting trigger-happy. Personally, I'd prefer relying on our own assets. In any event, whoever you use has to be capable of shooting this airplane down, which is a very messy last resort."

"No," Coltrane said, "we have to avoid that."

Davis pointed again to the white dot on the monitor that represented CB68H. "That's your call. But you should pray to God that this blip doesn't turn north. There's no telling how the Syrians or the Turks would react to a threat like this."

"And that," Coltrane ventured, "is where the chaplain comes in?"

Davis smiled.

# SIXTY-EIGHT

The odyssey of Charlie Bravo Six Eight Hotel continued to unfold on the main monitor in the Langley Ops Center. The flight plan was discovered within minutes. It had been filed electronically—when and from what source was put aside for the time being—and activated with Lebanese air traffic control as soon as the jet was airborne.

The most relevant sections were transparent: a proposed cruising altitude of fifteen thousand feet, and a route shaped by a more or less direct path through central Saudi Arabia, with a final destination of Abu Dhabi International Airport in the United Arab Emirates. The subterfuge Davis had predicted was also there—the aircraft type on the flight plan was not listed as an MD-10, but instead a Hawker 1000, a business jet with suitably comparable performance characteristics.

"They're into Syrian airspace," Sorensen said.

The jet was so far behaving normally, holding true to its filed track and level at the requested altitude of fifteen thousand feet. A conscientious crew undertaking an ordinary flight.

"So what are they after?" Coltrane said, voicing the question on everyone's mind. "Dubai could be a target. Banking and tourism, the tallest building in the world. We have the forged identity operation, so maybe this was sourced in Iran—there are a lot of Shiites who don't like the Emirati."

"No," said Sorensen. "I don't think we should fall into the trap that this is state-sponsored. Half the characters involved are not even from the region."

"She's right," Davis agreed. "This is terrorism, but I don't see religious or political aims. We're watching something else." He looked at a projected flight path that spanned hundreds of miles of empty desert, sand and hills and widely dispersed villages.

"Sir," said a comm tech near the front of the room. "I have CENTCOM requesting a secure link."

"What do they want?" Coltrane asked.

"They have a patch to the C-17 on the ground in Lebanon. Apparently the man we were watching earlier wants to talk."

Looks were exchanged all around the room.

"The Israeli wants to talk to us?" Coltrane asked rhetorically. "All right, maybe he can shed some light on this."

Coltrane chose a speaker option so that everyone could listen in.

"This is Thomas Coltrane, director of the CIA. Am I speaking with the former Edmund Deadmarsh?"

There was a significant pause, longer than necessary for the cross-continent link. "You are," the assassin answered.

Behind Coltrane the mood of confusion only heightened, no one in the room having ever heard the name before.

The man who answered to the name of Deadmarsh said, "I assume you know by now that the jet you're after was not contained here?"

"Yes, we're tracking it."

"Where is it heading?"

Coltrane paused.

The voice from Lebanon said, "Look, I'm sure you've been watching this place for the last thirty minutes, which means you've been watching me."

"Yes."

"Are you not convinced that I'm on your side?"

"I'm convinced," Coltrane said, "that you have some serious issues with these people. If I better understood your motivation I might be more inclined to—"

"No time, Director. Where is the airplane now?"

Coltrane was silent for only a moment. He relented. "They've flown east into Syria, and we think the jet is bound for Saudi airspace. They've filed a flight plan that runs all the way to Dubai. Can you think of any targets along that route?"

There was another hesitation that Coltrane read as thoughtfulness.

"I might know, at least in a general way. The details would take too long to explain, but I think it relates to oil supply. These people have made bets in financial markets that the price of crude oil is going to rise."

Coltrane glanced at Sorensen and could almost see the puzzle pieces linking in her head. She too was remembering the recent plays in energy markets they'd uncovered, all related to a Barclays account in the name of David Slaton—the man they were presumably talking to right now. That complication, evident as it was, had to be swept aside. There was room for but one question.

*Where would the strike occur?*

Analysts went to work, and in no time had assimilated the idea of a strike against oil assets into their pixelated big picture. On the central wall-mounted map a geologic survey of oil reserves was quickly laid under the aircraft's flight path. Every set of eyes in the room went to one spot.

"Christ almighty!" said Coltrane. "That's got to be it!"

# SIXTY-NINE

An accident of nature, the Ghawar oil field of Saudi Arabia was born some 200 million years ago. Shaped as a convex ridge, its Jurassic limestone reaches over one hundred miles south from Ain Dar in the general outline of a sleek nose-diving bird. The sheif beneath, a perfect geologic fusion of permeability and porosity, is ideally suited to the creation and retention of low-sulfur, high-quality hydrocarbons. Since first coming on line in 1951, Ghawar has produced nearly two-thirds of all Saudi Arabia's oil, and even after sixty years the field shows no sign of exhaustion. The managing corporation, state-owned Saudi Aramco, tirelessly pumps seawater, steam, and carbon dioxide into the earth to force more than five million barrels a day to the surface, this representing over 6 percent of the world's crude output. Fitting to its Jurassic origin, Ghawar is a monster without equal, and undeniably the largest oil field in the world.

In the Langley command center Ghawar was displayed as an elongated vertical blob on the map, and of prime interest was what perfectly intersected the oil basin's northernmost border near the place called Ain Dar—the projected flight path of CB68H.

"That's the target," Davis agreed.

"They're going to irradiate the world's biggest oil field," Coltrane said aloud and with some deliberation, clearly trying to wrap his mind around the idea. "It's a hundred miles long. Could they contaminate something that size?" The director shifted his gaze to Dr. Stan Zimmerman, a physicist from DS&T, Langley's Directorate of Science and Technology, who'd been summoned after the confirmation of radiological involvement in Al Qutayfah. "Could the amount of material we're talking about cover such a large area?"

Zimmerman, a bearded, professorial type, appeared thoughtful before answering. "We have to think in terms of radiation density. There's no way to tell exactly how the contamination will disperse—it depends on the method of release and atmospheric factors. As Mr. Davis has already suggested, wind, humidity, and precipitation can bring great variances in coverage. Putting that aside, the amount of radiation is static. Given what we know, I've estimated these sources will contain between fifteen and twenty thousand terabecquerels. Confine that to a small area, and the localized readings would be extreme. On the other hand, if these people spread that amount of material over an area the size of Ghawar, or even half of it, the local levels of radiation would be modest. Unfortunately, the impact in this scenario is far greater. Fear and uncertainty would reign, and every hospital and clinic within five hundred miles would find itself overwhelmed. Oil production would cease immediately, and the subsequent decontamination process—that would be measured in years."

Davis said, "In the military we call it area denial.

You can perform the same mission with land mines or chemical weapons. The idea is to keep an opposing force out, to shut down their ability to operate in a specific geographic region. We're looking at the same strategy applied to the world's most vital commodity."

"So that's it," Coltrane surmised. "These people silently invested in oil markets, and now they're going to shut down the world's largest source of crude for years."

"Supply and demand disruption, inelastic prices, fear," said Davis. "That's textbook economic terrorism."

"It leaves no option," Coltrane announced. "We have to shoot this airplane down."

"I'd be careful there," said Davis. "Shoot a Sidewinder into that monster, and you'll get a helluva midair fireball."

"He's right," agreed Zimmerman. "An explosion at altitude would create a significant cloud of radioactive particles that will carry on the wind."

"But it's the desert, for God's sake," countered Coltrane.

"I've flown quite a bit over this corner of the world," said Davis. "Parts of Saudi Arabia look like the moon. But you've also got villages, oil workers, Bedouin. Shoot the jet down anywhere on that track and people *are* going to die."

"He is correct," Zimmerman seconded. "Contamination of this magnitude cannot be contained. Wind and rain will drive it to populated areas. You can expect near-term fatalities, and serious health issues for decades to come. The only question is how many will suffer. Hundreds? Thousands? If you shoot that airplane down now, you lose control of the outcome."

"So what the hell do we do?" the director asked in

a raised voice, clearly nearing the end of his tether. "The House of Saud will pop an aneurism if they hear about this!"

"Probably a bigger one if they don't," Sorensen commented.

Zimmerman said, "To begin, I think Mr. Davis has a point. We must have a meteorologist involved. It's important to know the winds aloft in order to mitigate risk."

"He's on the way," said Coltrane feebly.

Davis remained quiet. He stared at the map, but unlike the rest of the room he was not seeing oil fields or towns, or even the floating dot that represented CB68H. He was looking south of the course line, toward the far end of the Ghawar field. He then alternated his gaze to a secondary screen that was still transmitting from Wujah Al Hajar Air Base in Lebanon.

"There might be a way," he said.

An exasperated Coltrane said, "A way to what?"

"A way to take this airplane down without people on the ground getting hurt. Without the radiation being released anywhere over Saudi Arabia."

"You do that, mister, and I'll put you in for a citation."

Davis frowned, but didn't bother to say that he already had a drawer full of citations—both the kind you wanted and the kind you didn't.

"Do you think we can trust him?" Davis asked.

"Who?" responded Coltrane.

He pointed to the screen where three white dots stood next to a C-17 in Lebanon. "The Israeli."

"What good is he now?"

Davis explained his idea. It was radical. Nothing like it had ever been attempted before.

"Could that work?" Coltrane asked.

Davis' eyes remained locked on the feed from Lebanon. "You've got a lot of fancy gadgets in this room. Right now, they're leading to nothing but paralysis. You need to take the initiative. And you need to realize that today's little war is like any other . . . in the end, it always comes down to a grunt with a rifle."

# SEVENTY

Slaton listened intently to Langley's plan, and he had to admit surprise. He'd expected them to simply shoot the aircraft down, because in his experience, Americans always went for firepower. Shock and awe. What they proposed was quite the opposite, a plan requiring precision and nuance. After three minutes the final question beamed halfway around the world.

"Can you do it?" Director Coltrane asked.

The plan was audacious. It was stricken with risk, and Slaton would have only one chance to get it right. Which was perhaps why he liked it.

"I don't know," he answered. "Nothing like that's ever been tried. I'm willing to give it a shot, but I do have one condition."

"Name it."

Slaton did, and then he handed the comm handset over to Lieutenant Colonel Bryan. The ensuing conversation lasted thirty seconds, the Mississippian clearly not liking what he heard. Slaton registered a second voice that was not Coltrane's crackle from the handset speaker, and Bryan was red in the face when he hung up.

464 | WARD LARSEN

He said, "Whoever you are, mister, you've got some pull." Turning toward his copilot, he said, "Fire her up. We're flyin' again."

"What?" the captain replied.

Bryan's hands were already working switches. "Our guest here has been given complete operational control of this aircraft."

"Where are we going?" the copilot asked, his eyes going back and forth between his aircraft commander and a stranger with a rifle—as if not sure who he was asking.

Bryan said, "Our immediate orders are to get airborne, head east, and establish communications with an AWACS air battle manager."

"Air battle?" said the former Marine. "I like the sound of that. And here I thought we just hauled trash so other guys could do the fighting."

"The Air Guard ain't no flying club, mister. When we get back stateside, you can tell all your buddies at your cushy Southwest day job what an adventure you had."

"Less talk, more movement," Slaton instructed from behind.

Both pilots turned a shoulder in time to see their jump-seater cradle his rifle, eject the magazine, and jack four rounds of ammo inside. Six minutes later the C-17 was rumbling down the runway into a darkening night.

The big jet was no more than a fading shadow when a convoy of three limousines—all bearing diplomatic license plates—careened in from a dirt road and skidded to a stop in the middle of the chipped concrete runway. A trim man dressed in a dinner jacket and powder blue Hermès tie got out, took one

look at the sky, and slammed both hands on the roof
of the car.

After a heated discussion with CENTCOM, it was
decided that the Saudi Air Force, competent as it
might be, would be roundly ignored. Two U.S. Air
Force F-22 Raptors, on temporary deployment from
Langley Air Force Base to Al Udeid Air Base in Qatar,
were quickly fitted with an internal load of air-to-air
missiles and their guns charged with a full quota of
20mm high-explosive incendiary rounds. Eighteen
minutes after receiving the order to scramble, the fighters were shrieking down the two-mile-long Runway
34 in full afterburner, each trailing plumes of orange
fire fifty feet long.

The Raptors' call sign was Ruger 22, and the pilots,
much like the crew of Reach 41, knew little about
where they were going, and nothing about what they
would face when they got there. The orders had been
simple: load two jets for bear, scramble, and fly southwest. From that point, Ruger 22 flight was to make
contact on a discreet air battle frequency for further
instructions. To the pilots, a major and her first lieutenant wingman, it was a mission of utter mystery.
There had been no briefing, no preflight planning,
and no rules of engagement had been discussed or
even alluded to. This void of planning only rein-
forced to the pilots the importance of their mission—
whatever it might be.

There was no hesitation as the jets turned northwest. Both remained in full burner a little longer than
necessary, credit that to the adrenaline rush, and they
climbed quite literally into the stratosphere, leveling

off at fifty-two thousand feet. There they established supercruise, a blistering Mach 1.7, and contacted a U.S. Air Force AWACS airborne controller. The AWACS had been diverted from a training mission two hundred miles north, and a pair of KC-135 tankers had also received an invitation to the party—or more accurately, what was fast becoming an intricate aerial ballet.

Ruger 22 steered a vector given by the AWACS, and soon both Raptors trained their powerful APG-77 radars on a lone target that was traveling, in relative terms, very low and very slow. The more the fighter pilots saw and heard, the more they realized they were involved in something exceptional. This would be a mission that did not exist in any manual, nor resemble anything they had learned in flight training.

Tonight, they realized, would be pure improvisation.

# SEVENTY-ONE

Jack Kelly cornered Sorensen in the Operations Center. "Boss, we need to talk."

Like everyone else, Sorensen was fixated on the aerial spectacle half a world away. "It'll have to wait, Jack."

"No—this can't wait."

She gave him her best *this better be good* look. The worry on his face held fast, and they stepped into the hallway.

"What is it?" she asked.

"There are eight."

"Eight what?"

"Eight people in this organization."

Her head cocked ever so slightly to one side. "And how did you come to this conclusion?"

Kelly waved a paper in his hand. "The dental clinic in Ahvaz—the forgery mill that connected the other seven. I went backwards and studied all the data NSA got from that hack. The original seven were grouped together because their docs were paid for all at once and sent in one shipment. But I found another order one month earlier, a single identity that was paid for through the same account. I'm betting whoever it is must be responsible for this whole scheme. He ordered an identity for himself."

"Okay . . . that's good, Jack. That's very good. Do we have a name?"

"Arslan Omer, a Turk if you believe the document. When I ran the name it came up blank in the database except for one thing."

Sorensen waited through a pause.

"Whoever it is entered the United States two weeks ago at Dulles. There's no record that he's left the country, so . . . apparently he's right here in our backyard."

Tuncay studied his navigation display and noted the distance remaining to their initial drop point. "One hundred and seventy miles," he said.

"Twenty-nine minutes," Walid replied.

"No, it will take slightly longer," Tuncay said from the left seat. "Remember, we must slow to two hundred and fifty knots for the delivery."

The copilot expelled a long breath. "I envy Ben-Meir and Ghazi. As soon as we took off, their share was complete. They are probably halfway to paradise by now."

A surprised Tuncay regarded his second, but quickly realized that the word *paradise* had not been used in a religious sense. His Druze copilot was as secular as they came.

Walid tugged his collar. "It is warm in here."

"So cool it off."

Walid reached up and adjusted the cabin temperature, but not without a wary glance aft. "That stuff makes me nervous. What good will money do either of us if we die of radiation sickness?"

"You heard what Ghazi said. As long as we keep clear of the holding tank we are safe."

"And what else would he say?" Walid grumbled.

The jet struck a wave of turbulence, bouncing gently on the cool night air. With the idea planted freshly in his head, Tuncay imagined their deadly cargo sloshing in the holding tank. He was every bit as uncomfortable as Walid, but he tried not to show it. Would he truly see his Mallorcan dream? He had long ago diverted his advance payment to three separate accounts, and twice that much awaited. Perhaps more now that fewer of the group remained. Five million? Ten? How much was enough to assume such risk?

He'd had a long discussion with Walid about the airplane they'd nearly collided with on takeoff, and in the end they agreed that someone had discovered their location and arrived with a planeload of commandos to put their scheme to an end. They'd escaped just in time. The first fifteen minutes of the flight had been nerve-wracking, both he and Walid expecting to be shot down at any moment. Now, after over an hour, he was sure they'd slipped away into the night. Luck was on their side. *But for how long?*

Not for the first time, it occurred to Tuncay that he could cut the mission short. They were established in Saudi airspace now, and he let his eyes rove over the map display. He saw two acceptably large airfields between their present position and the drop point. He could claim a mechanical problem, or even manufacture one. Shut down an engine or claim a fire. The group had long ago discussed this in detail as a potential weakness of their plan—such a complex, old aircraft had a significant chance of developing technical problems. He thought Walid might be with him, and Ghazi and Ben-Meir no longer had a say. Of course, if they aborted now their scheme would have little effect on the price of a barrel of crude. Not that Tuncay cared—his payment was not tied to it. Then there was the matter of his conscience, such as it was. He was not a cruel man, and if they never made it to Ghawar the horrid concoction behind him would not rain across the world.

On the other hand, diverting short of their target introduced new complications. Fire chiefs and airport police. In the ensuing confusion, he and Walid might find a way to disappear, and perhaps they could clear Saudi Arabia before anyone understood what they'd intended.

Their preplanned escape was waiting for them at an airfield in Kharj, only twenty miles south of the last coordinate set on their deadly run. They would land in the middle of the night, park the aircraft, and transition to a twin Beechcraft that was fully fueled and waiting in a nearby hangar. The chore of destroying the evidence had been assumed by Ben-Meir. A time-delay Semtex charge was implanted above the number two main fuel tank—it would be less than one-quarter full by then, and the roof of the tank thick with Jet A vapor. Ten minutes after activated, roughly when he and Walid would be lifting off in the Beech, the explosive charge, accelerated by their thousand-gallon fuel reserve, would create a fire of sufficient intensity to reduce CB68H to her component alloys in liquid form. By first light nothing would remain but a pile of highly radioactive debris, a monument to their success. From Kharj it was a simple dash south to the Empty Quarter, and finally Yemen, a land beyond the reach of even the mighty Americans. Altogether, it was a plan that had seemed rock-solid in the planning stages. But now? Now Tuncay saw a hundred things that could go wrong.

He surveyed the central panel, then locked eyes with Walid for a long, awkward moment. *Is he having the same thoughts?* Tuncay wondered. *Does he sense my doubts?* He averted his eyes and began toying with the volume knob on the secondary VHF radio. "Still nothing on guard frequency?"

"No, nothing," Walid replied.

Ten minutes earlier they had been given a frequency change by the air traffic controller. By design, they had ignored it, tuning the radio to the new frequency but not making contact. Since making the switch, the air traffic controller had not bothered to initiate contact either. In Europe or North America things would never have been so lax, but here, Tuncay knew, such carelessness was common. Perhaps the man controlling this sector—important jobs in the Kingdom of Saud were never trusted to women—had left his station for a cup of tea. Or more likely, in order to pray, leaving air traffic separation to the will of Allah. Whatever the case, for Tuncay and Walid it was an ideal circumstance. They would simply wait for the controller to call them on the radio. And if he never did?

All the better.

The secondary radio, tuned to 121.5 MHz, increasingly became their focus. If anyone became concerned that radio contact had been lost, a blanket call would be made over this emergency frequency, also referred to as "guard." The channel was monitored by virtually all aircrews, and in the worst case, if fighters were launched for an intercept, they too would attempt contact on VHF guard. So far there had been only silence.

In the navigation computer Tuncay typed in the name of the nearest of the two airfields he'd noted. It was twenty miles to the north.

"What is that?" Walid asked, pointing to the new circle on his map display.

"Only a reference point." Tuncay looked out the window and saw the moon disappear behind a cloud layer. The high stratus was comforting, as if they were slipping under a warm blanket. Tuncay hit the delete button and the fix he'd created vanished.

"It's not important," Tuncay said with a newfound rush of confidence. "We don't need it anymore. One more hour, my friend, and we will join Ghazi and Ben-Meir in our own versions of paradise."

# SEVENTY-TWO

The sidebar in Langley took place in a tiny conference room just outside the Operations Center. Sorensen and Kelly faced Coltrane.

"So we don't know who this eighth person is?" asked the director.

"No. We're going over the arrivals images from Dulles but nothing yet. If he's a professional that might not be much help."

Coltrane didn't argue the point.

Sorensen steered to what bothered her more. "Who is David Slaton?"

Coltrane shot her a look that said she'd overstepped her pay grade, but after a long hesitation he answered. "It happened before my tenure. The Israelis had an operative they wanted hidden . . . retired, in a sense. We were asked to facilitate his disappearance here in the States. Mind you, this was a direct favor from the president of the United States to the government of Israel. My predecessor personally made the arrangements, and it was kept at the highest levels. He briefed me on the matter when I took over as director."

"The cover name was the one you mentioned— Edmund Deadmarsh?"

"That's right."

"Why did Slaton warrant this special treatment?" Sorensen asked.

"The Israelis never said, but it was near the time of the Ehud Zak fiasco."

"The sniper who was involved? He was killed in London," Kelly argued.

Coltrane didn't reply.

Sorensen said, "So that's who we have in the back of our C-17—an assassin who was long thought dead."

"What I saw in Lebanon tonight was enough to convince me," said the director.

Kelly said, "Given the scope of this plot, I think we should be more concerned about whoever is here right under our noses."

"A valid point. If you get anything from Dulles, a good video image or passport photo—I want to see it."

"You think you might recognize him?" Sorensen asked.

"No," replied Coltrane. "But I suspect I know who will."

"Can't we fly any faster?" Slaton asked.

Lieutenant Colonel Bryan turned around from the left seat. He pointed to the airspeed indicator where a white cursor was nestled against a red-hatched limit. "If we go any faster the paint's gonna come off."

The entire crew was in the cockpit of the C-17 Globemaster. Bryan was flying, his copilot to his right. Slaton and the loadmaster were on a pair of jump seats behind the two officers. The cockpit was cramped, but it was the only place they could all be together. Slaton wanted everyone on the same page.

"What we're trying to do is straightforward in principle," he said, "but it's going to take serious co-ordination to pull it off."

"What we're trying to do is nuts," said Bryan.

Slaton couldn't argue. He'd hatched more than his share of bold schemes, but even he was stunned by Langley's plan.

"They had a hundred-mile head start," said Bryan, "but we're gaining fast. He's down low, and if our relative groundspeeds don't change we should catch him in twenty-one minutes."

"At that point how long will we have?" Slaton asked.

"Not long. If we assume they're going to drop on the northernmost portion of the Ghawar field—that gives us a ten-minute window to get in position and let you work."

"Just get me in position—my part takes about one-tenth of a second."

They were flying a tail-chase on the MD-10, and a pair of F-22s were closing quickly and would shadow their target from behind. The Raptors' assignment was to guide the C-17 closer. Then came the delicate part. Reach 41 would rendezvous with the MD-10 from behind in complete darkness and, in an inverted game of aerial leapfrog, Bryan would descend two thousand feet below, accelerate out front, and finally climb until they were precisely a mile in front of their target. There, the C-17 would lower its rear cargo door in-flight—as was usually done to airdrop pallets of cargo or deliver Airborne Rangers—and Slaton would take up his position. The C-17 would gradually slow to close the gap, and from the aft ramp Slaton would choose the right moment to issue two rounds from the SVDS.

Slaton remained skeptical about what would happen if he succeeded. "How can we be sure that jet is flying on autopilot?" he asked Bryan.

"We're relying on one thing—that these pilots will fly a programmed course over the oil field. I think it's a safe bet. Nobody flies a wide-body by hand except on takeoff and landing. If the pilots have a route programmed into the flight computer, it's almost a sure thing the autopilot will be flying it."

"What about at the end, when they reach the southern end of the oil field?"

"At that point it's all about escape. I figure they'll make a mad dash to the nearest airfield, and jump in a car or another airplane. They might fake an in-flight emergency to expedite things. They'll fly fast and aggressively, nothing you would program into a nav computer. So if it all happens like we think, the autopilot will take the jet to the end of its route at the southern edge of the oil field. If you've done your part by then," the skipper said, his eyes on Slaton, "it leaves nobody on the flight deck to intervene, and the airplane will just hold whatever heading it has. In this case, a more or less southerly course."

"So the jet just keeps flying a straight line?"

Bryan nodded. "Take the pilots out of the picture, and she'll fly south by southeast until she runs out of gas—somewhere over the Indian Ocean, I'd guess."

Slaton heaved a long sigh. "There are a lot of assumptions in this plan."

"Yeah, there are."

"But it makes sense to you, as a pilot?"

Bryan nodded to say it did. Slaton shifted his gaze

to the copilot, who also nodded. A two to zero vote. "All right, I'm convinced. Is there a way I can talk to you once I'm in position on the ramp?"

The loadmaster, an ebony-skinned sergeant named Willis, told Slaton, "I've got an extra headset. I'll plug you into the intercom and give you a hot mike."

"The big question for me," said the copilot, "is are they going to spot us?"

"Good point," said Bryan. He turned to Slaton. "I can tell you that when it comes to flying at night, almost every pilot focuses inside, especially during cruise—nothing much to see out the window. All the same, there is some moon out tonight. These guys won't be expecting another jet to materialize in front of them, but we have to do everything we can to not highlight ourselves. I'll make sure all the external lights are off, and the cargo bay has to be blacked out once that aft door drops." He looked at Willis. "Emergency lights, everything. Break 'em if you have to . . . and keep that damned iPad of yours turned off."

The loadmaster acknowledged.

"We'll need some light up here on the flight deck, but I'll make sure the door that connects to the cargo bay is closed. We also have to turn off our TCAS."

"What's that?" Slaton asked.

"Traffic collision avoidance system. If theirs is turned on as well, it'll sound a warning when we get close." Bryan reached down and turned a knob on the transponder. "Done. Now we're a stealth C-17."

"Radar?" Slaton asked.

"Big airplanes have radar, but it's only good for looking at weather—won't paint another jet. We'll be in contact with the Raptors, and they have the big picture. They'll vector us to a ballpark position. Once that aft door drops, we'll be less than a mile in front of him." He nodded toward Slaton. "At that point it's up to you. Tell me what you need. Left, right. Up, down. Slower, faster. Those are pretty much your options. Use increments I can work with. Ten knots faster. Fifty feet higher."

Slaton nodded to say he would.

The copilot, who was working the radios, said, "I have our fighters on frequency. The call sign is Ruger Two-Two. They're already shadowing the target, about five miles in trail. We're eighteen minutes from the merge."

Slaton picked up his sniper rifle. "All right. Let's see if we can make this work."

# SEVENTY-THREE

The three aircraft merged in an empty sky over an empty land. The first debate was short-lived.

Ruger 22, the flight of two F-22s, was established three miles behind and one thousand feet above the MD-10. They requested that Bryan join up high as well, two thousand feet above, and make his final approach from high to low.

"Not gonna happen," Bryan said on their discreet frequency, his tone suggesting that he outranked the woman flying the lead F-22. "I want to come in underneath. It'll be harder for them to see us, and also less chance that they'll be alerted by our wake turbulence, which tends to sink."

The flight lead of Ruger 22 didn't respond right away, which Bryan took as a victory of sorts. Then over the radio, "Ruger Two-Two copies. Reach Four-One, come five right."

Bryan banked into a turn to edge the compass 5 degrees right, then nosed over until the altimeter read five thousand feet above sea level. The MD-10 had descended and was now cruising at six thousand feet. Bryan speculated, and his copilot concurred, that there was only one reason for the MD-10 to be flying at such a low altitude—it was the height from which they would drop their poisonous load. It was also another bit of circumstantial evidence to confirm that an attack on Ghawar was imminent. Bryan was happy they weren't any lower because the terrain in the area was roughly two thousand feet above sea level. To be down in the weeds at night, in unfamiliar terrain, would have grayed what little color remained in his hair.

"You're nine thousand feet in trail, sixty knots of overtake," called Ruger 22, giving the first horizontal range estimate. The C-17 was a mile and a half back, but gaining fast. Both pilots looked ahead and saw nothing.

"Target speed two-hundred-twelve knots."

"Pretty slow," said McFadden from the right seat.

Bryan nodded agreement. "About how fast you'd go if you were preparing to open the belly doors on an airplane in flight. A release could happen any time. What's the distance to the estimated initial point we were given?" Langley had forwarded the MD-10's flight plan, and one navigation point had been highlighted near the northern edge of the oil field.

"Thirty-two miles."

Bryan nudged all four throttles forward, but it was a delicate dance. After passing the MD-10, they would have to slow to match speeds and then climb to the same altitude. Finally, in the most sensitive maneuver, they would gradually slow to put their sniper in position.

More corrections came from Ruger 22, and Bryan applied them. They were less than a mile in trail when McFadden, whose eyes were younger, said, "There!"

Bryan craned his head forward and looked out the window. Sure enough, a sleek dark shadow materialized. It was running dark, just as they were, no navigation or anticollision lights—a massive form floating in an obsidian sky.

"It looks like a KC-10 from here," Bryan remarked, referring to the aerial tanker, derived from the same airframe, that he and McFadden had rendezvoused with countless times in skies across the world.

"Yeah," said McFadden. "Only this one isn't carrying gas."

The two Guardsmen exchanged a look, then in unison watched the shadow that was quickly filling the windscreen.

"You know," Bryan said. "I sure hope them belly doors don't open right now."

"Exactly what I was thinking."

"At least the weather is cooperating. That high stratus deck is killing what little moonlight there is. Let's hope it stays that way." Bryan heard another correction from his fighter escort and this time ignored it—he was virtually flying formation on the aircraft above. That would change as soon as they moved ahead. At that point, they would be totally reliant on the fighters for guidance.

"Confirm external lights are off."

"Check," said McFadden.

"All right, two minute warning. Willis, you ready?"

"Yes, sir," crackled the sergeant's voice over the intercom. "Blackout conditions in place."

"All right—drop the ramp!"


Slaton had been in the back of many military transports. He'd even had the occasion to jump out of a few. Never had he used one as a shooting platform.

The wind noise was considerable, though not overwhelming thanks to the earmuff-type headset provided by Sergeant Willis. Slaton felt the eddies of a three-hundred-mile-an-hour breeze stir the stale air that had built inside the cargo bay, and he felt the controlled warmth ebb, drawn into the cool desert night as if into the vacuum of space.

Bryan's drawl crackled over the headset. "We're in front now. Another three thousand feet and we'll climb to go co-altitude with the target. From there it's up to you to put yourself in position."

Slaton checked his weapon was ready, including the scope.

Bryan again. "You never said—how close do you need to get?"

"You think I've done this before? It's not going to be an empirical thing. I just need a sight picture I can make work."

"TLAR," Bryan suggested.

It was a term Slaton was familiar with: *That looks about right.* "TLAR," he agreed.

"Fair enough. Be warned, I can't hear you very well—too much wind noise on your mike."

Slaton adjusted the thin boom microphone closer to his lips. "That better?" he asked.

"It'll have to do."

Slaton moved aft where Sergeant Willis was studying the situation. They stood ten steps from the edge of a loading ramp that was wide enough to accommodate an M1 Abrams main battle tank. And beyond that—a half-mile drop to an unseen ocean of sand swales. The wind swirled mightily, whipping Slaton's hair and snapping at his shirtsleeves.

As a trained sniper, he had worked with countless weapons in hundreds of situations. Never had he encountered anything like this. The wind, the engine noise, the intercom, a target and a shooting platform that both moved in three dimensions. What other challenges would arise? What complications had he not foreseen? His was a mind-set of preparation and routine. What he was about to do—shoot two men piloting a weapon of mass destruction—verged on madness.

The sergeant pointed behind the rear door. "Since we're coming from underneath," he said, "you won't see the jet until we're almost in position—our big-ass tail is gonna block your view."

Slaton saw the problem—the C-17's massive T-tail hovered high behind them. "How far back should I go?" he asked, gesturing to the ramp's aft edge where the heavy-gauge steel floor gave way to an abyss.

"The farther back you go, the sooner you'll see him. Take it as far aft as you can stand."

Slaton sighed. "Yeah . . . I was afraid you'd say that."


He settled into a prone shooting position, two sand-bags provided by Willis giving support to his weapon. He tried to project an image in his mind: the nose-on silhouette of an airliner falling into view. How many times had he lay planted on his stomach trying to vi-sualize a shot, trying to assimilate in advance all pos-sible variables? Tonight those variables were simply unknowable.

He was traveling at roughly three hundred miles an hour, his target slightly less. His standard 7.62mm round would have to penetrate a multi-ply wind-shield that—according to Bryan—was tempered to withstand a strike from a large bird at two hundred and fifty miles an hour. The windscreen he had to breach was also angled roughly 30 degrees upward and canted to the side. To further complicate things, the glass in front of one of his targets would slant to port, the other to starboard. Would his round penetrate cleanly or deflect? Would his sight picture be subjected to refraction, as when one looks into water at an angle?

How would the atmospheric conditions affect his bullet path? In sniper school, the instructors had quibbled over relative humidity and temperature. A three-mile-per-hour crosswind was a serious concern. Here Slaton was dealing with a tailwind of three hundred miles an hour, some small, incalculable component of which would be from the left or the right—no way to tell which. Bryan had also warned to expect aerodynamic turbulence at the nose of the MD-10, like the bow wave from a freighter plowing through heavy seas. Only this bow wave was invisible, no way to tell where it began and ended. In essence, he was facing the mother of all ballistic puzzles.

So Slaton did what all good shooters did. He took a deep breath and relaxed.

The shot would come naturally, as it always did. The hard part was the waiting.

# SEVENTY-FOUR

He lay on his belly in total darkness, his legs wide for stability. Slaton was three feet from the edge of the ramp, a lip of dull steel that gave way to a half-mile drop. He had positioned slightly closer to the edge moments ago, but the turbulent airflow induced movement on the gun's barrel, and so he'd pulled back.

The swirling night air was cold, countered by hot engine exhaust that shredded the slipstream on either side. Through his planted elbows he felt vibrations in the airframe, a constant thrum conducted through the ramp's thick steel into flesh and bone. If all that wasn't distracting enough, Sergeant Willis had walked through the cargo bay and disabled every source of illumination. The sparse desert outside shone an occasional light, and seemed to blend perfectly with the odd star peering through the clouds above. Altogether it gave Slaton the discomforting sensation that *he* was flying, but with no orientation of up or down. Simply hurtling feet-first through a hurricane-swept void.

He forced away the distractions and concentrated on his scope, elevated to where his target would soon appear.

"Climbing now," said Bryan over the headset, his tone hushed like a soldier patrolling enemy territory. "We're one mile in front, speed matched. Five hundred feet below."

Slaton saw something, blinked once, and there it was. The engines stood out most prominently, their hot sections evident in the low-light scope. He pressed the sight firmly to the orbit of his eye—at this range it didn't matter, but there was undeniable comfort in the fact that no light whatsoever could escape to highlight their position. He increased the magnification and settled his sight on the cockpit. Fortunately, the instrument lighting inside had been toned down, and even from a mile Slaton could distinguish two melon-like heads behind the angled windscreen.

The pilots were talking.

Bryan again over the headset, "We're level now, one hundred feet below the target's altitude. Beginning to slow. Range fifteen hundred yards."

Slaton sensed a drift to the right. He was about to issue a correction when he realized he was facing backwards and would have to invert every command. A complication he should have foreseen. "Five degrees right," he murmured into his headset. He felt the C-17 bank ever so slightly, and the drift was arrested.

At this range both targets were in the field of view of his scope. All things being equal, Slaton decided to take the captain first—an earlier discussion with Bryan had convinced him that the control mechanism for the drop system was likely on that side of the cockpit.

When Bryan called, "One thousand meters," Slaton began shifting between his two targets. He wanted to take the first shot from as close as possible, hoping that minimum range would overcome the long list of ballistic variables. Too close, however, and they might be seen. So far the pilots seemed focused inside, talking and referencing their instruments. Slaton shifted his optic to the belly of the MD-10, and had just enough angle to discern the irregular shape of the clamshell doors. They were still closed. But for how long?

"Five hundred meters," said Bryan, his voice growing tense. "We'll be over the top of the oil field in five minutes."

Slaton swung his sight back to the cockpit. What he saw was not good.


"I have to pee," said Walid, rising from his seat.

"Do it quickly, we are almost there."

Tuncay watched his copilot head toward the back, knowing he would be quick because the holding tank was in plain view from the lavatory door. He checked the navigation computer. Twelve miles to go. He reached down to the switch that activated the belly doors—it had been fitted with a red safety guard, lest anyone bump it by accident while reaching for a dropped pencil. In what could only be a reaction to stress, Tuncay found himself fantasizing, wishing he could release his five thousand gallons of radioactive sludge on the headquarters of Arabian Air, the airline that had discarded him after eighteen good years. The thought of having such vast lethality poised under a fingertip was remarkably empowering. It made him think of the end of World War II, when the crew of an American bomber—the name escaped him—dropped the world's first nuclear weapon on Japan. Was this how those men had felt? All-powerful? In truth, he was happy no mass casualties would result from what he was about to do. A few oil workers, perhaps some Bedouin—that would be the worst according to Ghazi. Maybe a handful of others in the cleanup effort. Casualties were not his intent, only an unavoidable side effect. Tuncay was no crazed jihadist—he was simply a man trying to reach a dream.

He flicked up the guard and saw a simple silver toggle switch. With one tap, a rain of radioactive hell would devastate the House of Saud's cash machine. Tuncay gazed through the forward windscreen. He saw nothing but a pitch-black night.

"One hundred meters! Shoot dammit!"

"One of the targets left the flight deck!" Slaton responded.

"I'm pushing up the power to match his speed," Bryan announced. "We can't risk getting any closer."

Slaton felt a change in vibration, then a surge of acceleration as the C-17's big turbofans spun faster.

"The second pilot might have gone to activate the release mechanism," Bryan said.

"I know," Slaton replied, having already reached the same damning conclusion. His finger touched the trigger, beginning the deadly pressure. At the range of one football field the captain's head looked like a pumpkin in his sight.

"We're two minutes from the expected drop point."

Slaton hesitated, then eased his trigger pressure. "If I take one down and the other guy comes back—he's going to find a body and a nice neat hole in the windscreen. He might move to a place where I don't have a shot."

"He might also be in back with his hand on a release lever," Bryan argued over the intercom.

There was no good answer. The entire plan rested on taking out *both* men. Only then could the autopilot transform the jet into a massive drone that would, with any luck, continue harmlessly into the southern ocean. Slaton tried to think of a way to make both men show themselves, and an idea came to mind. He turned and explained it to the loadmaster.

"You want me to *what*?" Willis responded.

"No time to explain—just do it!"

# SEVENTY-FIVE

*It was the oddest thing,* Tuncay thought as he stared out the front windscreen in wonder. Through his years in the sky he had seen a great many sights. Shooting stars, continuous displays of lightning, the Star Wars effect of traveling through snowflakes at 300 knots with landing lights ablaze. He had seen the aurora borealis and St. Elmo's fire. Never had he seen anything like this.

"Walid!"

He heard banging from the aft cabin, but got no reply.

He shouted a second time, "Walid!"

"What? Is it time for the release?"

Tuncay turned around and saw his copilot holding a Styrofoam cup with steam rising from the top.

"The coffeemaker still works," Walid said. "Do you want some?"

"No!" Tuncay barked. "Come here!"

"What's wrong?"

"Look out the window and tell me what you see."

Walid took a cursory look out front. "I see a dark desert. Is it the oil field?"

"No, higher, just ahead in the sky. I see a light."

Walid leaned forward, put his head over the glare shield. "Yes . . . I do see something. Turn down the lights."

Tuncay rotated a series of knobs and the lights on the instrument panel dimmed. He too leaned forward and saw it more clearly—flashing lights and movement, as if a tiny motion picture were floating in the sky. Then he registered something more ominous, a counterpoint to the tiny square of light. A massive shadow all around it.

Tuncay said, "It looks like another—"

The last word of the revelation never escaped his lips. Behind an explosion of glass and a rush of air, the Turk flopped back into his sheepskin-covered seat. Walid froze in place, stunned to see his partner splayed motionless, his head a bloody mess.

Walid's lower jaw dropped down, as if to speak. No words came before the second bullet arrived.


"Two down," Slaton said evenly into his microphone.

Through his scope he scanned the cockpit back and forth. The man in the left seat was clearly hit, slumped and motionless, but the second target was no longer in view. The damage to the windscreens was as he'd predicted, two cleanly riveted holes, spiderweb cracks around each for a six-inch radius. There had been no explosive decompression. This point had also been discussed during the course of their eastbound chase— due to the low cruise altitude, it could be assumed that the pressure differential inside the cabin would be minimal. Indeed, according to Bryan, the MD-10's cabin had likely been depressurized in order to vent the drop tank. Apparently, a valid assumption.

Everything seemed to have gone as planned, yet Slaton, ever the perfectionist, wanted confirmation. *Had he struck the second target a lethal shot?*

"Get me closer," he said into the intercom, "I need to confirm the kill. Climb so I can see the cockpit floor." The last thing Slaton wanted was a surprised but unharmed, or possibly wounded, copilot crawling to activate the drop release mechanism.

He heard the C-17's engines again rise in pitch. The cockpit of the MD-10, backlit by its fight instruments in a jaundiced yellow hue, came gradually closer until the magnification of the scope was no longer necessary. Slaton gave a series of commands until Bryan had them flying no more than a hundred feet in front of the MD-10, perhaps fifty feet above. Finally, Slaton got his confirmation. He saw the second pilot sprawled motionless on the flight deck floor, his bloody face ghastly in the amber light.

"All right, two confirmed kills." He was considering whether a follow-up was justified for either target when the MD-10 banked to its right. The geometry and closure suddenly changed, and the two jets began to merge.

"Climb!" Slaton shouted. "Climb now—their autopilot is maneuvering and we're getting too close!"

Bryan reacted sharply on the controls, the frayed nerves of a pilot who was flying a heavy jet in formation with another he couldn't see. The C-17's engines whined to full power, and a surge of positive Gs pressed Slaton's body to the deck as they bucked upward. He watched the MD-10 slide harmlessly underneath.

Bryan's voice chimed over the intercom seconds later. "All right, gentlemen—job done. I'm relaying a report to headquarters. Now we sit back and watch—and hope to hell we've got this right."

Behind Slaton, Sergeant Willis held up his iPad, which was still playing the animated Disney movie *Frozen*. "Can I turn this off now?"

"Yeah, I think so."

Willis did so, and said, "Man, I am *not* telling my daughter what I just did."

# SEVENTY-SIX

Christine couldn't say why she woke—she only knew it was abrupt. The kind of tense, alert stir derived from an unaccustomed noise in the middle of the night.

By a mother's instinct, she knew it wasn't Davy. There had been no gathering cry, no coo, no sound of the crib mattress being used as a trampoline. She sat up in bed and saw the usual stray light at her open hallway door. The television downstairs had gone quiet, but wind still rattled the window. Had that been it? A stray gust?

She went to the hallway, but saw and heard nothing unusual.

"Yaniv?" she called out.

No answer. She crossed the hall to the nursery. Davy was not in his crib. The first stab of fear.

*"Yaniv!"*

A terrible silence. Nothing but the wind.

She went cautiously to the staircase and looked down. Nothing amiss. Then she heard a knock. No, an intermittent banging noise. *Clunk, clunk.* She descended into the living room. The TV was on a news channel, but muted. "Yaniv?" Her tone was less demanding. Hopeful. "Davy?"

No response.

*Clunk, clunk*. The kitchen.

She edged that way, and before turning the corner Christine felt a cool gust. She found the back door swinging freely in the wind, battering against the house. *Clunk, clunk*. Davy was nowhere to be seen. Nor was Stein. Full-blown panic clutched her gut. She hurried to the door and looked outside, saw no one. In the old snow, however, were three sets of footprints. One coming toward the house, two going away—they ran up the driveway to the street, and then across on a diagonal.

*"God, no!"*

She ran for her phone but it wasn't on the counter where she always left it. Through the window she saw that Annette's place was dark—Tuesday night was chorus practice. She had to call for help. She went out the kitchen door and looked up and down the street, trying to calculate who might be home. That was when she noticed the garage door of Ed Moorehead's house—it was raised, and inside was the silhouette of a car. Could that be where Davy was? Inside, about to be taken away?

She reversed back inside and ran upstairs. In the nursery she rushed to the closet and flung open Davy's circus-theme toy chest. She tossed aside layers of Fisher-Price plastic and stuffed animals, and scooped out a layer of brightly colored wooden blocks. She tipped the heavy box on its side to reveal the false bottom. At the time she'd objected mightily, but of course David had been right. *It's the last place in the world anyone will look*. She removed the trigger lock on a Beretta 9mm and slipped it into her back waistband.

She darted downstairs, and out to the driveway.

The driver's door was open on the car in Ed's garage. Had it been earlier? She couldn't remember. Christine went back to the kitchen and ripped a spare key from a hook by the door, then dashed to her own garage. A light flashed on, causing her to freeze like an escapee caught in a prison-yard spotlight. Then she remembered—Stein had rigged it that way. She entered her garage through the side door, disengaged the opener, and heaved the big door up. Christine tumbled into the Ford. The engine cranked hesitantly, laboring in the cold, but soon the car was running. She slammed it into gear and hit the gas hard. The Ford lurched outside in reverse, slid into the street. She spun the wheel hard, slammed the gearshift into drive, and the car bounded up airborne over the opposite curb. She took out Ed Moorehead's mailbox, and closer to the house a snow-encrusted plant pot, but the car came to rest right where she wanted it—sideways in the driveway, blocking the garage entrance. Christine put the car in park. Removed the keys. Set the parking brake. *What else?* She pressed the keys into a gap in the backseat upholstery.

She studied Ed's garage but still saw no one. The door that connected to the house—through a laundry room, she knew—was hanging ajar. She got out, and looked up and down the street, hoping her demolition-derby run had been loud. Hoping every neighbor within earshot would call 911. Not a single porch light flickered on, nor were any heads peering out windows. Her neighbors were mostly professionals, people who worked and dined late. People who kept their shutters closed when they were home at all.

She saw no sign of either Davy or Stein. The cold Beretta pressed hard in the small of her back.

Never had Christine felt so alone.

She moved cautiously toward the car. There was no one inside, front or back. *Where are you, Davy?* Just then, the garage door began to lower. Christine stood frozen, unsure what to do. *Make it stop!* She looked near the door to the house, and where the plastic button should have been was a wire hanging out of the wall. The big segmented door was halfway down. She ran and kicked the tiny black box at the foot of the roller track, the motion detector whose beam would break and cause the door to freeze in place. The box flew clear out into the driveway. The door kept moving and hit the floor with a thump of finality.

Suddenly in near darkness, she was seized by fear. The only light was a thin shaft of white that spilled from the open laundry room door. Christine edged toward it and found a wall switch. She snapped it on and an overhead fluorescent light staggered to life. She looked up, searching for the rope-and-handle arrangement that would disengage the garage door opener, a mechanism like the one she'd pulled minutes ago to free her own car. It wasn't there. Not anymore.

The rope had been cut cleanly away.

# SEVENTY-SEVEN

The cheer at Langley was short-lived. Slaton's two bullets had given them what they wanted. Yet what they wanted was a pilotless wide-body aircraft hauling a deadly stockpile of radioactive cesium.

"That's half a victory if I've ever seen one," commented the army colonel on the line with CENTCOM.

"Are you sure this will work?" asked Director Coltrane, addressing Davis.

"Sure? Nothing is sure. But so far so good. There's no evidence of a release yet, and the Raptors have seen the aircraft make deliberate, coordinated turns. If the autopilot wasn't engaged that jet would be waffling around the sky like a drunken paper airplane. The heading would drift, and it wouldn't hold a steady altitude. There's no doubt in my mind—-so far that jet is hooked up to its flight computers. The question is whether anything has been programmed after the end of the delivery track. If it makes an abrupt turn toward an airfield somewhere, then we're out of options—we pick the least-risk terrain and shoot it down over Saudi airspace. On the other hand, if the last fix on their route is at the southern end of the Ghawar field . . . then she'll just hold that heading until the fuel tanks run dry."

"And you still think that's the case?" Coltrane asked.

"I do."

"Why?"

"Because," Davis reasoned, "that's what I'd do. After the drop, I'd want to hightail it away and get on the ground. You can fly more aggressively by hand than on an autopilot."

Everyone watched the central map as Davis' theory kept holding. Aside from the course the aircraft would take, there was one other vital unknown. How much fuel was on board the big jet? Reach 41, critically low on fuel itself, had already broken from the formation and was headed for Riyadh, Saudi Arabia. Ruger 22 was still shadowing the MD-10 when they reached the southern end of the Ghawar field.

For a few tense minutes everyone waited, hoping the MD-10's heading held steady. Twenty miles later the lead Raptor pilot, who would be the first to see anything amiss, confirmed the good news, her radio-filtered voice crackling over the speaker. "No turns, she's holding steady south. We show a one-seven-two-degree course."

A collective sigh of relief washed over the operations room.

Davis said, "We're not out of the woods yet. It's still a long way to the Indian Ocean."

"What else can we do?" Sorensen asked.

"Did that chaplain ever get here?"

For as long as possible, the crew of Reach 41 followed the drama over Ghawar on the tactical frequency, but the reception was weak by the time they landed at Riyadh Air Base.

As soon as the C-17 was shut down, Slaton followed Lt. Colonel Bryan across the tarmac toward base operations. They had not yet reached the door when a two-stripe airman burst out of the building with a message, and soon Slaton was talking for a second time to the woman named Sorensen on a secure line. She explained that they had unearthed an eighth conspirator, one who'd recently entered the U.S. at Washington Dulles International Airport.

"Do you know who it is?" Slaton asked.

"Actually, we were hoping you could tell us. We have a passport photo and we'd like you to take a look."

Slaton was guided to a computer and within seconds the picture arrived. It took his breath away. "What have I done . . ."

It was the last thing he would have expected. And it made perfect sense. Only then did he remember what Astrid had told him about the man who'd recruited her. *There was something strange about him. He seemed . . . how do they say it . . . unbalanced.* He had thought she'd meant irrational, but her grasp of the English language was more fundamental. She'd meant *physically* unbalanced. A man with a damaged leg. A man who, even more than Ben-Meir, had been aware of Mossad's dealings with Grossman.

Yaniv Stein was the force behind everything. And also the man Slaton had tasked with protecting his family.

He turned to the airman. "I need a phone right now!"

The door leading into the house stood open like an invitation.

Christine took a step back, then noticed something she hadn't before. The Chevy's trunk lid was cracked open, the smallest of gaps, and its lock had been damaged. No, it had been breached. Pried and gouged into submission. The back end of the car also appeared to be riding low, the tops of the tires high in the wheel wells. She moved in for a closer look and saw a long crowbar on the floor near the far wall—it was the only thing in sight not hanging on a hook or stacked neatly on a shelf.

She looked again at the door to the house, listened for any sound. There was nothing. She slipped her fingertips under the trunk lid and pulled. There was a hitch in the action, as if something in the lifting mechanism was damaged. She pulled harder and it opened. Christine stepped back and gasped. Gleaming inside were stacks of gold bars. There had to be almost a thousand, each slightly larger than a cigarette pack. She stood still for a long moment, until her trance was broken by a faint sound. It fluttered through the garage, soft and subdued, and caused her heart to miss a beat.

A cry from Davy.

In that moment, Christine's outlook underwent a seismic shift. She reached back and took the gun from her waistband. Gone was the constant of reason, replaced by something more feral, more elemental. A mother's protective instinct. Holding the gun with two hands, she moved slowly to the doorway. Seconds ticked by with no further sounds from above. Only a terrible silence. Without so much as a glance down, her foot found the threshold.

# SEVENTY-EIGHT

The house remained silent. But she *had* heard her child—of that Christine was sure. The laundry room was uneventful, nothing but a paired washer and dryer that hadn't been used recently—no shirts on hangers or stacks of folded towels. She emerged into the dining room where a four-chair setting gathered dust, and to the right was the kitchen. In the half-light she saw a plastic grocery bag spilling a can of soup and a half-used loaf of bread. She had been here before, most recently on the Fourth of July, standing around the center island and sharing hors d'oeuvres with Ed and Annette and a half-dozen other neighbors. It looked different now, empty and cold. The only illumination cascaded down the staircase from the second floor.

Then she heard it again: a gurgle she'd recognize anywhere. Her son was upstairs.

She bit her lower lip, and called up the staircase, "Yaniv?"

At the sound of her voice Davy wailed, the way he did when she came home from work. Stein didn't respond. Was he even there? One of the footprint sets in the snow must have been his. She wanted to call out to Davy, tell him she was coming in her most reassuring voice. She said nothing. Then, by some impulse she didn't understand, Christine slid the gun back into her rear waistband.

She took the stairs slowly, one at a time. A step creaked halfway up, and she cringed and wished she'd done everything differently. Done it as David would have. She should have stepped on the edge of the stairs and climbed in silence. She should never have announced her arrival. Christine was sure she'd done a hundred things wrong since rushing out her kitchen door. But there was no going back. Her son was upstairs.

She tried to remember the second floor. Big room in the middle, a living area with chairs and a TV, two bedrooms and a bathroom on the sides. She stepped more quickly, listening and watching, until her eyes reached floor level. She froze when she saw the body.

A man she had never seen was sprawled on the floor, and there was no mistaking the blank glaze in his eyes. As a doctor Christine was familiar with death, yet the manner of this man's demise was both obvious and chilling—there was an ugly wound on one side of his head, and blood had pooled on the carpet underneath. Her heart thrashing, she steeled herself and climbed the last few steps. The next sight brought a wave of relief.

"Thank God!" she exclaimed, exhaling for what seemed like the first time in minutes. "Why didn't you answer?"

Stein was across the room in a wide armchair, Davy sitting on his good left leg. Her son chirped when he saw her and lifted his arms, expecting to be picked up.

She took a step toward him, until something in Stein's level gaze caused her to stop. His left arm was wrapped around Davy, and resting casually on his damaged right leg was his handgun. She looked once more at the dead man. Graying fair hair, long and unkempt, a white-stubble beard. Hardly the image of a Palestinian assassin.

"Hello, Christine."

"What the hell happened? Did you shoot this man?"

"Of course I did."

His tone was light, as if she'd asked if he'd unloaded the dishwasher. The roller coaster in her gut hit bottom again. "I don't understand—who is he?"

"His name is Tony, or at least that's what he told me. Street people make a habit of not giving their real names."

"Street people?"

"He's been here since Friday. I found him living in a cardboard box under a Georgetown overpass. Lousy way to live in D.C. in February. I told him I needed a house sitter to keep an eye on things, which was true. All he had to do was stay inside, keep the blinds closed, and he could have all the heat, food, and sleep he wanted. I even told him I'd give him twenty bucks a day. Everybody was happy until he broke into the car and found my retirement fund. Then he got greedy, wanted to make a deal. Bad move on his part."

"Where did all that gold come from?"

"There's a very clear paper trail, one that leads straight to David."

"David?"

"I know you're playing catch-up here. There's a bit of terrorism taking place in Saudi Arabia as we speak. More damaging than September 11 in a practical sense, although it won't get as much press coverage—no crashing airplanes and burning buildings. If

David is still alive, by tomorrow he'll be world enemy number one."

*"What?"*

"He's going to take the fall for this attack. It's been in the works for some time—I rented this house over a month ago. I know how problematic David can be—but then, being married to him I'm sure I don't have to tell you. He let you believe he was dead, for God's sake. You see, when our strike went down I intended to lay low, and being across the street from you seemed like a good insurance policy. Come tomorrow, it's the first place they'll look for David, which means it's the last place he can go. My original plan was to sit right here and watch you and Davy from a distance until our mission was done. Imagine my surprise when David called and *asked* me to keep an eye on you." Stein chuckled.

Christine tried to wrap her mind around what he was saying. "So . . . there is no assassin."

"No, but you can blame David for that lie—it was his idea to get me into your house."

For the first time she noticed a television on the far side of the room. It was tuned to CNN, but muted, just as the TV in her own house had been.

"So what's going to happen?" she asked.

"You'll see very soon. The first reports should be—"

Stein was cut off by a phone ringing. No, by *her* phone—she recognized the ringtone. Christine watched Stein pull her handset from his pocket and study the screen. His expression went leaden. "You don't have any friends in Saudi Arabia, do you?"

When she didn't respond, Stein hesitated for a long moment. Then he swiped the answer button.

# SEVENTY-NINE

The transmission from Ruger 22 was straight and to the point. "On this course and speed we show twenty-one minutes to Yemeni airspace. Are we to maintain the shadow across the border?"

For five minutes the debate ran, by which time the president was directly involved. Coltrane was perfectly happy to punt that decision. The MD-10 was so far behaving as hoped, a straight track toward the Indian Ocean. The danger, however, was not yet past. While Saudi Arabia might soon be in the clear, another less reliable ally was coming under threat—or as more bluntly put by the Secretary of Defense, "under a fast-moving cesium cloud."

In the end it was decided that the two-ship of Raptors, each with the radar cross section of a wasp, could safely penetrate Yemeni airspace. Chances were also good that the MD-10, on the off chance it registered at all on Yemen's dodgy radar network, would not be considered a threat. The beleaguered government there had all it could handle with countless terrorist groups camping, quite literally, in its desert backyard. Threats from the sky were hardly a priority.

The Raptors backed off but kept radar contact.

Charlie Bravo Six Eight Hotel droned its southerly course steady and true.

Slaton stood behind the commander's mahogany desk at Riyadh Air Base, a secure phone to his ear. His call to Christine had been picked up on the fourth ring by the voice he'd hoped not to hear.

He began, "So help me God, if you—"

"Steady, *kidon,*" Stein countered. "Before you start making threats, I should tell you that your wife is standing in front of me and your son is in my lap."

"And you should know that your mission failed. The cesium cloud you aimed at Ghawar is heading harmlessly out to sea. Langley understands that I had nothing to do with it. In fact, we worked together to keep the drop from happening."

There was a lengthy pause on Stein's end.

Slaton turned the screws. "You haven't gotten any updates from Ben-Meir. Want to venture a guess why? You had me going when you told me he'd been kicked out of Mossad, and that it related to the operation with Grossman. Not only did I fall for it, I played right into your hands—I asked you to watch over my family."

"You know our creed, David. Trust no one. I made the same mistake. I trusted Mossad and they left me for dead in a desert in Iran."

"And *I* was the one who pulled your ass out! I saved your life!"

"Life? What life? I gave *everything* to Israel, and in return they spit me out with a cane and a disability check! I won't let it end there—I've earned far more."

"So that was your motivation—money? The rest of

your group are gone, Yaniv, all seven. You're sitting in the dark waiting for news reports about your strike. Only there aren't any. There should have been *something* by now, right?"

Stein didn't respond.

"Trust me, it's over."

"If so, then congratulations. But it only simplifies things for me—seven fewer paychecks to cut. All I have to do is disappear."

"Only you can't. Not from me."

Silence followed, and Slaton realized his mistake. He was cornering a man who was almost certainly armed, and who had his wife and child in the same room. Slaton was halfway around the world, his only weapon one tenuous fiber-optic connection. He could ask Langley to intervene, and he was sure they would try—but no hostage rescue team could arrive in time. For Slaton, the two most precious lives on earth were dangling by the thinnest of threads. If the call ended, he knew it would be over.

Stein was quiet, but the connection remained. Slaton heard Davy's tiny voice in the background. Never in his life had he felt so helpless.

Christine held out her arms.

Her son lurched toward her, his arms outstretched, and Stein was forced to use both hands to keep him from toppling to the floor. It was as instinctive a reaction as there was on earth—to protect an infant from falling. In that instant, Christine reached around and pulled the Beretta from her waistband and leveled it at Stein. Only it wasn't really level. The gun moved in her hand, wavering like a leaf-heavy branch on a blustery spring day.

Stein caught Davy and righted him in his lap. He saw immediately what she'd done. For an instant his expression was one of surprise, but then his relaxed demeanor returned. He almost seemed amused by her wavering aim.

"Please don't shoot your son."

Christine didn't respond, and Stein's right hand drifted toward his own weapon.

"Don't!" she shouted.

The hand went still.

Stein said, "You told me David didn't keep a gun in the house."

"No, I said I asked him not to keep one there. And I said I had never owned a weapon myself. All true."

Stein grinned. "You didn't trust me—a good intuitive move. Well done."

"I guess David taught me something."

"You know, you might have made a good spy."

Over the wobbling gun sight, Christine saw a good bit of Stein, her tiny child covering no more than his left shoulder and stomach. "Maybe so," she said. "But then, we all tell the occasional lie."

"Have you told me any others?"

"Actually, yes. I led you to believe that I didn't know anything about guns. Truth is, my father was a serious hunter, and he made damn sure I knew how to handle a weapon." The Beretta instantly went to stone in her hand, its barrel fixed on Stein's head.


Even at the speed of light, the sound of the shot took two and a half seconds to reach Riyadh. Slaton had heard both sides of the tense conversation on the open line, and tried to imagine what was happening, tried to visualize the scene. Now he heard Davy screaming, terrified by the booming noise.

For the longest ten seconds of his life, Slaton waited. That was all he could do. The next voice he heard was Christine's.

"It's okay, David. We're both fine—it's over. Please come home."

# EIGHTY

Every set of weary eyes in the Langley Ops Center followed the odd aerial procession through two border crossings and an aerial refueling. It was nearly an hour later, following an uneventful traverse of Yemeni airspace, that Ruger 22's flight lead made her last transmission of the night.

"Feet wet, we're handing off and heading home."

"Feet wet" conveyed that they had crossed the coastline and were headed out to sea. From there a pair of FA-18 Hornets, launched from the carrier *Stennis* in the Arabian Sea, took over the job of babysitting the pilotless MD-10. Within the hour, the Hornets also refueled as the gaggle headed south, passing the Horn of Africa and skimming uncomfortably close to the tip of Somalia. Six hundred and twenty nautical miles later, halfway to the Seychelles Islands, the end played out.

The Hornet pilots gave a running commentary as the MD-10's port and starboard engines flamed out almost simultaneously. The aircraft slowed as the autopilot tried to maintain altitude despite the loss of thrust. The number-two engine, mounted high on the tail, and thus having longer fuel lines drawing from the starved main tanks, ceased combustion one minute later. The autopilot did its best, but on reaching minimum speed gave up trying to hold altitude, reverting to a controlled descent.

No sooner had the new aerodynamic trim been set when, with the engine generators no longer supplying electrical power, the autopilot succumbed to a bus transfer and disconnected. At that point, CB68H was little more than a three-hundred-thousand-pound falling leaf. Her final downward glide took less than a minute. She hit the Indian Ocean at 02:58 UTC, bounced once in the gathering dawn, and cartwheeled in a massive splash that was recorded by the gun cameras of both Hornets. The old workhorse airframe—which had been rusting away in the Amazon only days earlier, and with two neat new holes in its forward windscreen—sank quickly in what would eventually be charted as 13,810 feet of water.

The Night Over Ghawar, as it would come to be known in Langley's internal after-action report, had reached its inglorious end.

# EIGHTY-ONE

For forty-eight hours the D.C. intelligence community held its collective breath. Yemen never so much as made an inquiry about the strange blip that had invaded its airspace on the night in question, only to disappear over the Southern Ocean on a course to nowhere. There were no reports from ships in the Indian Ocean of an aircraft going down, nor any mention of an emergency locator beacon sounding in the early hours of that morning.

More quantifiable was what happened in the oil markets, which was to say nothing. There was a blip the first morning when a Nigerian oil rig caught fire, and a burble the next day when Russia announced election results with a modestly nationalist sway. Not a whisper was heard of the disaster that had nearly befallen the Ghawar oil fields. Even unfulfilled, the very idea of what *might* have happened, had the plot come to public awareness, would have rocked the markets to their core.

The funds in the Barclays account, along with a half-dozen other deposits identified with Slaton's help, were quietly frozen. What to do with that bloodstained fortune was a question for another day. The Fairfax County Police were diverted away from a suspicious incident in a quiet neighborhood, the situation quietly addressed at some opaque federal level. The next of kin of a homeless man, one Nathaniel Morris, was notified of his passing, and no one seemed surprised that the longtime drifter had succumbed to the elements in the middle of a particularly harsh winter. A second body, whose identity was never made public, was quietly cremated and buried at sea, the only persons in attendance for the deep-sixing of the remains being the crew of the small Navy patrol boat and a rightly flummoxed rabbi. The house from which the bodies had been recovered was made spotless by a cleaning service that, professional as it seemed, was not listed in any online or print directory, and certainly did not advertise.

In Malta and Switzerland the investigations into a string of killings went cold, even more so when the U.S. State Department intimated that the man responsible had met a violent end in the hills north of Beirut. There was little hard evidence, and no body to prove the point, but a report, sourced from the charges d'affaires of the U.S. embassy in Beirut, made a convincing case that the suspect had perished in a firefight with smugglers in the shadows of Mount Lebanon. The report went on to certify that a man matching the description of the assailant from Europe had flown from Frankfurt to Larnaca International Airport on a timetable that meshed perfectly with the events on either end. This much was easily verifiable, and seemed enough to sate weary Swiss and Maltese investigators. Dead or not, the man was out of their hair.

The most disquieting loose end involved Iran. Certain equipment found discarded at Wujah Al Hajar Air Base, along with a stack of oil drums uncovered in a barn near Al-Basrah, were attributed with a high degree of certainty as being sourced from Iran. More definitive yet was the trove of identities NSA had revealed on the computer of a faux dental office in Ahvaz. The last and most speculative link came out of the blue, an NRO intercept suggesting that a shipment of gold bullion had arrived at Reagan National Airport, on an Iranian diplomatic flight no less, one week before the affair had begun. Taken together, the evidence hinted strongly at Iranian involvement. More was needed, however, to launch a formal accusation.

No more was ever found.

Two weeks later a slim letter reached Salvino's Ristorante in the village of Mosta. It came at the usual time, the carrier from Malta Post as reliable as the sun. Mario Salvino saw no return address on the envelope, and he opened it to find a bank check drawn in the amount of 10,302 euros. Attached was a typewritten note:

THANKS FOR THE LOAN. THE €302 IS REPAYMENT IN FULL FOR WHAT WAS IN THE CASH DRAWER. THE REST IS TO REPLACE THE PIZZA OVEN I LIKELY RUINED.

A stunned Salvino stared dumbly at the check, wondering if it was a joke of some sort. He checked his watch, saw the bank was still open, and fifteen minutes later had his answer. When he arrived back at the restaurant, drinks were on the house.

# EIGHTY-TWO

The Chesapeake of early April pledges neither hope nor despair. A day that begins with warmth and steady breezes can yield to gales and snow by midday. Calm waters seem only to be organizing the next battering swell, and fishermen mindfully track safe coves in which to lay up. On this particular morning the conditions had so far been agreeable, a cool breeze and steady sun, with a layer of marine mist clinging to the shorelines.

Where the bay turns seaward, near the discharging York River, a lone sailboat carved a path through the strikingly calm waters. Her name was *Windsom II*, forty-six feet of glimmering fiberglass, canvas, and rigging that had yet to be tested by the open sea. Christine was at the helm, watching with considerable amusement as her husband stood in the cabin trying to wrestle their son into warmer clothes. Hands accustomed to rigid gunstocks and impervious brick walls were predictably helpless against energetic infant limbs.

"All right," Christine called out, "let's try another."

"Barcelona, summer," Slaton said. "You see a car driving slowly, maintaining a block behind you. It's midday, so the traffic is ordinary. In front of you is a bank, an office building, and a big retail store."

"What day of the week is it?"

"Good question—Tuesday."

"How long has the car been following me?"

"You just spotted it. You don't know for certain if it's a problem."

A gust of wind brushed past, and Christine referenced the telltales before adjusting a few degrees to port. "I'd turn into the retail store because it must have another entrance. That will force them out of their car, right? If they're following me, it'll make them commit and show themselves."

Slaton came out on deck, leaving a freshly dressed Davy to cruise the cabin amid the low lying furniture. Their son was thirteen months old now, starting to walk, and clearly enjoying his strange new home. Slaton sat next to her on the lazarette hatch.

"Well?" she asked.

"Good and bad," he said critically, a teacher handing back a C+ term paper. "You're correct that the retail store forces their hand. But you don't want to do that. You don't want confrontation. The bank is out because there would clearly be no back door. That said, if you knew the people in the car were definitely coming after you, especially if they were armed, you could use the bank guards as a buffer—in Europe bank security is serious business, and they carry heavy weapons. But the office building is the best place to disappear. There are always multiple ways in and out, lots of hallways and doors and elevators—it's very difficult to follow someone in that environment."

She heaved a sigh of defeat. "I'll never be any good at this."

518 | WARD LARSEN

"You'll do fine—you only have to instill the right mentality. Just like I have to learn how to cruise the seven seas with an infant on board."

She watched Davy throw an Elmo doll at his playpen. "We'll have to be careful," she said, "very careful. But it can be done."

*Windsom* passed over the tunnel of the Chesapeake Bay Bridge, and soon they were heading east with the Atlantic stretched out before them.

Slaton regarded the cobalt expanse that would soon fill the horizon on all points of the compass. "Following the trade winds, no destination in mind. It's hardly a bedrock existence for raising a family. Are you sure you're up for this?"

"It's the only thing I *am* sure about, Deadmarsh."

"Not my name anymore."

"I never liked it anyway."

She looked across the deck at shining new winches and unfrayed lines. "We paid too much for this—I could have gotten a used boat for a fraction of the price."

"There was no time to shop. Besides, we can afford it."

"Can we? You never told me exactly how much gold was in that trunk."

"Do you really want to know?"

She turned away and pulled on the main sheet.

"Enough to take care of us for life," he said.

"Are you suggesting neither of us ever works again?"

"Not at all. You're a doctor—that's an act you can take on the road."

"I've been thinking about that. At some point in the last couple of years I've acquired a new perspective on things. Living in the States—it's a pretty sheltered existence. If my MasterCard gets compromised, I'm having a really bad day. I've never had to worry about whether the water will give me cholera or if there's a land mine in the schoolyard. The idea of getting out there and offering some basic care to help a small number of people in a big way—that appeals to me. And I never thought I'd admit it, but after what Stein and his cohorts tried to do . . . I think the world needs people like you too."

"A first-class stonemason?"

Her gaze went effervescent, the trace of a smile. "Exactly."

Neither spoke for a time, and soon the twin shorelines on the bay behind them faded to mist. "We're at sea now, David. You said you would explain the agreement."

"All right. We've been given our freedom, along with what you found in the trunk of that car. Where we go, what identities we use—that's up to us. If we ever need security, all we have to do is ask."

"And in return?"

"In return, both Israel and the U.S. will have a way to contact me. It won't happen often, but they can present proposals."

"Proposals?"

"All right—missions. I don't *ever* have to accept one. There will be stringent criteria, and only one source of approval."

"You?" she surmised.

"No—you. You have to make the call."

Her expression hardened. "You'd put me in that position? To decide whether to put you at risk? Whether to send you out into the world to kill someone?"

"Can you think of another way? One that we can live with?"

Christine considered the logic, and her voice softened. "It's a hell of a way to live."

"No, that *isn't* how we live—let's get that straight right now. You're a doctor, I build walls. Ninety-nine days out of a hundred, we raise our son and do our damnedest to make things better."

"And the hundredth day?"

They sat in silence for a time watching Davy, his legs moving in rhythm with the boat as gentle swells announced their passage into open water. Dark skies loomed in the distant north.

"Well," she said, "where do we go now?"

"I have no idea," he said, sliding an arm around her waist. "But if we turn right . . . in about a week things will get a lot warmer."